Within the Silver Mirror

The Nickelville Novels
Book 3
Tom Barnett

For Bill and Cleo, whose stories laid the foundation for who I would

become, and for the tales I would eventually tell.

Books by Tom Barnett

The Nickelville Novels

The Haunting of Nickelville Academy

The Goatman of Guarded Wood

Within the Silver Mirror

The Children of Nyx

Table of Contents

Chapter I: Reflections

The runestone felt strange in Megan's hand, oddly warm as if it had been sitting in the sun. She'd expected her grandfather to follow her to her grandmother's grove, but he remained at the old Formica table, his unfocused eyes resting on the note that her mother had left.

August, the man whom locals called Old Man Biggerstaff, waited for her ahead. His wolf-hybrid, Fang, greeted her on the path. Standing on his hind legs, he put his paws on her shoulders and rested the soft fur of his head against her cheek.

"Thanks, boy," she murmured, appreciating that this was the closest the hermit would come to doing this himself. But as much as she enjoyed the wolfy hug, it did little to diminish her anger.

She'd expected to find August standing at the edge of the spring that had risen when he'd created the grove for her grandmother so long ago. But for once, he was sitting on one of the stone benches. He looked thinner than she remembered, but given his active lifestyle, it wasn't exactly surprising that he wasn't overweight. He studied her as she approached, no doubt gauging the extent of her displeasure at being kept in the dark while he helped Emelia prepare to leave her behind.

"She made me swear not to tell you," he explained, not waiting for her to speak. His eyes searched hers, finding no comfort in their violet hue.

"That's no excuse," she snapped. "You knew that I'd want to know what it was that she was doing. You knew I'd want to go with her. If she dies, and I'm not there to help her, is your word going to be enough to justify what you did?"

"I'm not sure there's much in this world capable of killing that woman. Furthermore, in all of my long life, I've never broken my word," he added, an edge creeping into his voice. "I'm not going to start doing so now to save the feelings of a teenage girl."

That stung. It wasn't what she wanted to hear, but it was enough to remind her of the centuries that had forged him into the man before her. Yes, he might be sitting on a bench at the end of summer vacation in Nickelville, Texas. But like the Sentinels that marked the edge of his domain, his roots burrowed deep into a world that had moved on while he protected strangers from harm. Megan knew that he'd hated to keep this secret from her. She also knew, without a doubt, that he'd have gladly died before suffering the dishonor of breaking a single one of his promises. She closed her eyes and took several deep, calming breaths, willing her eyes to go back to their normal brown.

"I'm sorry," she said quietly. "You didn't deserve that. I'm just…"

"Frightened, angry and woefully under-caffeinated," he finished. "To be honest, I am too. Before you ask, I do indeed know where she's gone. I can't tell you where that might be yet, but I can tell you that she left you that information, as well as the answers to all of the questions she could never answer before now, in those runestones."

"Do you promise?" she asked, walking through Sam's yellow flowers, over the wooden bridge to sit next to him on the stone bench. Fang followed, then turned around once like an overgrown lapdog, before plopping his considerable furry mass on her feet so he could rest his head against her leg.

"On all the days I have left in this world," August replied, making her look up from the wolf and into his eyes, "and on any chance for finding happiness in the next."

"I guess that's good enough for me," she said at last. "So how does this thing work?"

It seemed to take more from August than it should have to rise from the bench. Motioning for her to stay seated, he crossed back to where his horse grazed on a patch of clover. She noticed something flat and metallic sticking out of one of his saddle bags. When he reached up and pulled it free, she thought at first that it was a serving platter like the ones her grandfather used to serve turkeys. When he brought it closer, she realized it was a very old mirror.

"This belonged to my wife," he told her, "and I want you to keep it when all of this is finished."

"Oh August," she said, holding her hand out to refuse. "I'm not mad at you. You don't have to give me your wife's mirror to make amends."

"This has nothing to do with that," he said quietly. "You're going to need this to access the memories embedded in the stones. But after all this is finished, I still want you to keep it. My wife and I never had children, and in all of these long years I've never met anyone who felt like they could have been one. Until I saw your grandmother that is. You are so much like her."

"Thank you," Megan said, touched by this rare admission of affection from her reclusive friend. "I'll cherish it."

"Good," he replied softly before resuming in his usual gruff manner. "Now, before we get to the method, I need to explain why we're doing it this way. Emelia came to me for help because it's my people, not yours that record memories in this way. We usually use quartz crystals for this purpose, and when they're made that way the memory bonds with the crystal permanently. However, recalling the information from them creates a sort of euphoria in regular folk...a euphoria that can both addict the mind and drain away the soul. Since the part of you that comes from your mother might not be able to handle a crystal, we decided to use runestones. They are each good for storing one memory. When it is retrieved, their power will fade, and they'll revert to common stone once again."

"So what's the mirror for?" she asked, noticing something odd about the reflections within.

"Not just any mirror," he said, handing it over to her. "It's made from a solid piece of polished silver. Silver, gold and platinum are extremely good conductors, not only of electricity, but also for the energies we create when we use our abilities. Copper works too, but it tends to oxidize and burn away. So, given that I don't have any gold or platinum laying around for you, you're going to have to make do with this."

"But how do I use it?" Megan asked, anxious to retrieve whatever her mother had left for her in the strangely warm rock.

"Place the mirror flat on your lap," he directed, watching with his usual critical eye as she did as he asked. "Put the stone in the center of the mirror. Now place your hands palm down on either side of the runestone."

She did as he instructed, assuming a position she could hold comfortably, not knowing how long this process might take. Through the extended senses that began with her touch but ended deep within her mind, the polished surface opened up into a world unto itself, one that waited for the spark of life to give it birth. It found that spark within the rigid matrix of the rune-carved stone and began to feed on what it discovered there.

"Do you feel that?" he asked. "Now close your eyes and look deep into the mirror and find what Emelia has left for you."

She found herself looking out of her mother's eyes at a younger version of Azarich. His dark hair held only a sprinkling of gray. He had a neatly trimmed mustache and beard that looked quite becoming on his lightly wrinkled face. He wore a western shirt with a pair of jeans just as he would in his later days, but the frame beneath was toned and muscular.

Behind him, a likewise youthful Alan Green loaded a mover's dolly into the back of the same truck her grandfather owned in the present. His limp was less pronounced than it would be later in life.

"Now don't forget," Azarich said, reaching out and putting his hands on her shoulders. "If you need anything, I'll be just a few hours away."

"I'll be fine," she heard herself speak in her mother's voice. "And I promise I'll call every Friday afternoon as soon as my classes are over."

"Don't think we won't come running if you don't," Alan said.

Several girls walked past, looking disdainfully at the old truck and then back at Emelia.

"I'm so proud of you girl," Azarich said, pulling her into a hug that lasted just a bit too long. More stares from the people who passed.

The two men climbed into the truck, waved and then slowly drove away. She stood there on the sidewalk, watching them pull in between two new cars she couldn't identify and then creep down to the edge of the block where they disappeared from view. She felt a sudden urge to chase the old truck down and make them take her back to quiet, comfortable Nickelville. But instead she closed her eyes, formed her energy into a silent prayer and set it free to work its magic.

The memory shifted, taking Megan to another time and place from her mother's past. She drifted into it without resistance this time, content to let her mother guide this journey toward the answers Megan most wanted.

Her roommate was pleasant enough, although there was enough hairspray in that big blond bouffant to protect it from all but the worst storms. And even though southern hospitality demanded that she treat this poor country bumpkin with some semblance of courtesy, the city girl's thoughts weren't remotely kind.

Emelia had never been around so many people at once, and she found it difficult to shield out stray thoughts. Sam had warned her about this during his numerous attempts to convince her to stay. So, even though the girl who slept a few feet from her at night never said anything mean, Emelia knew exactly how much the wealthy girl looked down on her small-town roommate.

Deciding that she needed some air, Emelia left to explore the campus. Everywhere she went, people looked at her strangely, the girls with their linebacker shoulder pads and short skirts, the boys with their billowing pants. It had taken only a short time to realize that Nickelville fashion was several years behind the times. No matter, she thought, too comfortable in her jeans and t-shirts to care. This was her time. Having people look down on her was nothing new. If she'd survived it before, she could do so again. Finding a deserted corner of the campus, she allowed her shields to drop. The strain of keeping them so rigid, even when she slept, drained her and it felt good to set her senses free from the confines of her body.

At once she felt the presence of an old tree nearby. It wasn't as old as the ones back in Nickelville, but it was the first thing she'd found here that reminded her of home. Around the corner, she spotted an evergreen oak that stood forgotten at the edge of the college's boundaries. Judging by the unkept lawn around it, not even the campus grounds-keepers came there. And even though it was just an infant next to the ones she'd left behind, she claimed it for her own.

She tossed her shoes at the base of its trunk and once again became Sam's squirrel. After exploring the canopy of its boughs, she settled into

7

a broad space where a particularly large branch split from the trunk. She closed her eyes and reveled in the way the breeze dried the sweat on her skin and rustled through the leaves around her. Her senses fused with the tree, and she could feel not only its questing branches above, but the roots that split the earth below. She would have fallen asleep there for the first true rest that she'd managed since her arrival had it not been for the realization that someone was watching her.

Standing far enough out that he could only be seen through a gap in the leaves, a dark-haired young man stared at her. He was smartly dressed in a way that was almost as far above her classmates as she lay in the other direction. He smiled and nodded her way as if to say, "Good day miss."

Feeling suddenly awkward in the tree, Emelia climbed down with as much decorum as she could manage. When she looked toward the place where he'd stood, he was nowhere to be seen.

The warmth of the day left her as she thought of another man she'd seen who was dressed as if from another time. A man who often disappeared as if into thin air.

Then the scene faded around Megan and she opened her eyes on the present. Vertigo tilted the world, but a familiar gnarled hand reached out to steady her.

"Easy, girl," he said. "We weren't sure how well her memories would mesh with your senses. How do you feel?"

"That was the first time she saw my father!" Megan burst out, ignoring his concern. "She thought he was a ghost like the Dark Man. That was so weird. I could totally see everything, and hear everything and feel everything. I was thinking her actual thoughts!"

"Breathe," he chuckled. "Slow down or you're going to pass out

8

from lack of air."

"Grandpa and Alan dropped her off at college," Megan continued, picking up the runestone which no longer felt any different than a normal stone. She placed the mirror on the bench next to her and was surprised to find that it was hot, like an electrical wire that had been carrying a heavy load. As soon as her hands were free, Fang began to nudge them with his head. "She didn't fit in at school."

"The special ones usually don't," he replied, watching her pet the wolf absently. "It's going to take a bit for you to sort through everything you just experienced. Take the mirror with you and sit somewhere quiet for a while. From what I understand, your mother found a way to give the stones to you when you were ready for them. And tell Azarich that I'm sorry about her leaving."

"I will," she said, slipping the stone into her pocket even though it no longer served any purpose. "Grandpa's a good man."

"He always has been," the hermit agreed, bracing himself before gripping the saddle horn and swinging his aging frame up into the saddle of the waiting horse. "I sure am grateful to Sam for giving me Shadowfax."

"You finally named him!" Megan said.

"No, Sam did when he gave him to me. He thought it would be funny to name him after Gandalf's horse."

"Gandalf?" Megan asked.

"Ask Bruce," the old man advised, turning his horse to go. "I'll see you soon. You don't have to have me present when you use the stones, but I wouldn't mind being there when you do."

"You helped her make them, right?"

"Yes," he answered. "But the process didn't show me what they contain, and to be honest, I'm a bit curious about what they hold. Get some rest, Megan. It's going to be an eventful time for you until this runs its course. If you need anything, just call and I'll come running."

"I'm sorry I snapped at you," she said. "I don't know what we'd do without you."

He smiled a little sadly and rode away.

The energy necessary to merge her mother's memories with her own left her feeling as if she might need a nap. Of course she'd just spent over a week unconscious in another dimension after an explosion nearly killed her, so it might be that as well. But this unhindered look into her mother's mind exhilarated her. She'd never expected to experience so many of her mother's personal thoughts. Emelia didn't even let anyone take pictures of her. Azarich had tried several times without success since they'd returned. Even though her mother had left Megan behind, the runestones felt like Emelia was still watching over her.

As she walked up the steps to the back porch, she glanced over to the swing and was surprised to find it occupied by a very large and very familiar black cat.

"I'd still like to know how you got all the way out here from the Academy," she said. "But Mr. Green told me you don't belong to anyone at the school, so I'm keeping you."

He stretched, jumped down and walked over to rub his head against her leg, clearly declaring ownership of her as well. She tucked the mirror under her arm and picked up the heavy mass of muscle and fur. He rewarded her with a rumbling purr.

Chapter II: Dream Therapy

Bruce woke in the total darkness of his bedroom from yet another nightmare of the Baker Hotel's basement. In this one, he was the only one Megan managed to send through the shadows before the explosives blew the foundation out from under the building. Even now, as he summoned a cold flame to banish the darkness that crushed him and sucked up all of the air, he could still hear their screams all the way from town.

He gulped air, but none seemed to reach his lungs. He wasn't sure if it was some sort of survival reaction, but his foresight cast off spasmic spurts of precognition that flooded his consciousness and threatened to carry him down into depths of madness.

He made himself banish the flame and return to the darkness. Then he forced his extra senses to retreat slowly back into the confines of his own mind. He ignored the monsters that waited just out of reach to drag him down into their lair. He ignored the difficulty of trying to confine himself to a body that no longer felt adequate to the task. But most of all, he closed away the part of his mind that monitored the webs of future potential that radiated outward from him into the dimension of time.

Imprisoned completely within himself, he opened his eyes and listened to the night sounds. He identified them one by one, taking his time as the roar of his heart receded like an outgoing tide. He could still smell the pizza that his brother had made from a recipe their big friend

had given him. The air from the ceiling fan cooled the terror on his skin, and the giant squeezing his chest went back to sleep. At last he could breathe again. He centered himself completely in the present, and his mind grew as quiet as the darkness around him. With each easy breath he allowed his extra senses to leak from the confines of his mind until he could feel the entire house and its inhabitants.

Paul slept fitfully. His dreams held a strange flavor that made Bruce suspect that his brother had once again returned to the hidden trails of Guarded Wood. Or maybe he was just courting a talented violin player with questionable taste in fashion. Bruce wished him luck in whichever dream he traveled and moved on.

He panicked at first when he couldn't sense Jade. But then realized she was just sleeping too deeply for the echoes of her dreams to reach him. Her future remained as solid as the rocks she loved, and the only times she crossed paths with danger were the ones when he took her there himself. He promised himself that she would have the life she deserved.

His mother, like Paul, slept fretfully just like she did every night that her husband worked at the station. He realized that he'd always known this about her, even though she'd never spoken of it aloud. Maybe everyone, whether they wanted to admit it or not, was a bit psychic when it came to their mothers.

Now he found peace in the heavily shielded confines of his house, a precaution he'd taken to keep his friend from feeling the anguish of his dreams. However, it was four o'clock in the morning, and the possibility of sleep had escaped him for the night. He supposed he could read or write in his journal, but neither felt particularly appealing.

On a whim he got up, changed into a pair of jeans and put on his shoes. He moved quietly through the darkness lest he wake his family. Then, relying on the house protections to hide his actions, he walked the shadows to the place where his night terrors had begun.

Although the containers of toxic sludge had been removed, their stench remained and likely would for some time to come. Of course, even as he thought this, his senses suggested a dozen ways to solve the problem. Beyond the newly flushed drains, the town's new filtration system stripped the last of the Jones legacy from the town's water supply.

Work lights exposed the darkened recesses where only Sam had been able to see when they'd been there before. Massive columns supported the fourteen stories of hotel securely above his head. He could still see where the explosives had been attached to them, but he wasn't quite ready to revisit the path where those memories led.

Unwilling to disturb the crime scene markers, Bruce walked the shadows to the base of the stairs and started to climb toward the ground floor. He stepped over the ashen dust which marked the final resting place of the missing sheriff, wanting no part of that memory either. Then, to his surprise when his hand settled on the banister rail, he realized he could feel more than just his immediate surroundings. His consciousness flowed up the iron castings beneath his hand, up into the girders hidden within the floors and through them to the rest of the building.

Something wasn't right about the hotel. It wasn't something wrong with the construction, which had been carried out to specifications far sturdier than seemed necessary. Rather he sensed within its design an alternative purpose.

"What have we here?" he said aloud, startling himself when his quiet voice echoed through the stairwell. Far above, he sensed that something had become aware of his trespassing.

Away from the stairway, the ground floor had an old, disused smell that he greatly preferred to the acrid odor of the basement. Although not immediately pleasant, it held within it subtle hints of old books and letters found in attics on rainy days.

He liked old books. He liked them a lot, and just like an old book he realized that this place held secrets. Future paths involving the Baker Hotel opened like an exotic flower all around him, and he knew that he'd be spending his sleepless nights here drinking in all that this forbidding structure could teach him.

He didn't make it very far in his explorations of the ground floor before the windows lost the purple hues of nighttime. But that was okay. Now that they'd saved the beautiful old building, she wasn't going anywhere. He fixed the location in his mind as the hermit had taught him, content with the knowledge that he could resume his exploration where he'd left off the next time. Then he walked the shadows back to his bedroom where a quick scan of his childhood home told him that his mother and siblings were still engaged in that willful, though ultimately doomed attempt to hold the morning away by sheer acts of sleepy will.

Smiling at the prospect of starting the new school year with a friend, something he'd never done before, he decided to make a cup of coffee for himself and scramble some eggs for the family. It wouldn't be as good as what his father or even Paul would have made, but he found himself hungry after the morning's secret adventure.

"So he just showed up?" Paul asked their neighbor, who rode shotgun with his sister in the restored car.

"I have no idea how he got all the way there from the Academy," Megan replied, watching the cornfields pass on her side of the car. "But he seems to cheer Grandpa up a little, so as far as I'm concerned, Mr. Bob is ours now."

"Millie will be glad to have him away from her fish," Paul said.

"But Mr. Harris will probably miss him," Bruce added.

"At least we won't have to go check the library every time something goes missing anymore," Jade said. "I thought he belonged to the principal."

"Alan told us that he just showed up one morning and nothing they tried kept him out of the school," Bruce said. "They eventually gave up and let him stay."

The morning traffic crept down Main Street, and Bruce found himself looking at the abandoned hotel with new interest. He'd always been fascinated by it, much as he'd been curious about the hidden places at the Palace. But unlike the theater, he felt an odd possessiveness for the hotel and wanted to see it fully restored. He made mental notes of what it would take for Sam to buy it. It would raise some eyebrows and give his big friend a reputation for being eccentric, but Bruce also saw that the big man wouldn't mind. He realized it had some part to play in the future that spanned out long past the time they had left in school. What that might be, Bruce had no idea.

When they pulled into the Academy's parking lot, he noticed Andrew Jackson (of no relation that he knows of to the former president of the same name) waiting next to the front door. As usual, he looked nervous and out of place.

Bruce allowed his eyes to rest on Megan for a moment while they parked. One of the many benefits of being able to see the future was that he usually knew when to look away before she caught him. The downside however, was that he had yet to have her smile in even one the visions when she did.

He liked the way his sister obsessed about her car, but no matter how much he assured her that he could fix scratched paint easier than he could walk an extra mile each week due to her preferred parking spot, she still protected the metal behemoth like it was her firstborn child.

The bus pulled up just as they reached the stone steps, and he wondered who had taken over the last two seats on the driver's side. Oddly enough, he found that he missed it. The windows had all been replaced and the worst of the dents from the previous year's hail storm had been pounded out, but it still looked lumpy and misshapen. The school board would likely replace it as the town began to recover in earnest.

"Hey Andrew," Paul called.

"Hi Paul," the boy answered without looking away from Jade.

"Are you ready for this?" Jade asked him, her hand seeking his before they turned and entered the front door. He smiled, but didn't answer.

"Don't forget you have to drop me off at Kate's on the way home," Paul reminded her. "She says I'm progressing faster than she thought I would."

"After all," Megan teased, "You've only got a couple of months left to practice so you can serenade the infamous violin girl."

Paul grinned in reply. He'd finally gotten used to them giving him a hard time about the mystery goth from last year's Jubilee.

"Wouldn't it make more sense to play a different instrument than she does?" Andrew asked, surprising them all by speaking.

"No," Paul said seriously, "I have to play the same one if I want to…"

"Make beautiful music together," they all finished, getting some strange looks from the other students. Bruce noticed Mr. Danders watching them from the office door as they passed.

They found the janitor and librarian sitting on the edge of the stage watching the students pass when they entered the cafeteria. After spending so much time with the two old men during the summer, Bruce could tell that they were talking about the librarian's wife. From what he'd heard in passing conversations at the McGeehee place, the doctors doubted that Esther would survive the school year. But both men still

17

brightened when they saw the youngsters approaching.

"Here comes trouble," Alan laughed. "Although Andrew might just be able to keep them in line." The boy blushed crimson.

"Look what you did," Jade scolded. "It takes him an hour to lose that sunburn! Anyway, we'll see you guys at lunch."

"And geometry after that," Megan reminded her.

"It's going to be so weird having a class with my little brother," the eldest Grimble replied before leading her boyfriend toward the door by Mr. Green's office.

"Any word from Emelia?" Mr. Harris asked.

"Not yet," Megan answered, her mood darkening the bond she and Bruce shared even though nothing showed on the outside.

He didn't mean anything, he sent. *He's just trying to cover that they were just talking about Esther.*

I know, she replied. *I'm just worried about her.*

I used to feel like that when people talked about my asthma. It would catch me off guard when I was happily thinking about something else. Have you noticed that we don't do this as much anymore?

Talk mind to mind?

Yes.

All of our friends know about the supernatural parts of our lives now, and it's just easier to say things out loud and not have to repeat everything we say.

It's probably like getting a phone for the first time. You spend every second on it for a while and then you just sort of lose interest, he sent.

I'll have to take your word on that. I was thinking about trying out another radio alarm. How does that work out?

He stepped to the side of the stage for a moment and focused.

It's fine as long as you don't want to have it for more than a week or so.

Oh well, I guess I can still dream.

If you want, I can just send Paul over to practice his serenading skills under your window, he sent, finally getting a smile in return.

"Jade assures me that he talks when we're not around," Megan said aloud.

"Andrew?" Paul asked.

"Yeah," she answered. "For some reason he gets nervous around us. But he's apparently pretty talkative when it's just the two of them."

"We are pretty intimidating," Bruce said.

"And he doesn't even know the worst of the trouble we get into. What do you guys say we try to go have a completely normal day without anything resembling a supernatural catastrophe?" she asked.

"Does that include teleporting felines?" Paul asked, pointing to the place where the stage curtains stood partly ajar.

When she and Bruce turned to look, Mr. Bob flopped down in the place where the light from the windows above merged and began to bathe himself.

Chapter III: Old Cotton and Confusing Dreams

After a gloriously mundane day of the three R's, as Mr. Green was annoyingly fond of calling them, Megan came home to an uncharacteristically quiet grandfather whose smile no longer lit his eyes. And in the instant when she saw him, she realized that a part of her had been looking forward to telling her mother about her day.

So now she sat on the edge of her mother's bed, looking over the room closely for the first time since she'd woken after the Baker. It already felt abandoned, the traces of her mother's presence fading away like her scent. With difficulty, she could call echoes of the woman forth, but even then, they felt washed out and lifeless, as if her mother fought having her image captured even in memory. Paperbacks that looked like they'd all been read repeatedly back when Emelia was still in school still filled the bookcase. Empty spaces on the walls marked the places where her mother had removed the unicorn and castle posters. However, with the exception of the partially completed watercolor of Emelia's crib that Azarich had framed and placed over the head of the bed, there had been no attempts to decorate the room.

Megan walked over to the closet door and discovered that her mother had never removed the clothing she'd left behind when she went to college. She'd merely pushed it back to hang the few garments she'd allowed Azarich to buy her from the catalog.

Megan pulled out a pair of jeans and held them up to herself. They'd be a little short on her, but otherwise they'd fit perfectly. Then she pulled out a Star Wars t-shirt with heavy wear around the hem and neckline, letting her know that Emelia had worn it often. She reached out with her mind long enough to confirm that her grandfather was still laying on his bed in his room with the door shut. Then she pulled off the shirt she'd worn to school and pulled her mother's old one over her head. It was soft in the way that only well-loved cotton can be. It felt good against her skin and when she concentrated, she could feel something of her mother's happiness still trapped within the thin fabric. Then she took a few other items from her mother's high school years and laid them down on the vanity's bench. She knew her mother wouldn't mind if she tried them on, and it might make her feel better about the woman's absence.

The dresser was the same. A few of things she still wore rested on top of the things she probably wore during her last year at the Academy. In short, every clue necessary to realize that Emelia had never intended to stay was laid out for Megan to see. She'd just been too busy playing with the kids next door to notice. She sank down on the side of the bed, twirling her hair around her fingers.

A loud purr made her jump up and look back to where Mr. Bob stretched out, watching her.

"How do you keep doing that?" she asked.

He chose not to answer.

She crawled over and laid down beside him, running her hand across the silky fur of his side. As if rewarding her, he reached with his paw under the pillow and slid something against her cheek. She knew it for a runestone even before she looked.

"I found another runestone," she called out to her grandfather.

There was a muffled grunt of affirmation from his room.

She carried the clothes to her room for later, picked up August's mirror and made her way downstairs to the back door. Her mind raced with possibilities of what the stone might contain, and she wondered if she should call for the hermit before she delved into its secrets.

She knew the grove wasn't empty before she left the path and entered its quiet shade. She crossed through the sea of yellow flowers and found Sam sitting on one of the stone benches that encircled the fire pit, his massive back toward her.

"Good evening, Megan," he said without turning. His voice was tired and washed out, like the memories of her mother had been back in the house.

"Hey Sam," she said, happy to see him. "I just found another one of the runestones that Mom left for me."

"That is good news," he said, though his voice didn't reflect any eagerness to find out what it held. Even though his shields were rigid, they were unequal to the task of holding back the full extent of his feelings.

"I'm going to have a look at it if you want to stay and see what it shows," she offered. She'd felt sorrow from him before, but it had always been tempered with the joy he found in her mother's presence.

"I appreciate the offer," he said, rising to his feet. "But I promised August that I would bring him some things he can't obtain from within Guarded Wood. I just wanted to stop here and reflect on better days for a moment before I crossed the boundary."

She knew he shielded her out to spare her from the worst of his sadness, and even though it was a noble attempt, she'd had enough of people moping around. So she put the mirror and stone down at the base of one of the trees and rushed up to give him her best imitation of one of

22

Jade's famous hugs.

His chuckle rumbled deep within his core, reminding her of the purring of the cat she'd just left. Then he enfolded her gently in his massive arms and kissed her lightly on the top of her head.

"I don't know what I did to deserve that," he said quietly, "but it is greatly appreciated."

When she backed away from him, he noticed her shirt, and his mouth spread into his first genuine smile since her mother had left.

"Where did you find that?" he asked.

"It was in Mom's closet," Megan answered, running her hands over the soft cotton. "It's really worn so I'm guessing it was one of her favorites."

"Indeed it was," he said. "She stole it from the back of my closet the summer after she learned to drive."

"You were this small once?" Megan asked, surprised.

"Yes, when I was nine years old," he answered. "I was wearing it the day we met. She loved how soft it was."

"That's what made me put it on," Megan said. "I really miss her."

"We all do," he admitted. "But I really do need to get out to August with these medicines. He's a bit under the weather."

"Tell him I hope he gets better soon," she said, giving Sam another quick hug. "Don't be a stranger."

"I could never be a stranger to you Megan McGeehee." Then he walked over to his horse, pulled himself into the saddle and headed off into the woods.

She watched him go, silently berating her mother for the misery she'd left in her wake. Then she retrieved the stone and the mirror before returning to the place where she'd unlocked the first runestone. In her eagerness to see the past once again through her mother's eyes, she hardly noticed the vertigo as she surrendered to its hidden depths.

It took Megan a moment to separate the stale odor of cigarette smoke from her other senses in the airport. This must have been before smoking had been banned inside of the terminals.

Although the narrow tunnel leading off of the plane opened into a larger space, the holiday crowds packed it with too much movement. A multitude of stray thoughts needled at her shields like droplets of high-pressure water. She felt a bit nauseous from the short flight, but it would be worth it to sleep in her own bed and lose herself in the familiarity of home.

"Emelia, over here," she heard her father call. She'd missed the sound of that voice so much, even though she'd kept her promise and called him every Friday night after classes let out. Alan was with him, just as he'd been when they dropped her off at her dorm that first day. The past few months felt as insubstantial as a dream, but then again, so did her life before. What if none of it were real? What if her dreams were the true reality, and this was nothing more than fantasy? She rushed into her father's arms, and for the first time in months, she felt truly safe.

"God I've missed you!" he whispered in her ear while he did his best to squeeze her in two. More like an uncle than her father's best friend, Alan joined in as well.

"I missed you guys too," she whispered back, closing her eyes in contentment.

"How was your flight?" Alan asked as he took her bag.

"It was really bumpy about halfway here," she answered, linking arms with her father as they navigated the crowds toward the front of the airport where she knew his truck waited. "But I'm home for a whole week!"

"About time too," Azarich said. "There's a certain young man that has been stopping by the office every day to ask if I've heard anything else from you."

"You'd think he got enough from the letters we write. I think he's only missed two or three days since I left."

"And do you answer all of them?" he asked.

"I write to him about twice a week. There just isn't enough going on there to write more than that."

"And your classes are still going well?" Azarich asked, steering her in the right direction when they got out of the building.

"Straight A's so far," she answered.

The memory shifted and she found herself sitting in front of the house on Beverly Road, perched on the tailgate of Azarich's truck when a beat-up muscle car with more rust than paint pulled into the driveway.

"What have you gone and done?" she asked as a lanky but still impossibly tall Sam climbed out of the driver's side door. "I mean, how do you even fit in there?"

"I got tired of driving my uncle's old Buick," he said. "I practically got it for free. Mr. Green helped me tow it to his place and showed me how to get it running again. He says I've got good hands for this sort of thing."

"Imagine what you'll be able to do when you finally finish growing into them, Boy Who Talks to Trees."

He crossed the space between them in two long strides, lifted her into his arms and hugged her so hard she actually grunted.

"I missed you too," she whispered in his ear. "But putting me in a body cast won't make me stay longer, so you'd better put me down while my ribs are still whole. The short hair is going to take some getting used to." she told him as she reached up to run her fingers through what

25

remained of his thick black hair.

"It kept getting in my way while I worked on the car," he explained, reluctantly putting her down.

The memory shifted again, and this time Emelia was lying awake in her bed. It was almost time to go back, and even though she'd spent almost every moment with her father and Sam, it wasn't enough. Every time she drifted off to sleep, she found the stranger that reminded her of the Dark Man waiting. But in her dreams, she couldn't fear him because she somehow knew he was like her. He had answers to the questions she'd never been able to find. That was what drew her to him. It had absolutely nothing to do with the way she felt when those strange violet eyes looked at her. She wished the dreams would stop. She'd never seen him again since that first time when she'd climbed the old tree at the edge of campus. But even so, she knew Sam had noticed that she was blocking off parts of her mind from him lest a stray thought betray her. This had led to more than one awkward silence where there had never been any before. She resolved to put the memory of the strange man aside and get some real rest. And though she remained firm in her resolve, her dreams betrayed her yet again.

Chapter IV: Paint Samples and Cannibals

Bruce felt a certain amount of pride as he looked over Sam's financial portfolio and compared its growth with the needs of the community. Nickelville had begun at long last to pull free of the recession that had gripped it for the past several decades. Several of the closed shops on main street had already reopened their doors to the public.

Hey Bruce, the thought came from next door.

What's up? He asked, his pulse quickening before he locked down his reaction.

Not much. I've been trying to make Mom's room look like someone actually lives here. How about you?

I just saw that the school board is going to approve renovations to the Academy next week, starting with the heating and cooling systems. Supporting the initiatives put forth by Tony Jones have become extremely unpopular with the community. By the time winter gets here, we should have heat that doesn't smell like swamp gas.

Nice! She sent, with just a hint of guilt at the evil man's name. *What is everyone doing over there?*

Jade is over at Andrew's house supposedly studying, and Paul is practicing the violin down the hall. You know, he's getting scary good. I'm pretty sure he just played part of that song he's always whistling from the Jubilee last year. It wasn't perfect, but I could tell what it was, and I don't get the feeling that it's a particularly easy piece to play. I can't figure out if he's super talented or if he just sounds good compared to the rest of us. How is the overhaul of Emelia's lair going?

I can't settle on a color. I've got a whole bunch of samples laid out in front of me, but I can't make up my mind.

You end up painting it a muted yellow.

That's what I was thinking! Being friends with you is certainly handy sometimes.

A small yet significant lurch in his stomach accompanied those words, down low enough that she couldn't feel it.

I was planning to take a run through Guarded Wood in a little bit. It's hard to believe that I'll have to race again in just a few months. Want to come?

As much as I'd like to pretend that I can keep up with you, we both know I can't. It's not fair to slow you down when you're trying to train. I think I'll go bully Grandpa into taking me to the hardware store again to get some yellow paint and painter's cloth.

He's already got some brushes and plastic in the garage that his father added onto the house. You just need the paint.

How did you know his father added it on if you can't see the past?

He told me about it after I mowed his lawn a few years back.

Good to know, thanks. Have a good run and check in on August. I haven't heard from him in a few days. Sam said he wasn't feeling good.

I will.

Her presence left him as quickly as it had come, creating an emptiness where there hadn't been one before.

He stuck his head into Paul's room long enough to tell him where he was going and then took off down the path that led to the tree house. He'd hoped that the guilt he felt every time he saw the Sentinel tree would fade over time. But here he was, several weeks removed from that night, and if anything he felt worse. Rationally, he knew the faun's sacrifice wasn't his fault just because he'd designed the treehouse, but the emotional part of him didn't always listen to reason. Just like the rational part of him understood that Megan didn't have to feel the same way about him that he felt about her.

August.

Yes?

Would it be okay if I went for a run in Guarded Wood?

That would actually help me out, the hermit sent. *There hasn't been anything going on here since the boundary was restored, and Fang is getting restless. Would you mind a running companion?*

That would be amazing, Bruce answered, excited by the prospect. He loved the wolf-hybrid and knew Fang wouldn't have any problem at all keeping up with him.

He's already on his way. Now that the protections are back up, you can go anywhere you want. He'll take you through some pretty sights so you won't get bored.

You're the best, August.

Bruce took off at a run down the same path where he'd once let Megan, Jade and Paul talk him into running in the Jubilee race.

True to the hermit's word, Fang soon joined him. But before Bruce could figure out which way to go, the beast knocked him down and nuzzled him affectionately.

"It's good to see you too," Bruce chuckled, losing some of his earlier agitation in the thick fur before climbing back to his feet and asking the beast which way he should go.

Fang took off at a fast pace, forcing Bruce to widen his strides and use the full depth of his lungs to get oxygen to his starved muscles. At first, he thought he'd have to ask him to slow down, but then he found his rhythm and started to enjoy the run.

The trees thinned then died away entirely as the two of them flew through one of the dense air zones that marked the transition from one realm into another. The path began to climb, and Bruce could see the tracks of the hermit's horse in the sandy soil. The rise wasn't steep, but it made the muscles in his legs burn nonetheless. At its crest, he came to a vast, green plateau with the ruins of an old tower silhouetted against the horizon. Fang shot ahead and startled a huge flock of white birds that Bruce couldn't identify. They squawked angrily and took to the sky.

Bruce had never realized how much he'd grown accustomed to the hints of exhaust in his own time until he had a chance to breathe air that was truly free of pollution. He thought he might be in Ireland, or possibly Scotland. The views looked like the ones in the travel advertisements he used to pour over in the days before Megan had come to Nickelville. The question, as was always the case in Guarded Wood, was whether this was another time, or another place that had never been. Perhaps he and the others could come out sometime with a sextant and some star charts to try and figure out where they were. He was pretty sure he'd heard Paul talk about programs that could identify the locations of constellations in the distant past as well.

But before he could think too much about such plans, Fang led him between two stone monoliths and through a passageway into another realm. Suddenly Bruce found himself half-skipping half-sliding down a rocky slope toward water. When he reached the bottom, he came to a sandy beach. The sun shone deep on the horizon of the bluest sky he'd ever seen. An inward wind salted the air and drove waves to crash on a shore littered with shells and driftwood.

The wolf opened up his strides. Bruce only managed to keep up for a minute before the resistance of running in the sand sapped his strength, and he had to admit defeat. Unable to maintain his stride, he slowed down, gasping for breath as he hadn't done since he'd collapsed after the race.

Throwing himself down at the edge of the water, Bruce laid back and looked up at the sky where three massive gull-like birds glided toward the open water. Fang was instantly there with him, rolling in the sand and showering him with small shells.

When he sat up, laughing, he glanced back to see how far they'd come down from above to find that the cliffs were gone to be replaced by jungle.

Now you know why it hasn't been so bad being in here for so long, the hermit's voice said in his mind where the sound of the surf couldn't drown it out. *This is just one of a thousand places I've explored over the centuries, and I doubt I've even scratched the surface of what Guarded Wood holds within her borders. Don't go into the trees here though,* he said. *There are some really nasty ants and spiders that will leave you covered in bites before you even realize they're there. That beach is one of my favorite places though.*

"Thanks for sharing this with me," Bruce said out loud, knowing that August would hear it through Fang's ears.

For the love of the gods, don't talk out loud! The cannibals will hear you!

Bruce scrambled to his feet, ready to run.

Fang knocked him down and started to lick his face.

You should have seen your face! the hermit howled, and even though laughter didn't transmit as sound in this type of communication, Bruce's thoughts were filled with it nonetheless.

Chapter V: Hypoallergenic Supernatural Beast

Megan had never been away from her mother for this long before, and it made her homesick in a way that had nothing to do with home. As much as it surprised her to think so, she'd have happily traded all of the answers she'd been promised to have her mother back. So she closed herself in her mother's bedroom and shielded herself from her grandfather's depression. Although she worried about the depths of his unhappiness, she had enough of her own to deal with. She'd cleared out her mother's closet and drawers of all but the clothing that she still wore. Some of the styles had come back, and Megan fully intended to wear them. Others however, she set aside to ask her mother if she'd ever worn them out in public. She couldn't bring herself to throw anything away though, so the rest went into a box that she sealed with packing tape and put on the top shelf of her mother's closet.

The room still smelled like paint, making her think about Bruce's asthma. She busied herself with folding the drop cloths and putting them away in the plastic tub her grandfather had brought in from the garage. All in all, it had turned out well, although it might have gone better if she'd asked Bruce to help. Of course, that would have led to more looks when he thought she wouldn't notice, and that would lead to the irrational irritation that always bubbled up within her when she caught him. Why couldn't she just be flattered by his attention? Unwilling to explore where that thought would lead, she opened the door and lowered her shields, allowing Azarich to fill her senses once again.

"Hey Grandpa," she yelled down the hall.

"Yes?"

"Didn't you say that Mom's new comforter came in?"

"Yes, it's on the couch in the living room. I think the sheets and curtains came in too."

"Thanks!" she called, already sliding down the banister.

Rather than carry the large stack of oddly shaped parcels up the stairs, she tossed them through the shadows where they landed on the floor next to the bed. Then she ran back up, taking the steps two at a time and wondering how Bruce's training had gone the day before. She thought about asking him, but decided against it. Sometimes when she did so lately, it felt like he was blocking a part of himself off from her. This, of course, made her remember the way her mother had hidden her dreams from Sam in the runestone memory. Something stirred within her before she lost her train of thought.

She enjoyed ripping the packaging open and dumping all of the scraps in the trash can. She doubted she'd ever get used to this constant stream of new things coming into her possession, especially when a part of her kept warning her that it was dangerous to own more than she could fit into her duffle bag.

She stripped the bed and carried the bedding down to run through the wash. Grandpa didn't like to get rid of stuff, and it still matched the bed clothing from the guest rooms, so she planned to just put it into one of those closets for future use.

When she'd finished, she looked over the room and thought, with the exception of the largely empty walls, that it now looked like a place that would suit her mother. It certainly looked better than any of the places they'd stayed before, which of course made Megan wonder where her mother was now. Had her travels taken her into the sorts of places Megan wished she could forget? Her good mood evaporated, and she considered once again going to find Bruce.

But that wouldn't be fair to her grandfather, whose sad and selective loneliness so nearly matched her own. So she wandered down the hall to the door to her grandfather's room where she found him sitting on his bed, looking at one of his many photo albums. Without waiting for him to invite her in, she crossed the room, climbed up next to him and looked through the pictures with him.

"This is one of my favorites," he said, pointing at a picture of her grandmother, Josie, standing next to some musicians at the Jubilee. One of them looked familiar, but she couldn't place where she'd seen the young woman before. Megan could just make out a fortune teller's tent behind them. Josie was casting Azarich a sideways smile, and even though the picture was black and white, she could still see mischief in her grandmother's eyes.

"It's almost frightening how much we look like each other," Megan said, looking at image after image as he turned the pages. There were pictures of Mr. Harris and his wife, and as always seemed to be the case, they were laughing. There was also a picture in which Mr. Green was looking at a woman in the distance. Even without color, Megan knew the woman's hair was red.

"Is that Kate?"

"I believe it is," he said, pushing his glasses further up on his nose to get a better look. "I'll have to take this one out and give it to her. She'll get a kick out of that."

"If you've got a moment," Megan said when he got to the end of the album, "Come and see what you think about Mom's room. And speaking of having time, I should be around more now that the Palace is doing well enough to pay actual employees. As much as I love watching movies there, I'm probably not going to be able to eat movie popcorn for at least a year."

"I'd love to look, and I always love having you around more," he said, rising stiffly from the bed. His knees popped loudly. "There must be rain coming. I'm really feeling my age tonight. Are your classes still going well?"

"Yes, it's so much better without any Joneses," she answered, leading him into the brightly painted room.

"It's good to see it looking like it's lived in again," he said, walking over to sit on the edge of the bed. He winced and rubbed his right knee again.

Mr. Bob chose that moment to saunter into the room, jump up onto the new bedding and curl up next to Azarich.

"It's also nice to have a cat in this house again," he added, reaching out and running his fingers through the cat's silky fur. "They usually give me allergy problems, but this one doesn't seem to do so."

"There's something strange about him," Megan said.

"Besides him being a kleptomaniac?" Azarich asked.

"Yeah, he's still showing up at the school too. Sometimes it's only been a few minutes since I saw him here."

"Well aren't you just the most perfect supernatural beast?" the old man asked.

Mr. Bob purred loudly.

Chapter VI: Terrible Trio Version 1.0

Bruce's nightmares had largely stopped since his first trip to the Baker Hotel, but a storm blew in during the witching hour one night, and he found himself lying awake in bed once more, unable to go back to sleep.

It wasn't a bad storm as they went, and unlike most of the others he'd seen over the past year or so, this one owed its origin to completely natural forces. Ever since finding out that storms often preceded the arrival of the Wild Hunt, he made a habit of keeping track of the weather so as to distinguish between an autumn shower and an invasion.

He felt guilty about not sharing his early morning explorations, but he still needed this. He needed to be alone in the dark as he worked out the puzzle of the mysterious building. In a way, it felt almost as if the strange hulk had been waiting for him to come. And even though he couldn't acknowledge it to himself, he needed to put some distance between Megan and himself. He loved her, of that he had no doubt. He also knew that she loved him in her own way, though not in the way he most wanted. But no matter how things eventually turned out, he couldn't allow himself to push her away from him as he could see in so many of the future paths.

As soon as he walked the shadows to the place where he'd been forced to end his previous exploration, he realized the roof leaked. From the torrents pouring in from collapsed ceiling plaster and running down the stairwell in rivulets, it looked like the roof leaked a lot. But given that the hotel had stood for nearly a hundred years without any maintenance, that was pretty much a given.

At first glance, everything seemed to be what he'd expect to find in a partially completed hotel that had been deserted for so long. Graffiti covered places where some of the more daring youth had managed to evade the now deceased sheriff and gain entry. Here and there he found signs of short-term habitation, though none looked recent. That of course, made him think of Megan.

The foyer contained a long counter behind which room keys would have hung had the hotel ever progressed that far. Unfinished concrete floors helped carry the sounds of his footsteps down hallways where ornate tiles would have been laid. Some of the walls sported a layer of cracked plaster that had warped in the Texas heat and fallen away in chunks to bust on the floor as the decades passed. Others were framed in to receive wood paneling that had never come.

Reasoning that any light might be seen from the outside, he relied on his extra senses to examine his surroundings. That suited him perfectly, since it was the darkness he'd come to defy. For him, this acceptance of the darkness proved he could walk alone, and that he wasn't merely an extension of the people he loved. It was also there in the darkness that he realized he was evolving in ways that he didn't yet fully understand.

In hindsight, he realized that it wasn't just actual events that shaped him, but rather the sum of the collected pathways and the continuous subconscious feedback of how his actions could affect the world around him. It also gave the part of his mind that had always reveled in the analysis of patterns an infinite supply of data to interpret. That, in turn, altered the way he interacted with the world and revealed things otherwise hidden, such as looking past the hotel's veneer to notice what should have been there but wasn't.

First of all, he sensed no rats or termites anywhere in the building. That suggested supernatural forces at work, yet he felt nothing of the like. As far as he could tell, no shields or wards operated anywhere in the vicinity except his own. He also knew the Baker had electricity. It had run the elevator and there were lights on the first floor. But as far as he'd seen, there wasn't a single electrical outlet anywhere. Furthermore, even though there were rooms marked as lavatories that held sinks and toilets, there wasn't any plumbing attached to them.

The more he explored, the more his findings confirmed that there was something fundamentally wrong with the Baker. What he found as he walked slowly through the darkened corridors and partially completed rooms suggested that the builder had possessed absolutely no training in the arts of construction. But Bruce didn't believe that for a second. The mere fact that the building had survived a century in this derelict state hinted at engineering genius.

When he came to the central elevator shaft, he located the water supply line and was surprised to find that there were two. One of them terminated a few floors above where he now stood and the other continued up to the top floor. Why would the builders do that? The obvious thing to do would be to run a single, high-volume line to the top floor and allow gravity to increase pressure for the floors below like the water tower did nearby.

"What were you doing here?" he asked aloud, and once again he felt something stir up above. But whatever it was didn't seem like any sort of a threat. For that matter, it didn't feel entirely human either.

Closing his eyes and casting his senses out through the skeletal structure of the building, he also found an intact electrical line that still supplied power to the top floor of the building. Given how much water currently poured down from up there, he considered going back home and returning on some future night when everything had dried out so as to avoid electrocution. Being an asthmatic, Bruce's least desired way to die was suffocation. But having his brain fried by electricity and living out his last days as a somewhat loveable vegetable wasn't far behind.

However, he was a teenage boy with the gift of foresight and he couldn't see anything bad in his immediate future. And yes, he knew that he should wait until Sam had the deed to the building safely in hand and come back with the rest of the bunch, but for now this was his secret. It was his adventure, and even though he had to strangle out the urge to tell Megan about it at least three times a minute, he also knew that she'd insist on coming with him on these outings. He might be over his nightmares about that day, but he still wasn't ready to see her here in the place where she'd so easily left him behind. For now, he'd keep his mouth shut and take a nap during English class after he finished his literary analysis essay.

He continued to explore the layout of the floors above, careful to study them closely lest he miss any clues about what had been going on here during the years when Azarich and his friends had been children. But though he searched closely, nothing presented itself.

Then he reached the fifth floor and everything changed. An oversized apartment took up the entire floor. Unlike the floors below, this one held the memory of habitation. He thought longingly of his friend's ability to read the past, but still didn't want her here. Had she realized yet that her ability to see the past was every bit as powerful as his foresight?

Everywhere he went, he found signs that people had lived there for what looked like an extended period of time. An old stove and refrigerator were pushed into a corner next to a table and broken chair.

There were cabinets full of cooking paraphernalia, and he thought he could sense the scent of food long since turned to dust.

There were rooms where the remains of bedding rotted on beds that sagged to the floor. Clothing hung in closets that hadn't been opened in decades. And though he sensed it had all been nice in its day, he doubted the furnishings on this floor had ever been up to the lavish standards of a hotel mogul like Baker.

He found nothing that explained the strange distribution of completed work in the building, so he returned to the stairway to explore what lay above. The next floor opened into a vast, unfinished place within the shell of the hotel. Between the fifth floor and the penthouse, he sensed nothing but the internal skeleton of girders and columns. Everything else was just a hollow husk, giving the impression from the outside that the building was much closer to completion than it actually was.

Although he wanted to find a way up to the top floor, he could tell by the lightening of the horizon over Guarded Wood in the distance that morning drew close. He felt tempted to walk the shadows to the top of the building, but even considering the action created an ominous blank spot in his foresight. Disappointed, he marked his location and walked the shadows back to his bedroom.

After a short shower to wash off the grime of his explorations, he ate breakfast with his family. Paul had scrambled some eggs since their father was still on shift for a few more hours.

"Hey Mom," Bruce said when they'd finished. "Would you mind if I came by sometime and looked through the Tribune archives for stuff on the Baker?"

41

"Of course not," she replied, placing some papers she'd been working on the night before into her battered briefcase. "I'm pretty sure the research I had Heather put together for me after the Jones incident hasn't been refiled yet."

"Awesome," he said, feeling Megan leave her house next door.

"Why do you want to know about the hotel?" she asked.

"I've been thinking about it a lot lately. It just seems like something I'd like to know more about."

"Well, let me know if you discover something interesting," she said, giving him a hug. "If there's anything that people love as much as Goatman stories, it's stories about the mysterious Baker Hotel."

They found Megan reclining on Christine's hood, wrapped up in a well-loved book when they came out the front door together. Bruce took it out of her hands as he passed, glancing at the cover with interest.

"Hey," she complained. "I was reading that!"

"Where did you get such an old copy?" he asked, returning it to her without losing her place.

"It was on the bookshelf in Mom's room," she answered. "It's pretty good. I think she and Sam must have read it several times each. I can feel both of them when I touch it."

"If memory serves, the first one in that series was the first fantasy book to ever hit the *New York Times* best seller list. That's the second, and I think it came out about the same time Emelia and Sam were teens. They probably read it when it was first released."

"Are there any more of them?" she asked.

"Tons," he answered, pleased that she was reading fantasy on her own.

"And Bruce probably has all of them," Jade said.

"Of course I do," he replied, climbing into Christine's back seat behind Megan. "As a matter of fact it was a book in that series that Chuck threw over the wall in the courtyard. And you're welcome to borrow any of them any time you'd like."

"I've got to stop and get gas on the way," Jade announced once they were moving down Beverly Road. "I don't suppose there's anything you

43

could do to improve her gas mileage. I love her, but she is an insatiable beast when it comes to fuel."

"Christine's engine was designed eighty years ago," Bruce replied, closing his eyes for a moment after the night's excursions. "This is as good as it gets unless you want me to swap the engine for a newer one."

"How about enchanting her to repair herself and kill my enemies?"

"No need," he said. "Allison is already gone."

"Chuck and Glenn aren't that bad any more either," Megan added.

"Oh well, a girl can dream. Anyway, now that they're almost done reupholstering the seats in both theaters, Kate has agreed to extend the concession stand to include a coffee bar!" the eldest Grimble exclaimed, drifting into the shoulder and hitting a pothole.

"So Kate took our resignations well?" Megan asked.

"She said to thank you for helping out for so long and that I was supposed to let you in for free for the rest of the year," Jade said.

"I can live with that," Bruce said happily, starting to drift off. Like Megan, he was ready to have his nights and weekends free again, especially now that school had started. "You going to miss it, Paul?"

The youngest Grimble continued to stare out of the window, making Bruce open his eyes and look over when he didn't answer. He had his violin case in his lap and his fingers were drumming a complex rhythm on the clasp.

"Earth to Paul," Jade said loudly.

"Huh?" the youngest Grimble mumbled, breaking free from whatever daydream had trapped him so thoroughly.

"Kate is letting us see movies for free at the Palace for a year," Megan said.

"Oh," he murmured. "That's cool." Then he was gone again.

He's got a calendar next to his bed, and he's been marking off the days to the Jubilee, Bruce sent.

How can he be so crazy over a girl that he's never even talked to? Megan asked.

The heart wants what the heart wants, Bruce answered.

Getting philosophical on me?

Never, but I do wish I could see more of his future. It's still clouded when I try to see anything more than a few hours out.

Later that day when the afternoon lethargy set in after lunch, Megan sat in Journalism, the only class she didn't share with Bruce. She tried to concentrate on the teacher's lecture over the need to be concise, but still yawned, unable to help herself and the teacher glared at her.

She'd slept well enough the night before, but she felt like she'd spent the night hiking through Guarded Wood. Maybe she needed to start taking vitamins or drinking more water. This wasn't the first time over the past few weeks that she'd felt like this.

Moments later, she caught herself starting to nod off again, so she raised her hand and asked to go to the restroom. Maybe some cold water on her face would snap her out of it.

She thought once again about the specter of Jacob Routh as she passed the isolation room. As always, something within the memories he'd given her tried to surface. She hated when they did that. His thoughts were strange, alien things inside her head, and she wished she could be rid of them. She doubted, however, that she could do that until she finally understood all of what he had attempted to tell her that day.

Once in the girl's restroom, she splashed water on her face in a vain attempt to wake up. She looked up at herself in the mirror, glad as she did so that she didn't seem to need makeup. She wasn't sure they even made cosmetics for her pale complexion. The only time she'd ever tried them had left her looking too goth for her taste. The last thing she needed was for Paul to see her like that, given where his romantic inclinations seemed to be taking him these days.

Nearby, someone started to cry.

Megan followed the sound toward the cafeteria where she climbed the wooden steps to the stage. Behind the curtain she found a young girl that she'd never seen before. One side of her flaming red hair was neatly braided. But someone had cut the other braid, and she held the severed end of it in her hand. She wore a flour sack dress like the ones that Mrs. Harris had described once, and Megan realized she was looking at an echo from the Academy's past.

"There you are," a familiar voice said, and Megan looked up to find herself walking up to the girl.

"Grandma?" Megan whispered.

"What's wrong?" Josephine asked.

"They cut my hair," the girl sobbed, burying her face in her folded arms and holding her knees close to her chest. "Papa's gonna kill me."

"There, there, Kate," said the young woman who looked so much like Megan, reaching into her purse and taking out a pair of scissors. All we have to do is even up the other side so that they match and your daddy will never notice."

"Are you sure?" the girl asked, looking uncertainly at the scissors.

"Does he really pay that much attention to your hair now?" Josie asked.

"He doesn't like my hair," the girl sniffled. "I think it reminds him of my mama."

"That's not very fair, now is it?" Josie asked, unbraiding the other

side of the girl's hair so she could see what she was working with.

"No, it isn't," Kate agreed, a little surer of herself now. "I sure do miss her."

"We all do," Josie said, moving the girl forward so she could see the back of her hair and start cutting. "It wasn't fair for her to die so young. My best friend and I always cut each other's hair," she added, probably sensing that her voice soothed her young friend. "There you go, just let me plait these back up, and you'll be right as rain." Then she stood up and pulled the girl to her feet, brushing the stray bits of hair off. "You're one pretty little cookie, you know that Kate?"

"They don't think so," the girl whispered, blushing at the complement nonetheless. "They all make fun of my clothes and my hair."

Josie pulled her into a sisterly hug, and Kate held her tight for a moment.

"It won't always be like this," Azarich's future wife whispered. "When you grow up you'll find someone who will cherish you."

"How do you know that?"

"Because I know a thing or two about being different myself," Josie answered. "Now we need to figure out what we're going to do to make these hooligans leave you be."

"What are hooligans?" Kate asked.

"Boys with big mouths and small brains," Josie answered.

"What makes you think I could do anything to stop them? Mr. Brown saw what they were doing to me on the playground, and he didn't even tell them to stop."

"Did he now?" Josephine asked, her expression going cold exactly the way her granddaughter's would many decades later.

"You see what I mean, what can I do to stop those three if the principal won't even do anything to help? I'm just a girl."

"I know you can do something because you're twice as tough and ten times as smart as the best of them. Here's what you're going to do…"

The image of her grandmother and the future owner of the Palace faded, leaving Megan to wonder what had happened afterward. Then she bent forward and pulled a strand of red hair from where it had caught in the baseboard. Maybe she could find some way to ask Kate. But then, how would she do that without her asking how Megan knew about it in

48

the first place?

No longer sleepy, Megan made her way back down the steps from the stage. But just as she opened the door leading back toward the high school side of the Academy, a figure in dark trousers, coat and an old beanie hat barreled toward her. In the instant before they collided, Megan noticed the end of a flaming red braid poking from under the cap.

She braced for an impact that never came. When she opened her eyes, she realized that three very wet and very angry young men were hot on the girl's trail. And even though the girl was fast, the boys were all taller and ran faster.

Turning to follow them, Megan saw a tall young man intercept the three bullies.

"Leave that boy alone!" he bellowed, and even though he looked nothing like the old janitor Megan would meet just a few yards away and some seventy years later, she recognized the rich baritone of Alan Green's voice. Reaching out to grab the first two by the collars of their coats, he shoved them backward into the third so that they all landed at his feet in a jumbled heap. Then he grabbed the biggest one and dragged him back up so that only the tips of his toes touched the ground.

"If I ever catch you lot ganging up three on one again, I will personally thrash all of you and then dump your worthless carcasses in the woods for Old Man Biggerstaff to deal with as he pleases!"

He dropped the frightened boy on top of his friends, and they scrambled quickly through the door behind them. Then he looked over his shoulder toward Kate, who was pressed against the door of what would eventually be his office, watching.

"Are you okay back there?" he asked.

"I am now," she called, already running for the door on the opposite side of the stage.

49

Later that afternoon while Megan hiked with the Grimbles toward Jade's preferred parking place, they passed Mr. Green coming in with a box full of plumbing fixtures. The sight of him made Megan think about the echoes of his and Kate's shared past as she tried to shove her spiral into her backpack. She'd been unable to do so before with Mr. Bob sprawled across her desk.

"Hey Alan," Jade called.

The janitor continued to walk, muttering to himself as if he hadn't heard them.

"Mr. Green," Paul called, making the old man jump. No one seemed to be able to resist the youngest Grimble's voice.

"Oh," Alan said, looking up at them in surprise. "You guys have a good evening. Paul, remind Kate that we're eating dinner tonight after your lesson."

"Will do," Paul replied. "You okay big guy?"

"I'm fine," the janitor answered. "Like I said, you guys have a good evening."

"That was weird," Jade said, watching him hurry toward the school.

Megan felt Bruce go distant for a minute then he broke into a broad smile.

"Spill it," she said out loud.

"Do you guys want to know now or be surprised when he does it?" he asked.

"He's finally going to propose to her, isn't he?" Jade squealed, dancing around them.

"Right now, he's still trying to get up the courage to ask her," he said. "But I think it will be another week or two before he actually goes through with it. She says yes in all of the possible outcomes, but there's one that works best for us. Megan, you've got to get Azarich to have one of his famous dinner parties for everyone."

"That's easier said than done," she replied. "Grandpa is even more moody than Sam these days. I'll see what I can do though."

Chapter VII: Feline Dreams

As soon as Megan walked through the door, she dropped her backpack at the foot of the stairs and stumbled up the steps to her bedroom where she found Mr. Bob waiting.

"Now you're just showing off," she said, kicking off her shoes and curling up next to him on the four-poster bed. "I'm going to take a nap before dinner, Grandpa."

"Okay dear," he called up from the kitchen.

"I'm going to have to snap him out of this if we want to have any chance of seeing it when Alan asks Kate to marry him," she whispered to the cat, who blinked sagely in response before she pulled him closer. "You still love me, don't you?"

His purr was deep as he nuzzled her chin.

When she drifted off, she found herself in the hallway of the Grimble house. The front door opened and Mr. Grimble walked in, carrying a duffle bag and looking as if he could use a shower. Dora met him there and took his bag, kissing him on the cheek before walking down the hall past Bruce's room, where her son was leafing through a thick manila folder.

"Thanks for bringing this home," he said.

"No problem," she replied. "It was still sitting on the archival table, and I didn't see any reason why you should have to take time away from everything else to come up there."

"You're the best, Mom."

"I know."

"Hello, Jade," Mr. Grimble called.

"Hey Dad, glad you're home," the eldest Grimble called back.

"I'll make that pasta dish you like for dinner if you'll go get your brother in half an hour."

"Deal!" she yelled back.

Megan flew across what felt like a great distance to a mountaintop where her mother neared the summit. Looking around warily as if feeling her daughter's eyes upon her, Emelia removed her pack, dropping it to the ground before continuing on with a pair of binoculars in her hand. Her face was hidden in the shadow of her hood, but Megan knew the way her mother moved better than anyone else in the world. Even though her clothing wasn't camouflage, it still blended with her surroundings, and the air around her shimmered with power. Her slow, almost languid movements at last brought her to the edge.

Far below at the rocky base of the next mountain, the entrance of a huge cave had been sealed with ornate black stone similar to that used in the construction of the Academy. A single entrance led within.

Nothing stirred below that Megan could see, but after several minutes during which her mother remained perfectly still, Emelia suddenly backed away from the edge, retrieving her pack and stowing the field glasses as she did so. She took off at a run and Megan realized she could hear sounds when the snarling yips of hunting wolves crossed the distance to Nickelville.

Ahead of her mother, a huge chasm stretched as far as she could see in either direction. Without slowing, Emelia sprinted toward the drop-off. But just as she reached the edge, a replica of the small woman broke away from the real one, turning to run parallel to the fall even as the small woman leapt a dozen yards to the safety of the other side. Rolling from the impact of her landing, she sprang up into the lower branches of a tree where Megan immediately found it impossible to distinguish her from the canopy.

Seconds later, huge black wolves appeared, snarling as they searched for her scent. Megan found their movements odd, and their behavior different than that of normal wolves. But of course, her only basis of comparison was Fang, whom she suspected represented something much farther down the evolutionary tree. As she watched, she became convinced that these were the prehistoric dire wolves that Paul had described in Guarded Wood.

With a bray of triumph, the largest turned toward where Emelia's decoy had run, and Megan noticed that he had some sort of metal collar around his neck. Then he bounded after the distant sound of the decoy's passage with the rest following close behind.

Megan dragged herself back to consciousness, rolling from the bed and locking her mother's location into her mind. She ripped a fighting staff through the shadows from its locker at the tree house as she prepared to walk the shadows with it held ready before her.

Don't interfere, the voice in her head ordered.

But she's in danger. She needs my help.

Emelia is more than capable of dealing with a handful of hellhounds.

How do you know that for sure?

She's fought them before and in far greater numbers. The only reason she hasn't dispatched these is because she's homesick, and they remind her of Fang.

You can't know that for sure.

Of course I can. I've been in her head even longer than I've been in yours.

Who are you?

I'm your friend and greatest ally. Or if you'd prefer, in a sense I'm one of your many grandmothers.

But why can't I go to her if she's safe?

Because you'll upset the balance and endanger everything she's worked for so long to protect. The answers you seek are close at hand.

Mr. Bob cracked one eye open irritably, as if their thoughts were too loud, and a runestone appeared next to him on the bed.

"That's bribery," Megan said, unsure of what she should do.

Think of it as you will, but you must leave your mother to finish what she has started. It has taken all of her considerable will to leave you and her father. If you distract her, she may not be able to maintain the focus she needs to pave the way for what must happen in the days to come. Your well-intentioned meddling could very well doom us all. The best thing you can do to help her is to summon the contents of that runestone so you'll be prepared when the time comes for you to fulfill your part.

Snatching the stone up from the bed, Megan turned to get the mirror, leaving the cat to sleep on in her absence. She walked the shadows directly to her grandmother's grove in order to avoid disturbing her grandfather as he cooked something that smelled wonderful for dinner. The cool wind brought the mingled scents of honeysuckle and approaching rain. She wondered where Charlotte had gone and what she might be doing.

Megan wasn't sure if she needed to be in the grove to view the memories, but she also didn't want to take the chance of losing what the runestone contained by doing it wrong. Spatterings of rain rustled the leaves of the trees while she sat down cross legged on the same stone bench as before. She put the stone on the mirror and placed her hands on either side, making sure she didn't make physical contact with the stone itself.

Emelia returned to college, and the confusion that had taken root in her feelings now spread through her every thought and action. Her roommate's inane mental chatter battered away at her shields, never giving her a moment's peace. So she stayed up late at the library, studying material she already knew to avoid the stray thoughts of the girl who slept just a few feet away. And when she grew too tired to fight her exhaustion, she dreamed of him.

She'd given up any pretense of trying to avoid him when she slept, and as insane as it sounded, she knew he dreamed of her too. They danced across the terrain of her subconscious, looping and spinning through celebrations in castles and battlefields where they vanquished her worst nightmares.

Then one day, while she ate her lunch high in the branches of her tree, a strange but beautiful woman quite literally dropped down next to her, startling Emelia so badly that she dropped the apple she'd been eating over the side.

With a flick of the woman's pale wrist, it flew up and landed neatly in her open hand.

"Sorry about that," the woman said with a thick accent. Possibly Irish? She dropped the fruit into Emelia's lap and sat down beside her.

Emelia had never felt such strong shields on another human being. Were it not for the fact that she could see the woman next to her and even smell the leathery musk of her unseasonably warm coat, she wouldn't have known she was there. Her skin was unblemished alabaster, and her eyes were the same strange violet as the man from her dreams. Her features were perfect in their symmetry and Emelia tried not to stare.

The newcomer's clothing drew Emelia's eye now that the shock of her unexpected arrival had begun to pass. Beneath the long coat, the woman wore some sort of leather breastplate embossed with an exquisitely detailed tree. Her pants were cut from some coarse yet supple, form fitting fabric and the leather of her high boots had been tooled with looping patterns that almost mesmerized Emelia as she looked at them.

"I can see why you come here so often," the woman said, looking around. "This tree has power. I don't think you're the first witch to be drawn here."

"You're obviously one too," Emelia said, finally finding her voice.

"Me? A witch?" the woman laughed. "No, I'm nothing nearly as special as that. I'm one of the Tuatha dé. So is he."

"He?"

"Don't play coy with me," the woman said. "The bond between you two is strong or he wouldn't have heard your call."

"Pardon me," Emelia said, completely forgetting about the apple in her lap and looking down, surprised to find it there. "But did you say I called him?"

"Yes, shortly before he found you in this tree."

"I don't know what you mean," Emelia stammered, unsure how to make sense of this strange turn of events.

"How odd," the woman said, leaning close and looking at her closely with those strange violet eyes. "I know that you did indeed summon him, and yet you do not seem to have done it intentionally. But that matters naught at this late stage. Where have my manners gone? I am Cara Breathach, Scathlahm to the heir, Daragh Mackgahe. And I am pleased to meet you, Emelia McGeehee." She reached over and grasped her forearm, and Emelia reflexively did the same in return.

"I'm glad to meet you too, but the rest of that didn't mean anything to me. You'll have to forgive me if I don't ever try to say either of your names. Are you some sort of elf?"

The strange girl's laughter echoed off the walls of the nearby building.

"Well met," she said, trying to be serious but still smiling broadly. "I see why he is so smitten with you. You are a refreshing breath of sincerity in an otherwise selfish world. Just call me Cara, and as you have noticed, his surname is similar to yours, making me wonder if your line might not descend from our vassals from before the Dagda brought us to Tyr Sgodl. As for being an elf, the answer is not as simple as yea or nea. I can tell you that there are no elves in the world the likes of the ones in the books on your nightstand. But the seeds of those stories might very well have been planted by those mortals we met in the old days."

"Are you saying that you've been in my dorm room?" Emelia asked in alarm.

"You don't think I'd allow just anyone to keep company with the Heir without first looking into who you might be, do you?" Cara asked.

"That's pretty disturbing," Emelia said.

"Then you should ward your room," Cara replied.

"That's easier said than done," Emelia explained. "My roommate has so many people coming and going that I'd never be able to concentrate on my studies if I warded it."

"There are ways to avoid that problem, but I haven't come to teach you magic." The strange young woman reached into her coat and pulled out an envelope closed with a wax seal.

"What's this?" Emelia asked, taking it reluctantly.

"To discover that, you shall have to open it. Now if you will excuse

58

me, I really must be going. It was a pleasure to finally meet you." Cara vaulted off the side of the branch even though it was a story and a half in the air.

When Emelia looked over the edge of the wide branch to see if she'd landed without injury, the other woman was gone.

Confused by this strange encounter, she broke the seal and opened the envelope. Inside, she found a single sheet of heavy parchment.

Dearest Emelia,

As much as I have enjoyed our time together thus far, I would be most pleased if you would accompany me to a gathering in your honor. I understand that the circumstances of this invitation are unusual, but as I suspect you have realized, we are an unusual folk. To accept, you need only speak my name aloud. For even though I have spoken yours often, I have not yet had the pleasure of hearing mine from your lips. If I have mistaken your interest, simply forget this overture, and I will leave you in peace. But if I am correct in hoping that your feelings match my own, then call out to me and I will hear.

Your servant,
Daragh

Over the next several days, Emelia put the invitation aside. She told herself that the opportunity had passed. She told herself that she'd dreamed the encounter with the strange Cara. But the letter remained a silent testament that the meeting up in the branches of her tree had indeed occurred. True to his word, this Daragh hadn't graced her dreams since the offer had been made, no matter how hard she looked for him there.

Her exams came and she busied herself in studies that seemed far less meaningful than they had just a few weeks before. Her roommate remained unpleasant, but Emelia found herself unable to care what the spoiled girl thought any longer.

Then there was Sam. She hadn't written to him in over a week. She'd started a letter to him several times, but the guilt always stilled her hand. She argued with herself over her motivations for wanting to say the name. Clearly this man had answers, and she had so many questions that no one had ever been able to answer before.

And so it came to be that on the night before her flight home, she walked down to her tree and said the strange name aloud, enjoying the way it felt on her lips.

Megan returned to herself to find that it had indeed rained while she explored the memory. Her clothing clung to her unpleasantly.

"Come on Mom!" she shouted into the night. "You know that was a terrible place to cut it off!" Though tempted to leave the spent runestone there in the mud, she snatched it up to add to the growing collection now gracing the top of her vanity. Her socks squelched as she walked.

Not wanting to return to the house dripping with water, she stepped under a tree where no one around would see, and caused a burst of warm air to blast outward, through her clothing, spraying the area around her with water. It worked in that she was no longer wet. However, it also shredded her shirt and ripped the outer seam along the entire right leg of her jeans. For just an instant she felt shame for the way she looked, expecting someone to laugh because of her clothing or where she lived. Then she remembered where she was and how far she'd come from when those feelings had been part of her daily life. She took a deep breath to calm herself, but she felt stupid and didn't like it at all.

Then, for reasons that had nothing to do with anything her best friend had ever done or said, she became suddenly angry with Bruce for his ability to see how to do things before he did them, thus avoiding humiliating mishaps like the one in which she found herself.

Hey, what did I do? he asked.

Nothing, I don't want to talk right now.

Then why did you want to flay me alive a few seconds ago?

Bruce, go study something.

Sudden mirth crossed through the bond they shared.

You can't see me, can you? She asked, hurriedly trying to cover herself.

No, but you just explained what happened in one of the other futures.

Tell that Megan she's a traitor and needs to keep her damn mouth shut! Leave me alone Bruce, or so help me I'll come over there and get Jade to help me beat you with your favorite books!

Not dressed like that you won't!

Blindingly angry, she reached into the muddy runoff from the spring next to her and dumped it through the shadows directly onto him. Then, feeling much better, she hardened her shields to keep him out, and walked the shadows to her bedroom, changed clothes and went down to eat with her Grandfather.

Chapter VIII: A Girl and Her Cat in the Doghouse

It had taken Bruce a long time to get to sleep, and when he woke only a few hours later, he knew even without the gift of foresight that he'd sleep no more that night. He didn't immediately travel the shadows as he usually did. Instead he thought about what he'd read in the files his mother had brought home from the *Tribune* archives. At least what he'd been able to read before Megan's little outburst.

Over the years his mother's newspaper had written several articles about Nickelville's most prominent landmark. They'd even included information about the sister hotels its owner had built in other places across the state. What he didn't find was a set of blueprints, which was one of the things he'd wanted most. A quick search online showed that there wasn't a set on file with the city either, which was not only odd but perhaps illegal as well. But once again the building was a century old and mistakes could have happened purely by coincidence during such a long period of time.

He didn't believe that for a moment. No inspector in his right mind would have signed off on that building. Of course he wasn't entirely sure that an inspection had been required back then.

As for the infamous Mr. Baker, there didn't seem to be any indication that the man had ever set foot in Nickelville, which was again, odd. All he knew for sure was that between the years of 1927 and 1929, extensive work had been done on the Nickelville Baker Hotel. Shortly after the stock market crash all construction on the building ended, leaving it in the derelict state in which it now remained.

But an even better question about the building's mysterious beginning was why a well-known hotelier like Baker would have built it there in the first place. Maybe it was just a coincidence that it shared names with the others. Perhaps it was just one of Chuck's equally foolish ancestors that had started the project. But then again, it was a near match for one of the other hotels, right down to the pool.

He finally got up, knowing even as he did so that he'd be completely dead on his feet the next day if he went out two nights in a row like this. But it wasn't like he was going to get any more sleep anyway. Furthermore, if he stayed busy he wouldn't think about how pissed off he was with Megan.

So he walked the shadows to the stairwell and began the odious ascent. Sweat soaked through his shirt by the time he reached the top, and the muscles in his legs burned. Post workout endorphins flooded his brain, and he thought he just might not kill his neighbor when he saw her later. But unless he'd lost count somewhere along the way, he was still several floors short of the penthouse level. He opened the door and reached out into the cavernous space he felt on the other side. As far as he could tell, there was no path to the top other than the conduits and pipes that supplied the penthouse with water and electricity.

"This can't be right," he said out loud, straining to sense where the response to his speech came from this time.

Once again, he felt something stir, something definitely not human, yet not particularly threatening either. Unwilling to walk the shadows into an unknown space, he went instead to one of the exposed girders that he could sense just below the top floor. Then, reaching out again through the cold iron beneath his fingertips, he searched every place where metal met metal within the whole massive structure.

"You're good, but you're not that good," he whispered, finding an elevator shaft starting on the fifth floor that went directly to the penthouse. "Gotcha."

Walking the shadows to the general location on the fifth floor, he began a meticulous search. He ran his hands over everything and probed with his senses below each surface until he found what he was looking for. At last, in the back of a storage room he found a secret door.

He'd always wanted to find a secret door, and now that he had, his first thought was how much he wanted to show it to Megan. He sighed irritably.

The elevator car wasn't a rectangular box as he'd expected. Instead he found himself staring at a cylindrical cage of gracefully curved silver bars. Deceptively delicate arches framed in the tops of the sides, and he could see a simple lever on the left side. It currently rested in the down position and the need to touch it was almost more than he could stand.

But even now that he stood directly before it, the elevator remained invisible to his senses, which brought on an even more disturbing realization. Whoever had built the Baker had protected the hotel from people exactly like himself. Yet the method of that camouflage remained a mystery. Its construction clearly incorporated both technology and magic, but who had created such a thing and what had been their motive for doing so?

"This is the point where I should go back for reinforcements," he whispered. The presence above seemed neither to agree or disagree. His foresight showed nothing beyond stepping into that heavily shielded cage, and the rational part of his mind reminded him that he might not be able to get out once he went in. Furthermore, no one knew where he'd gone or had reason to look for him here. Should something happen and he became trapped inside, it was doubtful he'd ever be found. Then he thought about the water dumping on him out of thin air, and he stepped into the elevator and closed the silver gate behind him.

His last thought before he pulled the lever up to start his ascent into the darkness above was that it would serve her right for taking him for granted if he never came back.

Megan woke with a start when the bond she shared with Bruce suddenly broke. She reached for her mother before remembering that she too had gone.

Bruce, she called, and for the first time he didn't answer.

She cast her senses toward his house and discovered that she couldn't penetrate the protective armor he'd layered around his room.

This isn't funny Bruce, I know you're mad at me, but answer right now!

She tried to walk the shadows to his room, but found herself unable to pass through the shields. The fact that they remained active meant he still lived, but what if something had happened to him? What if he needed her help?

The thought of him in danger sent jagged shards of ice slicing through her concentration, freeing some force she couldn't understand to geyser forth. Her bedroom glowed violet as she tried to focus. Summoning every bit of energy she could muster, she blasted the protections on his room apart and materialized in the middle of his room. The computer on his desk gave a single loud crack as her terrified energy arched across metal surfaces.

She tried to follow the feedback from his ward back to him, but it dissipated as soon as it was released from the structure in which he'd bound it. She waited for her power to blow out every circuit in the house, but his shields held just long enough to stop her from damaging anything beyond the confines of his room.

What the hell are you doing girl? August's thoughts came from where she could already feel him rushing toward the boundary. *As if opening trans-dimensional doors all the time wasn't loud enough! You know, you're a really lousy neighbor sometimes!*

Something broke our bond, and I can't find him!

And how did setting off a psychic nuke help anything? he asked.

His room was shielded, and I couldn't reach it through the shadows.

And you're too good to walk one house over like a normal person?

Now that she'd had a second to think about it, she could have just walked the shadows to the hallway outside of his room and opened the door. But that was beside the point. Why had the bond broken and where *was he?*

Megan, I can feel how worried you are, the hermit sent. *But Bruce is more than capable of taking care of himself. He's not in Guarded Wood, and there's been no indication of anything sinister in the area. Besides, if something bad were going to happen he would have seen it, right?*

Megan felt worse by the second. He'd already been mad about the water, which did seem pretty childish in hindsight. He was going to kill her!

Go back home, the old man sent. *He's a teenage boy, and sometimes teenage boys sneak out at night when they don't want people to know what they're up to.*

But why did the bond break? You don't think something happened to my mother, do you?

No, I don't. Emelia could take down a small country if she felt like it. She's fine. Go home and get some sleep. I'm sure he'll be back in the morning. Goodnight Megan.

Then she was alone in her best friend's room, wondering what she should do next.

The ancient elevator crept slowly up its cables, smooth movement showing that it had been well engineered in its day. Bruce felt the bond he shared with Megan break, and in spite of his thoughts just moments earlier, he really hoped he didn't die in there. As far as he could tell, it was just an elevator, doing normal elevator stuff. Of course, it might be designed to drop would-be intruders from the top of the building.

After a floor or so, something strange happened. Even though his senses never told him that he'd moved beyond the subtle ascent of the elevator itself, he no longer found himself in anything that looked like an elevator shaft. The framework of silver bars still surrounded him, but the interior of the building was gone.

Outside the silver cylinder, he moved up what appeared to be a tunnel made of the longest tree roots he'd ever seen. They twisted and turned about the open shaft, and blue light filtered through between them as if he were deep down in the ocean someplace. Although he had no reason to do so, he suspected that he might currently be traveling through some previously unexplored portion of Guarded Wood. That would explain why he couldn't sense it directly, since for all intents and purposes he couldn't sense what technically wasn't there.

His foot nudged something that he hadn't seen on the floor of the elevator, making him look down. There on the floor sat an old hacksaw,

but the blade had been melted to slag as if someone had tried to cut a high voltage power line.

The minutes it took to reach the penthouse were some of the longest in his life. When at last he arrived, in the most gloriously non-eventful way imaginable, he let out the breath he hadn't realized he'd been holding and opened the door. When he stepped out, expecting his sense of the outside world to return along with the reestablishment of the bond, he was sorely disappointed.

An eerie silence permeated the uppermost floor of the Baker Hotel, and beneath that an alien awareness teased his extra senses. So even though the only sound he could hear was that of his own breathing, which hadn't yet settled from running up the stairs, it still felt like alarm sirens echoed down the deserted floor. Further experimentation proved all of his abilities still intact and functioning, though he sensed he wouldn't be able to pierce the mysterious shields and walk the shadows until he left the confines of the penthouse.

No matter how hard he looked, he sensed nothing of the wards or shields at work here. Yet something definitely kept the inner part of this floor and the outside world in which it stood quite separate. His curiosity to discover the means by which that had been accomplished proved almost more than he could bear.

"I know you're here," he called out from the elevator. "I mean you no harm, so you might as well come out."

The presence stirred once again, much nearer than before. Something about it felt utterly alien, and yet he sensed something human in it as well. Furthermore, some quality in the way it displaced the energy around it made him suspect there was more than one of them, whatever they were.

Could they be more of the fauns? He didn't think so, since they'd said they couldn't leave Guarded Wood. But once again, he definitely felt a kinship between whatever lay up here and the presence of Guarded Wood's diminutive protectors. But if it wasn't them, then what?

The room into which the elevator opened was mostly empty. He couldn't feel much with his senses and decided that since there didn't seem to be any windows nearby, he could chance a light.

Summoning the cold flame he usually favored, he saw that the room had likely been some sort of a gallery. Several display cases stood empty, and one had been knocked over. The glass from its lid covered the floor next to it. Exposed wiring hung in regular intervals across the wall, marking the places where light fixtures had once hung. The patterns of lights and bare nails sticking out from the paneled surfaces made him think that light fixtures had once been positioned to illuminate spaces where paintings had once hung. Closer inspection of the wood on the walls revealed some species he'd never seen before with dense rings and swirls. Laying his hand on it revealed a level of craftsmanship that far surpassed that of Honeysuckle House.

As interesting as he found the room, Bruce's curiosity demanded that he go to the door and continue his exploration. Like the missing wall fixtures, the door handles had been removed sometime in the past by someone who, judging by the tool marks on the fine wood, had either been in a hurry or completely incompetent to such a task. With a gentle push it opened outward with a whispered creak.

The next room proved to be just as well constructed and just as stripped of the splendor that had likely been displayed there. The opposite wall curved inward, giving Bruce the impression that a massive round chamber lay beyond. Oddly enough, the doorknob hadn't been removed from the opposite door, making him wonder why the mystery thief had left this one while taking the rest. He looked around quickly, trying to find clues as to what had happened here, but because the room had been completely emptied of furniture, he had no idea what its purpose might have been. Curious as to what might lay on the other side, he crossed the room quickly and tried to open the door.

The ornate brass doorknob turned easily enough in his hand, but something on the other side seemed to be lodged against it. Using his abilities, he applied far more force than he could have done with strength alone. At first it held firm, then with a crack that sounded like splintering wood, it moved a fraction of an inch and he was able to shoulder it the rest of the way open.

A massive tree took up the space where he'd always been told an open-air ballroom had been constructed. It filled the circular space in which it took root and he could feel its upper branches touching the steel awning that hid it from the air above.

Something huge landed in the branches overhead, separate from the entities Bruce could feel just before him, but also linked to them. He stepped through the door, trying to figure out how to best communicate with whatever he might find.

Then the backlash from his bedroom wards slammed into him, giving him a blinding headache just as his bond with Megan reestablished itself. The pain almost drove him to his knees, and would have had he not been holding onto the doorknob.

"Damn it, Megan!" he growled and angrily closed the door behind him before crossing through the shadows to his bedroom.

Ignoring the advice of the hermit, Megan decided to wait for her friend to return and was perched on the foot of his bed in her pajamas when Bruce finally materialized in front of her. Relief flooded through her as she leapt up to try and to hug him, but he held her at arm's length.

What the hell? Bruce sent, the strength of his anger giving her a headache. *Do you have any idea how much that hurt?*

Where have you been? she demanded, her own anger rising to meet his.

Studying something, like you told me to do. She'd never felt him so angry.

That's not fair, she countered. *You have no idea how worried I was. I felt our bond break and you were gone! I had no idea if you were okay!*

If he'd been angry before, it was nothing compared to the rage that her comment invoked.

NO IDEA? You lost track of me for what, half an hour? How could I POSSIBLY know how you felt?

What are you talking about? she asked.

Were there any explosives involved other than the EMP you dropped on my bedroom?

Bruce, I know you're upset, but I don't know what you're...

Without any warning he snatched her up with his mind and cast her back through the shadows to her own bedroom. Then she felt a wall slam down between them, far stronger than the protections that had surrounded his room before.

She started to bend the shadows around her.

Let him cool down, the hermit sent.

You heard us?

I'm pretty sure Sam heard that all the way out at his place.

Why is he so angry?

That was about the worst thing you could have told him. You've apparently forgotten that you made him think you were dead for over a week when you saved the town.

But I was just trying to protect him! It's not like I was intentionally trying to hurt him.

And he knows that. But you have no idea how badly it hurt him to live in a world where he thought he would never be with you again. We were all worried about him during that dark time. To be honest, I wasn't sure he was going to make it through to the other side. As it is, I'm not sure he would have made it another week if you hadn't returned.

What are you talking about? she asked. *I knew he was sad and all, but you don't die from sadness.*

No, you don't, the hermit answered.

You're not suggesting that he would have...

As someone who has lost the love of his life and been forced to live on without her, I know what to look for, he explained.

I'd never do that, she argued. Something inside of her tried to come alive at the hermit's words, but although it smoldered for an instant, it didn't catch fire. *I can't believe that he would either.*

That kind of pain doesn't heal overnight he sent wearily. *Scars on the soul take much longer to heal than the ones you can see. He's not whole yet. I felt him shield his room from you when he did it.*

Why did he feel that he needed to block me out?

He's told you about his night terrors with the dark when he was young, the hermit sent.

What does that have to do with this?

Everything, I'm afraid. The first of his nightmares about losing you was so bad that it had Fang and I hiding in the corner of my cabin all the way out here.

If it was that bad why didn't I feel it? We're bound by the stone around his neck.

Your mother shielded you from it. As soon as he realized you might feel it, he walled his room away from you. Think about how strongly you reacted when you thought he was in danger. Now imagine what it would have been like if your roles had been reversed at the hotel that day and then he didn't show up for well over a week.

Now that she knew that he was safe, she couldn't understand the debilitating fear that had overcome her at the mere thought of him in danger. And in hindsight, she really hadn't had much of a reason to think anything bad had happened to him.

I'm so sorry...

And you'll have the chance to tell him that tomorrow, probably a few times. Now, I'm going to cut you off here and go back to bed...again. I have a strong suspicion that if I don't, this discussion is going to head into waters where personal relationships would be discussed. And if your best source of advice on that front is a six-hundred-year-old hermit, then you're in worse shape than I thought. Goodnight, and please let this be the last time I say that tonight. I'm old and cranky even when I do get enough sleep.

Bruce sat stiffly in Christine's back seat, ignoring his best friend's attempts to apologize. He'd tightened his shields to the point where he doubted she could even sense him in the seat behind her.

"Paul and I talked it over last night," Jade said happily. "We're making you an honorary Grimble for both audaciousness and artistic ability in the realm of pranks."

Bruce sighed loudly, and his siblings burst into laughter.

"I really am sorry," Megan said again. *You didn't tell them about the rest, did you?*

No, I wasn't feeling particularly talkative, and then I would have had to explain where I was.

And you're still not going to tell me that part, are you?

He turned toward the window.

"Are those cat scratches?" Jade asked, glancing down at Megan's hand.

"Yeah," Megan said, holding it up. "It was the weirdest thing. Mr. Bob was sitting on my vanity while I was brushing my hair this morning. There was something about the way he looked that made me think of this cool purple dragon statue I saw when I was a kid. So I reached out and called him my little dragon."

"I take it Mr. Bob doesn't like dragons," Paul said. "You put antiseptic on it, right?"

"Yeah," Megan answered.

"Come on, Bruce," Jade said, "it was just water!"

"That dropped on me while I was sitting on my bed," he said, not looking at them. "Extremely muddy water."

"And Mom heard him yell," Paul said, shaking with the effort to keep from laughing again.

"And nothing can stop our mother when she thinks something is wrong with her favorite child," Jade added.

"Of course I'm her favorite," Bruce snapped. "Like you two are competition!" To which his sister moved the rear-view mirror where he could see her and stuck her tongue out at him.

"I had to lock the door to keep her from coming in and finding the mess," he growled.

"And there are no locked doors allowed in our house," Paul explained.

"Which led to me having to let her in after I'd stripped the bed clothing off of the bed. I also had to draw all of the water out of the mattress," he said pointedly to Megan, "which I managed to do without tearing it to shreds."

"Low blow," she complained, but she was smiling when she said it.

"And then Mom thought he'd wet the bed because he wouldn't let her take them," Jade said, laughing again.

"Because every single future where she saw them led to us having to tell her the truth," Bruce explained.

"Why would that be so bad?" Megan asked. "I mean Grandpa handled it really well."

"My mother freaks out when she thinks I might get wet and catch a cold," Bruce answered. "How do you think she'd react if she knew about Paul nearly being eaten by a siren or the fact that you and I routinely travel through another dimension?"

"Ugh," Jade said, "Let's not allow that to happen if we can help it."

"So now Mom's probably going to make him go to a urologist," Paul said, cracking up again.

"No," Bruce winced. "That was before she called Dad. He told her that I was probably just doing something else."

"You don't mean…" Megan said, turning to look over the seat at him.

"Yes, Megan," he growled, finally looking her in the eye. "That's exactly what they decided I was doing. Now if you don't mind, I'd like some quiet while I try to find a future path that leads to me moving in with Sam and ignoring you ungrateful degenerates for the rest of my life."

But no, they did not give him the silence he craved. There were many, oh so many giggles before they reached the questionable safety of Nickelville Academy. And even though he could feel Megan's curiosity about where he'd been, she kept the secret of his night time explorations, and for that he was grateful.

Megan finally got him to accept her apology during art when his curiosity about what the runestone had contained finally got the better of

76

him. He still remained deeply irritated with her, but he understood why she was mad about the memory cutting off at that particular place even if it had not been his fault.

I don't know, he sent, *but I just thought that they would give you more answers about why you were running instead of, well, I don't know how to describe it.*

Instead of How I Met Your Father, Supernatural Edition?

He nodded, dipping his pen into the inkwell. Although he didn't have much artistic ability, he showed some potential with calligraphy. He found something pleasant in the precision of the curved and straight lines.

He looked over at Megan's paper and saw that she was freehand drawing extremely ornate Celtic knotwork around the edge of her paper. The precision of the ribbon she drew as it looped in and out over itself without ever changing thickness made his letter work pale in comparison. But of course, just about everything was like that for her. Yet she'd gotten mad at him just because she'd done something, and it didn't turn out perfect the first time she tried it. His mood began to sour again.

The bell rang, and they put their work into the bin reserved for their class. He was glad they'd made up before lunch. He hadn't known where to sit if it wasn't with her and his siblings.

"I thought Azarich still hadn't started making lunch for you since your mom left," Bruce said, noticing that she had a sack lunch in her hand. She usually just ate half of his.

"I am perfectly capable of making my own lunch," she said.

"You knew I was still mad at you and you didn't know if I'd share," he said and was rewarded with a sheepish grin.

"We'd never let you starve," Jade said, taking the seat next to Megan. Paul took the one next to his brother on the other side of the table.

"Yeah," Paul added, his mouth already full of chips. "You being orphaned and all."

Bruce slapped him across the back of the head, spraying Jade with partially chewed chip bits.

"Gross," she exclaimed looking down at herself.

"That's what you get for laughing at me so hard," Bruce said, massaging his hand. "And I can see why you do that so much. It's extremely satisfying."

"Right?" Jade said, brushing herself off. "I see you two have made up. Half the school thinks you broke up."

"We're not dating," both Bruce and Megan said in unison, making heads turn their direction from all over the cafeteria.

"Methinks thou dost protest too much," Paul said, then ducked away, coming to his feet before his brother could hit him again. "Hey Megan, have you had any luck with getting your grandpa to host another dinner?"

"Nope, it never seems to be the right time. I'll make it work though."

"I can't believe they're really going to tie the knot," Jade squealed, grabbing Megan in a fierce hug that made the smaller girl grunt with discomfort. "I wonder if…"

"Please don't ask her if you can wear a black tutu with your bridesmaid dress," Bruce said, rolling his eyes.

"Tutus aren't always bad," Paul said with a grin.

"Would you still say that if Goth Violin Girl hadn't been wearing one?" Megan asked him.

"It's rude to not let me at least dream out loud before shutting me down," Jade complained.

"For some reason I'm still not in a very polite mood," he said, looking pointedly at Megan.

"I really am sorry about that," she said, at last looking sincere. "I had no idea your parents would…" She trailed off and shrugged.

Just then a movement on the stage caught his eye where Mr. Bob was batting something around.

"What's that cat doing now?" he asked. "Is that a runestone?"

Megan spun on her seat. She opened her hand, and Bruce could feel the surge of her power as she attempted to pull it through the shadows toward her.

As if sensing her attempt, Mr. Bob fixed her with a baleful gaze and placed his paw directly on top of the stone.

Megan gasped.

"What's going on?" Paul asked, his mouth already full again.

"That furry little turd *blocked* me!" Megan growled, then turned toward Bruce. "Did you know he could do that?"

"I've never noticed before," Bruce said, after reaching out with his mind and finding nothing. "But I can't sense that cat at all. Not in the present and not in the future."

"I'm getting that stone," Megan said, getting up and crossing the walkway between the tables toward the stage.

Everyone turned to look, curious about what she could be doing. With the athleticism that came from several months of training at the dojo, she vaulted effortlessly onto the raised wooden platform.

"Oh I hoped she'd choose this path," Bruce said with a malicious grin.

"I thought you couldn't see Mr. Bob," Paul commented, watching as Mr. Bob effortlessly evaded her, at times batting the stone directly between her feet.

"I can't," Bruce answered, taking in the show with intense amusement. "And I can't lie to her when we communicate mind to mind either. But I can see Megan and the way the school is going to tease her about this for the next week."

"That's not very nice," Jade observed.

"I never thought I'd say this," Bruce said happily, resting his head on his hands as he watched. "But I really love that cat."

Chapter IX: Tyr Sgodl

Megan excused herself to go to the restroom, leaving Bruce and the others at the table to finish lunch without her. Food was unimportant as long as she could unlock the contents of the next runestone. The strength of that need stopped her suddenly there in the hallway, looking down at the stone in her hand and remembering August's warning about the dangers of a norm using this sort of memory recall. Was she in danger of addiction? She'd used the silver mirror each time to buffer its effects and she was fairly sure that what she felt now represented nothing more than strong, but normal curiosity. Finding the restroom deserted, she walked the shadows to the isolation room where no one would bother her.

Once there, she hurriedly pulled the mirror out from her backpack and unwrapped it from one of her t-shirts. Just before she hopped up onto the table, she noticed once again the musty odor she remembered from her last visit to the disused room. Wrinkling her nose in distaste, she closed her eyes and let her consciousness seep into the stone.

No sooner had the name left Emelia's lips than Cara appeared at her side.

"I knew you'd call for him," the young woman said, barely containing her excitement.

"Is he always in the habit of sending other women to collect his dates?" Emelia asked, surprised and a bit insulted that he hadn't come

himself.

"If he were a normal person it would be unusual," Cara admitted, looking her over. "But he is not. I'm his protector, and for the night I'm your chaperone as well. But don't worry, I'll take good care of you!"

Without warning, the woman with the strange violet eyes took Emelia by the hand, and the world twisted around them before solidifying into what looked like the interior room of a castle.

"What just happened?" Emelia asked, holding onto Cara for balance.

"We just walked shadows," Cara answered as if explaining the obvious. "You'll get used to it in time. This is Tyr Sgodl, home of the Tuatha dé."

Emelia hoped there wouldn't be a quiz at the end of the evening over all of these names.

"I wish we'd been able to give the grand tour," Cara said absently. "The views leading up to the castle are quite breathtaking the first thousand or so times you see them. And you simply must see the Queen Mother's monument sometime, but tonight you'll have to be satisfied with the throne room."

"I really just want to see Daragh," Emelia said.

"Well, you'll definitely get enough of him tonight. Now we have to get you dressed," Cara said, and four older women, all dressed in plain woolen dresses, entered the room. All but one of them had gray hair, and each possessed the finely formed features that Emelia was coming to associate with Cara. Each wore their hair tucked into businesslike buns at the backs of their heads. "These women will get you cleaned up before the fitting. Isn't this all so exciting?"

Emelia didn't have time to decide how she felt, let alone voice any confirmation before one of the women took her by the hand and did the shadow thing just as Cara had done earlier. It wasn't particularly unpleasant, but she really wished they'd warn her before moving her around like that.

In the center of the room stood a large tub crafted from heavy hammered copper. Judging by the steam rising from it into the cold air of the room, the water looked hot enough to brew coffee.

"You're not planning to put me in there are you?" Emelia asked in alarm.

This prompted a hurried flurry of discussion among them in a language she'd never heard before. Then without so much as a warning, they began to pull at her clothing, clearly intent on stripping her down.

"I am more than capable of undressing and bathing myself!" she yelled, pulling away from them to no avail. They apparently had their marching orders, and nothing could make them deviate from their mission. Soon her clothing lay in a heap on the floor and she was unceremoniously picked up and carried to the tub.

Reaching out with her senses, she realized the danger of being badly burned wasn't as improbable as she'd hoped. Writhing in their hands, she twisted free long enough to grip the side of the beautiful copper tub and shunt most of its heat into the stone floor beneath it.

This of course prompted another outburst of angry chatter from her would-be bathing assassins. Before the sour-faced matron that seemed to be their leader could finish shaking her finger in Emelia's face, the lost girl from Nickelville jumped in the tub and began to bathe herself. It was still far too hot, but she doubted she'd have any lasting damage.

Then, in spite of her repeated attempts to make them let her bathe by herself, the whole lot joined in with rough sponges and soap even going so far as to wash her hair and dunk her repeatedly to rinse the soap from her body. By the time they'd finished, she doubted she'd ever

been or would ever be as clean as she was in that moment.

By the time Cara returned with a thin garment of what looked like silk draped over her arm, Emelia's tormentors had yanked her from the tub and dried away any moisture that might have ever landed on her skin.

"Please tell me that I'm going to be wearing more than that," Emelia complained, eyeing the flimsy thing with apprehension.

"Of course," her chaperone laughed. "You're going to wear this under the dress they will create for you. Why are you so red?"

"They boiled me, and then damn near scrubbed the skin off of me," Emelia answered, having progressed far beyond simple regret for allowing herself to become involved in any of this.

"Why didn't you tell them to stop?" Cara asked.

"I did! Several times in fact."

Cara looked at her, puzzled, and then realized what had happened.

"I am so sorry," she whispered. "He's going to kill me. Why would you know our language when it hasn't been spoken on Earth in over two millennia?"

"No lasting harm done," Emelia said grudgingly. "But would you please let me know what's going on. I don't understand any of this."

"And they didn't understand that your skin is much less resistant to heat and abrasion than ours. They probably thought your tan lines were dirt."

"That would explain a lot," Emelia said irritably. "Now would you please let me have that? I'm not used to standing naked in the middle of a bunch of people I just met."

"Of course," Cara said, helping her slide it down over her outstretched arms and head. It wasn't much better than total nudity, but it was a start. "And I beg your forgiveness for not understanding your modesty. The Tuatha dé are all so similar to one another that once you have seen one of us..."

"You've seen all of you," Emelia finished, starting to relax in Cara's presence. "Just give me a minute to adjust to the fact that the number of people who've seen me in my birthday suit has just expanded exponentially in the last hour. So I'm going out with a man who has grown up in a place where every woman is as beautiful as you?"

"I don't understand your question," Cara said, dismissing the other women. "And what is a birthday suit? You weren't wearing a suit."

"Why would he want me when he could have you?" Emelia asked quietly, smiling at the strange woman's confusion.

"But he can't have me," Cara said, running her hands across Emelia's wet hair. In their wake, it was dry.

"Now that's a trick you're going to have to teach me. And why not?" she asked. "Can't the heir choose anyone he wants?"

"Yes and no. He can't choose me because I'm already married, and just between the two of us, royal or not, I'm fairly sure my wife would thrash him within an inch of his life if he were to ask. He's always been a bit scared of her. And as for choosing the one he wants, he already has."

"You don't mean me?" Emelia asked.

"Who else? Is it not you here in a place where no mortal has tread in hundreds of years? Is it not for you that he has risked the wrath of the Tuatha dé to court? Now before we move forward I need to make you understand something about him that is very different from humans or even the rest of the Tuatha dé. The royal family cannot choose their mates lightly. They mate for life. Should you change your mind after he has bound his heart to yours, he will be unable to love another in this lifetime."

"I'm not sure I can commit to that," Emelia said, panic rising. "I've never even spoken to him in person before."

"No one expects you to do so tonight," Cara said, holding her by the shoulders. "But before he can begin to court your favor, you must be presented to our nation."

"Wait, how many people are going to be at this dance?"

"Only a few score of us," Cara said, "Just his parents and the rest of the royal court."

Emelia didn't know how to respond to that, so she allowed Cara to whisk her away to another room where several other women waited. As soon as they saw her, they surrounded her and began to talk amongst themselves in the same tongue the bathers had used.

Like the previous room, this one lacked a window. She had the sense that they were deep within heavy walls. But now that she wasn't being distracted by amphibious assault, she noticed that even in this apparently unimportant place, masons had carved the walls with the same style of looping designs that she'd noticed on parts of Cara's clothing the day she met her.

"This will take a little while," Cara said from where she stood nearby. "Is there anything that I can bring for you?"

"Some heat," Emelia said. As the moments passed after her near-scalding, the cold air of the room leached the warmth from her skin and she began to shiver.

"I'm sorry," Cara said, shaking her head and with a simple gesture of her hand, the torches that surrounded the room changed from the heatless blue flames with which they'd burned up to that point into genuine fire and the small room began to warm at once. "We can feel heat and its absence, but only extremes bring us discomfort."

When the first bit of fabric fell across her skin, Emelia flinched. None of the women had left the small circle with which they surrounded her, and none of them had been carrying anything when they first approached. The sensation was faint and delicate beyond anything she'd ever felt.

"We call it moon silk," Cara said, noticing the way Emelia had reacted to its touch. "These artisans create it directly out of the ether

that forms this place."

"It barely feels as if it's there at all."

"An apt description. It has almost no discernible weight, yet it is quite durable as long as it is protected from the sun of your world. Then it degrades almost instantly. There are those among our scholars who argue that it may not actually exist at all since there are a very few among my kind who are blind to its presence."

"So you're sending me out there dressed in a material that some people can't see?" Emelia asked, hoping this didn't mean what she thought it did.

"There are only a few among us with this disability," Cara reassured her. "My nephew might be one such person, but he is as yet too young to tell with any certainty. It isn't as much of a hindrance as you might think. Moon silk is so rare that he'll likely live his entire life without encountering it."

As she spoke, the women layered Emelia in its barely perceptible weight. Under their hands, the dress took shape in shades of gray and black, fitting close about her small waist and hips only to flare out in a cascade of liquid night to the floor while still leaving her arms and décolletage bare.

"Is it a black and white ball?" Emelia asked.

"Moonsilk won't take dye, but don't worry," Cara assured her. "Only the Queen's attire will be as regal as yours."

When they'd finished, one of the artisans pulled a small pouch from the pocket of her smock. She upended its contents into her palm and Emelia gasped at the sparkle of the gems that spilled forth. Then, with a critical eye, the woman began to lift the faceted stones with her mind, and where they came into contact with the moonsilk, they fused into place.

"And what are those made from?" Emelia asked, watching as the artisan arranged them in the shape of a tree exactly like the one on Cara's breastplate.

"I don't know what diamonds are made from," the Tuatha dé answered.

"I can't..." Emelia began to argue.

"You can't go out there looking like anything less than the future queen," Cara reminded her. "That's the royal crest she's creating."

Emelia looked down at herself in wonder. The strange fabric of her dress moved like molten metal as she turned, catching the light and reflecting or absorbing it almost at random.

"Do you like it?" Cara asked.

"It's beautiful," she answered.

"Then we should be going," her chaperone said. "They're waiting on us."

"Who is?"

"Everyone."

Without further explanation, Cara whisked her away again, this time to a massive corridor lined with stone columns that supported arch supported alcoves on either side. Emelia glanced up to find her first glimpse of open sky in this secluded realm. Tinted in the dark gray of twilight, its frigid air leeched the warmth from her skin and made her breath steam.

This time her chaperone anticipated her needs and an invisible shroud of warmth embraced her before her teeth began to chatter.

"Thanks," Emelia whispered.

"That should protect you long enough," Cara answered. "Now try to look regal."

Emelia had no chance to contemplate how she might do that before *they arrived at two ornately carved doors that reminded her of the ones at the library back home. At the first glimpse of the crowd within, she readied her shields to block out the discomfort of strange thoughts roaring through her mind. But instead she found the mental quiet of those like herself, the quiet of a place where she might one day belong.*

The high court dressed as if their tailors had once worked for renaissance festivals but since moved on to red carpet cinematic openings. The walls had been constructed of white stone. Arched supports had been carved to look like the intertwining vines of a plant, and massive chandeliers hung from the high ceiling. Each held several hundred yellow witchflames.

Follow at my side, Cara sent. First, I need to introduce you to the court.

So, doing as she'd been instructed, Emelia entered the throne room of the Tuatha dé. If what Cara had said was true, and she had no reason to believe otherwise, then she was the first human to be here in a very long time. Standing just inside the open doors, the scathlahm spoke loudly to the assembled Tuatha dé in the language that Emelia had begun to find pleasant to hear now that the speakers were no longer old women with sponges. The only part she understood was her own name. At the head of the chamber stood the thrones of the King and Queen, and from these elevated seats they watched as Cara led her forward toward the steps where the Heir waited for her.

Be regal, Emelia chanted over and over in her mind as she walked.

Judging by the startled looks of the assembled High Court, Daragh's formal attire owed as much inspiration from the mortal world as this one. Unlike the long cloaks and tunics of the men around him, the Heir wore the most eccentric tux Emelia had ever seen. Tailored from what looked like heavily patterned black satin, the vest and pants fit tight

91

across his body, accenting the muscular form beneath. The gray of his scarf-like tie matched the color of her eyes perfectly, and his long coat billowed out behind him as if unable to wait for her to reach him. He strode out to meet her with the heels of his polished boots clapping the black stone beneath his feet in the silent room.

She gave up any attempt to appear regal when he looked into her eyes and smiled. When his hand reached for hers and brought it to his lips, the interaction of his magic with hers in that first touch sent little tremors of potential streaking up her nerves to invade her every thought. Suddenly it wasn't cold at all.

Then, refusing to release her hand now that he had it at last, Daragh led her to the raised dais where his parents waited to meet her.

What am I supposed to do? Emelia asked her chaperone.

He will take care of everything, Cara assured her. You won't need me until the dancing starts.

For several moments he spoke to the King and Queen. It was all that Emelia could do not to smile and nod like an idiot, lest they unmask her as the fraud she knew herself to be. While he spoke, she noticed a strange suit of armor on display directly behind and between the thrones as if placed there to watch over the happenings in court. Covered in strange designs, Emelia marveled at its small size.

She also noticed that most of the High Court wore clothing that was predominantly green, blue, red or black. Furthermore, they seemed to cluster together based on those colors.

Daragh ended the dialogue without warning, and led her to the center of the room. The black onyx of the floor absorbed all of the room's flickering light, making it look like the two of them floated across a midnight sea of calm water. But inside Emelia a tempest brewed. In horror, she realized the court expected them to lead the first dance, and *she had no idea how she should respond to any of this. Then his hands were on her waist and the moonsilk transferred their heat as if they were touching her bare skin. She looked up into the swirling violet of his eyes and nothing else mattered.*

She felt Cara's presence at the edge of her shields and happily let her take control.

The music began when the couple flowed into motion across the floor. And unlike any dance Emelia had ever seen, the two of them weren't really dancing to the same rhythm. Each of them moved around each other in a symbiosis that somehow merged into the music as if their choices were driving the music instead of the other way around.

She was unsure of how long the dance had lasted, but when the music came to an end, she found herself winded. She didn't know if others had joined them or if she and the heir had danced alone. But she'd found something strong in his eyes that was greater than either of them alone.

Another song and another dream, followed by drinking something cold that left her strangely warm. Although he never spoke, he never left her side.

Then as quickly as it had begun, Cara led her away from the throne room.

Why didn't he talk to me? Emelia asked.

"In a formal event like this where the two of you were under such close scrutiny," Cara explained, "it was best that you not speak in English as it would have been considered rude. But the King has given his consent, and Daragh may now begin to court you in earnest. I promise he will speak to you then. In fact, I often wish he'd shut up. You did well, Emelia."

When they walked through the doorway, Emelia found herself back in her dorm room, glad that her roommate hadn't been present when they appeared.

"You should change out of that dress at once," Cara said, glancing around the room. "It will degrade quickly in this world. I'm sure I will see you soon. If you need us sooner, simply say his name."

Then she was gone.

The first thing Emelia noticed when she'd had a second to collect herself was that the light was blinking on the answering machine. She pushed the play button so she could hear what was probably a reminder from her father about what time she needed to be at the airport.

And that's exactly what the first one was, but the tape was full, and in the messages that followed, Azarich became more and more frantic. He kept asking why she'd missed her flight and begging her to call him as soon as possible if she got the message.

Frowning, she turned on the television and stared in horror at the date on the bottom of the news station which said she should have flown home over a week ago. How could this have happened? How could she have been gone for so long when it had only been a few hours there? Then she remembered the fairy tales where people went to the home of the fairies, only to return hundreds of years later. Is that what she'd done?

"I assure you there is no one left in the building," a voice came from the hallway outside her door, followed by a loud knock.

She reluctantly opened the door, expecting to find her father on the other side. Instead she found Sam. He took in the dress, and then his eyes met hers. Before she could explain, he turned and walked away, his long strides taking him halfway to the parking lot before she could push her way past the startled RA.

Sam nearly knocked the door off its hinges in his eagerness to be

94

away from her, and he was nearly to his car by the time she finally reached the exit. But as soon as the light from the setting sun touched the moonsilk, it began to wither like a dying plant.

Let me explain! she called after him. But for the first time since she'd met him, he hardened his shields against her and began the long drive back to Nickelville while diamonds fell unnoticed to her feet like tears.

Megan came back to herself in the musty isolation room. She knew, without needing to be told, that this had been the last time her mother had seen him until that night at Gordon's. And even though the pain had been her mother's, she still felt the guilt and heartbreak as if they had been her own.

Megan wrapped the mirror up and returned it to her backpack. She held the runestone she'd worked so hard to retrieve for a moment, cold now that it held none of the past within its depths. She thought about leaving it there, but still slipped it into the pocket of her mother's old jeans. Then she opened the door and walked back to the cafeteria where she sensed Bruce and the others still finishing up from lunch. Like her mother's trip to her father's land, time here hadn't moved at the same pace. She felt as if months had gone by since she'd chased Mr. Bob on the stage.

Several people meowed at her when she returned, but she barely noticed. She pushed her lunch over to the ever-hungry Paul and put her head down on the table.

"Are you okay?" Jade whispered in her ear.

"Not really," she answered. "But I'll be fine."

The table lurched and she felt something nudge her head. She looked up to find Mr. Bob's luminous green eyes close to hers. She

wrapped her arms around him and used his purring mass as a pillow while the others put their hands on her back and shoulders to remind her that she wasn't alone.

"I love you guys," she said loud enough for them to hear.

We know, Bruce whispered in her mind, and strangely enough, it almost seemed as if Paul had too.

Chapter X: Wise Actions

As the hours passed, Bruce became more and more angry with himself. It angered him that his mother's gaze held a hint of disappointment when she looked at him. It angered him when he needed to borrow Paul's laptop to print some research. But what angered him most was that every time he discovered something, he immediately found himself reaching out to tell Megan as if doing so was the only way to make anything real.

In the beginning, his night time excursions had indeed been therapeutic, and not just for his night terrors. It gave him a sense of separation and self-identity that he'd found sorely lacking in his life recently. But the events of the previous night had traveled beyond self-help into realms of recklessness in direct conflict with large parts of who he believed himself to be.

He needed to share what he'd found with everyone soon, but for now it still remained in his control to determine when that would happen. Besides, as near as he could tell, glancing toward the horizon where he could see the silhouette of the Baker, the strange forces at work there had nothing to do with any of them.

Blank spots littered the future, but none of them looked particularly troublesome. The complexity of his brother's future continued to trouble him, but as far as he knew, it might have always been that way. With a sigh of resignation, he folded several sheets of paper and tucked them into his pocket before making his way out to the tree house where he could feel Megan looking out over the treetops.

"Are you drinking coffee at six in the evening?" he asked when he joined her, noticing the cup in her hand.

"I'm exhausted, but I don't want to go to sleep this early and be up in the middle of the night again. It makes for a long day."

"Me too. How was the sunrise this morning?" he asked, picking a path where she'd just fall into their normal rhythm and ignore the mystery of his actions during the previous night.

"He barely spoke the whole time, and I had to drag him out of bed to get him out there at all," she answered. She made as if to dump the cup over the side.

"Hey now," he said, taking the cup from her, "Let's not be hasty now. Some of us poor souls haven't had any coffee at all yet today. I woke up too late this morning."

"It's cold," she warned.

"Like that's a problem," he said, warming the liquid until the steam wafted upward through a beam of sunlight. Then he took a sip and grimaced. "How do you drink it with this much sugar?"

"It's the McGeehee way," she murmured. "When the spoon stands up by itself, you've almost got enough sugar."

He dumped it over the side, disgusted by the sugar sludge at the bottom of the cup. Then he took the printouts from his pocket and gave them to her.

"What's this?" she asked. "You're taking pity on my technological disability and giving me cat memes now?"

"Read it," he said, really wishing he had a fresh cup now to wash the taste of hers out of his mouth. He really should pay more attention to his own reactions to things in his visions.

"Cat Sidhe," she murmured.

"It's pronounced like sea," he advised.

"Supernatural beings from Irish folklore that closely resembled large black cats with a white marking on their chest," she read, starting to get excited. "Known for being tricksters and feared for their ability to consume the souls of the recently deceased."

"Sounds an awful lot like a certain furry little turd, as I think you called him."

Megan looked thoughtful and then he could have sworn he heard faint whispers coming from her. "This isn't completely right," she said, staring out over the treetops. "They remembered part of it, but it changed over time. It's not a species, it's one creature that's been alive for a very long time."

"And how exactly do you know that?" he asked, unsure that he wanted to know the answer.

"There's a voice in my head," she answered hesitantly, probably afraid that he'd take it the wrong way, particularly in light of their argument the previous night. "It's always been there. Sometimes it tells me things I need to know."

"That's useful," he said, also trying to avoid another argument now that they'd made up. But the casual way she mentioned the presence of a foreign entity that lived inside her head wasn't particularly comforting. "Did it tell you anything else?"

"The Cat Sidhe was *hers*," she said, frowning. "But I don't know who she was exactly. She was important to the Tuatha dé. Something about washing armor…"

"So we're sure that's who's been following you?"

"I saw their hidden realm in Mom's memories," she replied. "It was so strange to see them. I have their pale skin, but their eyes are violet all the time, not just when they get upset."

"Then the woman you're talking about might be the Morrigan," he said.

"Maybe…" she said, her eyes unfocused in the distance as she weighed the information, "That feels right. If he was hers, maybe that explains how he moves around. Do you think he's walking between the shadows?"

"Probably, but if he's one of the Tuatha dé, and they're the ones who've been trying to find you," he said, trying to piece everything together, "why hasn't he brought them here?"

"Maybe he's just stubborn and unhelpful like every other cat?" she said.

It took you two long enough to figure that out, August's thoughts drifted through their minds.

So you've seen him? Megan asked.

Only from a distance. He's smart enough not to pass the boundary.

Why not? Bruce asked.

You said it yourself. He's supernatural. Guarded Wood is a sanctuary for things like him. He wouldn't be allowed to leave once he came here.

August, you know about the memories in my head from Jacob Routh, right?

The specter of the old minister at your school?

Yes, Megan answered. *I've never been able to sort them all out, and I know you're good with this kind of stuff.*

I wouldn't claim to be any kind of an expert, that's more Sam Wise's area. If anyone can help you with untangling them, it would probably be him.

But not with the Well of Dreams, she said. *That didn't turn out so well the last time.*

I don't think he'd need to use the Well, but to be honest, what you told me about what happened there puzzles me. People of power lose all of their abilities when they die and the things they created die with them. For this Dark Man, as you call him, to have so much influence on the material world shouldn't be possible.

That's why we're glad he turned out to be one of the good guys, Bruce said, remembering a similar conversation he'd had with Megan last year.

How are you feeling? Megan asked. *Sam said you were sick.*

Like I'm several hundred years old, came the reply.

Bruce pulled out his phone, stepped a few paces away from Megan and tried to call their large friend, but it went straight to voicemail.

"That's weird," Bruce said, "let's go check at Gordons." He took her hand, and realized it was the first time he'd touched her since last night. It frightened him how much he wanted to be in her life. It took a few seconds to look through possible futures for the best time to cross over to the Palace. With Kate back from the hospital, they could no longer just assume that they could use the theater as a safe jumping point.

He chuckled in anticipation. No longer even noticing the instant of vertigo that accompanied this form of travel, the two of them appeared directly in front of Jade while she carried a fresh reel of tickets to the booth.

As he'd known she would, she yelped in alarm and dropped the tickets on the floor.

"Damn it, Bruce!" she yelled. "You know I hate it when you do that!"

"I just want it known that I had no idea he was going to do that," Megan said, trying to glare at him. However, it lacked the power to make

101

him feel chastised due to her barely controlled laughter.

"Jade," Kate called from her office. "Are you okay out there?"

"I'm fine," Jade yelled back. "I'm just getting ready to kill my jerk of a brother. Please don't call the police until the screaming stops."

"Which one is it?" the older woman asked with mild interest. "If it's Paul please don't hurt his hands. He's coming along too nicely with the violin."

"It's the bookworm," Megan answered.

"Oh, hello Megan. I didn't know you were here too. Carry on Jade."

"Megan, would you mind doing something spectacular so he won't see this coming?" Jade asked, advancing on her brother.

"Okay, okay, I'm sorry," he said, backing away from her and trying not to get upset by the number of future paths in which his best friend did exactly as his sister asked in spite of their new truce. "We're just going over to see why Sam isn't answering his phone."

"He's not?" Jade asked, immediately stopping her advance in her concern for her mentor. She pulled out her phone and tried as well with the same result. "The dinner crew is probably swamped over at Gordons. You know how he has to put his personal touch on everything that comes through that kitchen. Maybe he's just too busy to answer."

"When have you ever known him not to drop everything when we called?" Megan asked.

"Good point," Jade said then, moving faster than Bruce would have thought possible, she slapped him across the back of the head. "Our big friend is an awful lot like Paul on steroids. That's probably why I like him so much."

"What was that for?" Bruce asked, massaging his head.

"For trying to distract me from hitting you by making me worry about Sam," she answered, bending over to pick up the tickets. "Let me know when you find him, since I really am worried now, you jerk."

Outside, Bruce noticed with pleasure once again that more people were walking down Main Street. Most held purchases from the numerous shops that had reopened in the last few months. He glanced over at the Baker, but kept his deeper thoughts about it from surfacing where his perceptive friend might sense them.

"He's not there," Megan said, having already reached out to search.

"Let me have a look," Bruce said, turning down an alleyway where no one could see them. "He's at his house."

"I've never been to his house," Megan said. "How do we get there?"

"That's okay, I can see it in the vision," he said. "Are you sure you want to do this?"

"Why?"

"He doesn't look like he wants company."

"Then we definitely need to snap him out of this, and I think I might know how," she said.

"You're the boss," he said with a shrug, taking her hand in his and walking the shadows to Sam, who currently sat on the front porch of his house.

He looked awful. The long dark hair that he normally kept pulled back in a neat braid hung in oily clumps around his face and shoulders as he rested his face in his big hands. His shirt was torn and stained.

"You two have a serious disregard for personal space," Sam said irritably. "If I'd wanted to speak with you, I would have answered the phone."

"You can't keep going on like this," Megan said.

"Thanks for your opinion even though I don't recall asking for it," he said, getting up from the steps and walking back to the front door. He

103

slammed it hard enough to shatter the glass in one of the windows.

"Like I said," Bruce explained. "He doesn't seem to want company."

"Yes he does," Megan said, "He just doesn't realize it yet." Without even taking his hand, she took them both into the house.

They found Sam looking out the broken window at where they'd just walked the shadows. He nodded and sighed in relief, clearly thinking he'd scared them off.

"We're still here, Sam," Megan said quietly.

The big man jumped with a very un-Sam-like expletive and whirled to face them.

"Are you sure it's wise to make Sam this mad?" Bruce asked.

"GET OUT OF MY HOUSE!" the big man roared only inches from their faces, and for the first time, Bruce realized how frightening his friend could be.

"No," Megan said simply, utterly unaffected by what had just happened.

"What do you mean no?" Sam said, startled enough by the young woman's audacity to drop back into his usual voice. "I've done everything you've asked. I've invested in just about every business in town, even the ones whose owners wouldn't let my people through their doors just a few decades ago. I've put every one of my own interests on hold to help you people, and yet she…she…"

"Didn't even say goodbye?" Megan finished for him, dodging effortlessly between his outstretched hands to wrap both of her arms around his trunk-like waist.

"Don't," he said miserably, trying to push her away, but even in this miserable state, he was careful not to hurt her.

"Don't what?" she asked, still holding onto him as hard as she could. "Love you like the father I wish you were?"

Bruce held his breath, waiting to see what would happen next. Until that moment, he hadn't realized that strong emotions could blind his vision even more thoroughly than heavy use of magic. Or maybe, now that he thought about it, love might be the most powerful magic of all.

Sam's anger evaporated. He wrapped his arms around Megan, lifted her off of the ground, and set free the tears he'd held back since finding her mother gone.

Megan held onto him through it all, not that she had much choice in the matter. She looked like little more than a rag doll in his arms. At last his sorrow spent itself and he realized what he was doing.

"I'm so sorry, Megan," he sniffed.

"There's nothing to be sorry for," she whispered, reaching up and wiping his wet cheek with her thumb. "She left a big hole in all of our hearts."

"I mean, I'm terrified of her," Bruce admitted, "But I miss her too."

Not helpful, Megan sent.

"Did the two of you ever talk about why she didn't come home for Christmas?" Megan asked quietly. Sam stiffened.

"She told you about that?"

"No, it was in one of the memories she left for me," she answered, and then went on to relate most of what she'd seen so far. She didn't tell him anything personal about her mother and father since she didn't think it was her place to do so. But she explained everything else, including their last meeting.

"So she didn't even realize she'd missed her flight?" he asked. "She didn't ignore me on purpose?"

"No," Megan answered.

"I should have let her explain," Sam whispered after a long pause.

"Things might have turned out differently if I had."

"Yes, you should have," she agreed.

"I'm glad you didn't," Bruce added. "I kind of like the fact that Megan was born."

"Now Sam," Megan said, glancing at Bruce as she did so, her eyes softening for only a second in which Bruce forgot all about being upset with her. "I've got to tell you something, and I don't want you to get upset."

"Okay," the big man said, steeling himself for what might come next.

"You smell," she said, wrinkling her nose. "And your house is a mess. We're going to tidy up and open the windows while you go get cleaned up."

The big man's laughter went a long way toward healing their own wounds.

As soon as he left, Bruce went straight to the broken window.

"This thing was like a thorn stuck in my hand," he admitted, lifting the jagged edges with his mind and fitting them into place before he began to fuse them back together like he had Christine's windshield. "I was ready to sneak back and fix it while he was asleep. I knew he'd catch me, but I was pretty sure I could finish before he got all the way out here from his bedroom."

They opened the windows and aired out the place the same way they'd done at the Palace, but on a much smaller scale and without disturbing the piles of books and papers that filled much of the space.

"And people say I hoard books," Bruce said, looking around.

"Don't alphabetize them," she teased, contenting herself with straightening stacks of papers until she froze and picked up one of the pictures. "Oh my god, how did he manage this?"

Coming over for a better look, he saw that she held a picture of Emelia, apparently taken during Jade's last birthday party.

"No one takes pictures of my mother," she said in admiration. "I mean, there are probably more legitimate pictures of Bigfoot than there are of her. I wonder how many of his cameras she blew up before he got this."

"Look at these," Bruce said, holding up a stack of old black and white photos of the days when Nickelville was doing better than it was now. There were quite a few shots of the town's Native American population as well.

"I think he's been scanning them," Bruce said, looking over the big man's desk.

"That's right," Sam said from the door leading back to his bedroom, drying his long hair with a towel. "I've been trying to get everything digitized and stored with some of the national databases. One of the joys of being the last of my people is trying to document that we ever existed at all."

"This stuff is amazing," Megan said, looking at some of the artifacts he'd collected over the years. "Where did you get all of it?"

"This house belonged to my grandfather," Sam answered, gesturing around. "He spent a lot of his time gathering our history from the things my people left behind. I've found some of it in garage sales from the people in town who weren't sure where their ancestors found it. I fear a lot of it has probably moved beyond the town through online markets."

"That's awful," Bruce said. "Can we do anything to help?"

"No, but the offer is appreciated. I dream sometimes of creating a small museum to house these treasures and to preserve who we once were."

"Done," Bruce said.

"What do you mean, done?" Sam asked, sitting down on the floor so Megan could braid his wet hair. She still had to stand in order to reach it comfortably.

"You don't think the improvements we've been making in town are just to get the local economy going again, do you?" Bruce asked, stepping away from the overflowing bookshelves. Since some of them were written in the sing-song language he'd heard Sam speak with the hermit, he knew he'd found his worst nemesis: clutter he couldn't organize.

"Well, yes," Sam answered, "that's exactly what I thought we were doing."

"We're helping Nickelville find its way back to itself," Bruce explained. "And your people make up the foundation of this town's history. It would be both unethical and irresponsible not to create a museum here. And it doesn't have to be small. Did you have any particular place in mind?"

"My Uncle's store," Sam answered without hesitation.

"The one with the hitching post that you used to walk like a balance beam?" Megan asked.

"That rail fell down when I was six," Sam said. "And everyone else who could possibly know about it is either dead or moved away. How did you know that's what it was from two rotten posts in the ground?"

"The first time my mother brought me here, I could see this area like it had been," she reminded him. "And I promised to show you what I saw some time."

"That would indeed be nice," the big man said.

"Hey Bruce," she said. "Do you have anything you have to be doing right now?"

"Not since that dragon ate Allison and died of indigestion," he joked, "It's a shame, really. I really wish we could have saved the dragon."

"Are those horses in the coral across the street broken?" she asked.

"One of them is," Sam answered.

"You get that one," she told Bruce.

"You can ride wild horses now?" he asked.

"Can't everyone?"

It only took Sam and Megan a few minutes to calm their mounts enough to ride. Bruce doubted that anyone but the two of them would find them to be the least bit tame though.

"Is there anything out here that we need to be on guard against?" she asked.

"Your places are the only ones nearby except for August if he's on this side of the woods," Sam answered.

"Then completely lower your shields. I'm going to open my eyes to the past and show you what it's like to live in my world."

At first everything looked normal to Bruce. The ruins of old houses sprinkled the raised plateau of Sam's ancestral home. But soon after they gave their horses their heads and let them pick their own path, the three of them started to notice faint shadows across the landscape. As they approached a roofless building that owed most of its survival to the layers of trumpet vine that held what was left together, they could see shadows of people moving around it. There was an old station wagon out front with the back end loaded to capacity. As they watched, a young couple with two young girls got in and drove away.

"I never knew who lived there," Sam said. "In my earliest memories it was already abandoned. "I did find a homemade doll there. It's in an airtight container back at my place."

Further on they came to the echo of a small pond that had dried away to a cracked indention in the ground. Several boys knelt along its edge, tossing out lengths of twine with pieces of meat tied to the end.

"How are they going to catch fish without any hooks?" Megan asked.

"They aren't after fish," Bruce answered. "Paul caught enough for Mom to cook once and Dad told us that they were just like shrimp."

"What are?" Megan asked, just in time for one of the boys to pull out a large crayfish and put it into a bucket at his side. "Ew…"

"I can't say I ever liked them much either," Sam said. "And no, they aren't just like shrimp. They've got much tougher flesh. Or at least that's what they were like when my grandfather cooked them. I did enjoy catching them though. Emelia did too."

The horses made their way to the old store, and Bruce understood at once why it had caught Megan's eye. The overlapping images of Sam's past moved in a chaotic swell. And sure enough, a young boy walked across the hitching post like a balance beam.

Sam's eyes widened in wonder and he quickly dismounted, almost hitching his horse to the long-gone rail. He spent some time wandering slowly through the crowd, studying each face before moving on.

When he was satisfied, he returned to the two of them.

"Thank you, Megan," he said, reaching up to cover her small hand with his large one. "This is a gift more wonderful than you could possibly imagine. I remember so many of these people. That's my uncle you can see behind the counter inside, and that's my grandfather sitting on the bench smoking a cigarette. I almost knocked it out of his hand before I remembered he was gone. Those things were what killed him."

"I can see why you want to use this site for the museum," Bruce said. "It's amazing. We might have to add onto it though. I'm not sure it's big enough for all of the stuff you've accumulated so far, and we'll want to have room to grow as you find more. And then there's storage, preservation rooms and office space for the workers. And you'll need a break room too. Maybe an outdoor amphitheater?"

"It became the heart of our community," Sam said, smiling at his young friend's enthusiasm for a moment before becoming lost in the scene before him again. "By the time my uncle died, there weren't enough people left to keep this place running. When it closed, the few people who remained decided it was time to go. We weren't really allowed at the store off of Main Street, and as you can imagine, it was quite a drive to another where we were treated no better."

"But that was illegal even then, wasn't it?" Megan asked.

"Laws are only as strong as the people who enforce them, and Chief Pullin's predecessor wasn't much better than he's been. Grandpa and I got by though. We grew or raised most of what we needed, just as our people always had. And in time, Nickelville accepted me."

"Then it's time something was done about this. We'll make it happen," Bruce said. "I think we should bring in professional help to catalog and preserve everything though, or at least get some interns from the college. There's just too much work for one person to do alone, and an expert would better know how to preserve things so people can see everything you've done here for generations to come."

"And Bruce is afraid that this might cut into the quality of his pizza if you spend too much time out here," Megan teased.

The world blurred around Bruce as he laughed at Megan's words, and he had a clear vision of people, real people living in the present, returning to this area once again.

"Are you okay Bruce?" Sam asked, reaching out to steady him so he wouldn't fall off of the horse.

"I think we need to start restoring some of these houses," he said. "Sooner rather than later."

"Why?" Megan asked.

"I just think we should," Bruce said.

"Well," Sam said, frowning, "Since your foresight hasn't steered us wrong yet, I guess I'll get some contractors out here to get started."

"There are people coming. I couldn't be sure, but most of them looked like they could be your people," Bruce said, motioning to the echoes of the past which still surrounded them. "And you're going to buy the Baker Hotel."

"Hold on now," Megan said. "You want to buy the building we almost died in a few months ago?"

"It's not the Baker's fault that Jones tried to kill us all," Bruce answered defensively.

"If you say so," Megan said, frowning. She knew there was more to this, but she also knew better than to pry.

"I must admit, it would be nice not to be the only person of color in Nickelville," Sam said happily, looking toward Megan with a mischievous grin. "The newcomers just keep getting paler and paler."

She rolled her eyes in response.

"And now that you two have suitably brought me back from the brink of despair, what was so important that you had to barge into my house uninvited?"

"Hey now," Megan said defensively, "We might have come to ask you if you could fix the Dark Man's memories that are stuck in my head, but we broke into your house because we were worried about you."

"Fair enough," the big man replied.

"Do you mind?" he asked Megan, motioning for her to dismount.

She threw her leg over and slid down the horse's flank.

Although they all knew it wasn't strictly necessary to make contact when they did work like this, Sam still fanned his fingertips across the sides of her head and started to probe.

"Your mind is very interesting in the way it works," the big man said. "I've never seen anything quite like it."

As soon as he began to probe deeper, an angry female presence blew through their minds.

GET OUT! It demanded with such force that it actually knocked the big man to the ground several feet from where Megan stood.

"Did you just blow Sam out of your mind?" Bruce asked, shocked by the possibility.

"That wasn't Megan," Sam answered before she could, already rising. "That was something incredibly old. Old and female."

."But Bruce has been in my head tons of times without that happening," Megan said, rushing over to make sure Sam was okay.

"Maybe I should look," Bruce offered.

"I don't want to hurt you," Megan said, turning toward him.

"Just don't dump any more water on me or blow up my bedroom again," he teased, moving closer.

Sam appeared to be too dazed to question them further although he did look puzzled by this remark.

Entering her mind this way differed from anything they'd ever done before. In spite of what had happened to Sam, Bruce was far more worried that he might inadvertently hurt her than he was for his own safety. Even though he'd shared her thoughts on more than one occasion over the past year, he'd never entered her mind as an outsider.

He immediately became aware of the presence of which Sam had spoken. And while it was indeed an old presence, it felt nothing like that

113

of the Dark Man. Whoever this was felt infinitely older, making him wonder once again if it could be the spirit of the Morrigan.

Are you the voice she hears sometimes?

Don't try my patience, boy. The only reason I'm tolerating your presence here is because I will have need of you in the days to come. What you're looking for is over there.

He felt her roughly move his consciousness to the place where the Dark Man's memories resided.

"Are you okay?" Megan asked. "That felt weird."

"I'm okay," he said out loud where Sam could hear as well. "I just got forcefully redirected to the nearest information desk. And I thought your mother was tough. I think I can see what the problem is. Sam is right, your mind doesn't work like ours. It's like it works on a different operating system or something."

"If you're done geeking out in my brain, do you think you could do something to fix it?"

"I don't think so, it's just not compatible with you. But it feels like it wants to come to me. I think it would cross directly into my mind if I let it."

"I've never been particularly fond of having a dead man's memories in my head," she admitted. "But I warn you, it really hurt when I got them."

"I'm willing to take that chance," Bruce said. As soon as he opened a path to his own brain, the images flowed painlessly into his mind.

"Oh, that's just like getting a big splinter out," Megan whispered, massaging her temples.

"And you?" Sam asked, watching Bruce closely.

"Well I'm not unconscious or bleeding out of my nose," he said. "So that's a plus."

"So what's in there?" Megan asked impatiently.

"Are you sure we shouldn't discuss the ancient presence inside your head that's strong enough to knock Sam on his butt?" Bruce asked. "I mean, not even the duck cows of doom could pull that off."

"She's always been there to help me out of bad situations," Megan said dismissively. "If she wanted to do me harm, I think she'd have done it long before now."

"Okay," he said, holding his hands up in defeat. "Jacob became convinced that there was a gate into the afterlife somewhere under the school. There was a cave behind the carved doors that now lead to the library. He went down there with his wife's surviving two sisters. The older, Crina, was what they considered to be a witch for lack of a better term. She's the one that Megan and Emelia are descended from. The other one, Luminita, had power, but it was tied to her music."

"Like a bard from the stories?" Sam asked.

"I think so," Bruce agreed. "Anyway, Crina wanted no part of Jacob's attempt to open the gate. She said he was insane to even think about it. But Luminita and her betrothed agreed to help him. Something went wrong and they caused an explosion. Jacob doesn't know anything about what happened after that and I don't know how anyone could have survived what the memory shows."

"Why does he want us to know this?" Megan asked.

"I think he wants us to find the gate," Bruce said. "But that's not the weirdest thing about this memory."

"Weirder than opening gates into the afterlife?" Sam asked.

"Remember the girl I had the vision about before the boundary was restored?" Bruce asked, frowning.

"The one who will eventually replace August?" Sam asked.

"I recognize her now," he said, more puzzled than ever. "It's the sister that died in the accident. How can she be the new caretaker of Guarded Wood if she's already dead?"

Chapter XI: Wellness Check

"Where is all of this sand coming from?" Mrs. Grimble asked as she swept the entryway where Bruce normally kicked off his shoes after his morning run. Paul shot him a curious glance from the living room couch where he'd been for the past hour, writing something in a spiral that required a great deal of humming the same series of notes over and over. With a look that said *I know you're hiding something* without saying anything out loud, Paul let him know he wasn't fooled. After all, if anyone knew that there wasn't any sand to be found in the area it was Bruce's rock hound brother.

With a twinge of guilt, Bruce realized he still hadn't shared August's beach with anyone else, not even Megan. And of course, that made him think about all of the other things he'd been keeping to himself.

"I'm going for a run in the woods," he said, grabbing his shoes on the way.

"Be careful," his mother said absently. "Make sure you take your phone in case you turn an ankle."

He almost told her that phones didn't work there before he caught himself. If he didn't start getting more sleep, he might very well spill everything by accident.

He started to run as soon as he left the driveway, circling the house and heading for the woods. As always, as soon as he started to move it felt like most of his worries fell away. He knew it made no difference in the problems that plagued his idle moments, but at least while he ran he felt as if he was making progress.

As he'd expected, Fang soon fell soundlessly into step beside him, but Bruce felt nothing of the hermit's presence within him. Although the absence was unusual, Bruce wouldn't have been concerned had it not been a while since he'd seen the old man. The beach would have to wait.

Instead of taking the paths that led to what he'd come to think of as his own personal resort, he stretched out his senses and combed the woods for traces of the old man's passage. By taking the forks that held the strongest memories of August, Bruce found a place that even his siblings had never discovered.

He knew he was going in the right direction when the twisting sandy trail he'd been following passed beneath the gnarled branches of a bois d'arc tree only to come out in a valley surrounded by either small mountains or extremely tall hills. Early fall scrub suddenly gave way to a riot of wildflowers balanced on the edge of going dormant for winter. But even so, it was one of the most beautiful places Bruce had ever seen.

The path widened as he slowed to a jog. Oddly enough, Fang didn't bound ahead like he usually did but instead seemed content to follow the pace set by his two-legged friend.

Although large trees still dotted what he could see of the valley before him, most were smaller and bore signs of human intervention in the shapes of their limbs. Many of the leaves had already begun to turn, leaving freckles of color along the path.

He passed the ruin of what might have once been a tower, but couldn't be sure as it was almost completely enveloped in wild grape vines. Although he sensed August within the remaining walls, the presence felt old and irrelevant. He continued on with the panting wolf at his side.

Low in the valley, the sun dipped below the surrounding peaks and cast a chill over the land. Then he and his running mate entered a gentle fog which, rather than hiding the features of the place, seemed to soften its focus. He thought it looked like some drowsy artist's rendition of Eden.

He passed through orchards from which the fruit had already fallen, some familiar and some not. Here the rough trail became a cobblestone path. Fruit trees gave way to ornamental gardens plucked straight from the pastoral English countryside. Bruce gave up any premise of knowing what might come next. Although he'd attempted to envision what the hermit's home might have looked like, this paradise seemed too perfect to be real.

Statues in the style of the ancient Romans dotted the area, some set upon marble pedestals, and others rising unfinished and forgotten from the foliage as if the artist had lost interest and moved on to something new. As he drew closer, it looked as if they might all be of the same woman.

At the bottom of the valley stood a huge, calm pool through which a lively stream passed and into which a weather-worn dock jutted. Sitting there on an old lawn chair with a modern fishing pole in his hands sat August. Fang trotted straight up to the water's edge and splashed several feet in before starting to happily drink.

"I wondered when your wanderings would lead you here," the old man said. "I thought for a while that it would be your brother and sister, but they don't come out exploring as much anymore."

"Jade found boys," Bruce replied. "And Paul found the violin."

"He's really quite good for one so young," August said, reeling in his empty hook. "So what brings you out here instead of yonder beach?

Or did the cannibals scare you away?"

"That was so wrong," Bruce said, although he'd long since lost any real anger at the prank. "Did you catch anything?"

"Enough for dinner if you'd like to join me. And just so you know, no self-respecting cannibal would eat someone as scrawny as you."

"You know," Bruce said, ignoring the taunt, "I will if you don't mind."

"Of course I don't mind," the old man said, rising to his feet. "Do you see that rope looped around that spike at the end?"

Bruce reached out with his mind and pulled it in, revealing several good-sized trout.

"You do know that you're still allowed to do things without magic, don't you?" the old man asked, raising one of his bushy white eyebrows. "And since you're joining me, grab the chair. I've only got the one in my cabin."

"August, are you okay?" Bruce asked soon afterward, carrying the string of fish as well as the old lawn chair as he followed the old man up a stony path.

"Why do you ask?"

"Sam said you were sick a while back, and this is the first time I've ever entered the woods without feeling your presence in Fang."

"Are you implying that I shouldn't just let him run free?" August asked. "Just so you know, I always send him off when I'm going to spend any amount of time fishing. I don't know what kind of dog he's mixed with, but it must have been one of those water breeds. I can't catch anything with him splashing around in there."

"Can't you just make him stop?" Bruce asked, noticing that his furry friend was getting awfully close to the fish.

"Sure I could," the old man said, glancing back at Bruce. "But I'd have to force him, and that isn't any way to treat my best friend. Besides, now that the boundary is guarding itself for the first time in decades, I think Fang and I have earned a chance to take it easy for a bit."

"That's for sure," Bruce agreed. "How old is he?"

"A lot older than he should be."

121

Tucked in among the rocky outcroppings on the hill, a small stone cabin came into view. Spongy moss covered the ground as well as the roof, making it impossible to see what lay underneath or to tell exactly where his home ended and the hill behind it began.

"Home sweet home," August said. "Did you pass the tower?"

"Yes," Bruce answered, his senses already exploring the front of the structure as August leaned his pole against the wall next to the door.

"I built that when I first came to Guarded Wood," he said. After about a century and a half of trying to keep that huge thing upright and watertight, I gave into an inspirational bit of common sense and built this place. It's easier to heat in the winter, and it doesn't echo as much when Fang gets riled up and starts to bark."

"He's been around that long?" Bruce asked, scratching the wolf between the ears. As soon as he stopped, Fang moved over to a spot in the sun and stretched out for a nap. Then several chickens ran out from where the path disappeared behind the hill. Not only were they unafraid of the huge beast, but one of them began to eagerly pick at some of the debris in his fur.

"I couldn't tell you exactly how old he is, but he's definitely what your generation would call a senior citizen," Azarich answered. "Now, since you're so eager to show off your magic, would you mind filling the pot in the hearth with water from the stream? And don't be messy about it or you'll drench my kindling."

"Can't we just dry it out if I do?" Bruce asked.

The old man glared at him in response.

Snatching moving water and sending it through the shadows to a stationary container without letting the stream's momentum slosh it back out again proved to be extremely difficult. By the time Bruce finished, he felt more winded than he had from the run, and August had finished cleaning the fish.

But that wasn't the end of Bruce's involvement with dinner. A quick tour of the hermit's cabin followed which revealed not only numerous bookshelves, but also that it extended far back into the hillside. August talked him through peeling potatoes with magic, an exercise that turned out to be similar to making Paul's fossils turn loose from the matrix. Then he was back outside gathering the last of the year's carrots and onions from the garden. All of these ingredients passed through the old man's gnarled but surprisingly dexterous hands to be chopped and added to the pot along with the pungent contents of several jars that sat on a shelf near the hearth.

At last August seemed content to let the stew cook and joined his young friend at the roughhewn table.

"Remember when I told you about the woman who will follow you?" Bruce asked, holding a cup of cider that the hermit had made himself.

"The one who belongs here?"

"Yes," Bruce answered, uneasy about taking away the hope he'd given the old man a while back. "We took your advice and had Sam look into Megan's memories. That didn't work out very well, but we finally got them all moved over into my head."

"Sensible, since you have so much empty space in there," the old man teased.

"Ha-ha," Bruce replied. "The thing is that the woman I saw before is in those memories. I don't know what went wrong with my foresight, but she's already dead."

"You're sure?" August asked, looking concerned. Bruce nodded.

They sat in silence for a while afterward, watching the fire lick the bottom of the iron pot. It wasn't long before it started to smell good.

"I've never had fish stew before," Bruce said, trying to draw the old man back out again.

"It's pretty good the first few thousand times," August replied.

"So what made you choose this particular spot?" Bruce asked, changing tactics. "Was there a small cave that you enlarged or did you mine the whole space out?"

"I wanted to be closer to where I laid my wife to rest," the hermit answered.

"I didn't see a grave," Bruce said.

"Follow me," August said, draining his cup and putting it down on the table. "The stew will cook faster without us watching anyway."

The trail hugged the side of the steep hill, wide enough to walk comfortably, but not wide enough to keep Bruce from looking down over the side. His dislike of heights hadn't gotten any better since that day with the rocs, but he liked the way the old man was allowing him into this brief glimpse of his long life.

The few trees that managed to eke out enough open space to take root sprouted from the crevices, twisting windswept branches into strange patterns. Because Bruce was so focused on the path and making sure that he didn't fall, he didn't notice that they'd reached the end of the trail until August stopped in front of him. Perched at the pinnacle of the hill, overlooking much of the valley below stood a mausoleum.

Just high enough to reach the rays of the sun, it glowed against the late afternoon sky. With a square stone base and a circular peak that rose two stories above it, the entire surface had been carved in relief with scenes that Bruce couldn't quite discern from where he stood. Stone columns surrounded it and helped to support the domed peak. It was the sort of thing that would have taken artisans a lifetime to create, and for all he knew it might have taken the hermit just as long.

"That is where her remains are held," the old man said, looking at it with longing. "We normally cremate our dead, but I just couldn't do that to her."

"It's beautiful," Bruce said. "You're an amazing stone mason."

"Anyone with our gifts can be an amazing mason," the old man answered, but he looked pleased by the compliment just the same. "It took me a while to find the stone and get it here though. As you can see, there was something here before I came, but there wasn't really enough of it left to tell what it might have been. I did make use of the flattened peak it was built on though. Having you and Megan would have been useful. Sending the raw blocks through the shadows would have shaved decades off of the project."

"We would have loved to help," Bruce said, thinking suddenly of the graves of Sorina and her child. "Wait a minute, you said you could still leave Guarded Wood all the way up until the sixties, right?"

"That's correct."

"Were you still going into town when the Academy was a church?"

"Yes, though I was more interested in the woodland magic that permeated the woods nearby. The diminishing of my senses came about the same time the Reverend disappeared. I met him a few times."

"You met Jacob Routh when he was still alive?" Bruce asked in surprise, looking away from the beautiful building above. "Why didn't you say so before now?"

"He was a good man with a head full of dreams for this town. That was actually before it was a town though. Why didn't I mention him? I don't know. As you get older it's easy to get focused on the things that directly affect you. And I've had a lot longer than most to fixate on Guarded Wood to the exclusion of everything outside. But in his day, Jacob Routh was a powerful magician, although a bit reckless. In hindsight, I suspect whatever it was that created the unnatural hush that descended afterward must have been the result of this accident you spoke of. Do you know what it was that he was trying to do?"

"Open a gate to the afterlife and bring his wife and son back."

August didn't react at first, but his eyes returned to the mausoleum

126

while he thought.

"It was a foolish thing to try," he said at last, "but as someone who's been where he was at that time, I understand. I can't say with any certainty that I wouldn't have done the same thing were our roles reversed. But gates are dangerous things, and the people who meddle with them do so at their own peril. Only the Beloved can do so with impunity."

"The Beloved?"

"That was an entire branch of study where I came from, and I don't think I've enough decades left in me to properly explain them," August evaded. "Let's head back. The stew should be close to ready."

"What about the Baker Hotel?" Bruce asked, following his friend down the hill.

"Is that where you've been poking around when you should be at home asleep?" August asked.

Bruce nodded.

"What did you find there?"

"I don't think it was ever intended to be a hotel," Bruce answered, feeling better now that he'd started to talk about his night time excursions. "The ground floor and a few above it looks real enough if you don't know what you're looking for, but the fifth floor is set up like one big apartment. But not penthouse level furnished."

"That's what I saw as well," August admitted.

"You've been inside?" Bruce asked.

"I suspected things were not what they appeared," the old man admitted. "So I went to check it out after the construction stopped. I never found a way to go to the top of the building though. The stairway leading up wasn't completed."

"Did you try sending a bird to the top?" Bruce asked.

127

"Even when I could still leave the woods, my control over the creatures that lived here only extended a short distance from the Sentinel boundary."

"There's a hidden elevator that goes all the way to the top," Bruce said. "It's behind a secret panel in the back of a storage room. It took me forever to find it."

"That's not possible," August said. "I would have seen it when I was looking out from the stair exit."

"So you went during the day when you could see?"

"Of course," August said. "That hotel wasn't a particularly comforting place to be back then and I'm sure it hasn't gotten better during the years since. You're still trying to gain control over your fear of the dark, aren't you?"

"Honestly, the dark doesn't bother me much anymore. Not unless I'm having a nightmare, and then for only a few seconds after I first wake up. My extra senses are much more dependable than my sight. But even so, I wasn't able to sense the elevator shaft at first. It wasn't until I let my extra senses travel through the iron girders like a highway that I found it."

"So you traveled through the actual structure of the building since you couldn't see! It never occurred to me that something might be hidden from sight in that way so I never looked deeper," the hermit exclaimed. "Here I am centuries old, and you're already coming up with uses for a power you've just inherited that I haven't thought of with all this time and experience."

"Admit it," Bruce said. "I'm an absolute genius."

"You're certainly something," August said, frowning. "But I'll never accuse you of being humble. What did you find?"

"The elevator was really old, but it still worked. What I didn't take into consideration was that the same shielding that made it almost impossible to detect, would also sever the bond between Megan and me."

"Which led to her going on a rampage through your house like the proverbial bull in a China shop," August said.

"They did a special on that on a show I used to watch. It turns out that bulls are actually quite careful about where they walk," Bruce said.

"Why would anyone take the time to test such a thing?" the hermit asked, before shaking his head in irritation. "Don't answer that. I want to know what you saw."

"First of all, the elevator shaft was really weird," Bruce began, trying to figure out how to describe the strange place. "It was filled with tree roots, and I'm not talking about a few. It's like the whole shaft was *made* out of the tree roots. There was this blue light that filtered through from somewhere, even though it was completely dark inside the building from what should have been the outside of the shaft."

"Although there are ways that the shaft could be camouflaged from detection," August said thoughtfully, "There is only one group of people I know of who can do it, and I'm certain that they had nothing to do with the construction of that hotel. Did you experience anything like you do when you walk the shadows, or when you pass from one portion of Guarded Wood into another?"

"I did," Bruce replied, remembering the sensation. "As a matter of fact, I wondered if I might not be in a part of Guarded Wood when it happened."

"What else?" the hermit prompted.

"The penthouse was much nicer than the fifth floor, but it looked like everything had been carried off. I found places on the wall where paintings had hung along with a lot of empty display cases. I meant to go back and take a closer look at them, but I kept sensing that there was something alive up there that reacted to sound but not power. I was trying to find out what it was, but when I got to where I felt it, I left the shielding on the place and the backlash from Megan trashing my shields hit me. I had to come back in a hurry before she tore the whole house down and woke up my mother."

"Let me get this straight," August said, closing his eyes in dismay. "You rode up an elevator that hid you from even the girl who is bound to you, not knowing if it were some kind of trap. Yes, I know you understood how dangerous that was, and the only reason I'm not going to scold you is because I am not your parent and it is not my place to do so. Then you went looking for something you couldn't identify in what was a clearly magical place, even after spending the entire summer dealing with dangerous magical creatures here in Guarded Wood. But after all of that, the thing that finally made you quit was the worry that your mother might wake up and become angry with you?"

"My mother has gifts stronger than magic when it comes to keeping her kids in line. Besides, I didn't see anything bad in my future," Bruce said defensively.

"Ah, so you knew what you were going to find before you got there?"

"Well, no," Bruce said. "It was in a blank spot. I only had a second at the top, but there was an enormous tree and a ton of plants up there growing wild."

The old man gave him a long hard look.

"Okay," Bruce admitted at last. "It was a stupid thing to do."

"You are going to have to go back there," August said at last. "But you must promise me that you will never go alone again. I was young once myself, and I know how tempting it is to fly in the face of danger. But I for one would be very hurt if something happened to you, and I

130

never heard from you again."

"I'll take Megan and Sam," Bruce promised, unable to look the hermit in the eye.

"Take Jade and Paul too," August suggested. "They may not have magic, but they are as keenly observant as any I've ever seen. And take lots of pictures. I want to know everything about what is there. I really wish I could come with you."

"Me too," Bruce said. "I have a feeling your experience would catch things we'll miss. I'll take some video too if you want."

"I'd like that."

They walked back down to August's home in silence with the hermit likely thinking about what his young friend had revealed about the hotel and Bruce worrying about what would happen if a weak spot in the path gave way. When they arrived, Fang still slept but now a marbled black and gray hen had joined him.

The wolf woke for the stew though, which August ladled out into wooden bowls. Like the walk, they ate mostly in silence. Bruce liked the stew, which surprised him since he'd always been a picky eater.

"So you won't mind if I drop in on you from time to time?" Bruce asked when they'd finished and the sun had begun to dip behind the hills.

"I'd be terribly disappointed if you didn't. And Bruce, if there's a gate in that school, I'd strongly advise you and the others to leave it alone, lest you set something nasty free."

"Wait a minute," Bruce said. "That reminds me. Do you know anything about some ancient scary lady living inside of Megan's head? Megan isn't worried about it, but I don't know."

"Yes I do," August said, "And the runestones will explain it soon. Just leave it alone and everything will reveal itself in due course."

"Now you sound like Emelia," Bruce said, and August looked at him hard again for almost a full minute before he spoke.

"There was a time when I would have been offended by that remark. But even old men who've seen the passage of centuries can still be horribly wrong. I am honored to be compared to her, though nothing I've done can ever compare to what she's had to endure. Now go, so Fang and I can get some sleep or I really will have him lead you into a nest of cannibals."

Chapter XII: Redneck Wizard

Enough was enough. The rising sun painted the clouds in crimson hues, but the most Megan could get from her grandfather were a few grunts of approval. It was time for him to come back to her from wherever he'd gone when her mother left.

She leaned forward, picked up one of the large plastic buckets he used for various tasks around the porch and sat on it, turning her back on the sunrise to face him.

"You're going to miss the best part," he said without much enthusiasm.

"This is going to stop," she said, willing her voice to take just a hint of her mother's. "I know it hurts that she left the way she did. But I'm still here, and I promise I won't leave you like she did. If something happens and I have to go, I'll take you with me."

"I'm sorry if it feels like I'm not appreciating you," he whispered, "but this is too much like before. I don't have thirty more years left to wait for her. I didn't even get to say goodbye."

"She's not gone forever," Megan assured him, leaning close so that her forehead rested against his and taking his hands in her own. "And even though we all miss her, we've got to stop letting it drive us crazy."

"Has Bruce seen her come back yet?" he asked.

"He can see that she does, but he can't tell when."

"So it's probably a long time away," he said.

"Not necessarily," she assured him, squeezing his hands. "He only gets detailed visions about a month out. And if she comes back when we're doing something big it could hide her return as well."

"I'm sorry I've been so distant from you," he said. "I'll try to do better."

"It's not me who needs you most right now."

"Who?" he asked, leaning back away from her to better see her face.

"When was the last time you talked to Alan?"

"He's got the renovations at the Academy and Kate to keep him occupied right now. He doesn't need me anymore," he answered bitterly.

"Are you seriously jealous of him right now?" she asked, feeling his emotions spill over her shields when she did so.

"I know I shouldn't be," he said guiltily, "but after Josie died, it was Alan that stayed by me and made sure I was okay. He did the same thing when your mother didn't come home from college. He came with me to her wedding. I don't begrudge him the chance to finally settle down, but with Emelia gone, it feels like everyone is leaving me behind."

"Look at me," she said, holding his stubbly face between her hands. "I swear on everything that I've ever loved that I will *never* leave you behind. I love you too much to waste any time we have together." Then she stood up and hugged him as hard as she could.

"I love you too, Megan," he said, finally starting to sound like himself. "Now what is it that Alan needs me for?"

"Well, he doesn't realize he needs you yet, but you've got to have a barbeque up in the tree house," she said.

"Of course I can do that," he said. "But why?"

"He's also going to need you to give him some advice," she said, enjoying the look of confusion on his face. "And after you help him

134

figure out how to ask her, he's going to need you to get fitted for a tux."

"You're not saying that he's going to propose?" Azarich exclaimed, jumping to his feet and then falling back into the swing when it hit him in the back of the knees. "Is he going to do it at the barbeque?"

"He'll do it even if you don't host one, but then we won't be able to watch," Megan said, standing up and pulling him to his feet again so she could hug him. "So you'll do it?"

"This will be the best meal I've ever cooked," he said, only half hugging her in his distraction. "Burgers or chicken simply won't do for this. Definitely steak and maybe some ribs too. You know what? I haven't smoked a brisket in years. I'm going to make the butcher down at the market a very happy man. And my grill isn't big enough for this much meat. I'll call Tom and ask him if I can borrow his and run both of them."

Tell him not to bother, Bruce sent from next door. *When you suggested the meal, it solidified the future. I just had this really cool cascade of visions that started with us having this conversation and ends with me doing some really cool stuff with stone and scrap metal that I never would have even thought of before now. This barbeque pit is going to be EPIC!*

A short time later, Bruce watched as Megan arrived with her grandfather under the tree house, pushing a wheelbarrow full of scrap metal that they'd scavenged from around their place. Then Jade and Paul added their last contributions to a big pile of stones, and Bruce could feel Sam and August approaching on horseback. Even Mr. Bob came to watch, though he stayed perched in one of the trees a safe distance from the boundary of Guarded Wood.

135

Bruce couldn't remember being so excited, and his nervous energy infected everyone around him. For a short time at least, no one thought about the woman who wasn't there.

"Okay everyone," he said, clearing his throat. "Hopefully this goes the way I see it in my head, and I don't make us all mutate into flying monkeys."

"I've always wanted a prehensile tail," Paul mused. "I could probably live with that."

"Here goes nothing," Bruce said.

He could feel Megan's surprise when he didn't open himself to her for help. But on some level, he knew this held the potential to hurt her if she did, and that simply wasn't acceptable. First, he scraped the sod off the top of the ground with a gesture. Then, with palms facing downward, he compressed the soil into something like stone. When it happened, it looked like someone had dropped a giant invisible brick onto the cleared ground.

"Maybe you should stop hitting him in the back of the head," Paul muttered to his sister as they watched. "I'd hate to see you under that…"

The stones began to rise in sequence, shedding mass that didn't fit into Bruce's mental blueprint and squaring themselves off so that they fit together with seams so perfect that a knife's edge couldn't fit between the gaps. Then the pieces of scrap metal began to rise from the wheelbarrow, glowing with heat as if they were in a forge.

"You guys might want to stay back for this part," Bruce warned.

The metal glowed white hot and began to twist into a molten mass as if an invisible baker were kneading dough. When he felt it was ready, a portion broke free and formed itself into a latticework of glowing metal that continued to float in the air. Another portion split away, forming itself into a cylinder that hollowed itself out and elongated to become the

smokestack. Then what remained flattened itself out to become the lid and ash door. Then they fitted themselves to the stone.

"I'm glad we didn't use sedimentary stone," Paul muttered. "Or it would have exploded when he did that."

"Don't distract the wizard while he's making me a barbeque pit,"

Azarich whispered, making Bruce smile. Thunder rolled in the distance as the area tried to balance the energy he expended.

He brought the temperature of the metal up far beyond what should have caused it to disintegrate, and held it that way with the strength of his will until it had the exact properties he wanted. Then, unable to resist a theatrical ending, he brought it all down to the ambient temperature with a flourish of his hands, and it was done.

But his cockiness lasted only until a wave of vertigo washed over him. He staggered and would have fallen if Megan hadn't hurried forward to steady him.

"Are you okay?" Jade asked, rushing up too.

"Yeah," he answered sheepishly, "It just took a bit more out of me than I expected."

"You're sure?" Megan asked, staying close to him just in case. He felt her probing him for damage, and her eyes softened in that way they sometimes did, affecting him far more than the enchantment. Every time she did that it was like an engine trying to start within him. No, it felt more like a nuclear reactor trying to come online. But like the mirage of an oasis in the desert, it faded again and whatever energy it evoked in him drained away as well.

"Ladies and Gentlemen," he announced when the worst passed. "I give you the world's first enchanted barbeque pit. Its parts will never rust or get dirty. And I have never felt like more of a redneck than I do at this moment!"

Everyone laughed except August who, Bruce noticed, looked deeply troubled.

They all moved forward to admire the grill from every angle, and Azarich admitted that it should be adequate for his needs. Bruce rolled his eyes in mock disgust.

"Well," Jade said reluctantly, "This was fun and all, but I've got to go to the Palace and invite a certain couple so they can get married and stop acting like teenagers. Worse than teenagers actually." She shuddered. "I don't suppose any of you can remove memories?"

"Why?" Megan asked.

"I walked in on them while they were making out in Kate's office."

"I could try," Bruce said. "But you might lose most of your childhood instead."

"If the nightmares don't stop soon, it might still be worth it," she said, looking haunted.

"Am I still banned from cooking when I eat here, or can I bring an assortment of sides?" Sam asked.

"That would be wonderful," Azarich answered happily.

"And I'll bring homemade bread," August said. "As long as we're still planning to have it in the Sentinel tree."

"I didn't know you could cook," Paul said with interest.

"He cooks very well," Bruce added, realizing that once again, he'd kept his visit to himself.

"What did you think I'd been eating all the time I've been living out there?" August asked, gesturing toward the woods on his way to his horse.

"I don't know," the youngest Grimble answered thoughtfully, "Locusts and wild honey?"

The old man fixed him with an icy stare after he pulled himself into the saddle.

"Sometimes I regret not letting the siren eat you," he called back as he rode away.

139

Chapter XIII: Supernatural Philosophy 101

Bruce knew he'd find the hermit on the beach, he just didn't know why the man had chosen this time to come and speak with him. But he'd noticed August's displeasure at the creation of the new barbeque pit and suspected he was about to hear about something he'd done wrong.

"So have you figured out where or when this part of Guarded Wood originated?" the old man asked, looking out over the waves as he sat on a large tree trunk that had washed ashore from someplace else.

"It must be pretty far back or there would be trash washing up everywhere," Bruce answered, reasoning it through.

"I tried to figure it out with an astrolabe when I first found it and later a sextant," August said. "We're lucky it's one of the places that still experiences a full night and day. There are parts of the woods that seem to be permanently stuck in one or the other. I think it must be pretty close to the equator since there don't seem to be any seasons."

"You didn't come out here to talk about this place," Bruce said, sitting down next to him on the log.

"It might not be the only reason, but I did actually want to talk about it. How would you go about trying to figure out the where and when of it with modern technology?"

Bruce thought for a moment.

"We can't use GPS since the satellites they use haven't been launched yet," he said. "Our best bet would be to take pictures of the night sky and try to match them with archeological data bases."

"And what are those?" the hermit asked, interested.

"Archeologists figured out that many prehistoric sites are built on alignments with astronomical bodies, like the North Star. And sometimes they are positioned in such a way that light will pass through something on the solstice or something like that. After they started to notice that, they got astronomers to create charts based on where stars were in the heavens at certain times in the past."

"I wasn't aware that they moved," August said, smiling up at the sky.

"They don't, but the Earth wobbles on its axis, and over time it changes the way the night sky looks from earth."

"I have lived to see such wonders," the old man mused. "Would you mind seeing if you can find out the where and when of this place?"

"Sure," Bruce said. "Is there any particular reason why you want to know this one in particular?"

"My wife saw this beach in one of her last visions," the old man replied, his voice distant as if he were looking back across the centuries to that very moment. "She led me here on the day she died. I had to carry her, but that wasn't a problem. We watched the sun rise in this very spot, and then she was gone."

"What was her name?" Bruce asked.

"Aurora," August said, "Which made this a fitting time and place for her to pass. She always had a poetic soul. It was our people's word for the dawn."

"I promise I'll do everything I can to find out what you want to know," Bruce said, making a mental note to include this in his journal of stories with which he'd been entrusted.

"And you're right of course," August continued. "That wasn't the

141

only thing I needed to talk to you about."

"The barbeque pit," Bruce said.

"Yes," August replied. "Your enchanted barbeque pit."

"What's so bad about it?"

"Science is a wonderful tool," the old man began, looking away from the waves to the young man next to him. "But be careful of making it into a religion or using it to justify things that are not actually within its ability to analyze. Take this ability we have to move things with our minds, to summon fire, or in your case to move across vast distances in an instant. Do we create levers of force to do the work, or do the things we move do so of their own accord? Do we somehow produce heat from nothing at all? When you study all of the things we can do it all seems to come down to the fact that this world seems to like us enough to do what we want. We pay for that cooperation with the energy we give these efforts, but there isn't any way to understand how that energy translates into action. The only thing that appears to be constant is that when we die and that energy dries up, the things we created with our power end as well."

"There are very few exceptions to this natural law. As we saw but a few weeks ago, Guarded Wood is maintained by the willing sacrifice of one's life. That's a powerful source of energy, and one I hope to never use myself. Another is when something permanent is created by one of the Beloved. And no, before you ask, I have no intention of getting into a discussion about them. Just suffice it to say that if the world likes us enough to bend the rules for the short span of our lives, she loves the ones we call Beloved enough to honor their memory forever."

"And there's one more that applies to me," Bruce said, suddenly afraid of what the hermit had to say.

"Yes," he answered. "And in hindsight your ability to do so much that no one else can do should have told me what you were."

"Besides an amplifier and seer?"

"You are one of the greater smiths," the old man answered. "You have the ability to create artifacts of great power by infusing portions of your soul into their making."

"So the grill?"

"Will likely be around for millions of years after the last human dies. And part of you will be trapped inside of it."

"That's why it drained me so much when I finished," Bruce said, feeling nauseous.

"Yes, and you not only have to refrain from making any more artifacts, but you also have to make sure no one else learns of what you can do. Otherwise, there will always be those who would willingly trade your soul for a chance to gain more power for themselves. And yes, they'll always have some compelling reason why you must make such a sacrifice. But this is your soul we're talking about here. Keep it whole, and let it move on with you to wherever it is we go after leaving this world."

"This has happened before?" Bruce asked.

"Among my people there was a man who created weapons to fight against others who were similar to us. He died in their creation, and they lay forgotten for two millennia before they were dusted off and used in battle."

"Did you see them used?" Bruce asked. This was better than any story he'd ever heard.

"I had already come here when it happened, and I cut myself off from my people when I learned of what they'd tried to do. And the ones most responsible? I am bound to them by marriage. Sometimes I think my wife was the only good that came out of that cursed bloodline. They had a fascination with artifacts from the past and not just the ones created by our own. They had quite a collection of them when I left. Hopefully they haven't added to it since."

"And all of these artifacts hold parts of the souls of the men and women who created them?"

"Yes," August said.

"Has anyone ever tried to get the souls out?" Bruce asked.

"I'm not sure anyone could," the hermit replied. "I mean, a great part of what makes an artifact powerful is that it can outlive its creator. That imbues such objects with a certain permanence."

"I guess so," Bruce said.

"I just thought you should know the real cost before you created anything else," the old man said, rising to his feet. "Have you talked to anyone else about what you found at the hotel?"

"Not yet," Bruce answered. "That's going to stir things up, and right now we all just need to focus on Alan and Kate."

"That's true enough," August agreed. "Just remember your promise until you do."

"Cross my heart," Bruce promised. "No more solo missions, even though I really don't think there's anything dangerous up there. But I'll wait until the newly married Mr. and Mrs. Green are safely on their honeymoon. Then we'll go and see if we can't get some answers. That way we should also have the deed to the property in our hands."

"You convinced Sam to buy it before you even told him what you knew?" August asked.

"I didn't know much then either, but my visions implied that we needed to own the property. And it's the perfect time to buy it. For some reason the Jones estate seems eager to rid itself of any connection to the place."

"Toxic waste spills and associations with domestic terrorism do have a way of bringing down property values. Right now, I'm thinking about taking a page from Azarich's book and starting to take midday naps. Now that the boundary is completely functional, I'm pretty sure that Guarded Wood can survive for an hour or so without me each day."

Chapter XIV: Rockin' Round the Sentinel Tree

Megan waved to Paul where he sat whistling on the lowest step of the treehouse's circular staircase. One of his Dutch ovens sat nearby, giving off sweet smells, maybe of cobbler. It was hard to be sure with the aroma of smoked brisket in the air as well.

Her grandfather happily manned the magical grill, opening the lid to check on the steaks. He was wearing that hideous yellow shirt he reserved for happy days, and he would probably get his hair cut soon since it had recently reached the length where it began to curl. Normally he'd have been whistling himself in such a situation, but he probably didn't want to compete with the youngest Grimble.

"Here you go," she said, putting the last of the meat down on the table that usually sat next to the smoker by the house.

"Thanks, favorite granddaughter of mine," he almost sang.

"I'm your only grandchild," Megan replied, smiling at his good mood.

"And you would have been my favorite even if there had been more," he said with a grin.

"Because I look like Grandma Josie," Megan said knowingly.

"Because I see the best parts of us in you without any of the bad," he answered, drawing her into one of his one-armed hugs. "Where are you off too?"

"I'm going to saddle up and meet Bruce on the trail to August's place," she answered, hugging him back. "Apparently our reclusive friend makes good homemade bread. We're going to help him bring it here."

"That sounds wonderful," Azarich murmured. "I'd better wear my loose trousers for dinner with suspenders. That way I don't have to worry about a belt getting too tight."

"Whatever it takes to make you happy," she answered. "We should be back in a little over half an hour by horseback. Maybe a little more or less."

"I'd say take care, but I think Guarded Wood might be one of the safest places around since you fixed the boundary."

She hugged him again quickly for good measure and headed down to the corral they'd built for the horses. Bothering with a saddle only because she needed the saddlebags to carry bread, she found Bruce waiting for her at the next fork in the trail a few minutes later.

"You did good," he called when he saw her. "Everyone is going to have a great time."

"Does it ever take the fun out of things when you see everything before it happens?"

"Not really," he said. "I mean, this is all still new to me, and I guess I might get tired of it in the future, but for now it's okay. More than okay, really. I hate blank spots and worrying all the time, but it's nice not to have to wonder how it will turn out when I do something. Have you ever had a situation where you wonder what would happen if you did something differently?"

"All the time," she answered.

"When I do that, I can actually see what would have happened," he explained. "If you'd like, I'd be happy to let you know all of the possibilities when something like that comes up."

"Unless doing so messes up something else," she heard herself say and wondered at once why her mental houseguest was taking an interest in this discussion.

"And then I'll tell you I can't answer."

"Unless it messes up something to do that," the voice in her head persisted.

"What are you really asking?"

"Do you ever keep things from me for my own good?" she asked. She looked straight ahead when spoke the words.

"I can feel you trying to sense if I'm lying or not," he said, hurt. "When have I ever shied away from letting you see what was in my mind?" He dropped all of his shields and invited her in.

"That's not what I mean," she said.

"Do you remember when I promised you that I'd never make you feel like a freak for what you could do?" he asked, and now he was the one who wasn't looking at her.

She knew where this was going and didn't want to hear it.

"I guess I should have made you promise the same thing, and not just about my asthma," he said in little more than a whisper. "And no, I'm not going to stay mad at you. I can tell this whole line of questioning came from *her*. You know, the one I'm not supposed to be worried about. Please don't lecture me about not telling you everything. Do I filter out things that will hurt you for no purpose? Absolutely. Do I sometimes choose paths that will save you pain? Of course I do. And before you tell me that you don't do the same thing, I'd like to remind you that you dumped me into your grandmother's grove instead of letting me help you at the Baker. You might have protected my body when you did that, but you took everything that makes me who I am with you when you left.

148

And I'm not talking about my power. For over a week I thought you were dead. And then some guy who can walk the shadows brought you back. But I suppose I'm not supposed to ask about him either."

"I'm so sorry, Bruce," Megan said, reaching out and taking his hand while the horses continued to walk. "I'm just so…"

"Worried about Emelia," he finished. "I know. And you're worried about Azarich… and Sam… and me. But if you ever find yourself not trusting me, just ask. No matter what, I'll still let you into my head any time you want."

"I know," she said. "I really am sorry."

"I know that too, But I want you to think about something in the future."

"What's that?"

"After what happened at the Baker, I get absolutely crazy when I can't see your future. Every single time it happens, I wonder if you might do something like that again, and maybe the next time you won't come back."

She didn't have to answer.

"And if the situation comes up that way again," he said, pulling his hand from hers. "You won't hesitate to do it again. And since I'm still sharing what I'm learning, you should probably know that I can't see it coming when the scary lady in your head interferes."

"Bruce, I don't know what to say," Megan said.

He took a deep breath and reached over to take her hand again.

"You don't have to say anything," he said, forcing a smile that gradually became genuine. "We are going to have a wonderful evening. Paul and Kate are going to play for us and August's bread is positively sinful. You're going to have an interesting conversation with him about getting flour from a medieval miller and his wife who never remember him no matter how many times he's traded with them. Make sure you ask him because you're going to talk with Azarich about it later when you're remembering how much fun the day was. But while you're talking to August about it on the ride back to the tree house, he's going to catch me admiring the color of your hair when the sun comes out for a minute, and he's going to give me a knowing smile that will make me blush even though I know it's coming. And I'm going to completely forget that we had any of that discussion before this because it wasn't you talking. Well, that's not completely right either. I'm going to trust that the voice had a reason for putting me through this, and that she knows what she's doing. After all, if she's been there for your entire life, then she was a part of you when you became my best friend. So I guess I love her too."

Megan started to speak and he cut her off.

"Please don't say anything," he whispered. "I know every variation of what you're about to say. I know about the difference in feelings and the uncertainty and all of the big sordid ugly mess. This is where I'm supposed to be, and I'm perfectly fine with that. Now if we don't get to August soon, the bread is going to cool down too much for the butter to properly melt. And then I will be incredibly angry with you."

He flicked the reins and his horse took off ahead of hers. By the time they reached Azarich's home they were both laughing and life was good again for a while.

Bruce heard Sam's laughter from the tree house before they got there. Even August smiled long enough to stop fussing over the way the bread was packed away in their saddlebags.

"You seem awfully nervous for someone who's just going to dinner," Megan observed, echoing Bruce's thoughts.

"I haven't done anything like this in a very long time," he said.

"I ate with you yesterday," Bruce said.

"And that was the first time I've cooked for anyone since I came to Guarded Wood," August admitted.

"I'm sorry we didn't think to move these get togethers to the treehouse before now," Megan apologized.

"To be honest, I didn't realize I missed this sort of thing until Emelia sent me a doggie bag," the hermit said, enjoying the pun with Fang trotting beside him as they rode.

Ben Grimble had joined Megan's grandfather at the enchanted grill by the time the three of them rode up. Bruce couldn't help but give it a sidelong glance, wondering how the part of his soul that was now trapped inside was doing.

They heard Alan and Kate coming up the path from the McGeehee place before they saw them. She was telling him about the new renovations at the Palace, and he was carrying a crate of what looked like Emelia's famous meade. For once, he didn't look as if he minded letting her do all the talking as his mind was clearly elsewhere.

Mrs. Harris teased Sam as he carried her up the staircase. She'd dressed in her Sunday best, as she always did for these events. Bruce could tell that she'd lost the last of her hair to the treatments. Tom carried her wheelchair and looked winded. In light of everything he was doing for his wife, he'd probably begun to neglect his own health.

After Bruce unloaded the bread, he hurried to catch up to the librarian and help him.

"How is she doing today?" Bruce asked, taking the wheelchair.

"It's a good day," the man answered with an affectionate smile when he found his favorite student at his side. "We've both been looking forward to this."

No matter how many times he climbed the stairs, it still struck Bruce that they'd done an extremely good job on the tree house. As hard as the work had been, he still missed the way the project had drawn everyone together. He missed the camaraderie. He missed stories those three men had told while outworking men and women a fraction of their ages. When he remembered how no one except Sam had been able to keep up with the three old men, he couldn't help but notice how all of them seemed somehow less substantial than they'd been just a few months before. Of course, Azarich and Tom both had good reasons to be sad. And even though Alan seemed to have slowed down a bit, he was happier than Bruce had ever seen him except for the fact that he was currently trying to work up enough courage to propose to Kate.

On more than one occasion Bruce noticed Azarich's friends looking at the hermit with puzzled expressions, as if trying to place a familiar face. But after Sam introduced him as a friend he'd met out of town, they seemed to be satisfied enough to forget his uncanny resemblance to someone they'd met so long ago.

It took a while to bring up the mountains of meat that Azarich and Ben had grilled. Both men praised at length the performance of the grill. Bruce worried that he might throw up if they continued.

When everyone had been seated, Alan cleared his throat and stood up next to Kate. Ironically, Bruce realized that most of the people gathered there already knew exactly what was going to happen. Frankly, he was amazed Jade hadn't slipped up and mentioned it before now.

"Kate," Alan said, then paused and took a deep breath. "We've known each other for a long time."

Everyone sat in quiet expectation as the man turned several shades of red and for the first time that anyone could remember, seemed at a loss for words.

"I'm not going to say yes until you ask properly," Kate said, prompting laughter from around the table.

Alan made a great show of getting down on one knee and pulling out a small box.

"Will you marry me?" he asked, presenting her with a ring.

"Of course I will, you great hulk of a man," she said, smiling broadly. "It sure took you long enough! I would have said yes on our first date!"

The rest of what she said was drowned out by the cheers of everyone present. He stood up and gathered her into his arms, lifting her from her feet and almost making her drop the ring which needed to be resized. But as wonderful as the moment was, no one seemed to be able to concentrate on the couple with so much good food on the table before them.

It had been too long since they'd done this, and it was readily apparent that everyone had missed it. From his vantage point at the end of the table, Bruce watched everyone, and even though he'd seen almost every variation of its outcomes, it still held him riveted.

Megan worked hard to keep her grandfather too busy to remember the absence of his daughter, although at times even Bruce could tell that his mind was elsewhere. Sam and the hermit seemed to have become close friends since that day when he'd introduced them. The old man's bread proved to be a favorite with everyone present. Bruce's parents looked happy and relaxed now that the power of the Jones family had been broken. Alan and Kate seemed decades younger, and Bruce could see what Azarich had meant about them being oblivious to the presence of anyone else.

Then his eyes fell on the librarian and his frail wife. Like Alan, Tom Harris narrowed his world to the woman at his side to the exclusion of all else. But Esther's eager eyes took in everything, the sights, the sounds and the energy that could almost be tasted in the air.

When her eyes met his, Bruce didn't need foresight to know that this would be the last time she'd attend one of these dinners. And in a communication not so different from the way he and Megan spoke mind to mind, the woman with the powerful laugh told him that she knew it as well. With the tilt of her head she asked him to watch over the man she loved when she was gone. With a nod that only she witnessed, he accepted.

He wondered to how many of the others she had given such duties. Looking around at these people whose love and friendship had spanned nearly a century, Bruce wished he could have seen what they were like when they were younger. But then again, he thought, looking at his friend and his siblings, maybe he already knew.

Paul and Kate took up their violins. Their duet was beautiful, but the real show started when Paul played his solo. Judging from Kate's reaction, she'd had no idea that he'd composed his own piece. It was fast and furious, then it was soft and heartfelt. He never gave them more than a second's respite before he was onto something else, playing their emotions even more skillfully than he did his second-hand violin.

Paul had always been a person of strong passions, and when he found something that interested him, he poured everything into it whether it was scouting, paleontology or now, music. But this new hobby felt different, almost as if the youngest Grimble had spent his life up to this point trying to find that one thing that would define him. Bruce suspected he finally had.

Chapter XV: Esther's Secret

Megan didn't understand why Paul was smiling at her until she realized she was humming his song while they cleared the table. They'd already packed away enough leftovers to keep several families and a grown wolf busy for a week. But the task of getting all of the serving dishes going in the correct directions was proving a bit of a job since all of the adults were currently making wedding plans at one of the picnic tables that dotted the treehouse deck.

Now that Alan had finally popped the question, the adult portion of the treehouse crew eagerly took up a whole new project. Megan wasn't sure how much work they were getting done, but there was certainly an infectious enthusiasm coming from their direction. The only thing that could have made it better would be to find her mother hovering at the edges of her senses, ready to come back into their lives. Glancing over at the table again, she knew there were at least two of them who were thinking the same thing.

August had left soon after the meal ended, not feeling as if he belonged in their plans. Well, he also wasn't sure that he could keep Fang from climbing the steps to join them much longer. He probably didn't know about the steak that Bruce had sent to his furry friend early on in the meal, but Megan did and wholeheartedly approved.

Esther had settled into the bunkhouse for a nap, but judging from the number of times Megan found Tom looking toward the tree house door, the librarian was worried that his wife might need something. As soon as she finished cleaning up, Megan walked up to listen for a moment.

"Want me to peek in on her and make sure she doesn't need anything?" she whispered in his ear while the others talked about the logistics of having the wedding at the Palace.

"If it's not too much trouble," he answered, relieved. "I'm sure she's probably asleep, but I'd like to know for sure."

"Neither of you are ever any trouble," Megan assured him. "And as I recall, I still owe you a favor or two for keeping me out of trouble when I wanted to make Allison eat a dead cell phone last year."

She found Esther sitting up with her back resting against a pillow, looking out over Guarded Wood through one of the windows.

"He sent you to check on me, didn't he?" the frail woman asked.

"I volunteered," Megan replied, walking over to sit on the edge of the bunk with her. "I could tell he was torn between being with you and helping his friends, so I offered my services."

"What a thoughtful young woman you are," Esther said, reaching over and patting Megan on the hand. Although Megan had spent a lot of time with old men over the past year, Esther was the only elderly woman. Kate was at least a decade younger and thus held onto more of her youthful vitality. Megan wasn't sure if it was the cancer or just the difference between the way age treated men and women that made her skin feel so different. It had grown paper thin and barely seemed to hide the ligaments and tendons that struggled to move fingers and joints. Bruises marked much of the skin not covered by her long-sleeved blouse, some of which appeared to be the sort that might not heal. Yet in spite of the deterioration of her body, Esther's vibrant spirit warmed Megan's extra senses like sunshine.

"Everything bruises or chafes me now," Esther explained when she caught Megan looking. "And that poor man feels guilty for each one as if he made them himself. You get that from Josie, by the way."

"Get what?"

"Being so thoughtful," Esther answered. "She was two years younger than me, but even before I started going with Tom, she became my best friend. Josie could talk to anyone, and if someone needed a friendly ear or just a bit of encouragement, they'd likely look up and find your grandmother."

"I didn't know that," Megan said, eager to hear more. Her grandfather and his friends told many stories, but they were usually centered around the mischief that they got into with their fourth friend who hadn't returned from the war. And even though Azarich never hesitated to answer any question Megan might have about the most important person in his life, he never volunteered Josie's stories like he did the others. It was almost as if he feared that speaking them out loud might somehow diminish his memory of her, and he was loath to let any escape from him. This was a rare opportunity to find out more about the woman Megan so closely resembled.

"I understand you found her special place," Esther said. "Where she painted."

"I did," Megan agreed, "And something about the way you say that makes me think you already knew about it."

"We talked about everything," the woman said meaningfully.

"And did she show you how to get to her hidden studio?" Megan asked.

"I'm the one that suggested using the boat to hide the entrance."

"I'll bet that was hard for the two of you to move," Megan said, trying to draw Esther out.

"No," the old woman said with a knowing grin. "She just moved it with her mind, as I suspect you and Emelia can."

"Does Mr. Harris know?" Megan asked.

"No," she snorted as if the idea were preposterous. "The boys had their own secrets. Well, it might be better to say they thought they had secrets. We had our own. Dear lord child, you are the spitting image of Josie at the age when I first met her. That's probably why I don't feel so bad about telling you her secret."

"Did she ever say why she didn't tell Grandpa?"

"The dance that the two of them shared circled around Josie's magic. She didn't mention it, and he pretended not to notice. You have to realize that she and I lived in another time. It might as well have been another world when you put it next to this one," Esther explained. "It might have been the golden age after the War to End All Wars, but here in Nickelville, Texas, ideas about what to do with witches weren't as far lost in the past as they should have been. I mean they even tried to tie the Goatman stories to witches if my memory serves."

"They still do," Megan replied eagerly, hoping for more.

"Since we're being honest, and I'm sure you've seen her painting by now," the frail woman whispered as if this next thing was something even more surprising than what she'd already said. "She saw a whole bunch of them dancing around that spring that popped up on the back of the property one night. Imagine that! I guess they must live out there in the woods."

"You have no idea how much I wish we'd had this conversation a few months ago," Megan said. "And since you're sharing with me, I'll share some with you. August created my grandmother's grove."

"What do you mean, he created it?" Esther said, frowning.

"He has abilities like the women in my family, and he's been living out in Guarded Wood for a really long time."

"But the only person who ever lived out there was," Esther brought her hand to her mouth in a way that wouldn't have looked out of place in one of the black and white movies Emelia loved. "You don't mean to say that he's Old Man Biggerstaff?"

"The one and only, although he doesn't really like that name. As far as we can tell he's been here since before the Mayflower landed."

"Well isn't that something!" Esther laughed. "I guess I wasn't the oldest bat at the party after all! I'm so glad you came in to check on me. It's almost like getting to spend one last afternoon with Josie before I go."

Megan went quiet, not knowing how to respond to the sweet woman's acknowledgement of how little time she had left.

"Don't feel bad for me," Esther said. "I have lived such a wonderful life in this strange little paradise. I've seen wonders that stretch the limits of imagination and belief. I've had the unfailing love of the most amazing man to hold this cold world at bay. And even if the two of us were sometimes sad because that one little room in our house never held a crib, we've had the chance to watch you and your friends grow. Tom has always said that he wished he'd had a son like Bruce. Now that I've seen you and your friends together, I realize that even though you are the only one of them that's related to our little circle of friends by blood, you are all our children in the exploration of this wonderful town. I can almost taste the wild energy that flavored every second of our youth when I look at you. And that makes me remember something Josie told me once that had come from one of her ancestors. She said everything in this world is just a series of echoes like the ripples on a pond moving out over and over into eternity. It doesn't matter that we lose the names and the faces in the passage of time, because each and every one of them will

160

be reborn. And in the years since her death, I don't think she was talking about reincarnation. She meant that it's like some of us are cast in the same molds as the people who came before us, and that some of our stories are destined to be told over and over for as long as there are people to play the parts. I don't know if she was just really wise, or if she had that as part of the lore that her family had passed down since the time of Crina."

"It's so strange to hear you speak of things that I've only just learned about myself. Do you know much about the daughters of Crina?"

"Not really," Esther said. "I was fascinated by all of it, but even though I was her best friend, I was still an outsider in those matters. She only shared the smallest part with me. And as much as it hurts my pride to admit it, I've likely forgotten a great deal of what I once knew."

"I seriously doubt that," Megan said. "You, Mr. Harris and Grandpa are probably the smartest people I've ever known."

"But not Alan?" Esther teased.

"Oh," Megan said, guiltily, "I mean…"

"It's okay. The only reason he passed his schoolwork was because all of us helped him study," Esther confided. "But he has more love and loyalty in his heart than the rest of us put together. I'm glad he finally stopped finding excuses to go to the movies each week and actually started to court her properly."

"You've known all this time?" Megan asked, starting to wonder if there was anything this quiet old woman didn't know.

"Tom and Azarich might have suspected, but it was Josie and I who knew. If your grandmother had lived a bit longer I have no doubt she would have found a way to make this happen sooner. I should have continued after she was gone, but that wasn't my role."

"Your role?"

"It was like your grandfather was the courage of our group, and he drove us forward in the things we did. My husband was the brain who knew or could find out anything we needed to know. Alan was the loyal glue that held us all together. I was the one who told everyone that things were going to be okay."

"And my grandmother?" Megan asked.

"She was our heart. The first time any of us started to feel old was when we gathered around that grave and watched them lower her into the ground. Up until that time, it was like we were immortal, and nothing, not even the passage of time, could hold us back. But when Josie died, the warmth left our town. Maybe it was just because she was my best friend, but it seemed like everyone felt it."

"What about the one who was lost in the war?"

"Carl?" she asked and then fell silent for a moment. "I'm not sure that there are words to describe what role he played. I don't think any of us could have defined what quality it was that he brought to us. But it was special, and we were all diminished when we realized he wasn't coming home."

Then she fell silent and Megan could tell that her strength was starting to fade.

"Would you like me to let you rest now?" Megan asked.

"Not really," Esther replied. "What I'd really like is to see what the view is like from up there." She pointed toward the ladder leading up to the tower. "Any chance you can get me up there the way Josie would have?"

"I've got something even better," Megan said, helping the frail woman up from the bunk. I have a few abilities from my father as well."

Sam, can you make sure that no one comes in here for a little while? I'm going to take Esther up to the tower, and I don't want to

162

explain to the ones who still don't know how I did it.

Of course. I take it she's been initiated into our unofficial order?

Apparently, she's been one longer than anyone except August.

Your grandmother told her? I'll let you know if Tom gets worried or *says they need to leave.*

Thanks.

"Okay, Esther, this is going to feel a little bit like taking the plunge on a big roller coaster. Do you think you can handle that?"

"Oh, I love roller coasters," the old woman giggled.

"Why does that not surprise me?" Megan asked and took the librarian's wife through the shadows.

Her eyes were wide, but her gasp was one of excitement. She looked out over the treetops for several minutes, taking it all in.

"Thank you, Megan. Josie would have been so proud of you."

"No, it's me who should be thanking you. Because of you, I know her much better than I did this morning."

"Oh, the adventures we had!" Ester whispered happily. "My only regret is that we had no way of knowing when it was our last. Josie passed so quickly. It felt like she was there one minute and then gone the next. Even now, after all this time, I don't feel like she's really gone. I do so wish we could have had one more adventure together though. I would have liked that. But I'm glad that you and the Grimbles are carrying on the tradition. I want you to do something for me, Megan."

"Anything," Megan promised.

"I want you to make sure that you live while you're alive," the old woman said, holding tight onto her hand. "No matter how bad things get, a time will come when you'll wish you could return to even the bad times. Almost no one is wise enough to realize when they are living their best days. That always comes when it's over, and the only thing left are the memories."

Sam warned them that Mr. Harris was coming in to see what had taken Megan so long. They whisked back to the bunkroom and Esther's laughter could be heard all the way back to the ground where the Grimble children sat around the fire pit, considering the possibility of spending another night there.

Chapter XVI: The Tuatha dé

After the Harrises left, Megan returned to the house to find Mr. Bob sitting on the kitchen table, staring at her with his green eyes. Given how intelligent she knew him to be, she strongly suspected that he'd chosen the spot because he knew how the yellow Formica contrasted with his sleek black fur.

Well hello there Mr. Cat Sidhe.

He purred.

You know, you look quite dashing for someone who's been around since at least the Bronze Age, she told him.

His purr rumbled deep in his chest.

"I don't think Grandpa would like it if he saw you on the table though," she said, and he gave her a look that clearly said, *I sit where I like, mortal girl.* "You've got another runestone for me, don't you?"

He turned his head to look at the table next to him and the next stone faded into existence.

"This one doesn't end as badly as the last, does it?"

He stretched out his considerable length, put his paws on her shoulders and nuzzled the spot where her neck met her jaw. Unable to help herself, she wrapped her arms around him and squeezed.

Then he was gone.

She stared at the runestone, feeling curiosity rise within her. But unlike the times before, it was tempered by the realization that some knowledge came with an emotional price and left her far less eager than she'd been with the previous stones. At last she picked it up and went up to her room where the mirror awaited.

Emelia tried to call Sam repeatedly and wrote him a letter every day, only to have them return unopened. She'd hurt him deeply, and even though she'd done so unintentionally, she also understood that the blame still rested fully on her. No matter how it had played out, she'd known that either Sam or Daragh would be hurt. Maybe it was better this way. After all, now she didn't have to choose between them.

Her Tuatha dé suitor now appeared often and took her to places both well-known and hidden across the world. He took her to an impossibly green valley dotted with standing stones and circular earthworks, surrounded by scrub clad hills. As they walked hand in hand, he told her of a great battle fought there long ago.

"Did the Tuatha dé build this?" she asked.

"We raised the stones in honor of our dead," he said, pointing as he spoke. "But the great circular ditches cut into the ground were made by the humans who lived alongside us. They treated our Beloved Dagda like a god, although he never asked them to do so."

"What is it called?" she asked.

"Mag Tuired."

Then he took her to the place where two massive slabs of moss-covered stone rested against one another, forming a simple arch. Emelia could feel power in their placement, as if this Dagda had left a portion of himself there in its making.

"Do you feel it?" he asked.

"I think so, but I can't tell what it does," she replied.

"I brought you here at this time of the day for a reason," he

166

explained. "First I want you to stand on the flat stone and face the arch."

When she did so, she noticed that the cleft between two of the distant hills stood directly below the peak of the stone arch, making an opening like a diamond. She also noticed that the sun had begun to set just a short distance away from the window created by arch and hill.

"The power you feel is a very powerful magic that waxes and wanes across the span of each year," he explained. "On the night shortly after the sun sets between those two hills, a doorway between the mortal world and Tyr Sgodl opens for just a few hours."

"But you don't need such a passage," Emelia observed. "You can walk the shadows there any time you like."

"That's true," he said, smiling at her. "But it is a part of who we are. It was through this place that the Tuatha dé first entered our realm. And it was through our connection to this place that the Beloved Dagda gave us the gift of walking through the shadows."

He took her to dinners in fine restaurants across Europe and Asia. For some Cara appeared with fine dresses for her to wear, and the waiters seemed to know that they served royalty. For others he simply whisked her away as she was and they ate in little out of the way places with only a handful of tables crammed within their walls. She even cooked for him once. To his credit, he kept a straight face while he ate, and she fell in love with him when he lied so beautifully to tell her how good it was.

He took her to a lagoon fed by waterfalls hidden deep within the jungle. The roar of the main torrent filled her ears. An earthy scent of moist decay surrounded her, surprisingly similar to the woods near her childhood school. It was a place of vibrant growth, of life layered on top of layer in a cycle of death and rebirth.

Water fell from the cliffs overhead, dancing through the channels it had worn though the rock. *The largest of the streams had washed away any vegetation that might have hidden it, making it stand out among the smaller ones that burst into the open only to pass through crevices over which lush vines and small trees grew, heard but not seen until at last they splashed into the blue-green waters below.*

"It's beautiful," she said, leaning back against him as he held her at the peak of a rocky prominence that looked down over the water below. Reaching out with her senses, she probed the water's depths.

"It is," he agreed.

They stood there for a moment, enjoying the sights and sounds of this hidden, magical place. Still dressed in the finery of the opera they'd just attended, he didn't question her when she bent down to remove her shoes.

"I'm really sorry," she whispered, turning to take both of his hands in hers.

"You've done nothing wrong," he said, looking into her eyes but not knowing her well enough to read the signs there.

Without warning she threw her weight backward, taking them both over into the water below.

When she asked him about who the Tuatha dé were and where they'd come from, Daragh took her back to the castle where there were rooms upon rooms of books and paintings. But before he did so, he summoned her a heavy coat and gloves. And instead of taking her directly into the castle as Cara had done, he brought them to view it from just within the gate that led from Mag Tuired.

She'd never seen the barren landscape of Tyr Sgodl before, and the sheer expanse of its lifeless beauty surprised her. She'd known it was cold from her brief trip down one of the open castle corridors. And she'd known from Daragh's descriptions that the land there was barren and devoid of any life but what the Tuatha dé had brought with them.

When open, the gate would pass from the green fields of Mag Tuired into a valley of similar size in Tyr Sgodl. But any similarities ended there. In spite of her high grades in writing classes, Emelia could find no words to describe such an inhospitable place. Even with the warm clothing she wore, she doubted she could survive there for more than a few hours.

At the foot of the nearest mountain, she saw an opening, too perfect in its symmetry to be a cave. It didn't look terribly large, but distances were hard to judge due to the magnifying nature of the frigid air.

"The only way into our lands lies through that tunnel," Daragh yelled above the wind that blew across the open space, cutting through her winter clothing as if it were nothing. "I'm going to take you to the other side so you can see the castle."

Then, still holding her hand tightly, Daragh walked her through the shadows. A wall of ice some six stories tall rose before them, broken only by a seam that ran up its center. There a stairway rose, cut directly into the perfectly transparent walls on either side. Tall stone columns stood along the wall's perimeter, topped with an eternal violet flame the color of the Tuatha dé eyes.

"What is this?" Emelia asked, huddled close to him against the cold he barely noticed.

"This is a frozen lake," he told her. "When the Dagda brought us here, he carved the ice out of this portion of the valley and then created the tunnel to the other side of the mountains. The columns are one of his artifacts. Should the reigning King or Queen wish it, the columns will melt the lake instantly, sweeping through the tunnel and returning to ice afterward, sealing off Tyr Sgodl from the Mag Tuired gate."

"In case of an invasion?" she asked. He nodded in reply. "Why did he create the gate if he was so worried about it?"

"He didn't create it," Daragh answered. "This place was already here when we came to Earth. He merely made use of it. And keep in mind that he did all of this with a mortal wound."

She tried to respond, but the tremors along her jaw rendered the sounds she made incomprehensible.

He placed his hands on her coat for a moment and it filled with warmth.

"Oh that feels good," she murmured in pleasure.

"I'm sorry I didn't think of it sooner," he apologized. "I knew it was cold…"

"But not how little I'd be able to handle it," she answered for him. "It's okay, I'm fine now."

"That was part of what he did for us when he made us what we are," Daragh continued. "Before he reshaped us, we had similar tolerances to heat and cold as humans, and I believe our eyes were green. But we'll go indoors before I explain that part. First, let's go to the top of the staircase."

A moment later they stood at the base of a long stone ramp perhaps ten feet wide that rose into the distance until it met with an island rising up from the ice below. But that wasn't right, she realized. What was an island but the top of a mountain rising up from the ocean floor? Other peaks rose in the distance, though not as tall as the peaks that hemmed in the place the Tuatha dé called home.

On its peak stood a castle of such vast dimensions that the word hardly seemed sufficient to fully name it. Impossibly delicate spires rose majestically into the air like inverted icicles, supported by buttresses that angled off from them like the folded wings of dragons.

170

For just an instant there was something about its construction that reminded her of the Baker Hotel. She swept it away in irritation before it could summon the memory of swimming there with a big awkward boy who liked to talk to trees...

Although Daragh didn't need to do so, he brought her directly to the place where the ramp met the landing. An armored figure stood in the center of the walkway, blocking their path with a wicked-looking spear gripped in her left hand.

"Who seeks entrance to our fair castle?" a pleasantly sonorous woman's voice demanded.

"Adair," Daragh said irritably. "You know full well who I am."

"You bear a striking resemblance to the Heir," she replied, somehow sounding serious and playful at the same time. "But the Heir is required to keep his faithful Scathlahm in attendance, and you travel in the company of this beautiful girl with obvious poor taste in men. So how can you be him?"

Emelia took in this familiar banter with great enjoyment. Up until this point, the only person she'd seen who felt comfortable around Daragh was Cara. Something about the way this woman teased him made her suspect who she might be.

"You're Cara's wife, aren't you?"

"Yes, and you must be Emelia McGeehee," the woman said, removing her helm and handing it to the Heir as if he were her squire. Then she reached out and clasped Emelia's arm in the same semblance of a handshake that her wife had used the first time they met.

Now that she had a better sense of what was armor and what was woman, Emelia was surprised to find that Adair wasn't as large as she'd appeared at first glance. If the armor was as form fitting as it appeared, she was muscular without being dense the way some female bodybuilders

171

became. And although she was taller than Emelia, which really wasn't saying much, she was slightly shorter than Daragh.

"I guess I'll let you in since Cara has already vouched for you," Adair said, making Daragh sigh in resignation. "But seriously, you could do better."

"It was nice meeting you," Emelia said warmly.

"Oh no," the warrior said with a smile and something akin to a bow, "It was definitely my pleasure to meet you. And Daragh, even with the warming enchantment you put on her coat, you need to get her inside. Their lungs can't handle how dry our air is for very long."

"I will," he said, looking at Emelia with concern as if her life had suddenly come into peril in the past few seconds. "Thanks for telling me."

"Any time..." she said with a smirk. "Your Highness."

In an instant Emelia found herself in what was clearly a library.

"Cara told me that you were afraid of her wife," Emelia confided, indeed breathing easier now that they'd left the cold wind behind.

"Anyone with sense is afraid of her," Daragh admitted.

"Why?" Emelia asked, thinking that she should take off her coat but realizing it was still too cold, even indoors. "She doesn't look that scary."

"She beat the previous Captain of the Guard with nothing more than her side knife at the age of thirteen," he said. "The only time I've ever seen her lose a fight was eight on one and five of them couldn't walk unaided for days afterward. Another didn't wake up for nearly a week. So yes, it might be better to say that I respect her instead of that I'm afraid of her. Not because I want to impress you with any false sense of bravado, but because I wouldn't hesitate to trust her with my life."

"Good answer," Emelia replied, far more relaxed than she'd been before meeting Adair.

Together they walked down a vast corridor lined with long tables and comfortable chairs. Pendant lights hung from the archways that supported the stone roof in patterns almost as intricate as the ones she'd seen in the throne room. The light they gave off threw the library into noon radiance, contrasting sharply with what she'd seen outside.

"We grew accustomed to the light of your world, which was so much brighter than the one from which we came," he explained when he noticed her squinting up at the ceiling. "And even though the Beloved Dagda made us well suited to this dark place, we never wanted it. So we live in sunlight when we can. And over the centuries we've become so good at replicating it that the plants we brought from your world flourish in its glow."

"But isn't it too cold to grow crops here?" Emelia asked, having already wondered how they grew food."

"There are vast caverns deep below where our farmers grow crops year-round," he answered proudly. "We've become quite good at it, although we've never had much luck with livestock. We maintain enclaves in different parts of your world where we either raise our own meat or buy it. Either way, we have everything we could possibly need."

"So why did you bring me to the library?" she asked.

"You wanted to know who we are and where we came from," he answered with a shrug. "Everything you could ever want to know is here. Everything we've learned in our time here."

"So this is a study date?" she teased.

"Just try to keep up," he answered, leading her deeper into the catacombs of knowledge.

As they walked, they occasionally came upon men and women seemingly of all ages and positions. Some dressed in the rich clothing of the High Court. Others wore the rough-spun robes of the servants. But no matter who they were, all dropped to one knee in respect to the Heir, making Emelia realize just how brazen the Scathlahm's wife to be.

He showed her paintings and tapestries of their history as he spoke, relating that the Dagda brought his people with him to this land when the world they'd come from could no longer support them. And even though the primitive people of this world looked much like the Tuatha dé, they were not similar enough to intermarry and produce offspring without a significant expenditure of power.

The first of this land's inhabitants to encounter the Tuatha dé thought them to be gods, and nothing that these immigrants from another world did could convince them otherwise. At best the humans gave them their name, which translates as children of the gods. Over time, the Tuatha dé allowed their language to merge with the Gaelic of this new land as their old largely described things no longer relevant in this new world.

This world was a paradise compared to the dark realm from which they'd come, a world corrupted by the improper use of magic and populated with nightmares crafted by those whose abilities surpassed their good sense. Earth was an Eden for the Tuatha dé, perfect in every way. Well, it was perfect in every way except one. Soon after they arrived and began to fashion tools and weapons of bronze, they encountered a strange substance that disrupted their magics. But that one ill omen was of little importance laid next to the raw, untarnished potential of their new home.

Like all of the Beloved, the Dagda created artifacts, objects of such power that their use could survive the death of their creator. Prior to bringing the Tuatha dé to this world, the Dagda had crafted four such artifacts. The first was his Harp, for although he loved music and excelled in most anything he desired to accomplish, he lacked the gift of music. Many suspect that the harp might have first been constructed as the actual instrument for which it bears the name, but whatever its original appearance, it became a twenty-sided near spherical object of gold that could reproduce any sound that its user could imagine. But the

Harp was lost in Dagda's battle with another of the Beloved, the self-proclaimed goddess, Nyx.

The next of the Dagda's treasured artifacts was his cauldron, which could create food from the air itself and feed multitudes in times of famine or drought. In the last days before they fled from their dying world, the Cauldron had been their only source of sustenance. This artifact was also lost in the battle, for the fighting took place on an island far to the west where the Tuatha dé had planned to flee ahead of the human discovery of iron which so disrupted their magic.

The third artifact was the Dagda's staff, which, like his harp, could assume the properties of any weapon he could imagine. It was immune to the influence of magic and invisible to all but the physical senses. This was the only one of the Dagda's original artifacts to survive to the present and has been passed down from Scathlahm to Scathlahm in the service of protecting the Heir to the throne.

The Dagda created the fourth artifact, the Ark, for a single purpose. Should this new world prove unsuitable for the Tuatha dé, it would return them to the spoiled lands of their birth. And though it was not used as it was intended, the Ark proved instrumental in both the Dagda's victory over Nyx and in his own death as well.

But the Dagda's artifacts were not the only ones that the Tuatha dé possessed. The Morrigan herself was not only a seer of great battles and their outcomes, but also one of the greater smiths. Knowing that Nyx could not rest while the Dagda lived, the Morrigan forged for herself a suit of armor impervious to the cold bite of iron. It also gave her the speed and cunning of the goddess she was later worshiped to be. But like many well intended plans, the armor was not to be used against Nyx.

In a surprise attack, Nyx mortally wounded the Dagda with a javelin of iron hurtled from such a great distance that he was wounded

176

before he knew she'd come for him. As soon as the first drop of his blood touched the ground, the Morrigan saw that he was doomed. For though he was Beloved, this was not the land of his birth, and this world loved her own daughter far more than her adopted son. He would not be allowed to prevail against Nyx.

So the Dagda fled with his followers into the shadows and found a place between day and night where he breathed a new life into the loved ones he'd brought with him through the vast emptiness. To the Morrigan, he gave dominion over the others and decreed that her line would forever rule them so that they could never take up arms against their own. To them all he gave the power to walk between the shadows, the power to turn evil in judgment on those who deserved it, and lastly, he gave the Tuatha dé control over the elements so that they might protect themselves after he was gone. As the last of his gifts were bestowed, they opened their violet eyes and bid him farewell.

Guided by the cunning words of the Morrigan, The Dagda left in her hands his beloved staff and returned to the world of mortal men. There he traveled to an island far to the west, covered in the ruins of a mighty civilization. He used his harp to call forth a mighty fog and to sound a call to war which he knew Nyx could not ignore. Then he made a throne of stone from the rubble around him and there he rested, losing his life's blood from the wound in his side. With the Ark in his lap, he understood at last why his wife had insisted it be made in the semblance of a small boat.

Knowing that the death of her enemy was near, Nyx rushed to his side, abandoning her plans for battle in her desire to bear witness to his last moments.

"Get down from your beggar's throne and kneel before me as you die. Then I shall spare your children the death they deserve," she

177

commanded, but he knew that her words were false and her honor hollow.

"I am weak from the wound you have dealt me," he said. "You must help me to kneel if you wish it to be so. Otherwise I shall occupy my last moments as I see fit." Then he held the Ark up before his eyes as if studying its craftsmanship was far more interesting than the professed goddess before him.

"Your pain has robbed you of your senses," Nyx snarled. "And I will tell your children that their father chose to play with toys rather than save them. I swear to you by the gods that birthed me that those who loved you will curse your memory before I allow them to die."

With this she strode forward and grasped the Ark, meaning to crush its seemingly fragile form before his eyes as he died. But the trap was sprung, and the artifact fulfilled its purpose, if not in the way its creator had intended. Designed to transport the entire nation of the Tuatha dé, it took not only the two warring Beloved back to the world of the Dagda's birth, but also the island of the lost civilization, leaving only legends to hint that it had ever existed at all.

Before Nyx realized that she'd been taken from the world where she could not be defeated, the Dagda took his revenge with such malice that he broke the world of his birth and left it forever malignant.

Knowledge of these deeds passed on to the Tuatha dé even though the Dagda himself had decreed that no man or woman born among the Children of the Gods would bear witness to his final hours. For there was one among them, a trickster by nature, who escaped the binding words of the Beloved by means of being neither man nor woman. The Cat Sidhe, himself a groom's gift from the Dagda to his wife on the day of their handfasting, wielded all the power of the Tuatha dé but answered only to his mistress, the Morrigan. And if truth be told, he only did that

*when it suited him. But he was there on the fabled island in the last
moment before it was ripped from existence and as he was wont to do
sometimes, he allowed the Morrigan to see through his green eyes.*

*When the Morrigan felt her beloved husband pass from this world,
she swore an oath so strong that it bound all of her descendants, though
it was not her intention at the time. When she swore that she would never
love another again, something changed within the aspect of who she was
and who her descendants would become, and from that day forward, the
royal line mated for life.*

*This would, of course, prove problematic with succession. Unable
to conceive a child with one of the Beloved while the Dagda had lived,
yet needing to produce her own heir lest the Tuatha dé die when her days
came to an end, she took one man from her clan into her bed and
conceived the first king, Lugh, on the first night. And because she was
mindful of the power her sacred promises had on her people, she made it
known that she would remain chaste for the remainder of her days
without actually promising.*

*"Now you know the full extent of what this means," Daragh said,
getting down on one knee to respect the ways of Emelia's people. Then
he gave her a necklace and a promise that would bind their descendants
forever.*

Chapter XVII: Keeping Promises

The waning moon cast sparse light on the beach where Megan watched while Bruce set up the camera equipment. Luckily the moon had neared the horizon where its light wouldn't interfere with the exposure as he photographed the night sky. It did, however, provide just enough light to highlight the incoming waves. The air was cool but humid and filled with the salty tang he associated with the ocean.

"You greedy boy," Megan murmured. "Keeping something like this to yourself."

"Hey, I told you about it didn't I?"

"Eventually," she teased. "Did you know that I've never been to the beach before?"

Bruce stopped setting up the tripod on which they planned to mount Emelia's camera and turned to face her. Her pale skin glowed in the faint moonlight as she looked up at a sky so filled with stars that they reflected in her eyes.

"I thought you'd lived just about everywhere," he said, "You mean you lived in California and Florida, but never went to the beach?"

"It wasn't for lack of asking," she answered, sitting up and looking out over the restless undulations of the water. "Mom didn't like the idea of having our backs to the water where it would limit our choices for where to run."

"Maybe she just doesn't like the water," he suggested, returning to the setup of the camera and then checking its orientation against the compass he'd borrowed from Paul. But of course, it didn't work very well in Guarded Wood, so he used the general direction of the setting sun to determine the direction of the west.

"Not everyone is scared of the water," she teased, "I wonder if it would be okay to go swimming."

"Places like this are exactly the reason I'm scared of the water. As far as I know there could be prehistoric monsters out there."

"I'm surprised Paul didn't come with us," she said. "Or Fang for that matter."

"I offered, but he said he'd rather come out when he could see better," Bruce replied, changing the camera to a different alignment. "And I guess August has started sleeping more soundly since the boundaries are up and running again. I've been in several times now without him seeming to notice me."

"He's certainly earned the right to get a good night's sleep. So why did you need my alarm clock?" she asked.

"My phone isn't reliable out here. For whatever reason, this spot seems to have high levels of magnetism that interfere with the charge. I've been coming out off and on all day to nail down exactly when the sun came up and set. Then I needed to know what time we were taking these pictures. That apparently makes a difference on what stars should be in the sky at any given time. Paul made it pretty clear that we needed as much information as possible if we were going to have any chance of figuring this out."

"The shows on tv made it look pretty easy," she said.

"That's because they can automatically know where they are just by pulling out a phone and checking their location. There's nothing that will give us that information without some sort of star chart." He paused for a

181

moment, deep in thought.

"What is it?"

"If I did a time lapse it would tell me which one is the North Star, but that would only work in the northern hemisphere. And the only star that would work like it in the southern hemisphere is Polaris Australis, which isn't bright enough to see in modern times with all of the light pollution. But it might work for prehistoric times, depending on the earth's wobble."

"I'll take your word on that," Megan said, looking back out over the waves. "And I get that once we know where and when this is, we could leave something to tell us if we're really in the past or if this is a copy of the real world that's stuck in the limbo of Guarded Wood."

"Have I ever mentioned how attractive I find it when you tap into your nerdy side?" he asked.

She glared over her shoulder at him long enough to make it clear she didn't find it funny, but still didn't say anything because she was trying not to lash out at him like she'd done when the voice in her head had taken the wheel.

"So finish catching me up on the latest installment of your mom's memories," he prompted, collapsing the tripod and placing it in the backpack he'd borrowed from Paul.

"That was pretty much all of it," she said, getting up and dusting herself off before falling into step as they walked. "I know who my father's people are now, but I still have no idea why we're hiding from them. He seems like a really nice person. Likable even."

"And we have confirmation that Mr. Bob is possibly the oldest living creature in the world," Bruce said, still not sure how he felt about that. "And if he has all of the abilities of the Tuatha dé, it might also explain why the legends say the cat sidhe could steal the souls of the dead. If a person didn't know about judgement, that's a pretty close explanation."

She stiffened next to him.

"Sorry," he murmured. "I know you don't like to think about that."

"The sad thing is that it's not the fact that I've done it that bothers me," she said. "I don't like you thinking about me that way."

"You're not a monster," he said, clearly seeing the pity spiral she was about to slide down and wanting to head it off. "Would you like to come with me the next time I go to explore the Baker?"

"Is that where you've been going?" she asked. "Why would you want to go there?"

"I haven't been sleeping well lately," he answered.

"August told me about your nightmares and why you shielded yourself when you slept."

"I know he meant well," Bruce replied irritably. "But he had no right telling you about that."

"Why?" she asked.

"Because I don't want you to see me that way."

"See you how?" she pressed.

"As weak."

"Bruce, I've fought off ghosts with you at my side. You've gone against your peaceful nature to learn how to fight all because you worry that I might someday be in danger. What you risked to save me from the roc," she whispered, shaking her head in dismay. "August said that your first nightmare was so bad that he and Fang hid in the corner of their cottage until my mother shielded you."

"I never got a chance to thank her for that," he whispered.

"Those dreams would frighten anyone," she said, making sure that he looked her in the eye. "You are the bravest person I've ever met."

"Except for your mother," he said, hoping she couldn't tell he was blushing.

"That's not bravery," Megan said. "I love her and owe her everything, but that woman is probably more than half insane."

"August said something about him being proud to be compared to her," Bruce said. "He's really come a long way from when I was afraid she'd kill him."

"I thought you said you didn't know which way it would go if they fought."

"No, I said I wasn't sure how badly they'd react. I'm not sure anyone could stand up to her with that weird knife in her hand."

"That's the staff of the Dagda," Megan said, thinking about the last memories that the runestone had shown her. "It's an artifact."

"Made by one of the Beloved," Bruce murmured in awe.

"Yes," Megan said. "That's what my father called him. How did you know that?"

"August and I have been talking about magic," he answered, realizing at once that he didn't want to discuss that with her yet.

"So when do I get to find out what you've found so far at the creepy hotel where we almost died a few months ago?" she asked, sensing his discomfort.

In answer, he kicked off his shoes and laid down on the small blanket they'd brought with them. She did likewise and stared up at the sky next to him.

He opened his mind to her and she allowed her thoughts to merge with his. Now that he'd been made aware of her mental stowaway, he could feel the ancient presence within her and wondered how he'd ever missed it before. He denied her nothing, and allowed Megan to search his memory of the explorations as she saw fit.

Once again, it was clear that her mind didn't work the same way his did. She found the mystery of the hotel's chaotic construction barely worthy of notice and locked onto the moment in which he'd entered the elevator at once.

"I'm sorry," he whispered. "I'd forgotten about that. It wasn't very nice of me."

I'm sorry I made you feel that way, she sent. *I had no idea how much it would hurt you to lose me.*

You wouldn't feel the same about me had our places been switched?

You know I would. Like you said, I just about leveled your house when I felt you disappear. Can we make a promise to each other?

About what? he asked.

That neither of us will ever do anything like that again. Each of us will wait for the other to join them. We will never go off into danger alone.

I think I could get behind a promise like that.

He held his hand up with the pinky extended, but she pushed it aside, laid her head on his chest and held him there as the sound of the waves crashed against the sand at their feet.

Was it everything that he wanted? Maybe not, but having her that close with her thoughts focused entirely on wanting to be with him was more than he'd ever dare to hope for. He let the moment burn into his memory to use as a candle in the night when he should ever be afraid.

His foresight warned him when the moment was in danger of lasting too long, and he let his ability guide him lest he ruin it.

"Oh man, I just thought of something," he said.

"What?" she asked, rolling back onto her shoulder. He already missed the warmth of her against him and not just for what it meant to him. It really was starting to get cold.

"So am I supposed to be addressing you as Your Royal Highness? Or is Grand Poohbah of the Tuatha dé more appropriate?" he teased.

Her laughter would always be his favorite sound.

"Not if you want to take me to the dance," she said at last.

"I wasn't aware that I'd asked you to the upcoming frivolities," he said in his best Paul imitation.

"You were going to," she said.

"And here I thought I was the only one around with the gift of foresight," he teased, grinning in spite of himself.

"Seriously, I'd like to go to at least one school dance," she said. "And Jade could use the support since Andrew already asked her."

"Andrew Jackson of no relationship that he knows of to the president of the same name?"

"I believe that's the one," she giggled, remembering the first time she'd heard Sam call him that.

"Or do you mean the one I caught practicing CPR with my sister when they were supposed to be studying geometry in her bedroom?"

"You didn't!" Megan giggled.

"Oh yes I did, and let me quote her on this: There are some memories you really wish you could get out of your head."

This set her off on another bout of giggles that pushed evil thoughts safely back where they belonged.

"You do know that this isn't going to be anything like what you saw in your mother's memory of the Tuatha dé, right?" he said, getting up again.

"Oh god, I hope not," she replied, looking around to make sure they hadn't forgotten anything. "I don't think I'm ready for anything resembling moonsilk. Although Mom did look regal in it."

"Good, because if it's like everything else in this town, it's likely to

186

be tacky beyond belief. We should probably start paying more attention to our surroundings now that we're getting to the edge of the wards we put up. There could be some pretty nasty things out here hunting in the dark. I really wish Fang had come with us."

"Okay," she said, and he could feel her mind stretch out before them. Then she giggled as she thought of something.

"Why are we about to go pull Azarich away from that Louis Lamour book he's clearly enjoying to go and see Mr. and Mrs. Harris?" Bruce asked. "I mean, I know he's read it before, but still."

"Because I don't need foresight to know that if you and I go in and tell him that we're going to our first dance at the Academy, it will unlock a whole slew of memories and stories. And the subject would probably do a lot to brighten Esther's night. She might even tell me more about Grandma Josie."

"You're not wrong," he said, watching the woman in question throw her head back and laugh at something her husband said. And he realized that was exactly where he wanted to be too. "We've got to pick up Jade and Paul too."

"Why would they want to go?" she asked. "I know Jade would probably be interested in the dance since she's going, but why would Paul care? He won't be allowed until next year, right?"

"Because Esther had a good spell about an hour ago and she made brownies."

"Then we'd better get a move on before they get cold!" Megan laughed, grabbing him by the hand and running so fast that he barely had time to grab the pack.

And as Shakespeare said in the poem they'd discussed in English class that week, at that moment Bruce would have scorned to trade places with kings.

Chapter XVIII: Full Circle

The day of the wedding came faster than Megan would have thought possible, weaving a fog of sadness around her that she couldn't at first identify. But when she took a moment to think about it, she realized that she'd hoped her mother would return before now. There wasn't any reason to have expected it to happen that way, but it still sapped some of the happiness from an otherwise wonderful day.

It felt like the last piece of a puzzle falling into place, a puzzle that had taken seventy years to complete. Each of the other good natured, if mischievous, boys had met and married the woman of his dreams. Now Alan's day had finally come.

Gone were the Palace's threadbare carpets and moth-eaten wall coverings. In their places were period accurate replicas in a seamless transition between the original fixtures and the replacements. Having spent most of the summer working in the concession stand, Megan marveled at the new glass and newly re-chromed edging around the display. The popcorn maker was all original since Bruce had worked his own particular brand of magic on it inside and out, but the gourmet espresso machine and accompanying gear were new and top of the line.

But it was the Grand Theatre that left her speechless. The newly upholstered seats still gave the cavernous room a new smell and the red velvet curtains had been replaced. Wood glowed and metal gleamed. To Megan it seemed as if the Palace had been transported back to the days of its original splendor and at any moment, the first of Nickelville's residents might come through the front doors.

As if in response to her musings about days long forgotten, her unpredictable ability to see the past came alive, and the room filled with men and women. American flags hung everywhere, and many of the young men on stage wore uniforms. As Megan scanned the room, she saw herself, or rather her grandmother on the front row, wearing a blue skirt and red blouse as she waved at the men walking out onto the stage. For that matter, there was a lot of red, white and blue to be seen in the audience. Next to her was Esther and a young woman that Megan had never seen before. On the stage, her grandfather and his friends waved enthusiastically at the women on the front row. But even in the jubilant excitement of the moment, Alan looked a bit distant, as if he were the only one who truly grasped what lay in store for them.

"Well hello, Megan," Esther said from her side where Mr. Harris had paused.

"Hello, Esther!" Megan laughed in delight, bending down to hug the frail woman who, in spite of the hat she wore to hide her sickness, shone with such happiness that it was almost impossible to believe she was ill.

"Would you mind rolling me down to the front?" the smiling woman asked. "Tom needs to get back and make sure that Alan doesn't explode with eagerness before the music even starts."

"I'd love to," Megan said, taking the handles from the librarian after quickly hugging him as well. "Where would you like to sit?"

"The groom's family is supposed to sit on the right," she answered. "And since Alan doesn't have any living relatives that he still keeps in touch with, it's going to be our little circle who make up the family section."

Megan pushed her down the aisle to where she'd pointed, still exploring the energetic past with her eyes as they walked.

"Did anyone tell you why they're holding the ceremony here?" Esther asked while they walked.

"No, they didn't," Megan answered.

"This is the first place she saw him," she explained. "There was a big get together here."

"When they were heading off to war," Megan finished, looking at them on the stage.

"I wondered if you had Josie's ability to see the past. If it was the one that I'm thinking about, Kate would have had to be much younger than she made it sound."

"Grandma could do this too?" Megan asked. She'd always thought it was from her father's side since her mother didn't appear to have it.

"Do you mind letting me see what you've been looking at?" Esther asked and reached out to take Megan's hand in her own. "Oh yes, this is the day when it happened! Don't they all look so handsome!"

"I didn't know that someone who didn't have gifts could join in like this," Megan said, looking at the elderly woman in awe.

"Then it's a good thing I confided in you the other day. Do you see the young man standing on this side of my Tom? That's Carl, yes, the one who didn't come back from the war. I've always hated the way everyone tacks that onto his name as if that was the only thing he ever did. He was a delightful young man. A bit strange at times, but weren't we all at that age? And do you see the woman standing with your grandmother and me? That was Elizabeth, his fiancé. Oh, this is so exciting," Esther said, turning to scan the rest of the theater. "She must be here somewhere. We wouldn't have noticed her back then. I mean she was only about eleven at the time. And even though he didn't notice her until she started working here at the age of eighteen, to hear her talk she must have really noticed him. You're younger and your eyes are better than mine. Help me look for a girl with long, flaming red hair."

"I already know what she looked like," Megan confessed. "But this isn't really the first time they met. Kate probably doesn't want to talk about the first time. If you can share this, does that also mean I can share my thoughts with you?"

"Of course," Esther replied.

Over the next several minutes, Megan shared the sequence of memories that started in the cafeteria with Josie and ended with Alan thinking Kate was a boy.

"Josie never told me about that," Esther said, surprised. "I guess she had secrets of her own. Judging by the way Josie was dressed and the fact that we were still in school, I'd say that was probably about six or seven months before what we're seeing here."

Megan couldn't find Kate in the crowded theater at first, but then she noticed a girl off to one side of the crowd, standing on the back of one of the seats to get a better look. Her hair was braided and likely tucked into the back of her coat so that only a bit showed, but the look of rapt concentration gave her away. Megan pointed her out to Esther.

"Oh yes," the woman said. "I wish you could push me over there for a better look without making everyone wonder what we're up to. I do remember her from back then. Some of the boys liked to tease her because of her hair, which is probably why she's still hiding it. The story was that she eventually got tired of it and found them one by one and made them all cry. All of us girls thought it was amazing that a girl could fight back against not one but three boys. I had no idea that Alan or Josie had anything to do with it."

"It does explain why she took such a quick liking to Jade, though,"

Megan said. "Look, they're leaving the stage."

Although it was faint in the present, they could hear a band playing nearby as the uniformed men exited two by two. Esther sighed happily as she watched her younger self run up and hug the man who would, shortly after returning from the war, become her husband. Josie and the girl Megan now knew to be Elizabeth did the same. But Alan stood a few feet apart, staring up at the bright lights that shone down on the stage, likely already looking at the way everything had been built. He didn't notice when the hat he'd slipped under his arm fell to the ground, but the young Kate certainly did. She darted through the crowd with the dexterity of a dancer and snatched it up.

"Mister," they could hear her say from a long way away, "You dropped this."

Alan turned, and seeing what she held, gratefully took it from her hand.

"I'm no mister, little lady," he said, patting her shoulder in a brotherly manner. "I'm just Alan. Alan Green." Then, noticing that his friends were leaving without him, he pulled a stick of gum out of his pocket and gave it to her. "You take care now. And thanks for giving me this, I 'spect I would have been in trouble if I showed up without it tomorrow," he said with a warm smile and walked away.

For several minutes after the friends had left the theater, the girl put the hand not holding the gum on the shoulder where he'd patted her, and mouthed his name silently.

With a loud sniff, Esther fumbled with the purse in her lap and pulled forth a small package of tissues.

"This doesn't bode well at all," she sniffed, handing some to Megan and blotting her eyes. "I promised myself I wouldn't cry, and here I am with tears ruining my makeup and the bride and groom aren't even in the room yet. Of course, you've got Josie's complexion, and you probably won't ever need to wear anything of the sort."

"It's cool that Grandma could share the things she saw with you," Megan said, ignoring the comment about her complexion which definitely came from her violet-eyed father. "I've done it with Sam, Bruce and of course my mother already, but Jade, Paul and Grandpa will like seeing things like this too. We were sort of afraid it would hurt them."

"Well, I can promise you that the only harm that comes is from the jealousy of not being able to work such miracles on our own. At least that's the way it always was for me. Now I couldn't help but notice that I couldn't see any of the decorations up there on the stage while we were looking at the past. Have you seen them yet?"

Realizing that she'd had the same problem last year when visions of the Academy's past had overshadowed the present, Megan closed her eyes and centered herself in the present. When she opened them, simple white ribbons decorated the armrests nearest the aisles. Floral arrangements surrounded the podium where the happy couple would say their vows.

"Kate said she wanted to keep it simple," Esther confided. "They just want to make it official, so they can get on that plane and start their lives together. By this time tomorrow they should be out to sea, and neither of them will give today another thought. At least that's the way it was for Tom and me all those years ago. Neither of them has ever been on a cruise. I hope they like it."

As people started to trickle in, Megan noticed the sides filling unevenly. The groom's side had Alan's friends along with a smatter of teachers from the Academy. Mr. Danders had even come. But on Kate's side there was only an uncomfortable looking Andrew since Jade was going to be the maid of honor.

"Let's go sit with him," Esther said, having made the same assessment herself.

Bruce hovered near the main doors to the Grand Theatre, feeling unneeded since very few people had been expected, and all of those had already made their way into the Grand Theatre. It felt strange to see Mr. Danders away from the academy.

The low numbers surprised Bruce, knowing as he did that Azarich and his friends had been extremely popular in their day. Of course, their unusual longevity made it easy to forget how old they really were. As morbid as the thought was, the main reason they didn't have more friends present for this important day was that the majority of the people they'd grown up with were already dead.

Even though Kate was almost a decade younger, from what Bruce could tell, she had almost no life outside of the running of the Palace. Andrew was sitting on her side of the theater, but there weren't many others expected. He peeked through the doors and noticed that Megan and Mrs. Harris had moved over to the bride's side.

"Hey Paul," Bruce said, drawing his brother back from wherever he went these days.

"Yeah?"

"Mind if I go see how things are going? I think we're planning to start in about another fifteen minutes."

"Gee Bro," Paul said, trying to look concerned without much success. "I don't know if I can handle this by myself. We do need to cash in on that free year of movies though."

"I know, maybe after the Jubilee we'll have time to come in and see

194

what's showing," he agreed.

Bruce made his way over to the smaller theater where the men waited. As soon as he walked through the doors, he could feel Alan's anxiety, not because the man didn't want to get married, but because he wanted everything to turn out perfectly for Kate.

Azarich and Tom stood next to him, ready to give whatever help they could. But it was Sam who kept things under control. His soothing voice traveled all the way to where Bruce stood, and even though he couldn't hear what the big man said, it clearly showed that the old Sam had returned. Or at least he was keeping his sadness at his missing friend hidden well enough that not even Bruce could feel it leaking past his shields.

Bruce felt his sister approach before she tapped him on the shoulder.

"Is everything okay in there?" she asked.

"Alan looks like he's about to tear his tux off," Bruce said. "I don't think ties agree with him."

"Tell him the tearing off of clothes comes later," she said and then covered her mouth in horror. "I've been around Kate too much. If she's this wild now, I can only imagine what she was like when she was young. I'm not entirely sure Mr. Green could have survived her before now."

"Sounds like he would have died happy," Bruce said, deciding not to move out of the way when she punched him in the shoulder. "How about Kate, is she almost ready?"

"Everything is on schedule," Jade replied. "I wish she would have let us decorate more, though. She said she saw no reason to spend a bunch of money making a mess that she'd just have to clean up before the next show."

"Aren't they going on a cruise?" he asked, confused.

"Yes, but you know her," his sister said, then switched into an eerily good imitation of the bride. "I want this place clean enough to eat off that stage before we go, or I won't be able to enjoy myself on the trip!"

"I don't miss that," Bruce said. "I love her, but I think the only reason we were able to do any of the renovations was because she was pretty much on her deathbed. And knowing her as well as I do now, I really can't believe that she gave you the all clear to do what we did without her."

Suddenly his sister looked guilty.

"Jade," Bruce groaned, horrified by the implications. "She did say that she didn't care, right?"

"I might have exaggerated her willingness just a tad," Jade said and then added quickly, "But the important part is that she wasn't too upset with me when she saw how well everything turned out."

"You seriously have a death wish," he said, shaking his head in reluctant admiration. "You're aware of that, right?"

"Says the boy who will eventually have Emelia as a mother-in-law," Jade teased. "I know, I know, you're just friends. But I've known you your whole life, little brother, and sometimes, when she's not paying attention, you look at her like she's a new book by your favorite author."

"Look at you using similes!" Bruce teased. "You're not one to talk. He, of no relation to the president of the same name, seems pretty head-over just about everything when it comes to you."

"He does, doesn't he?" she agreed pleasantly. "Well, if everything is good here, I'm going to go start the music. Make sure you keep Alan fully clothed, okay?"

"I'll do my best," he answered grimly. "But he's a force of nature,

196

that one. Even if all of us need therapy by the end of this, as long as they're married, and we don't have to do it again, I say we let him do it his way."

"Gross," Jade mumbled and then hurried off. He wasn't sure if it was to get things going or to get out of the conversation. But making siblings uncomfortable was the sign of a good brother, and no one would ever accuse him of being lax on that front.

When he got back to where he'd left the Paul, Bruce found him speaking with the minister who'd agreed to conduct the ceremony. He'd only seen the man a few times before, but the man seemed nice.

Moments later, the music started, and everyone took their places. Bruce took the seat next to Megan opposite to where Esther had moved from her wheelchair. Andrew sat behind them and looked grateful to not be alone any longer. Although the decorations were minimal, the grandeur of the restored theater made it difficult to think of what could have made the place look more splendid than it already did. Paul sat down next to him along with their parents.

Having decided to forgo the use of a flower girl in spite of Jade's insistence that either one of her brothers would be perfect, Jade walked first down the aisle with a smooth rhythm that Bruce had seen her use when performing her martial arts katas.

For what might have been the first time, Bruce saw Jade not as his sister, but as a girl on the edge of womanhood, and a pretty one at that. She took her place to the left of the minister.

Alan entered, followed closely by the friends who had stood by his side since childhood. They took their places to the right of the minister, with Alan waiting at the head of the aisle, looking expectantly toward the main entrance.

Although the newly oiled hinges made no sound when the doors opened, anyone looking at Alan Green's face knew exactly when he saw the woman he'd admired from afar for so long. Impatient to be closer to her, he looked as if he might meet her halfway down the aisle, probably dragging the minister with him. But he held his ground, helped by the firm hand of his best man, Azarich, on his shoulder.

When they all turned to watch, they found that Sam had taken the place of Kate's father, who had died many years previous. Up close, Bruce realized he'd never seen the big man in a tux before and suspected they might have had to get one special-made to fit him.

I wish Mom could see him, Megan sent.

I'll bet he does too, Bruce replied. *I've never seen him with his hair down. Well except for that day at his house, and I don't think that really counts.*

It looks good, she agreed. *And you wouldn't believe how thick it is. I had a lot of fun braiding it that day. But I really do wish my mother was here. She loves Alan.*

She'd be here if she could.

I know, but it would be nice if she could see it from more than my memories, she sent.

She can see the video and the pictures. Mom brought two of the staff photographers with her. Fear not, there will be an extensive record of what happens here for Emelia to see when she returns.

When everyone reached their places, the ceremony was, as promised, short. They spoke familiar words, but Bruce suspected that they held slightly different meanings for all of those present. But whether those meanings sank roots in anticipation or memory, they touched them all. And if the kiss exhibited there on that stage in any way resembled the one Jade had interrupted in Kate's office, he understood why she'd been so surprised.

Chapter XIX: The Fates of the Baker Hotel

"So I finally get to find out why I spent a week in negotiations with lawyers from the Jones estate to buy a derelict building in the middle of town," Sam said, standing in the doorway to the Grimble's garage where Paul had almost finished outfitting them with enough gear for a month-long expedition into a jungle cavern.

They'd intentionally chosen a Saturday morning when both Grimble parents would be safely tucked away at work. So much excitement filled the air that even those who couldn't read emotions sensed the change. Paul had dug out and tested enough flashlights and headlamps to ensure that no one would be caught in the darkened interior of the hotel. Sam had even brought his newly purchased climbing gear should they need to overcome some obstacle Bruce had not already sensed in his previous explorations along with hard hats for the areas where the ceilings were collapsing.

Before they left, they returned briefly to the tree house where the hermit waited.

"I've always wanted to see what was in that place," Paul said eagerly, "As a kid I thought it was rude to put something like that in the middle of town where everyone could see it and then not let anyone go check it out for themselves."

"It's not what it seems," August said.

"You've been inside?" Paul asked. "I knew the place was old, but I didn't realize it had been there since the dark ages."

"Bruce," the hermit said, glaring at the youngest Grimble. "If I show you where the siren's lair is, would you consider dropping your brother off there?"

"As much as I understand your desire to do so," Bruce said sadly, "I'm pretty sure Mom would kill me if I did."

"Damned parental attachments," the old man muttered.

"So are we going to walk the shadows there?" Jade asked.

"Not if I can help it," Sam said quickly. "We own the building now, so we can park on the street and walk in the front door."

"Should I pack food?" Paul asked.

"No, Patty would be happy to bring us a couple of pizzas," Sam answered.

"Do you ever get sick of pizza?" Azarich asked.

"I almost never eat it," Sam answered.

Many of the people out shopping on Main Street stared at them as they climbed the clay tiled steps to the center of the three arches that lead up to the front doors of the Baker Hotel. The edges of the tiles were broken off quite a few, probably the result of skaters trying to use the iron handrails for tricks. But once again, given the age of the place, it was in remarkably good condition. Doric columns framed three archways, beyond which three sets of double doors lead into the main foyer of the hotel.

The early morning sun shone brightly, and Bruce looked forward to seeing the difference it made in the way the place felt. He was still glad that he'd had a chance to work through his nightmares of the place alone, but he'd reached a point where nothing really felt real until he shared it with his friends and family. He only wished August had been able to come too. The old man's curiosity made him seem younger, even if his movements had slowed in the recent months.

The sound of the key turning in the tall ornate door echoed through the foyer and beneath the masonry of the entrance. The pressure inside must have been greater than without since the door seemed to exhale a musty gust of mold and decay when the big man opened the door.

Inside, several inches of fallen plaster and debris covered the floor. A few pieces of scaffolding stood in one corner, likely left behind when the last of the workmen had left. A few rickety looking chairs were stacked against the check-in counter. Huge holes gaped in the ceiling where the plaster had fallen.

"I can't believe we're finally here!" Jade squealed, looking around as she entered. "Paul and I used to make up stories about running away and hiding up there."

"How about you, Bruce?" Megan asked.

"Oh, I had wonderful daydreams about them running away and leaving me at home in the peace and quiet to read," he replied. Then he met Jade's eye and finished quickly with, "I'd miss them now though."

Something stirred far above them.

"Did you guys feel that?" Bruce asked.

"There's definitely something up there all right," Sam said, looking toward the holes in the ceiling as he did so. "And you're right, it doesn't feel like a person. There's something familiar about it, as if I've felt this before, but I can't quite remember what it was or when I felt it."

"Didn't you say that you and mom used to sneak in here?" Megan asked.

"We were young and hadn't fully grown into our abilities," the big man replied, "and to be honest, we were far more interested in swimming

201

than urban exploration."

"Do you guys want to search floor to floor or just go up to the interesting stuff?" Bruce asked, trying to figure out which direction he should take them.

"How did you search all of this in the dark without being seen from outside the windows?" Jade asked.

"He searched the whole thing in complete darkness," Megan answered for him. "We can sense our surroundings well enough to know everything that's around us, even when we can't see. But even so, his memory alone was enough to scare me, and I've lived in places that weren't much better than this."

This drew a startled look from Azarich, and he moved closer to her so he could give her one of his quick one-armed hugs.

"But weren't you afraid of the dark when you were little?" Jade asked, craning her neck to get a better look at one of the chandeliers.

"Terrified," Bruce admitted. "But I got over it."

"I'll say," Paul said, his voice echoing across the room from the domed alcove in which he stood before walking to a nearby doorway and looking down a darkened hallway that was still light enough to see shapes in the distance. "But if you've already checked all of this out, I'd rather go up to where the cool stuff is."

"Me too," Azarich said. "I'm still well rested, but I suspect there's going to be stairs, and I'm still not completely recovered from our Goatman temple excursion. I wonder what this place would have looked like if they'd ever finished it."

"I'm not sure they ever intended to," Bruce said. "They sealed in walls without running electrical lines or plumbing. They'd have had to rip out half of what they already put in to make it a fully functioning hotel, even if they only planned to do it on the lower floors."

"More and more mysterious by the moment," Sam said in his deep voice.

"Ooh, say that again, Sam," Jade begged. "I got goosebumps from the first one!"

Bruce walked up to the tarnished bronze doors of the main elevator, placed his hands on the frame and stretched his senses out into its structure. Unlike many of the building's amenities, the elevator did seem to be in working order, but the motors that drove it on the fifth floor were disconnected from the building's power supply.

"Wait here a minute," he said, walking the shadows to the access door to the shaft that he'd found during his previous explorations. It was completely dark this deep into the interior where the light from the hotel's outer windows couldn't reach.

Megan appeared instantly at his side and turned on the headlamp that Paul had given her.

"I'm not doing anything dangerous," he promised, secretly pleased by her concern. "I'm just hooking the power back up to the elevator so Azarich doesn't have to use the stairs any more than necessary."

"You're sure you know how to do this?" she asked, watching as he found the high voltage line and, without touching it, reconnected it to the motor and tightened the fittings.

"Doesn't everyone?" he asked slyly. "Would you like to ride down with me? This one isn't shielded, so we could just walk the shadows to safety if something goes wrong."

He pushed the button to open the doors and they slid open fairly smoothly given how long the thing had likely been closed. He stepped inside to study the controls which consisted of a large brass disk with a lever handle sticking out of the top. The metal shone inside the elevator, making him think the shaft must not leak as badly as some other parts of the building.

"You're sure about this thing?" she asked, reluctantly stepping inside with him. He closed the doors and pulled the interior folding gate across.

"At least sixty percent sure it won't fall like a rock when the brakes come off," he said, pulling back on the lever. The car lurched, then started to descend and for just a second Megan became opaque as she reached out to take him with her to safety.

"Jerk," she said, realizing he'd known it was going to do that and how she'd react.

When the car arrived on the ground floor, everyone was waiting expectantly.

"It seems sturdy enough," Bruce said, "but it's not automatic like the modern ones. Megan and I can jump back and forth to the fifth floor to retrieve it, but if anyone ever does it without us, you're going to have to use the stairs if it's on another floor."

"What about the one you said leads to the penthouse?" Azarich asked.

"That one is shielded so tight that we can't do anything supernatural in it," Bruce replied. "The protections on that car are so strong it completely severed the bond that Megan and I have with each other, and it didn't come back until I stepped outside on the roof. I could walk the shadows to the roof now that I've seen it, but I can't go anywhere inside the protected area except by mundane means."

"What's the weight limit on this elevator?" Sam asked, looking at it skeptically.

"I checked it over as we descended, and it was made stout. We're just lucky that none of the water that comes in when it rains comes through this way. It should be okay for about four people at a time."

"I think I'm going to take the stairs," Sam said. "I'm a big guy, and there's no need to put an unnecessary strain on the cables."

"I'll come with you then," Megan said. "That way Bruce can take everyone else up. I can't say I like that thing much either," she said, motioning to the elevator. "I hate the sensation of falling."

"It smells like old crayons in here," Jade observed, moving as far back into the corner as she could to allow Paul and Azarich enough room in the musty car.

"I don't know what they make crayons out of these days, but I've never used any that smelled like this," Azarich said, wrinkling his nose in distaste.

Paul slid the gate closed and Bruce pulled the lever back slowly so as not to lurch the way it had before. He grinned as he did so. He could feel that Megan and Sam were already nearing the top and would get there before the four of them did.

The noises that the elevator made as it slowly ascended were not particularly reassuring in spite of the sturdiness of the cables. Even knowing that he could easily hold the car in place should something go wrong, Bruce was still relieved when the fifth floor descended in front of them and they could get off.

"Megan," he said when she walked up with their big friend, sweeping the room with her flashlight. "Can you see anything of the past here?"

"Are you sure there's nothing here that we need to be afraid of?" she asked. "Esther showed me how to project so that she could see too. Apparently, she used to do it with Grandma Josie all the time."

"I can't say that takes me by surprise," Azarich said, smiling fondly. "I don't think those two had any secrets from each other."

"So we do it like we did in my neighborhood?" Sam asked,

lowering his protections to see what she did, "and Azarich and the Grimbles will be able to see too?"

"I'll have to bring them into it," Megan said, "but it shouldn't hurt them in any way."

Bruce followed suit and in much the same way that it had happened before, the past slowly came alive around him. Children had lived here, he realized as phantom youngsters came into focus. But unlike the echoes of Sam's childhood at his uncle's general store, these didn't smile, run or play. They wore stiff, uncomfortable clothing and could be seen most often standing behind couches and chairs, watching adults who largely ignored them. The girl had brutally short black hair and wore dresses and shoes in all of her echoes, never going barefoot even in the comfort of her home. The boy wore short dark pants with a coat and tie. Like the girl, he never went without his shoes and seldom could be seen without his hat.

The father wore suits and always looked as if he might don the top hat that was never too far from hand. For the first time Megan was able to draw a smell forward from the past in the form of the sour cigar smoke that billowed from his mouth like a smokestack as he read the newspaper or yelled at the severe woman with short wavy hair. Although she dressed in expensive clothing, she always looked as if she were ready to hide at a moment's notice.

"This doesn't look like it was a particularly happy home," Jade observed, glaring at the man.

"Not from the look of those kids," Paul agreed.

The same pattern of images greeted them as they moved deeper into the rooms that branched off from the elevator. Children hiding under Art Deco tables and in spaces behind well-padded armchairs that had been positioned in corners. Although the echoes of the past never showed anything bad happen, it was still impossible to ignore the implied presence of menace that filled these walls.

"I'm not sure what I was expecting to find here," Azarich said. "I don't know any of these people. The children must not have gone to school, or I would have seen them there. I wasn't that much older than they were when this happened.

"Don't open that," Megan said, when Sam reached out to open a side door when they were moving down the hall toward where the hidden elevator waited.

"Why not?" Bruce asked. "It's just a closet."

"It's a bad place," Megan whispered.

"Why would someone put a lock on the outside of a closet door?" Paul asked grimly. "They locked the children in there, didn't they?"

"Sometimes she hid there with them as well," Megan added, watching the wife pass.

"I don't like these people very much," Jade said, frowning at the doorknob. "Who were they?"

"That's one of the mysteries we're here to figure out," Bruce said. "There's not much about this place in the city archives. I know it was supposedly built by Theodore Baker, who also built other hotels around the state, but I've looked at the blueprints for those, and this building isn't like any of them. What it really looks like is a building that was supposed to look like one of the others, but was constructed for something else entirely."

"How could you expect to get away with building a hotel in someone else's name and not get caught?" Jade asked.

"In the 1920's, Nickelville was just a quiet little backwater where no one ever went," Azarich answered. "I remember how surprised my parents were when they heard that this place was going to be built. We had a poor economy even then, and the only people who ever came to Nickelville were lost. Everyone hoped that it meant times were changing for us, but a grand hotel in the middle of nowhere seemed pretty foolish. As for not getting caught, you have to remember that it would be well over half a century before the internet connected all of us. Until then, it wouldn't have been hard for someone to hide the real origins of this place from the rest of the world. By the time people might have noticed, the Baker Empire had crumbled, and no one really paid attention to the oddity of this place until now."

"This place gives me the creeps," Jade said. "Let's go check things out upstairs. Maybe it will be better there."

"As much as I'm not looking forward to going up in that little cage," Sam said, "I agree with Jade."

"Have you noticed how much was left behind?" Paul asked. "Most everything from Megan's vision is still here. Why didn't these people take their stuff with them when they left?"

"Wait a minute," Megan said, turning back to a room she'd been about to pass. There was a nail eye level sticking out of the moldy plaster.

"What is it?" Bruce asked.

She reached out her hand and Bruce came over to her and clasped it. Then she focused as hard as she could on the empty bit of wall before her. Eyes furrowed in concentration, the rest of them watched as a portrait slowly faded into existence before them. In it, the family from her visions came into sight, as grim and joyless as the life they'd led within this large space. Below it, the placard read, Jones.

"So how does Allison fit into all of this?" Megan asked.

"The boy must have been her great grandfather," Azarich said. "He didn't go to the Academy. I always assumed they lived outside of

Nickelville proper. I do sort of remember his father now that I know that's who this was. There were lots of rumors about them. The Jones family was a strong force in Nickelville's early days, but then they lost everything. My father always said they'd made a deal with the Devil to go from nothing to riches again in such a short time."

"They weren't always wealthy?" Bruce asked.

"Yes and no," the old man answered. "They were wealthy and then there were stories about gambling and bad investments. Then all of a sudden, the father we saw in these visions turned up with a ton of money and founded Jones and Jones Industries."

"I still think we should head upstairs," Sam said. "Maybe we will learn more about this there."

It took longer to get everyone up to the penthouse than it had the fifth floor, and it turned out that Sam was positively claustrophobic when the shields cut off his sense of the outside world. Bruce had to talk him quietly through it as they ascended. Everyone else took it well, and Bruce found himself at last on the fifth floor with his best friend.

"I told everyone to stay in the foyer until we were all there," Bruce said. "I sure hope this doesn't fail now when we're both in the car together and no one is outside to help us."

"I'm sure it would have done so before now if it was going to," she said. "I still can't believe you did all of this by yourself in the dark."

"That's all in the past," he said.

"I know," she whispered. "I can see you here by yourself. Would you mind taking me to the spot where you can see the empty shell of the Baker?" she asked. "I'd like to see that before we go up and get stuck where we can't walk the shadows."

So he took her hand in his own and walked them through the shadows to the stairwell door that opened into nothing. It was a very different experience during the day when they could see the cavernous space before them. Even though everything was where he knew it would be from his explorations with his extra senses, it was still not what he'd expected to find.

It was both more and less impressive. There was a sense of ominous permanence when he sensed the space through the rigid iron of its skeleton that didn't carry over to his sense of sight. He could see where water had seeped down from several places in the roof, rusting the beams and girders that allowed the Baker to rise fourteen stories into the air above the sleepy town of Nickelsville. But the rust was only cosmetic, and even the worst of the corrosion would take several more centuries to truly undermine the structure.

"I think I've looked at this place every single time I've passed it," Megan said. "Surely I would have been at the right place to see through to the other windows at some point. Why does no one know the thing is hollow up here?"

"Don't freak out," he said, "I'm going to go have a look. I promise I'll be careful."

Then he walked the shadows to one of the window sills, balancing precariously on the narrow ledge. As soon as he touched the glass, he had his answer and he returned to her side.

"Was that your way of telling me that I should let you know before I do something stupid?" she asked.

He grinned in reply.

"Well?" she asked.

"It's one-way glass. I didn't even know they had that stuff back then. It must have been prohibitively expensive to glass in this many openings with it. Let's head back and see what we can find upstairs."

"Where is the elevator shaft?" Megan asked.

"It should be right about there," he answered, pointing to the general location of the entrance on the floor below them.

"Why can't we sense it?" she asked.

"I have no idea," he admitted. "August said there were ways to do it."

"I wish he was here," Megan said quietly.

"Me too."

As soon as the gate closed them into the elevator a short time later, the hush descended once again, and Megan reached out to take his hand.

"I don't like this," she said.

"Sam didn't either."

"This is like it was when I first got to Nickelville," she added. "I wonder if the source of Nickelville's mystery silence might be up there."

"I didn't find anything to suggest that," he said grinning. "But I didn't get much of a chance to look around before someone tried to blow up my house."

"I was worried, okay?"

"It's kind of sweet now that I don't want to dump you in the spring at your grandmother's grove," he said.

"You wouldn't have!" Megan said.

"You had just dumped water from said spring on me while I was in bed just a few hours earlier as I recall, and you did actually dump me in there when you went off to save the world by yourself. From several feet off the ground I might add."

"I did?" she asked. "I didn't know that."

"You had a lot on your mind at the time, but you have to admit that I showed a lot of restraint when I dropped you off next to your bed. I'm just glad we're together this time. It still makes my heart race every time the bond breaks. I hope it's not freaking out your mother," he added.

211

"I worried about that the first time too," she said.

Then the roots began to close in about the shaft, leaking blue light as they had done before. Her hand tightened on his as she looked around in mild alarm.

"Are we in Guarded Wood?" she whispered.

"I wondered that as well," he answered. "It felt a little bit like a boundary too."

"Maybe the reason why we can't see the shaft from the outside…" she said, looking around for an opening through the tangle.

"Is because it doesn't go through the interior of the building," he finished.

"It wouldn't be the strangest thing we've seen," Megan added thoughtfully, as the floor overhead descended toward them and they found the eldest Grimble kneeling next to the opening.

"Come on guys" she said impatiently, "Sam won't let anyone go exploring without you."

As soon as Megan stepped out of the elevator, she knew the penthouse was going to be very different from the floor on which Allison's ancestors had lived. The penthouse's memories of itself were such that she completely lost her hold on the present and was swept up in the vibrant images of the past.

Are you okay? Bruce asked.

"I'm fine," she said out loud, knowing that she probably looked like she was in some sort of trance, which she supposed she was. "Can you guys see this?"

She heard Jade say yes from a long way away.

The walls of the huge room hadn't been covered in paintings as

212

Bruce had thought, but rather in tapestries that spanned the history of the human race. A crude rendition in which dark skinned hunters battled creatures for which Megan had no names hung on the far right, woven from coarse cord and dyed in earthen tones that nevertheless radiated a sense of power. Both the weave and texture improved in the next one, which showed a cluster of dwellings around which people had been captured just living their daily lives.

"That looks like the deserted village in Guarded Wood," Paul said. "It's not the same one, but the dwellings look the same."

"I didn't know anyone was making textiles that early," Bruce said.

"It's hard to know," Paul replied. "Things like this don't survive as well as pottery. All the historians can do is work with what survives and edit the narrative when we find out more."

The next several depicted scenes of birth, death and harvest in that order. With each new weaving the quality and technique improved as if the weaver had learned new skills over time. As they progressed, new colors decorated the scenes as well. By the time they reached the end, the craftsmanship of the tapestries surpassed what any of them knew to be possible using only colored thread.

The one that stood out from the rest in both size and detail was a tapestry that covered the entire wall opposite the elevator of a single massive tree. And it was this tree that evoked such a deep sense of age and wonder in those gathered that for a time they lost all sense of themselves and of their reason for coming.

Woven with such fine detail and skill, it appeared that the individual leaves moved in response to some unfelt breeze back through the erosive winds of time, calling them back to the beginning, to the place where everything that truly mattered had begun. At the base of the otherwise perfect tree was a rift in the silver bark, a dark space that whispered of passage into places where mankind could only travel in dreams or nightmares.

A menagerie of ancient tools, weapons, and sculptures filled the display cases. And like the tapestries, they progressed from the crude to the breathtakingly crafted.

Megan felt Bruce take her hand and lead her toward the base of the tree which she now recognized as the door to the next room. The strength of the vision would have frightened her just a few short months ago as it had at the Academy. But in spite of the strange presence she could feel somewhere up ahead, she felt safe within the walls of this forgotten place.

Though not as grand as the previous, this next room held the warmth of habitation. Even though it had been filled with grand furniture, tables, armchairs and lounges, it was the books that drew her attention. Shelves crafted from dark woods with rich grains overflowed with books that also covered tables and sat open in chairs as if their owners had stepped out for just a moment.

It was in this place of study that Megan first saw the three women, with their dark skin and long flowing garments. The youngest was a girl barely crossed over into womanhood. Megan knew that she was a person who never simply walked, but rather flowed into empty spaces like rainwater on parched land. The second woman had moved beyond the stage of maidenhood, though she was handsome in her own right, and the angles of her face were perfect in their symmetry. Although there wasn't any real resemblance between this dark-skinned beauty and her own mother, Megan still sensed that this woman also possessed the protective love that could overcome any obstacle to protect the ones she loved.

The last, withered by the passage of eons, sat unnaturally still, reading or watching the other two move about her as she pondered the importance of all that she'd seen. And for just a moment, the old crone, long white hair contrasting perfectly with the darkness of her withered skin, looked up and seemed to see Megan watching her.

The shock of those eyes upon her, with the sense that they saw not just her appearance, but every moment and element of the physical world that had shaped her, cast Megan out of the past and into the darkened present where almost nothing of the room's splendor remained.

"Did she just see you?" Sam asked.

"It sure felt like it," Megan answered, massaging her temples. She'd never maintained her visions of the past that long before, and it had taken a toll on her. "Want me to see if I can get it back?"

"No," Sam said. "There's something on the other side of that door, and I think we should probably stay in the present until we've discovered what it is."

"The shielding stops when we go through there," Bruce advised. "That's as far as I got the last time I was here. It's really overgrown, and there's a big tree. I didn't have time to notice anything else before I came home."

"How did a big tree get up here?" Jade asked.

"It might have been a sapling when they brought it up here a hundred years ago," Paul offered in explanation. "Maybe it was just intended to be an ornament and it got out of control when everyone left."

The door opened much easier for Sam than it had for Bruce, but given how much stronger their big friend was, that didn't come as much of a surprise. Light poured in through the opening and at once, Megan could feel the world outside again.

It took a moment for her eyes to adjust, but during that transition her hearing filled with the sounds of birds. The air held a green scent, one that she'd smelled many times in the depths of Guarded Wood where

215

pockets of time still existed before mankind had reshaped the world in his image.

"How can no one know that this is up here?" Paul asked in awe, following Sam out into the open air.

Megan followed him with Bruce and had to remind herself to keep moving lest she block Jade and her grandfather inside. The tree rose from the center of the circular depression in which they stood, rising up from the earth with a trunk so massive that she suspected it would have taken all of them to link hands around it. Gnarled and twisted limbs stretched out on all sides, touching the edges of the stone enclosure in which it had grown. Green moss covered much of its surface and hung down from its branches.

"This is so much cooler than an open-air ballroom!" Paul exclaimed. "But this just isn't possible. That's a live oak and judging from its girth I'd say it was at least two centuries old when this building was first constructed."

Sam pulled his phone out and started to take pictures.

"Good idea," Bruce said. "Maybe August will have answers. The decorative stone cap on the top of the building completely hides all of this. But even so, how has no one seen this from the air?"

"Who would look?" Azarich asked, "Paul, didn't you tell me once that Nickelville doesn't even show up on that satellite map thing?"

"That's right," the scout said, already exploring the lush underbrush. "And the mystery deepens. This isn't one tree."

"What do you mean?" Bruce asked.

"It's also ash and laurel," Azarich said. "Look at the leaves."

"Aren't those the three types of dryad in the woods by the school?" Megan asked.

"Yes," Bruce said. "And now that I think about it, each of the clearings has two big trees of the same type at their centers. The parking lot has the Gateway Oaks."

"There are two big ash trees in the middle of the Academy courtyard," Azarich said.

"And the stage in Jubilee Field sits between two enormous laurel trees," Paul finished.

Birds fluttered among the branches, disturbed by the presence of people in this place where none had been for so long. Bruce couldn't identify many of them and wondered if they'd stumbled into a place like Guarded Wood.

Flowering vines climbed the walls, and moss grew over stones and parts of the masonry, giving the space a sense that, like the tree, it had been here long before the building of the hotel in which it was located. Small lizards and frogs could be seen here and there, watching their unexpected guests without fear.

"Uh, guys," Jade said, "Have you noticed the really big bird?"

Megan looked where her friend was pointing and was astonished to find a very still, yet very large raptor looking down on them. It was easily five or six times the size of a normal eagle and though its plumage was predominantly brown, the feathers on its head were white like a bald eagle with the exception of the fiery red of its crest. The claws by which it clung to the massive branch of the tree looked longer than Megan's fingers. She'd read one time that a golden eagle's beak was strong enough to sever an adult deer's spine, and given how much larger this beast's hooked beak was than its diminutive cousin, she decided she was as close as she'd ever need to get to it no matter how beautiful it might be.

"That's got to be the biggest bird in the world," Paul said in awe.

"I've seen bigger," Bruce said sourly.

217

"Someone check its nest and see if there are any library books in there," Jade said, smiling wickedly at her youngest brother. Even he laughed.

The bird stared back at them as they watched it, neither anxious or particularly interested in their presence.

"Okay, I know that weird stuff has pretty much become the norm where we're concerned," Paul began. "But that thing has to leave in order to eat. Why hasn't anyone ever seen it."

"I think it's what I felt fly up right before I left," Bruce said. "Which means it flies at night."

"But raptors don't fly at night," Paul argued. "Their eyes aren't designed to see in darkness like an owl's."

"Explain that to him," Jade said.

"It's a she," Megan heard herself say, "And she's the last of her kind."

"How do you know that?" Azarich asked.

"I have no idea," Megan answered, frowning. "I can't remember…"

"I am so going to research this when I get home," Paul said, reluctantly tearing his eyes away from the magnificent creature.

"There's another door behind those vines," Bruce said, closing his eyes to better concentrate with his other senses even though he still didn't trust the bird. "And two more to align with the compass points."

Further exploration yielded only more empty rooms, although one of them was clearly a kitchen whose appliances had been stripped away like everything else. Even the bathtubs and sinks had been taken.

Only through once again opening herself to the past could Megan determine anything from them. The three strange women came alive again as she moved from room to room, admiring the regal decor and piecing together what she could of what they'd done here.

The oldest was most often found doing exactly what she had before, reading or writing in a journal. More than once, Megan had the feeling that the white-haired apparition was aware that prying eyes were on her as she went about her business.

The matronly woman often worked at a loom, weaving tapestries like the ones that had graced the foyer. She was also the only one that they ever saw cooking the meals they ate together either inside the kitchen or outside in the shade of the tree. Megan was surprised to see the raptor there in her visions as well as in the present.

"This still doesn't tell us who they were or what they were doing here," Sam complained a while later. "We've been at this for hours. What do you guys think about taking a break and heading back down so we can get some lunch?"

"I'm always good for lunch," Paul said, once again moving through the overgrown enclosure beneath the tree. "I think I just saw a newt. How do you think everything got up here? I mean, the eagle could have flown in and someone clearly planted the tree, but what about everything else?"

"Hold on a minute," Megan said, feeling a change in the space and opening herself to the past again. "This is really hard. Those women must have had a really strong presence to create such an echo now. There are so many things going on here that they're stacked in layers."

"Like sedimentary rock?" Paul asked.

"Yeah," Megan answered quickly before he could launch into an explanation. "It's hard to separate them all out."

When at last she stabilized the vision, they found the three women huddled together beneath the tree, and it was clear something was wrong with them. All three were coughing and the youngest had dried blood dripping down her chin and front of her flowing garment. As they watched, the white-haired crone placed the hands of her two companions on the trunk of the tree and held them there firmly until all three grew still.

Looking closely at the spot, Sam moved slowly through the dense undergrowth and gently began to search the moss-covered soil. Almost immediately he found the first bones.

"So they died here?" Jade said.

"That looked like tuberculosis," Azarich said, still looking at the spot where the women had died. "But it looked like it killed them fairly quickly. Consumption normally took a lot longer than that. We did have an outbreak about the same time that the Baker construction stopped though."

"There's more," Megan said, concentrating on making the images flow faster.

The Jones patriarch from the fifth floor entered from one of the outer rooms with what looked like an ornate box filled with gemstones. He paused in the doorway leading back toward the elevator and started coughing. He brought out his handkerchief to wipe his lips and it came back flecked with blood.

They followed him through the display room where multiple versions of him dismantled displays and took down tapestries which he carried away down the elevator. The crudest one, and likely the oldest tore in his hands and he tossed it on the floor behind one of the displays before moving on.

Azarich moved quickly over to where it had landed.

"It's still here," he said. "I'm afraid to touch it though. It looks extremely fragile."

"Let me see if I can restore it," Bruce said, coming up next to Megan's grandfather and gently spreading it out on the floor. "Good, I don't think any of it is missing."

As they watched, under his tender care fibers began to reattach themselves and reweave the pattern which had been destroyed by the greedy man's haste.

"Open that display case," Bruce said to no one in particular. "I need to put this somewhere safe. I don't dare restore the elasticity of the fibers for fear of changing its reading with a carbon test."

"Why is that important?" Jade asked.

"Because that might very well be the oldest piece of textile in the world," Sam answered, staring at the cloth with reverence. Laying his hands on the case, he warded it heavily to keep out any moisture. "We need to get something specifically designed to hold something like this. I don't like leaving it here, but for the time being it's probably safer than it would be in one of our houses."

"I think we're seeing how the Jones family made all of their money," Azarich said distastefully. "Grave Robbing. Megan dear, would you mind not including me in the rest of this unwholesome business. I don't think I've got the stomach for much more, and I'd really like to enjoy whatever it is that Sam plans to feed us."

"Yeah," Jade said. "This has been fun and all, but my brain is full. Can we go eat now?"

It took much less time to descend than it had coming up since only Sam refused to be taken through the shadows to the ground floor from the roof. After making sure that everything was closed up tight, Bruce took the group down to the foyer while Megan went with her mother's childhood friend.

When she emerged from the elevator, she asked Bruce if he'd noticed the partially melted hacksaw.

"Yes," he answered, wondering what she'd seen.

"Jones tried to cut the Bars with it," Sam chuckled. "I think they

221

might actually be made from pure silver. Anyway, the three women must have left protections on it of some sort."

"I'll say," Megan added. "It nearly electrocuted him when he tried.

It turned out that they'd been inside the building longer than they'd expected, and it was well past the lunch hour when they finally walked out through the hotel's front doors. It was while Sam was locking up that the past intruded once again on Megan's senses.

"Enough!" she said, centering herself to banish them as the apparitions of the Jones family walked past.

"Wait," Bruce said, reaching out to take her hand. "The women are with them."

Bringing up the rear of the group as they left the building were indeed the three women that Megan and the others had been watching throughout the afternoon. But instead of wearing the flowing garments they'd adorned themselves with in the privacy of their home, they'd dressed as servants.

"That explains a lot," Azarich said sadly.

"What does?" Jade asked. "Why are they dressed that way when they were clearly the ones in charge?"

"That's the early twentieth century," Sam said quietly. "Not only during the height of prohibition, but segregation as well."

"They had to pretend to be servants in order to avoid problems with the locals," Bruce answered, understanding. "Equality wasn't very far along yet here."

"Some might argue that it still isn't," Sam added, following the women with his eyes as they descended to street level. "Wait a minute."

Moving quickly he ran over to get a better look at a big man who looked a lot like Sam. He nodded in recognition to the white-haired crone as he passed her. She moved her finger to her lips in an unmistakable

222

request to remain silent.

"That's my grandfather!" Sam said in excitement. "I think he knew them! This changes everything. Let's get our food to go and return to Guarded Wood so we can tell August what we've found. And then we're going to visit the Well of Dreams."

"Jade," Paul said, looking up the steep face of the building.

"Yes?"

"There was something I was going to look up while we ate," he answered, frowning. "But I can't remember what it was."

"It must not have been that important," Bruce said. "Let's go."

Chapter XX: The Third Battle of Mag Tuired

Although August listened to what they had to say with great interest, he offered little in the way of illumination. Aside from acknowledging that the women indeed fit the description of the three Fates and pointing out that they also looked like the statues in the faun memorial, he knew nothing more about the reclusive women who had, for a time, watched over the entire town from within their hidden garden.

The Well of Dreams offered little more in the way of information, but it was on this account that another mystery arose. In the following days, Sam became convinced that the Well was actively resisting his attempts to discover more about the Baker's strange occupants.

When Alan and Kate returned from their cruise, things went, for the most part, back to normal until the night of the school dance. Then Megan found herself standing in front of a mirror and second guessing her choice in a dress. She'd picked one out from a catalog and wished, once again, that her mother had been there to help her. As it was, her only source of guidance was the eccentric girl next door whose only advice had been that it shouldn't be floor length.

Megan felt uneasy about showing so much of her legs, remembering how both Bruce and Paul had stared at her even though her bathing suit had been modest. At least the dark violet velvet covered her shoulders.

Mr. Bob appeared at the foot of her bed while she looked at herself in the mirror.

"What do you think?" she asked. "Do I look as ridiculous as I think I do?"

He purred, and she wasn't sure which answer that translated into. But he purred louder when she walked over and gave him a good scratching. Then he summoned the next runestone and slid it over to her with his paw.

"So if I play nice and give you belly rubs, I don't have to chase you down for these?" she asked.

He nibbled at her fingers in what she thought might be an affectionate manner, and then curled up on her pillow to take a nap.

I think you should come to your grandmother's grove for that one, August sent from the woods.

Why? And are you stalking again?

No, and I can't see into that beast's mind any more than you can.

The purring became louder.

But I know where your mother put them until you were ready for them. I marked that one so I'd know when the cat gave it to you. I'm probably going to need to talk to you after what it shows you, and I'd rather do it in person than like this.

You really know how to take a girl's mind off mundane things like poor self-body image. I'll be right down. This won't take long, will it? I don't want to be late for the dance.

It will seem like a long time on the inside of the memory, but the transmission is almost instantaneous. It shouldn't make you late unless you waste any more time asking questions.

Ah, there's the grumpy hermit I know and love.

Moments later, she arrived in the grove with the mirror under her arm and the stone in her hand. August was sitting on one of the four benches at the center of the grove.

"I'm not going to like this one, am I?" she asked.

"I don't know about that," he said. "But she told me about this one, and I doubt you're ever going to look at your mother the same way afterward. She knew she was running out of time when she made this one, so it may contain more in it than the others. I want to make sure that there are some things you don't misunderstand. But you won't know what I'm talking about until you jump in and get it over with."

He stood up, walked over and took off his coat, placing it on the stone bench nearest to her.

"Thanks, but just so you know, you're not very good at pep talks," she mumbled and then sat down on his coat so she wouldn't mess up her dress.

As Emelia began to spend more time with the Tuatha dé, it became apparent that some among them considered her an unworthy candidate for queen. She'd been the brunt of enough crude remarks back at the Academy to recognize such at the castle even though she spoke no Gaelic. And then there was an openly hostile noblewoman named Nimue, who Cara hated above all others. Emelia sometimes felt like she was back at the Academy, but that would change, the Scathlahm assured her, when Daragh ascended and became king. Then he would know the thoughts of all his subjects, and none would dare his wrath.

Before the two of them could marry, they needed to submit to a ritual that would overcome the differences of their genetic makeup and allow them to produce offspring. She'd had no idea what it would entail or how it might change her.

Cara offered to explain, but like a fool, Emelia declared that their love was such that it didn't matter what she had to do. And, being Cara, the Scathlahm told her that she was either incredibly brave or incredibly stupid.

Emelia and her betrothed entered a small round chamber that held an odd bench that was flat on each end but rose to a high point in the middle. Daragh went to one side, threw his leg over as if straddling a horse and leaned his chest against the raised middle. The top of it stopped just short of where his collar bones almost touched.

She took her place on the other side and he guided her hands to his forearms and he grasped hers in return. He rested his cheek against hers so that they each could see down the other's back.

"This is going to be very painful, and for that I am sorry, my love," he warned her. "But I will be here, and I will experience it all with you."

A small group of the Tuatha dé entered the room wearing white robes that hid all but their general size. Since even their hands were covered, she was unsure if they were men or women. Half of them took places behind the Heir and the other behind her.

As she watched, one of the figures stepped forward and, lifting one feminine hand, reached out to his back, and ran a finger down the fabric of his shirt which parted at her touch. Emelia felt the same happen to her own shirt, followed by the band of her bra, leaving her back as bare as his.

"Because you are not Tuatha dé, there will be no shame if you cry out," he assured her.

She vowed to herself that even if he broke, she would not.

"In order for our bodies to be similar enough to conceive, we are now going to be marked with an ink made from each other's blood," he explained. "It will look like a tattoo when they finish, but because we are alien to one another, our bodies will treat this invasion of cells like an infection and will react accordingly. Once again, I am sorry, but this is

227

the only way that we can be together, for the Tuatha dé were given the gift of life in trust that there would always be a descendent of the Morrigan to rule them."

"Why did you choose me?" Emelia asked. "Why go through this when one of your own beautiful women would have been a better match?"

"Because I never understood what beauty was until I found you in that tree."

For an instant her thoughts turned to another meeting that began in a tree. She hurriedly pushed it back to where it always hid, ready to come back to her in dreams. That path had closed behind her, and it was time to embrace this life fully.

When the finger touched his back again, Emelia's blood caught fire. She clenched her jaw against a cry born in the pit of her stomach. Her knuckles locked on the flesh of his forearm, and she knew his fingers would leave bruises on her own. But that fire only encompassed the smallest part of what happened within them.

She forced her eyes open to watch as the woman's fingertip slowly traced intertwining lines on her betrothed's back. His flesh smoked ebony in its path, a perfect contrast against his alabaster skin.

The combined stench of their burning flesh turned her stomach and made it difficult to breathe. She felt the pressure of his hands on her forearms lessen and she looked quickly into his eyes, which had half closed.

"Stay with me," she ordered resting her forehead against his.

Using the three points where their bodies touched, she wove her consciousness through him, stealing his pain as she went, braiding a core stronger than iron through him.

"No," he whispered, coming alive in the fire. Back and forth they

228

danced through rising tides of agony, and with each pass it forged them into something that had never been before. Perfectly matched in their stubborn resolve, they fought for possession of the fire that burned through them, scorching nerves and opening new pathways unlike any that had ever existed before in either of their races.

Then a childhood memory, sparked by the sight of that black line trailing down Daragh's back, returned vividly to Emelia's mind. It was Kermit the Frog, in all his green splendor, drawing letters in the air with his magic finger. Forgetting her need for silence, Emelia opened her mouth and filled the crowded chamber with a throaty laugh.

Intertwined as their minds were, he laughed as he'd never had reason to laugh before, even though he had no idea what was so funny about this strange amphibian. But his soul had bound itself to hers, and he vowed that there would never be a place where she went that he would not follow.

Around them the witnesses bowed their heads in wonder and knelt before the future king and queen. It was on that day that the voice which would guide Emelia through this strange life began to whisper in the back of her mind.

Because relations had further deteriorated with the Children of Nyx, Emelia agreed that it would not be safe to stay in touch with her father after the wedding. If their enemies thought they could harm the Heir through his future queen's family, they would likely do so.

But the voice that had awoken within her whispered that she should take one more precaution to ensure Azarich's safety. So it came to be that she told her husband one small and seemingly insignificant lie, which was really only a lie by omission. When asked where her father lived, she told them it was in Texas, but did not specify which town. This small dishonesty was not done in mistrust, for she knew that Daragh would die rather than betray her. She did so because if she alone knew her father's true location, it could not be learned through stealth. And even though the Tuatha dé knew much that was hidden from the outside world, they were unfamiliar with the naming of places in the mortal world, and never noticed the omission.

Plans for their wedding continued, and at times Emelia traveled back to the world of her birth. When she did, she always inquired about the date so she could better construct the phantom life she believed her father and his friends to have resumed in her absence. She never allowed herself, however, to wonder about her childhood friend, because she could not find it within herself to hope he'd gone on without her. She loathed herself for that hypocrisy.

But as the day approached, she found herself unable to cut her ties with her father as quickly as they'd planned. She had to see him once more, she argued, so he'd know that she'd married and was okay. Otherwise he might hire others to find her and inadvertently lead the Children of Nyx to his doorstep.

Since he could not travel to Tyr Sgodl for the actual wedding, a second ceremony would be held near her college. That way he could drive himself there without giving away the location of his actual home, and he'd think that she was going to live nearby.

Dressed in moonsilk, she stood through her wedding with no comprehension of what went on around her. Nothing had been changed in the throne room to indicate that a celebration of any sort was under way. Conducted entirely in the Gaelic tongue that her husband's people spoke, her mind darted through her memories, at least the ones she allowed. As a race that traced its origins to another world, their customs held nothing in common with what she knew. They exchanged no rings. They spoke no vows. Yet she felt the weight of responsibility settle over her just the same.

Cara offered to translate for her, but after a few moments, Emelia asked her to stop.

Near the end, the King bound her hand to Daragh's with a strip of moonsilk. He spoke words she couldn't understand while he did so, but that mattered little to her. For it was in that moment that her husband looked into her eyes with such joy that it made up for the rest. Ignoring the gasps of surprise in the throne room around her, she kissed him eagerly. Judging from his response, he didn't mind at all.

Then Emelia returned to her own world, and marveled anew at the old church they'd found. The Tuatha dé craftsmen, using nothing more than an image that Cara had taken from her mind, transformed the space into something to surpass her most elaborate childhood daydreams.

The heavy wooden doors leading into the chapel had been adorned with live climbing roses. Each white blossom was in perfect bloom and placed with such artistry that it looked as if it had grown there on its own years in the past instead of overnight as she knew it had.

Inside, white rose petals covered the length of the aisle in a fragrant carpet. And although the old chapel had been constructed with dark vaulted arches and too few windows to properly dispel the gloom, candles had been lit in clusters at the ends of the pews and in candelabras along the wall. The previously chilly space held the warmth of a thousand fragrant flames.

Behind the podium where they would soon say their vows, a white petaled tree rose in perfect imitation of the royal crest, just reaching the walls to either side of the chapel. Like the rest of the room, it held hundreds of white candles, giving the impression of fireflies dancing among its branches.

Flower laden garlands climbed the arches to the ceiling above where minuscule flames lit the darkness like stars. Emelia loved the way they looked, but hoped her father didn't look too closely at these witchlights since they'd never hold up under close inspection.

When Cara appeared with an unfamiliar, though beautiful woman, it took Emelia a moment to recognize her. She'd never seen the Scathlahm dressed in anything besides the armor-like garb she'd worn that first day in the tree. Now she looked like a pale angel in her black dress.

"Why aren't you dressed yet?" Cara asked.

"Unless the bride doesn't do that until after the wedding?" the woman with her said in a startlingly familiar voice.

"Adair?" Emelia asked in shock.

"She looks better without the armor," Cara said, "doesn't she?"

"But I feel a great deal less protected," the Captain of the Guard replied in irritation, adjusting the dress.

"Stop or you'll tear it," Cara said, moving her wife's hands from the fabric and straightening the wrinkles she'd created.

"Just don't expect this to become a regular thing," Adair grumbled.

"Like you couldn't just summon your armor in an instant if you needed to," Cara purred, clearly enjoying her wife's discomfort.

"I still don't understand why I couldn't just wear a leg sheath like you are," Adair complained.

Emelia looked down at Cara's leg and realized she could indeed see the outline of the Scathlahm's Blade faintly beneath the folds of her long dress.

"My oath doesn't allow me to be parted from it for any reason other than by royal command," Cara explained, taking Emelia by the

232

hand and leading her back toward the doors at the back of the chapel. "As you well know. Now don't take it off or tear it while we get Her Highness dressed."

"There won't be any bathing this time," Emelia said, just to be sure.

"Not this time," Cara agreed with a guilty smile. "He was so afraid that I might have scared you off with that."

The fitting of her dress was neither as mystical or as stressful as it had been the night of the ball. The craftsmen had already tailored it to fit perfectly. Among the yards of white satin and silk, knotwork patterns had been skillfully embroidered, lending a supple grace to the way it moved.

"I didn't know it was going to have a train," Emelia said uneasily when at last she had it on. "It's beautiful, but won't I have to worry about it catching fire with all of those candles down the aisle?"

"Your attendant will make sure it stays clear," Cara assured her. "My vow of protection now covers you as well. No harm shall come to you while I live. And if I were to die, my successor would take over."

"Who is that?" Emelia asked as several women styled her hair.

"He or she hasn't been chosen yet," Cara answered. "But I'm sure you'll like whoever it is. Besides, this isn't a day for such thoughts. Just rest assured that you need worry about naught this day."

"Has my father arrived yet?" Emelia asked.

"Yes," the Scathlahm answered. "Adair is talking to him right now. His friend is telling her a story she finds quite amusing."

"I'll bet that's Alan!" Emelia said, excited by the discovery. "I shouldn't be surprised that he came, though. He's been backing my father up ever since I was born. He's practically an uncle."

"I believe all is ready," Cara said when the women had finished with Emelia's hair. "You are so beautiful, Your Highness."

"You don't have to call me that," Emelia said.

"I'll only call you that until you are Queen," the Scathlahm promised.

A short time later, Emelia walked through a door at the back of the chapel and found her father waiting there for her. She'd known he'd worry for her, but she wasn't prepared for how much weight he'd lost or how gaunt he'd become. His eyes were hollows of sadness, and it was all her fault.

Until now her absence and the way it had affected the ones she loved most had remained an abstract concept, known but not truly understood. She rushed up to him, and he held her close without speaking for several minutes while those assembled in the chapel waited.

"I've missed you so much," she whispered.

She felt his desire to scold her for not staying in touch, but he held it back under firm control. He didn't want to ruin her day, so he smiled a smile that only made the pain more visible, and she almost changed her mind. But the hour for that decision had passed, and she would stay the course, no matter how much she might wish to do otherwise. After all, she loved Daragh and wanted to spend the rest of her life with him. She only wished she could bring her father with her.

"I've missed you too," he whispered at last. "You look so beautiful. I wish your mother could be here."

"I'm sure she is," Emelia answered. "Are you ready?"

"I think I'm supposed to be the one asking that," he replied, taking a deep breath and looking a little more like her iron-willed father. "But yes."

When the two of them stepped up to the end of the aisle, she saw Daragh, and all doubts left her. Although the first ceremony in Tyr Sgodl already bound them together, she would always consider this her true

wedding, the one where her father gave her away. Tuatha dé musicians
played while they made their way to the front, and her attendant fell into
step behind them, guiding her train with subtle flickers of magic away
from the multitude of fragrant flames.

Her father's strong voice broke when asked who gave her hand in
marriage, and part of her broke with it. The hand on her arm clung just a
bit too hard and a bit too long, but in the end, he let her go.

So it was that even though the man behind the podium spoke her
language, she heard less of it than she had in Tyr Sgodl. Hope and loss
filled her in equal measure as she looked into the lightly swirling violet
of her husband's eyes. It startled her when he spoke, reciting his half of
their vow, and his voice brought peace to her heart. He placed the ring
he'd forged with his own magic on her finger, and she felt its power
spread through her, awakening the full power of the Tuatha dé within her
and giving her their abilities through his blood that flowed through her
veins. When she followed and placed the ring she'd created on his hand,
it bound the two ornate bands of platinum together and allowed them to
find each other, no matter how far the distance that separated them.

When they kissed, the chapel exploded with applause, for the High
Court had not been invited to this ceremony, especially not the dour
Nimue who would have cast a pall on the whole affair. As it was, the
pews on either side of the aisle had been filled with the craftsmen that
worked so hard on both ceremonies, members of the Guard who made up
the bulk of her husband's childhood friends, and a few of the castle
servants so quiet that the reigning queen knew none of their names. But
they'd all had a hand in raising this prince who would one day be king,
and they approved of his bride even if the nobility did not.

Then the crowd caught them up and flowed through a doorway that
took them through the shadows to another place. For just a moment

Emelia panicked, worried that her father and Alan might be left behind or notice the unnatural transition. But she need not have worried, since the Scathlahm and Captain of the Guard had smoothly caught them up in linked arms and brought them along.

It was then that she realized that in spite of their best efforts to look normal, the Tuatha dé had made yet another mistake. With the exception of her bridesmaids and the two men who stood in as groomsmen, the whole of the guest party had dressed the same as they would have for their own tightly regimented affairs. The men all wore the exact same suit with knotwork woven into the weave, making them look somewhat like players from a Renaissance festival. The women all wore the same slightly modest dress, also embossed with knotwork. As an unintended result, Azarich and Alan stood out in their gray and brown suits like weeds in a neatly manicured lawn.

Apparently, the craftsmen had been given free rein to decorate the dining hall as they saw fit. White drapes covered the walls in a rippling sea of white mist, catching the light of the candles which stood on the many round tables. Miniature versions of the tree from the royal crest dominated the center of each table, rising several feet to meet the strings of flowers that descended from the ceiling like shooting stars.

"I know," Cara whispered in her ear. "Adair is keeping your father's friend too occupied to notice, but I don't think he will be distracted by anyone but you."

"That's okay," Emelia said, already moving toward him. "I want to spend as much time with him as I can."

Her father rose from the seat next to where Alan continued to talk to the beautiful captain of the guard. The musicians began to play, likely under the guidance of Cara.

Emelia held her father close while they danced, taking in the smell *of his cologne as she rested her cheek against his chest. They didn't speak at first, and that was probably best. Talking might lead to questions she couldn't answer, and more than anything she didn't want to add any more lies to the one she knew she'd have to tell him at the end of the night.*

So she and her husband showered him with questions and kept him talking and telling the stories she could likely have repeated word for word without this refresher. But even though she'd heard them all hundreds of times each, she listened and she laughed, taking every chance to study the way the light lit his face and the way the hair on the back of his hands felt when she rested her hands on his.

But although Alan might not have noticed, they were the outsiders here, cast adrift in a sea of pale skin, black hair and violet eyes. Azarich's eyes left hers often during the night, trying to make sense of what he saw. And even though she held him above the rolling waves, he was drowning.

Because of this, she could feel his relief when it came time to leave, and this time it was she who held onto their final embrace too long. Slightly tipsy from meade, Alan hugged her too.

"Don't be a stranger," he told her, trying to give her a stern look and failing miserably.

"I won't," she lied.

Her father looked deep into her eyes, and on some level, she thought he knew.

"I love you," he told her, cupping her face in his hand like he'd done when she was a child.

"I love you most," she replied, hugging him again both in need and so she wouldn't have to look him in the eye. "I'll call you soon, and we'll get together," she told him, expecting her last words to him in this life to

be a lie.

The scene in the memory shifted, taking Megan further into the future.

"You're definitely starting to show," Cara told Emelia while the latter stood in front of the bedroom mirror, admiring her side reflection.

As far as she could tell, she was almost three months into her pregnancy. It was difficult to tell exactly how long it might last though, seeing as Tuatha dé pregnancies normally lasted closer to eleven months. She didn't care how long it took as long as the future Heir was healthy.

So far, she hadn't experienced any of the stereotypical symptoms. She hadn't been nauseous or sensitive to certain smells or tastes. The only odd craving she'd experienced was for Hamburger Helper, a request that had positively traumatized the royal cook. Luckily, Cara and Adair had happily procured the necessary ingredients, and on discovering that they liked it as well, now cooked it for her once a week in their quarters where Emelia felt far more like herself.

At once the Scathlahm froze where she stood, her eyes going distant.

"What is it?" Emelia asked.

"We're mobilizing for war," the woman answered, frowning.

"With who?" Emelia asked. As far as she knew there had been no hints of such danger on the horizon. Of course, she knew the answer even before the other answered.

"The Children of Nyx have massed on the plains of Mag Turied," she answered. "And the night of the gate's opening is at hand."

"How did they move so many into that location without being noticed?" Emelia asked. "I thought we kept watch there."

"We do," Cara answered, getting ready to leave. "My guess would

be that they either cloaked themselves and killed the sentries or took them out with snipers. Once one of their steel jacketed bullets penetrates us, we lose almost all of our abilities. It wouldn't be the first time that the cowards have acted thus."

Emelia moved to follow Cara when she moved toward the door.

"Where do you think you're going?" the Scathlahm asked.

"To help," Emelia answered.

"You're going to stay here where it's safe for the future Heir," Cara ordered. "You know I'd support you if you weren't with child, but the King and Prince will be fighting. If anything happens to them, then the child you carry will be the only thing separating the whole of our nation from oblivion."

"I'm coming," Emelia insisted.

"No you're not," Daragh said from behind her where he'd just appeared.

"You can't order me around like you do your people," Emelia snarled, rounding on him where he stood.

"And I will never try," he promised. "But you know in your heart that what Cara said is true. The safety of our entire kingdom relies on your continued safety. Please don't risk us all for this. You know I want you by my side. That's not why I ask this of you."

"Why have I trained to fight if not for this?" Emelia asked.

"For the times after," Cara replied quietly. "You will not be with child forever. Conflict is part of our lives. This is but one battle in a war we've waged with the Nyx kids for millennia. I beg you to sit this one out."

"There must always be a descendant of the Morrigan to rule," he pleaded. "Please don't risk yourself this night."

"After all," Cara said with a wicked grin, "You know the queen

would make him marry Nimue if anything happened to you."

Emelia's eyes flashed with a hint of the violet in her blood.

"By the gods don't even joke about that," Daragh winced. "I'd rather take my chances with Adair while she wields your blade!"

Though it broke her heart to do so, Emelia agreed to stay behind.

Because time moved much more quickly in the mortal realm, their preparations were short, and Emelia soon found herself alone. Perhaps it was the vast silence of the castle that allowed her to hear the voice in her mind so much louder than before. She followed it down silent corridors, cloaked in enchanted warmth. It led her to the throne room.

In hindsight, she'd always known that the woman's voice in her mind came from the strange suit of armor displayed behind the thrones. But where it had whispered before, its call had now grown deafening with need.

Cara had told her about the Morrigan's armor when she'd asked, surprised by its small stature. It was an artifact of great power, created with arts left behind in their old world by the Morrigan herself. It was of such power, in fact, that it killed any who dared touch it. While the mother of the Tuatha dé wore it in battle, it enhanced her strength, speed and agility.

It had always frightened Emelia, this strange attraction to something so deadly. She found herself lost in the patterns embossed upon its surface, looking like the feathers of a raven edged in hints of gold from one angle and the hidden veins and capillaries of a rose petal from another. No one knew what substance it had been forged from, but its surface reflected iridescence in the light, and could become almost invisible the darkness though it often glowed around between the joints

240

and plates as if containing an inferno within.

*It called to Emelia with an urgency that almost made her reach out
and touch the forbidden substance of its making, and only the fear for the
life of her unborn child stilled her hand. This did not, however, keep her
from leaning in to look closer.*

*The arm of the artifact moved of its own accord, and the articulated
gauntlet rested one finger on her hand.*

*Her mind's eye opened on a scene of carnage. The Tuatha dé lay
dead or dying by the thousands, besieged on all sides as they were slowly
forced to give ground and flee back through the gate. Their dead had
been left behind to be ravaged by clouds of ravens that swarmed like flies
over the corpses.*

*Bottlenecked at the gate, her husband had been driven to his knees
upon the death of his father. The former king lay sprawled on the ground
next to him with a large bullet hole from a sniper's rifle leaking onto the
churned and muddy ground. Emelia knew at once that Daragh had been
paralyzed by the power of the ascension in which the memories of his
ancestors going all the way back to the Morrigan herself became his
own. Likewise, his dominion linked him to each and every one of his
people as she watched. Worst of all, they couldn't move him until it
passed for fear of killing him and themselves with him.*

*Fighting almost alone against nine spider-like abominations, Cara
and Adair held them at bay only yards away from where Daragh knelt.
Wielding the Staff of the Dagda, though still in the form of a long knife,
Cara darted in and severed an arm from one of the multi-legged artifacts
that had been brought forth from hell to wipe the Tuatha dé from
existence. While Emelia watched, a shot rang out and a small hole
appeared in the leg of the Scathlahm's armor.*

Unable to walk the shadows with steel lodged in her body, the following swipe of the automaton's other scythe-like arm passed through her left shoulder and knocked her to the ground at its many feet.

Forgetting about the king, Adair rushed in and shouldered the thing aside before it could crush her wife and pulled Cara back to the questionable safety of the few defenders left standing.

"How can I see this?" Emelia sobbed. "This cannot be true."

You see this because I have shown it to you, the armor spoke as it flowed around her, encasing her in its protective embrace. You must join the fray and save the king, otherwise we are lost.

But I can't endanger the unborn Heir that I carry!

If the king dies, you will lose the ability to pass through the shadows and be trapped here while they hunt you at their leisure. The defenses that my Beloved Dagda put in place will only slow them. In time they will reach you. This is the only path which gives my children a chance.

And so it was that Emelia Mackgahe, who had unknowingly become queen of the Tuatha dé, crossed through the shadows at a run and found herself in the last battle of Mag Tuired.

The sounds of the dying filled her ears, and the stench of blood brought bile up her throat, but she held firm. Dimly aware of her husband's presence behind her, Emelia snatched up the Staff of the Dagda from Cara's numb fingers. In her own gauntleted hand, it became what it had been so many centuries before, a staff of great power.

Up close, the enemy artifacts possessed the upper torsos of men fused to the bodies of six-legged spiders. But instead of human limbs, each of the Nine had been given the scythe-like arms of a praying mantis. Sensing a weakness in the defenses before them, the nine monstrous

242

automatons began to advance, including the one that Cara had damaged.

Before they could realize what new threat she presented, Emelia slammed the Dagda's staff into the one nearest to her with such force that she separated the torso from the spider-like base and sent the top flying some thirty feet into the enemy ranks, crushing all in its path.

Because the artifacts looked so much like the robots of science fiction, she expected to see shorting wires and gears within the one she'd dispatched, but with the exception of a cloud of noxious steam that escaped like a tired sigh, the thing appeared to be hollow.

Just as she turned to bring the full force of the staff down upon another, something slammed into the side of her helm with enough force to knock her off balance. An instant later she heard the report from the rifle and realized someone was shooting at her. Although it proved little more than an annoyance, she worried that the cowardly shooter would target her husband as he rose up from the depths to which his ascension had taken him.

Reaching out into the ravens that plagued the field, she sent them after the hidden riflemen and gloried in the sounds of their screams.

Shrieking an ancient battle cry in a language she didn't understand, Emelia thrust and parried, whirling to appear and disappear as she walked the shadows between the iron soldiers, ripping pieces off as she sated her rage with their destruction. Intoxicated with the combined power of the armor and staff, she never considered what changes they might bring upon her unborn child.

The remaining four artifacts fled from her onslaught, compelled by some unseen master to quit the field rather than be destroyed. The Children of the Nyx fled before her as well, and she burned them to cinders by the hundreds for having dared to harm her people.

Her own scattered troops rallied behind her and she sensed Daragh's presence in their minds. But so few of them remained! Why had she taken so long to heed the Morrigan's call?

Using the ravens to seek out the one who had brought this army to the very gates of her kingdom, Emelia found him safe on a ridge, predictably far away from the danger in which he'd placed his troops.

Sending the ravens first to strip his guards to the bone, she walked the shadows to confront them. When the chaos of the ravens lifted, the enemy leader and his grown son found themselves face to face with her wrath.

Emelia had never seen a Child of Nyx in person, and this portly middle-aged man hardly impressed her. He scarcely fit into ornate armor that had never seen actual battle, and his small dark eyes were wide with terror. She could see the violet glow of her eyes reflect in them as her wedding ring and her husband's blood gave her the power to judge him.

She wrapped the son in the rigid chains of her will and turned her attention to the father.

His terror was sweet as it flowed into her through this first judging. The molten glow of her armor grew brighter as the life left him. Then his memories began to flow as well.

Within his dying thoughts, Queen Emelia saw his sister, a seer of great power, give him the key to bring the Nine to life and with it, the power to wipe out the Tuatha dé. She assured him that he had nothing to fear and that he would be known forever as the one who avenged their race on the ones who'd killed their goddess. At last they could strike down the King and his Heir, eliminating their alien pestilence from the land.

His last thought before Emelia drained him dry was to wonder how his sister could have been so wrong. With the power of his life force she burned his generals alive. The remainder of the Children of Nyx fled the field, having witnessed the death of their leader and his weapons. Suddenly tired of the carnage she had wreaked upon them, Emelia allowed the rest to flee.

"You can't do this!" the son cried, managing to free himself from her control just enough to do so.

"Your father might argue otherwise," she replied wearily.

"The Children of Nyx will avenge us," he said and spat at her.

"You tried to wipe us from the earth," she whispered, her rage beginning to rise to the surface again.

"That's what you do with vermin," he snarled.

"Have you ever seen a rat caught in a trap?" she asked, lifting her hand and noticing that the fingers of her gauntlet ended in claws. She opened her hand as if to reach out and grasp his throat, and then slowly she began to close it.

His armor began to creak and groan like a tin can in a slowly tightening vice.

"You can't do this," he repeated, though without as much conviction. Or perhaps it was for lack of air since his armor had become quite constricting in the last few seconds.

"You're right," she said, leaving him there at the edge of being crushed. "This would take far too long, and I'd much rather return to my husband."

He burst into flames.

As she walked the shadows back to her husband's side, the voice of the armor whispered that she should wipe them out as they had tried to do to the Tuatha dé. But that voice was quickly distracted by the cries of recognition that came from the survivors at the gate.

"The Morrigan has returned!" they cried and she was surprised that her husband had joined them. From deep within, Emelia felt the pleasure of the Morrigan. Even after all of these centuries, her children had not forgotten her!

But Emelia herself couldn't feel anything but loss as she knelt beside Adair who rocked slowly back and forth, holding her wife's lifeless body against her.

August remained quiet after Megan returned to herself, knowing that it would be a lot for the girl to take in. She sat there, knowing it had only been seconds, but feeling like months had passed.

"You're never going to think about her the same way again, are you?" he asked quietly.

"How could I?" she asked with a mixture of pride and horror. "Those were your people, the Children of Nyx, weren't they?"

"Yes," he agreed. "And now you know why I wanted to be here for this one. By the time that happened, Guarded Wood had already claimed me, and I could no longer leave her borders. I wouldn't have obeyed the summons even if I'd been able to though. I never felt much love for your father's folk, but I could never have condoned genocide. And that's exactly what my sister-in-law pushed the Children of Nyx toward that day. Had your mother not turned the battle, the Tuatha dé would be nothing more than a fairy tale. As it is, they remain a nation of children ruled over by a broken king. Most of the adults died on the field that day, leaving only the old unto which the protection of the children had been given."

"And the rest of the world didn't notice this happening?" Megan asked, trying to get her head around what she'd just been given. She found herself almost missing the days when it had only been the Dark Man's memories in her head.

"The world wasn't as connected back in the early 90's as it is now," he said with a shrug.

"What does that have to do with the 90's?" Megan asked in frustrated confusion. "My mother was pregnant with me and I was born almost two decades after that."

"And there you have an explanation for why she looks so much younger than the people she went to school with," he chuckled. "Fifteen years passed here during the nine months she carried you in Tyr Sgodl. Emelia looks thirty-five because she *is* thirty-five."

"I'm really going to have to take some aspirin for this headache before we go to the dance," Megan murmured, laying the mirror down on the bench next to her.

"You're the one who wanted answers," August chuckled. "If you really want something to hurt your brain, consider this. When my people realized that the next Heir would be a hybrid, and possibly immune to the effects of iron and possessed of both the power of a witch and the Tuatha dé, they took steps to create their own. And even though he was conceived just a few months after you, he's almost thirty now."

"There's someone else like me?" Megan asked, surprised.

"Not like you," August explained. "He was created to be your opposite."

"What's he like?" Megan asked.

"I have no idea," August said. "Shortly after the battle, I cut ties with my people and let them believe that I'd died out here. To be honest, I was never very popular when I lived at Haven. I was, after all, just a scholar who taught their children. My wife was the only one who ever really understood me. She was a bit of an outcast herself, partially for being a bit too outspoken with questions about why we spent so much time focusing on a feud several millennia old. This of course wasn't appropriate behavior for a Child of Nyx, even if she was a member of the ruling family. When she fell ill, her sister actually said they'd be better off without her. So we came here. I doubt any remain who knew we ever existed at all."

"So you don't care if I have questions?" Megan asked, rubbing her temples and closing her eyes.

"I'd be worried if you didn't."

248

"What is Haven?" she asked.

"Our capital," answered without hesitation. "It's the first place we came after leaving Europe back in the early sixteenth century. It's located deep within one of the Rocky Mountains in Wyoming. The gate made of black stone you told me about in your vision of Emelia is its entrance."

"Your wife was a member of the royal family?"

"We don't actually have kings and queens like the Tuatha dé," he said. "We are, after all, Roman in origin. But yes, my wife came from the closest thing we had to royalty. Try not to hold it against her. It wasn't her fault."

"So that means my mother…" Megan couldn't speak the words aloud. It was still hard to accept that her mother was the same person she'd seen in the vision.

"Killed my brother-in-law and nephew," he said without emotion. "Along with about half of the males of fighting age."

"And you were okay with this?"

"My in-laws were horrible people on the best of days," he said. "Although I was a bit upset when it first happened. Emelia didn't wipe out their line though. My nephew had already sired children of his own. And considering what they were trying to do to the Tuatha dé, I'd say Queen Emelia showed tremendous restraint. If it had been me in her place, I'd have been tempted to wipe them all out just to make sure they couldn't rise up against you again."

"So this is why Bruce had so much trouble finding a path where you two could meet and not kill each other," Megan observed.

"Excuse me?"

"Bruce agonized over that meeting for weeks before it happened."

"I may have to have words with that presumptuous little upstart," August remarked, abandoning the neutral tone he'd used thus far.

"He only did it to keep you safe," Megan said defensively. "And the voice in my head just had a go at him for it a few days ago. You should probably leave him alone."

"Like she's got any room to talk," the hermit said irritably.

"Okay, you've got to stop doing that. Who is she?"

"You've already got all the information you need to figure that out," he said.

"Come on," she pleaded. "My head really hurts."

"Haven't you wondered why the Cat Sidhe is drawn to you and your mother?"

"Because he senses the Morrigan within my mother," Megan said, getting confirmation of what she and Bruce had already suspected. "But how can she be in both of our heads at one time?"

"Because each of you contains a part of her soul," August answered. "But not the whole thing."

"When my mother used the armor, it allowed the Morrigan to infect us, didn't it?"

"Personally, I'm not sure I'd use that particular word to describe the presence of the Celtic goddess of war and death if she were inside my head," he said, "but you come from a long line of extremely powerful and stubborn people. On both sides actually."

"I feel like I could stay out here all night and still not run out of questions," she said, reluctantly getting down from the stone. She wasn't really used to moving around in a dress and doing so with the mirror made it even more awkward. August moved forward to help her.

"I'll still be here tomorrow," he reminded her, "And likely the day after that. Much further beyond that and I can't make any promises," he joked.

"I'll hold you to that," she said, starting to head back to the house and even more importantly, toward a very large bottle of aspirin her grandfather kept in the medicine cabinet.

"By the way," he added. "You look beautiful tonight, Your Highness."

Chapter XXI: The End Comes Unnoticed

Bruce thought about borrowing his Mom's SUV now that he could legally drive, but in the end, everyone decided to let Jade drive them in Christine like she always did. An energy filled the car that he couldn't explain, reminiscent of the way they'd all felt during the summer while still working on the treehouse. This time he wasn't sure what to make of it. Maybe it just meant that things were starting to look up for them. The Joneses were a thing of the past, the town was on the mend, and he was about to take the most beautiful girl in the world to a dance.

The only oddity of the night had been an unexpected premonition that had come to him at roughly the same time Megan had been talking to the hermit in her grandmother's grove. In this premonition he saw his brother attending the dance even though he remained a year shy of being eligible to do so. Of course, having learned to trust Bruce's premonitions, Paul jumped at the opportunity and quickly dressed.

"I mean it's not like they'll say anything if Megan says he can go," Jade said while she pulled out of the driveway. "She does sort of own the school after all."

Unlike the dress the eldest Grimble had worn for the wedding, this one fit her own personal style. The cut of the red satin and black lace screamed Jade, and she'd already indicated that she looked forward to finding out what sort of reaction it got from a certain young man with no known relation to someone of the same name.

Bruce let Paul go to the door to get his friend and tried not to be hurt by the fact that his brother could tell her she looked beautiful without upsetting her. The prospect of attending a dance forbidden to him by the school administration animated him more than anything but playing his violin. Bruce hoped that whatever Paul had planned to get the attention of the goth violin girl he'd obsessed over for the past year worked or at least didn't hurt him too badly.

"Paul informed me that you told him to crash the party," Megan said, looking over the seat at him when she got in.

"You're handling those heels better than I could," Jade marveled.

"I was just as surprised when I saw it myself," Bruce said, trying not to stare at her and readjusting the partial shielding he'd learned to fashion from the visions. Now he could open his mind to her without anything leaking out beyond the emotions she deemed acceptable. "About Paul, not the heels. But aside from a couple of raised eyebrows and Mr. Danders rolling his eyes and throwing his arms up in disgust, nothing happens."

"I'm pretty sure I can survive that," Paul said excitedly. "So Andrew is meeting us there?"

"Yes," Jade answered, turning onto the road that would lead them into town. "And no teasing him about the president thing this time. He's getting self-conscious about it. It's not his fault his parents are so uneducated that they didn't know the name was already taken."

"You seriously take all the fun out of life sometimes," Megan replied. "Every single time I hear his name I hear Sam's voice overlapping it."

"Me too," Jade admitted, giggling in spite of herself. "But seriously guys…"

"He's important to you," Bruce said, watching the first of the main street shops pass by. Several of them had extended their hours now that people were starting to spend money in town again. "And you don't want him to be hurt if you can help it."

"Yeah," Jade said, looking at him in the rearview mirror in surprise.

"I can't see any problems arising when you decide to tell him about us," Bruce offered. "So feel free to spill the proverbial beans. It would be nice to talk freely around him."

"August called you a pretentious twit for controlling how he and my mom met," Megan said. "But he backed off when I told him you were just trying to protect everyone."

"He wouldn't have been if he'd seen how much damage she can do with that knife of hers," he murmured, still looking outside.

"And that's while it's still a knife," Megan said with a shudder.

"You found another runestone, didn't you?" he asked, almost asking with his mind but not wanting to leave his siblings out. "Was it a bad one?"

"Let's just say that it answered a few of my questions and created about a million more," she said. "But I did get confirmation on the identity of the cranky lady in my head."

"And?" he asked, leaning forward to see her face and test his partial shielding to the fullest. She looked amazing.

"The Morrigan," Megan answered and he could tell by the stiffening of her shields that she was worried about what this news might mean to him.

"Did you seriously just refer to a goddess of war and death, not to mention prophecy, as a cranky old lady while she is actually present inside your head?" he asked.

"Have you guys ever noticed how much he sounds like a younger version of August sometimes?" Megan asked his siblings, earning more laughter than he thought necessary for the comment.

He hardened his shields against her and went back to looking out the window.

"There he is again," Megan cried before suddenly disappearing from the front seat of the car.

As possible futures fractured before him, Bruce threw his hand out in front of a startled Paul in his panic and caught Megan with his mind before she flew into the wall of a shop where the alley opened to Main Street. The effort of stopping her without the sudden deceleration killing her took every bit of reflexive protection he could muster. Next to her, stood a very startled man in a trench coat.

Jade hit the brakes when she noticed her friend's absence and slammed Bruce's face into the back of her seat. He almost blacked out from the strain, but his worry for Megan kept him alert. Then, before Paul could finish asking him if he was okay, he walked the shadows to her side just in time for the oddly dressed stranger to disappear.

"Damn it, Bruce!" she yelled. "I almost had him. Why did you stop me?"

"You're welcome," he growled, trying not to vomit from the piercing ache across his entire skull. "I don't suppose it occurred to you that thanks to my sister's lead foot, we were doing about forty when you chose to jump out? We don't lose momentum when we pass through the shadows. The only reason we're not scraping you off of that wall is because I saw you die with just enough time to keep it from happening. Have I ever told you that I experience the future as if it were *real*? So okay, I'm *sooo* sorry that you missed the Lost Boys wanna-be. And I'm sorry that I want to tell you how beautiful you are, and I know that none of this is your fault," he said, running out of steam and swaying on the spot. For just a moment he considered calling it a night and walking the

255

shadows directly to his bed where he could sleep for a few years.

"Your nose is bleeding, Bro," Paul said. Ever the prepared scout, he handed Bruce some tissues from his pocket.

Now that the adrenaline had faded, he sat down hard on the stone step of the next shop and held the tissues to his nose. He closed his eyes and begged the world to stop moving so fast.

"Are you okay?" Jade asked, and even though she did so quietly, each syllable pierced the back of his eyeballs like nails.

"Just give me a minute," he said, slowing his breathing. He felt Megan directly in front of him and reluctantly opened his eyes.

"Can you dry chug these?" she asked, holding out a couple of aspirins she must have had in her tiny purse.

"Oh God, I love you," he said, eagerly taking the pills from her hand and swallowing them whole.

"We know," Jade replied.

"Give me your left shoe," he said, mainly to end the awkward silence.

"Why?" Megan said, pulling it off and handing it to him.

With a theatrical flick of his finger, the heel snapped off and fell to the ground. He took the two pieces in his hands, willed the glue that had held the heel in place to return to a liquid so he could reattach it again before fusing both pieces back together.

"You have no idea how tempted I was to let you fall on your butt while we danced," he admitted. "But like I said, the future feels real to me, and pointing and laughing at you once is good enough, so I guess I'll forego the reality. Jade, Andrew is horribly afraid you've stood him up, so you'd better give him a call and tell him we're running late."

Megan hugged him when he stood up, and he knew she was close to crying. For the first time, down a path that started with those tears he caught sight of a life in which she became his girlfriend. It started with her feeling badly about the way she'd taken him for granted. She'd allow herself to enter that sort of a relationship even though it wouldn't change her actual feelings toward him. But maybe that would come in time? Maybe, maybe, maybe. It all came down to justifying a life he knew wasn't best for her just to kiss her the way he wanted to. It was then that he realized that he really did love her, because he cared far more about her happiness than he did his own. There were no guarantees of any kisses at all down the other paths, but he'd wait until they meant as much to her as they did to him. And if they never did? Then he'd love her enough for the two of them. But even so, it hurt to watch that opportune instant come and pass while she stood before him with tears brimming in her eyes.

"You've had a rough night," he told her. "And I'm going to need some serious laughter to get that vision out of my head." Then he put one arm around the girl he wanted to marry someday and the other around the sister he'd only recently come to appreciate. Paul happily moved to Megan's other side as they walked back to the still idling Christine.

"You should seriously text Andrew," he told his sister again, settling into his seat with a great deal of pain that he hid from the others lest it ruin their night.

"Nope," Jade giggled wickedly. "This way he'll be even more excited when he does see me."

The rest of the drive was quiet for a mixture of reasons. He already missed the energy from before since he'd expended almost all of his back on Main Street. He closed his eyes and leaned his head back against the seat, praying that the aspirin kicked in soon.

"Is that the ward you guys are always talking about?" Paul asked when they drew close to the school.

"You can see it?" Megan asked, looking back at him in surprise.

"Shimmery wall with hints of blue," he said. "Sounds like the hornet's nest Jade and I found in the woods that time."

"Jade, can you see anything?" Bruce asked, opening his eyes and wondering if he might not have a concussion.

"Still nothing," she answered, squinting hard at the road ahead before giving up and casting an envious glare at Paul.

The aspirin seemed to have taken the edge off of the pain when the school came into view. He'd heard about these dances, but until this year he'd never been able to attend one. He fully expected cheesiness in the extreme and from what he could see through his foresight, he was not going to be disappointed.

Megan unexpectedly linked arms with him as they went up the stone steps and stayed that way when they walked into the cafeteria. She hadn't been that comfortable with touching him since the early days of their friendship.

Judging from the pulsing beat of the bass, the PTA had used a sizable chunk of the money Sam donated for the event to buy a new sound system, which was probably for the best since they'd been forced to use the school's ancient PA system in the past.

Furthermore, considering the way the balloon arch at the cafeteria entrance glowed, they'd bought a set of black lights as well. This certainly wasn't for the best because it made Megan glow in the dark. Jade took one look at her and burst out laughing.

It doesn't matter, Bruce sent when he felt her start to release his arm. *This is fun. You were about to say that you look ridiculous, but you don't. The only way that you stand out is that you're the most beautiful, exotic thing I've ever seen. Everyone looks weird under blacklights, and they really should have warned us. Wait until you see the girls who wore white dresses. Now be quiet or you'll miss this.*

"Did we know it was going to be an under the sea dance?" Paul asked, staring at the archway. "I mean, someone totally nailed the look of two sea anemones fighting."

Maybe it was the stress of knowing that he'd soon have to dance in front of other people, or maybe he just really liked the comparison. But Andrew started laughing and couldn't stop. Within seconds Jade's concern turned comical and spread to the rest. They could barely walk by the time they passed through the twisted conglomeration of long, brightly colored and glowing balloons.

But the PTA wasn't finished. Hundreds of loose balloons covered the floors, lit by the swirling pinpricks of a disco ball. If this weren't enough, they'd also mounted several mini laser light projectors above the stage which now sent a swirling array of beams across the room, blinding them every few seconds.

Just then Mr. Danders strode across the room, kicking balloons out of his way as he walked grimly toward the office. The teacher chaperones parted before him, unwilling to slow his escape.

"It's going to be a miracle if no one has a seizure," he grumbled as he passed where their small group stood, still recovering from their uncontrolled laughter. Then, realizing that they'd heard him he added, "I hope you guys have fun. I'm going to go lock myself in my office and take a good long look at my life decisions."

"You too," Paul said before remembering that he wasn't supposed to be there.

The assistant principal turned quickly and looked hard at the youngest Grimble.

"Seizures," Andrew squealed, unable to contain his laughter any longer and setting them all off again.

Mr. Danders threw up his hands in disgust and turned on his heel to make a very hasty if not so dignified retreat.

"My eyes actually hurt looking at this," Paul panted quickly, holding his stomach in discomfort.

"I love it," Megan said, dancing along as she dragged Bruce toward the dance floor, all signs of her previous discomfort forgotten. Seeing that she'd lose the tiny purse in her hand before the night was out, he took it from her hand and made a show of putting it in the pocket of his slacks while actually sending it to Christine's glove compartment where it could be easily retrieved if needed.

They passed through several couples who lined the edges of the floor as if unsure how to proceed. From the corner of his eyes Bruce saw something black streak across the stage.

It's not every day that you see one of the oldest creatures on earth chasing a laser, he sent, directing Megan's gaze toward Mr. Bob just in time for him to pounce a balloon, causing the first of many loud bangs that would punctuate the night.

"This is so perfect," Megan yelled over the music.

Watching her as the music began to flavor her movements, he had to agree.

Jade and Paul had been teaching him to dance ever since that night on the beach, and with his martial arts training, he felt mildly adequate. Megan was pulling him along by the hand, and even though a part of him couldn't even daydream about her ever loving him, he could see that they were going to have a lot of fun.

"Good luck at the race, Bruce!" one of the upperclassmen called from somewhere in the direction of the punch bowl.

Startled, he waved in response. Nearby, he noticed Glenn and Chuck watching him, apparently not knowing what to do without Allison to rule over them. For so long his entire world had centered around avoiding those two. Now he barely gave them a moment's thought even when they were clearly watching him. His extra senses would warn him if they tried anything, and his abilities would make them regret anything they tried to do to him. But this realization didn't give him any peace. In place of that simple fear, he'd taken on the responsibility for everyone he knew. Checking and rechecking all of their futures until sometimes he'd missed half the night's sleep in worry.

Jade reached the balloon strewn floor before them with a reluctant Andrew in tow, and even though the boy looked even more terrified than Bruce felt, he still danced. When Jade smiled at him, Bruce worried that he of no known relation might very well explode. Or maybe it was just the way the black lights made them all look as if they'd spent a week camping at Chernobyl, and Andrew was really feeling pretty good about life.

Paul ran up to a girl several grades his senior, grabbed her by the hand and dragged her from her chair and out on the floor with him. The girl, though shocked by his audacity, took one look up into his handsome face and came willingly. Just like that there were two couples dancing with balloons bouncing all about them.

In the instant before he and Megan started to dance, Bruce was given the gift of one impossibly clear and unobstructed vision. It didn't matter what they did right now. Nothing in how well or badly they danced on this psychedelic nightmare of a dance floor would make any difference tomorrow when they woke or even in the years to come. They wouldn't remember what songs played or how they'd moved to them. But they'd remember the laughter and the camaraderie for the rest of their lives.

Megan felt him come alive as he took her by the waist and spun her,
making her laugh so hard that the overworked electrical system surged.
But the visions showed him what to do, and he became the lightning rod
that grounded her power and allowed her to pretend that she was nothing

more than a glowing teenage ghost girl, even if she'd never be anything less than everything to him.

And though it might have gotten off to a bit of a rocky start, it proved to be a glorious night that would forever come to their minds when they thought of the last days of their childhood.

For a moment, Bruce noticed Jacob Routh near the doorway to Mr. Green's workroom. Once again, he noticed that the specter appeared more substantial than he had in the past. Or maybe he felt more at place among the other ghosts in the room. But when Bruce looked closely, he noticed something odd. The Dark Man wasn't focused on Megan like he normally was. Following his gaze, Bruce realized he was looking at Paul as if noticing and recognizing him for the first time.

Chapter XXII: Return to the Jubilee

Megan could feel Paul's agitation all the way from the road to her room when Christine pulled into the driveway, giving birth to a light headache near the base of her skull. Stopping by the medicine cabinet, she downed two aspirin and grabbed a couple for Bruce too.

"Are you sure you don't want to come?" she asked her grandfather, running into the kitchen and giving him a hug.

"No," I'm going to go see the Harrises," he answered, happily returning the hug. "You kids have fun and tell Paul I hope he gets the girl."

"I will," she giggled.

Paul had already gotten out of the car to let her slide into the middle of the back seat since Andrew would be riding up front with Jade. A cloud of cologne assaulted her senses before she even got to the car.

"Wow," she said, hesitating to come closer. "And I thought your anxiety was going to be the strongest thing coming off of you."

"I told you," Jade called through the open door from the driver's seat. "Just because it won't kill Bruce any more if you wear cologne, it doesn't mean you have to wear the whole bottle at one time."

"Is it really that strong?" he asked in horror.

"Stay there," Bruce said, getting out of the car and walking around to his brother. Then, holding his hands about an inch away from his brother's chest, he focused and a faint mist rose from the would-be

Romeo's shirt to float away in the breeze. It immediately became easier to breathe.

"I thought you might need more of these," Megan said, handing him the aspirin which he happily swallowed.

"You're an angel," he said, rubbing the back of his neck. "I've had a headache all day."

"Thanks, Bro," Paul said, relieved. "Sorry about that. I've never been able to wear anything like that before, and I wasn't sure how much to use."

"Are you still hurting from last night?" Megan asked when she slid into the seat next to him.

He shrugged in response, wincing when it moved his neck.

"Did you get your dad to look at it?" she persisted.

"Then I'd have to explain how it happened without explaining how it happened," he replied. "I'm okay. Don't worry about it. I'll sleep on a heating pad tonight, and I'll be better in the morning."

As the car began to jounce down the poorly maintained road, Megan straightened up in her seat so she could get her arm up over the back. Then she held her hand just a fraction of an inch away from the back of his neck.

No matter what she did or how many times she accidentally hurt him, he never wavered in his trust. So he just sat there, waiting to see what she was going to do. Of course, he might have already seen it through his foresight. But judging from the look of blissful surprise that came a second later when she allowed heat to radiate from her hand into the damaged muscles in his neck, she thought not. The hardest part was judging how much heat would make him feel better without hurting him. His tolerance was far removed from her own.

"So the Jubilee is always on a Friday? she asked as his eyes rolled back into his head. She almost laughed when she realized how much he looked like Fang getting his stomach scratched at that moment.

"It always starts on the same day of the month," Jade answered from the front seat, turning fast and pressing them all into each other in the backseat, which wasn't as bad now that Bruce had taken care of the cologne. "You were lucky that your first one was on a weekend. They're not nearly as much fun when your parents know you've got school the next day."

"Not that Emelia was likely to care even if it did," Paul added before remembering that he shouldn't talk about the missing McGeehee.

"It's on a Friday again this year because it's a leap year and those years are divisible by seven. We've got plenty of time to get there before they open," Bruce explained, noticing that Paul was checking his watch again for the third time in as many minutes. "And as you probably remember from that time Jade tried to sneak in, there's no early admission."

"You guys probably think I'm crazy," Paul said, trying to occupy his hands by drumming on the back of the seat. "I mean I've never even talked to her."

"Yes," Jade said, "And if you don't stop doing that while I'm driving I'm going to pull over and lock you in the trunk until the race tomorrow."

Paul stopped abruptly.

"Be nice," Megan said, patting him on the leg with the hand not working on his brother's neck. "I think it's sweet."

"You wouldn't if he'd made you spend the morning helping him tune our old piano," Bruce countered, reaching up and removing her hand reluctantly from his neck. "Thanks, that feels a lot better. But you're going to get hurt trying to sit like that while she's driving."

"Hey, when I realized you could fix the cracked soundboard it was just the right thing to do," Paul said, starting to fidget again.

They pulled up in front of a well-kept if small house near Kate's place. Andrew immediately came out the front door.

"Hey guys," he said, climbing into the front seat with his girlfriend. "I've been meaning to tell you, Bruce. You did an awesome job on the restoration of this beauty. You'd never know Christine was sitting in the woods for decades with the way she looks now."

"I still think Big Bertha sounded better," Paul said.

"Keep it up, and my trunk will reek of cologne for months," Jade said.

Paul clamped his lips shut.

"Thanks, but I had a lot of help," Bruce replied, trying to take his sister's irritation away from Paul.

"And the main projector at the Palace?" the curly haired boy pressed.

"Same thing," Bruce answered, wishing Andrew would find a new topic, or that his sister would decide to let him in on what was happening. "I think it's already having problems again. Kate is thinking about updating it with one of the newer ones so the Palace can start running more new releases that don't come in older formats. I like your house, Andrew."

"Why?" he asked. "I mean, it's nothing like the ones where you guys live."

"I love Mid Century Modern houses," Bruce answered. "There were some really cool things they did during that period. Just because it's not incredibly old or incredibly new doesn't mean it's not great."

"Well, thanks," Andrew replied. Then he looked around in concern, trying to find something else to talk about.

"Jade told you that you had to talk more, didn't she?" Megan asked.

He looked guiltily at his girlfriend, and then the car filled with the kind of laughter they'd shared at the dance. Even Paul seemed to loosen up for a second. And in the midst of that moment, the voice of the Morrigan whispered to Megan.

This is the last time it will be like this.

Megan asked for an explanation, but the presence departed as quickly as it had appeared.

"It's hard to hang out with the cool crowd," Andrew said with such sincerity that it startled her.

"What do you mean?" Bruce asked. "They need to let you out more if you think we're the cool kids."

"Who else?" Andrew asked, puzzled by their reactions. "You guys single-handedly ran the Jones cartel out of Nickelville. You're friends with Mr. Wise, who not only saved the factory where both of my parents work, but also seems to be investing in every business in town. For the first time ever, we've got more jobs than we have workers to fill them. My dad reckons we should save up and buy some real estate so we can cash in on it when people start moving here from out of town to fill the empty positions. So yeah, I'd say I'm hanging with the cool kids."

"Geeze," Jade said, thinking over what he'd said. "When you put it like that, all I can do is wonder how I'm supposed to rebel against the system when it sounds like I've become part of it? I'm so ashamed of myself."

The chatter that followed felt much less forced. But by the time they pulled into the parking place where the attendant directed them, Paul had withdrawn into himself again. Tensed like the trigger of a steel trap, he had the door open and was already halfway to the admission line before Christine rolled to a stop.

"Good luck!" Jade called after him, but whether he couldn't hear or couldn't think of anything beyond the girl he'd seen the year before, he left them behind and disappeared into the woods.

Both Bruce and Megan sighed in relief as his deafening emotions moved out of range. Jade cast them a knowing glance as they climbed out of the car.

"I wish Grandpa had come," Megan said, walking with them toward the path that would lead them into the Jubilee clearing.

"He's still feeling under the weather?" Bruce asked.

"I think it has more to do with not wanting to be here without Emelia or Alan," she answered. "And he is probably right to go visit Tom and Esther. She's getting worse faster now."

"That's Mr. Harris and his wife, right?" Andrew asked Jade.

"Yes," she answered, taking his hand and falling into step with him. "She's got cancer and not much time left."

"That's sad," Andrew said. "She looked good at the wedding when she was talking to Megan, though."

"Mr. Harris said that was one of her good days," Megan said. "I really like her."

"Everyone does," Bruce added out loud, but inside Megan's mind he added, *Can you feel the Jubilee field from here?*

No, she said after casting her senses in that direction. *Was it that way last year?*

I have no idea, he replied. *I'd only just started to realize something weird was going on by that time. I know being inside the torches that surrounded that field felt amazing though, more than they ever had before.*

Same here. But surely if anything was amiss, Mom would have warned us. If I remember correctly, her exact words were to tell me not

269

to worry, that it was always like this.

And what a shock, I can't see anything for the next several days. What little I can see then doesn't make any sense.

He fixed her with an icy stare.

I promise I won't rush off to certain death without consulting you first.

"No," he said out loud, making Andrew look back at them, puzzled. *Not without taking me with you.* He extended his pinky, and she reluctantly hooked it.

Andrew looked at Jade, and she shrugged as if to say, *see they're totally crazy.*

Megan thought about what Bruce had told her while they waited in line. What could possibly block out his foresight that completely? As far as she knew, everything was going pretty well. Guarded Wood no longer wanted to eat them, and Bruce wasn't courting death in the form of magical elevators any more. Maybe her mother was coming home?

They followed Jade and Andrew down the woodland path, which had been lined, probably to Mr. Grimble's delight, with glow sticks instead of paper bag candles. Once again, the woodland creatures chose not to show themselves although Megan could feel them at the edge of her senses. As they walked, it was hard not to think about the previous Jubilee. So much had happened in the short space of a year. Tomorrow would mark one year since Bruce had won the race and put Glenn Floyd in his place. It marked one year since she'd met Sam, and it also marked one year since she'd discovered the power of judgment with the now absent Allison Jones. Even though the events of that one day were life-changing, the things that came after were even more so. She'd finally communicated with the Dark Man and fulfilled the town's promise to him. They'd built the tree house, met August, saved the boundary, and explored Guarded Wood. Had it really just been a little over a year?

Without understanding why she'd done it, she realized she'd taken Bruce's hand in her own while thinking about the race. But they'd held hands a lot that first time, and it only seemed right that they continue the tradition. After all, he certainly didn't seem to mind.

When they reached the edge of the trees, both Megan and Bruce found themselves standing at the boundary of a huge and powerful ward. Like the one that encircled the school, this one flared slightly in the visible spectrum, a band of translucent green light that climbed from deep in the ground at their feet to form a dome around Jubilee Field.

That would explain why we didn't feel anything in here from the outside, Bruce sent. *It's a really weird ward though. As far as I can tell, it doesn't actually do anything. And it feels old.*

It's watching... and waiting for something to happen, she sent. Jade and Andrew passed through without any disturbance at all. *I can feel something familiar in this. I don't think it's malicious. Should we round everyone up and leave anyway?*

I'm not sure even Jade could get Paul out of here. Your mother said it was safe last year, and she would have definitely felt this. Even though she's withheld a lot from us in the past, she'd never do anything to put us into danger.

Well, except for letting us detonate bombs and repair magical barriers that almost eat us, she replied with a grin.

You're right, he sent, chuckling aloud as he did, *aside from those things she's never once put us in danger. I say we go for it.*

Still holding hands even though it had been months since they'd needed to do so, they crossed the ward. It passed across Bruce without noticing, but Megan could feel it take note of her, as if it had been waiting for her to return to Jubilee field.

271

The energy that flooded their senses when they entered the field made it impossible to think about anything else. Their senses strengthened by an order of magnitude, filling them to the point where they feared they might not contain it all.

"They should definitely bottle this and sell it as a headache remedy," Bruce whispered in ecstasy.

Linking her arm through his, Megan hurried to catch up with Jade and Andrew.

"I hope she doesn't like corn dogs," Bruce said and both Jade and Megan laughed. Andrew looked confused, but happy to be there with Jade just the same.

"Should we see if we can find Paul?" Megan asked.

"No," Jade answered. "He doesn't need us there for this. I don't want to see what happens if whatever he's planning works, and I might have to kill her if she breaks his heart. Whatever happens, we'll see him when he needs us to."

They all nodded in silent agreement.

"So Andrew," Jade said, clearly intending to change the subject.

"Yes?"

"You indicated that you were in possession of, and I quote, mad skills, bordering on the supernatural when it came to the ring toss."

"I do recall making such a claim," he replied, seeing the booth under discussion nearby.

"Would you care to test your skills against mine?" she asked.

"How would a mortal like me ever hope to compete with a goddess such as yourself?" he answered.

"Now you see why I like this one," Jade whispered to Megan, loud enough for everyone within ten feet to hear.

Not trusting themselves to play without skewing the results with their abilities, they watched Jade and her boyfriend compete for several rounds. The boy with the non-existent relationship that they no longer spoke of was indeed good.

"I think we should leave them to this and go try out the knife throw," Bruce suggested. "I know I'll lose, but it will still be fun."

"Do you think it's because of her?" Megan asked, tapping her head.

"She was a goddess of war," Bruce answered with a shrug. He was pretty sure that the carnie running the knife throw remembered Megan from the previous year as well and looked none too happy at her return.

"Should I just give you the choice of my inventory now?" he asked when Bruce gave him enough for several games.

"Where would the fun be in that?" Megan asked, motioning for Bruce to go first.

He'd improved greatly under Emelia's tutelage, managing to stick every one of the knives within the second largest circle without his abilities. But the man who ran the booth obviously wasn't the only one who remembered her. Several of the operators from other booths left their posts in order to get a better view when she threw.

Megan sunk the first blade in the bullseye with a flick of her wrist. Like Bruce, her form had improved.

"Lucky shot!" a young man not much older than Bruce called. "Do it again!"

Giving Bruce an evil grin to which he responded with a shrug, she picked up a handful of the knives and began to throw them in rapid succession until she'd filled the bullseye and then proceeded to place one perfectly in the dividing lines between each distinction of the target.

The crowd burst into applause and even the carnie in charge of the booth clapped.

"I'd stay on her good side if you want to live to a happy old age," the man told him. "Now which of my treasures do you intend to deprive me of?"

Bruce watched Megan as she looked, likely thinking about how much she'd like to repeat last year's experience of making him carry a truckload of stuffed animals around the whole night.

"She wants one of these," Bruce said, reaching out on impulse and picking up a ring that he recognized as hematite from Jade's ramblings.

"I do?" Megan said, eyeing the big ring speculatively. "That's not even my size."

"Hush, ye of little faith," he said. "Are you willing to count us even for this?"

"I'd be more than happy to get off that easily," the man answered. "As long as the deadly lass agrees."

"She thinks he's crazy," Megan replied, "But she does have faith in him. So against her better judgement, she agrees."

"Why is she talking about herself in the third person?" Bruce asked, taking the ring.

"I wondered the same thing," the carnie admitted, "But I was too afraid of her to ask."

"It's a family thing," Megan said, frowning at the ring.

"But if you change your mind," the man said quietly, leaning close so only they could hear, "Come back for something better. You just guaranteed me at least three times my normal business as every one of those boys out there tries to one up you. And it's unlikely that they'll hit a thing."

"Bruce," she said when they were further away. "Why do I want a ring that I could probably fit on Sam's big toe?"

274

"Do me a favor and stand in front of me so no one notices what I'm about to do," he said. "Now clasp it between your hands like this." He placed both of his hands around hers, took a deep breath and channeled his power as a smith into the ring. Her eyes grew wide as she felt it grow warm within her hands and begin to move. He made sure that it never became hot enough to be uncomfortable, although given her heat tolerance, it probably wouldn't have mattered. He'd seen her grab glowing coals from the campfire without burning herself. Light leaked through their overlapping hands and even outlined the bones within.

Bruce staggered when he finished, just as he'd done with the barbeque pit, even though he hadn't imparted any of his soul in its forging.

"What did you do?" she asked, opening her fingers to reveal an ornately carved ring. "What did making this do to you?"

"It just sapped my strength," he answered, steadying himself. "There's no lasting harm done to me. But wait until you find out what it does."

"Um," she said, not wanting to sound ungrateful but feeling the need to point out the obvious, "It's still too big for my fingers."

"That," he said, picking it up and sliding it past the knuckle on her right thumb. "Is because I never intended for you to wear it on your finger." Then he pulled his phone out of his pocket and placed it directly into her open palm.

"What are you doing?" she cried. "I'll fry it." Then she waited for the inevitable hiss of smoke which turned out not to be so inevitable after all. She looked up in surprise. "I don't understand."

"I'm sorry I didn't think of this earlier," he explained, taking his phone back long enough to unlock it so she could play with it. "It's pretty ingenious if I do say so myself. The iron in the hematite absorbs the stray emissions you give off all the time and keeps it from interfering with electromagnetic fields. It shouldn't interfere with your abilities in any way, and you should still be able to pulse if you need to knock something out on purpose. But you know what the best part is? Your waste energy is what powers it. Given how much you normally give off, the thing should be almost indestructible. But because it is powered by its contact with you, it would probably destroy it if you took it off."

"This is so amazing," she said, handing him back his phone. "Why did you make it to fit my right thumb?"

"So there wouldn't be any confusion about what it might mean," he answered quietly then added, "This is the first time you've ever been able to play with an electronic device. You don't want to try it out?"

"Another time," she replied, taking his arm in hers. "We're here, now. I don't want to miss this. Electronics will still be there tomorrow. Let's leave your sister and her boyfriend to duke it out over the games. What do you want to see?"

"Call it professional curiosity, but I'd like to see the fortune teller you saw last year," he answered.

"Are you sure?" she asked, frowning in concern. "That woman spooked Jade and me pretty badly."

"All the more reason to go," he said. "Anything scary enough to frighten either one of you is something I've got to see."

They found the tent where they remembered it and realized just as they opened the flap that there was no sign on the outside to mark what they knew it to be.

"Excuse us," Megan said when they stepped inside and found the same woman wearing exactly the same costume that she had the year before. "I'm sorry if we're intruding, but I wondered if you remembered me?"

"As if it were only a few hours ago," the woman chuckled.

"So you wouldn't mind reading our fortunes?" Bruce asked.

"I always have time for those who share the burden of foresight," the woman said, startling Bruce with her easy recognition of his abilities. "And for a Daughter of Crina as well."

"You called me that last year!" Megan exclaimed, remembering at last. "Do you know what that name means? Will you tell us what you know?"

"Before the sun makes a full trip around the earth, you shall have your explanation from one far more qualified to answer than I. Though she may be a bit cross with you. The custom of your clan bade you to visit her the last time you were here, and you did not do so."

"We don't understand," Bruce said.

"By this time tomorrow, you will," the strange woman replied. "But I must not say more than I should at this time, or I risk bringing you misfortune. If you leave now, you might just get a chance to eat before things get interesting."

Chapter XXIII: Luminita Returns

Luminita could tell by the way the night sky brightened ever so slightly that she and the others had leapfrogged through time yet again. Then came the rising tide of emotion, the hope and the horror that he might yet find her even while losing hope that he ever would. She closed her eyes before the strength of her emotions could summon the phantom wisps of her lost magic, willing herself to be calm. If she didn't, she put everyone around her in danger of being chosen. Even that, however, was at best a stalling tactic, because Jubilee Field would have its sacrifice before the night ended. But this way it wouldn't be quite as much her fault. At least that's what she told herself. So she breathed, forcing herself to live in this new present even though it would be a year past in only a few hours. When at last she silenced her thoughts, for just the tiniest fraction of an instant, she heard a whispered echo of familiar magic, faint as the memory of a taste on her lips. It teased and taunted her, threatening to snare her in dreams of what lay too far behind in the past.

I'll always find my way back to you, he whispered in her memory.

When she opened her eyes again, she looked down to confirm the presence of the numbered stake which marked where she'd faded out the previous year. It had been Crina who realized that she reappeared in exactly the same place where she'd faded out the year before, and likewise, it had been her idea to mark the spot with a wooden stake.

Sadly, Luminita looked across the spike-studded field and waited for the others to arrive. Two hundred in all, one for each year of her long confinement. Before the night ended, her magic would snare one more.

As she watched, the others began to fade in as well. Each of them, like her, trapped within this endless night, doomed to walk eternity within the torches that marked the edges of their prison for a few short hours before her curse snatched them all away yet again.

"Welcome, Eldest," a young man said with reverence, dressed unknowingly in the period costumes of a dozen different decades, all of which she remembered like they'd been only weeks ago.

"Don't call me that," she said wearily, ignoring his overly bright smile and lingering eye. "Did anything happen here during the lost time? I thought I felt something."

"Just a handful of teens who snuck in a few months ago," he replied, dropping his eyes to show his shame. "I chased them away, and they did not return."

"Very well," she said, moderating her feelings lest the magic around them fixate on this young man. She had no desire at all to spend eternity with this one following after her. "Is there anything I should know about this year?"

"It is no longer the town's anniversary, so things should be fairly uneventful. Will you need to sleep again soon?"

"No," she answered, starting to walk toward the main festival ground, careful to avoid any of the other stakes. "Last year was my first in this cycle. I shouldn't need to rest again for several more years."

Her eyes traveled the perimeter and the torches that marked it. She knew it hadn't moved in all of the years since the accident, but sometimes it felt as if it were slowly drawing closer to the center. Maybe it was only a premonition of what would eventually come to pass. Maybe

279

in a thousand years there would be so many traveling through time with her that they'd run out of room in the clearing and no one would be able to come in and sacrifice themselves to the next cycle. In the beginning such thoughts had frightened her. Now she wished she'd ended it while she could have done so without taking all of the others with her. Wisps of magic began to creep through the edges of her vision.

"How do you do it?" the young man asked.

"Do what?" she asked, grateful for the distraction.

"Go so many years without rest?"

"Do they no longer teach the young about us?" she asked, wanting to be irritated, but determined not to give in and bring this idiot permanently into her orbit.

"They do," he said sadly, "but I am often a poor student."

"I see," she said, deciding that the best way to make him leave was to answer his questions. "Were you here last year when we faded away?"

"I was given the honor of marking the location of your return," he said as if driving a stake with the number one on it into the ground was the greatest of his short life's aspirations.

"For me, there was no passage of time between that moment and the one when I just returned. I gained no wisdom or insight during that time. I have not become something holy as some among you claim. I was given no visions of our salvation. Only an echo of what may never be again."

She could tell her curt reply upset him. She also knew he'd given himself over completely to the cult of her preservation, and his adoration sickened her. Not enough to make her seek the oblivion of sleep for another decade, but enough to make the phantom remnants of her magic gather closer. She reminded herself yet again to get herself under control or he might be chosen. Spending eternity with one talkative idiot was more than enough.

"Please forgive me for my impertinence, Eldest," he said, making her sigh in disgust. "I apologize for taking up so much of your time here. I hope this doesn't hurt my chances…"

"Your chances for what?" she snarled, motioning to the clearing where others continued to appear next to numbered stakes in the ground, "To share my punishment as these poor souls do?"

"It is a great honor," he pressed, bowing his head.

"An honor to be plucked from everyone and everything you ever loved?" she spat, "To watch them grow old and die while you barely age?"

Drawn by the strength of her emotions, the tendrils of energy, invisible to everyone except her, grew bolder, seeking the source of her anger. She closed her eyes and took several calming breaths.

"You need to go," she whispered.

"I have offended you," the young man said, backing away from her.

"My betrothed died in the accident that caused this travesty two hundred years ago, but for me little more than a month has passed. I would never wish this curse on another."

"But I would be honored if you chose…"

"What do you think of me that I would ever knowingly choose someone for this fate?" she yelled, no longer caring if this idiot's feelings were hurt.

"Someone showed up in a bad mood," the seer said from behind her. "Young man, I'd go find something to do elsewhere if I were you."

Luckily for him, he finally listened.

"Alas," the seer said, watching him go appreciatively. "At least you woke up to a handsome one. I don't think mine has bathed since the last Jubilee."

"By all means," Luminita said, happily shifting her anger to someone safe by virtue of having already been chosen. "Feel free to follow him. I wouldn't mind at all if I didn't see you for the rest of the night."

"It's not time yet," the seer said sadly. "And he's not the one."

"Why did you have to be one of the ones to follow me here?" Luminita asked. "I wasn't particularly fond of you in the old days."

"Is that any way to talk to one of your oldest friends?" the fortune-teller asked.

"Just because I've known you longer than anyone else here doesn't make us friends," Luminita replied, glad to see the magic dissipate.

"And here I thought you'd want to know that the Daughters of Crina have not passed from the world," the seer taunted.

"You saw one of my sister's descendants?" Luminita asked, opening her eyes. "Why didn't she greet me as custom demands?"

"I don't think she knows who she is," the seer answered. "She and another young woman came to my tent for a reading, which shouldn't have happened."

"Why not?" Luminita asked.

"I'd already taken the sign down," the seer answered. "I was to begin my sleep cycle last year. But they came in and asked me for a reading, clearly knowing the tent's purpose. But that's not even the strangest part. I gave her friend a reading easily enough, but when I tried to read your sister's descendent, someone took me over and did it in my place."

"How can that be?"

"I have no idea, but I can say with certainty that I don't ever want to repeat the experience." the seer answered with a shudder. "I've never felt power like that. She just pushed me aside until she'd relayed her prediction to your sister's descendant."

"So you're sure it wasn't this girl who pushed you out?" Luminita asked.

"Definitely not," the seer answered. "It was female, but felt older than the world."

"Why didn't you send her to me?"

"It wasn't the right time yet," the seer answered ominously.

Luminita held her with an angry stare.

"She will return tonight."

"How will I recognize her when she does?"

"She looks exactly like the last one, but if that one was a candle in the night, this one is a forest fire."

"Very well, now that you mention it, I think I might have seen her at the closing performance," Luminita said, wondering if she could trust what the irritating woman said at face value. "Send Jasmine to me. I want to speak with her about the costume she chose for me when last I was here. I was not amused by the way I stood out, and I will not tolerate such treatment again. I am not a doll to dress for her amusement."

"And you're sure you don't wish to sleep?" the fortune teller asked her slyly.

"What, and dream as I always do of all that might have been had I not listened to Jacob Routh? I think not. And have Jasmine bring me my violin as well."

Dressed in a comfortable dress that drew far fewer looks than the previous one, Luminita walked through the festival grounds, nodding in recognition at those she remembered from the early years. She tried to ignore the way the carnival folk watched her in cautious admiration, alternating between the ones who hoped for immortality and those who made the sign to ward off evil when they thought she wouldn't notice.

As she approached the small wooden stage they'd built between two towering laurel trees, she listened to the old man play a few runs on the battered upright piano to make sure it didn't need last minute tuning. He'd told her his name when she first met him as a young man, eager to win her favor and the gift of eternal life. She couldn't remember it, even though it had only been a few days ago from her perspective. Neither did she know the name of the old woman who'd played cello before this new one. That one had been young in the beginning too, but eventually her arthritis forced her to stop. At least Luminita had summoned enough presence to thank her for her long years of service even though she didn't honestly care.

Luminita was neither unfriendly nor narcissistic by nature, but this half-life had taken so much from her while only providing the chance to see her sister's descendants in return. But then they'd stopped coming as well. When that happened, she'd withdrawn into herself and slept for a dozen years, which was long even by her standards.

She realized she'd drifted off into thought when she found everyone watching her expectantly. She wanted to tell them not to stare at her, that she was just a woman with a broken heart. But she needed them to keep coming every year. She needed them to bring an audience to play for, because that was all she had left to keep her sane. And of course, she needed them to be here so she wouldn't wait out the hours until she left again in the dark without even this tiny glimmer of hope.

Her people gathered around the stage as she took out her violin and checked it over. It was a tradition practiced by many, but only understood by those who'd been traveling with her the longest. It was those early victims, the ones that Crina had lured herself, that knew Luminita's oldest sister thought her magic might eventually return on its own. So they gathered dutifully, the ones who understood that being chosen was no gift at all, and prayed that this would be the year she set them free.

Just before she brought her instrument to her shoulder, she noticed an unfamiliar young woman. She had a violin case at her side and watched with an expectancy that drew Luminita's eye.

"You there," she called, surprising the girl so badly that she almost fled. "Is that your violin?"

The girl turned quickly to the woman next to her, one who, given her resemblance to the young musician, almost had to be her mother. The older woman nodded, and the girl came forward, probably worried that she'd broken some unwritten law.

"Would you like to join us?" Luminita asked.

"I couldn't possibly," the girl said, shaking her head vigorously while staring at the ground before her.

"Aside from the closing performances, I haven't played with another violin in…" she paused, not wanting to put voice to the rest of the thought. "Well, let us say that it has been a very long time indeed. If you do not enjoy the experience then you are welcome to return to the audience when they admit the townsfolk."

The girl, with the encouragement of the crowd, reluctantly joined Luminita on the stage.

"Just play whatever you want and I'll join in," Luminita encouraged.

When the girl began to play, the Eldest brought her bow to the strings and joined her. As had happened each time she'd played since that fateful night beneath Jacob's church, there was an instant in which it felt as if her magic would come when she called. But even though she could sense it in the air around her, it no longer obeyed.

Crina had spent the rest of her life trying to free Luminita. But in the end, her only success was in convincing their clan to continue serving her sister after she'd gone.

Even without her magic, Luminita remained a master musician. But she remembered when she had been so much more. As she played with the girl at her side, it occurred to her that these musicians must practice without her during the rest of the year, and that someone must play with them in her place. Listening to this girl and the way the three of them played together, Luminita became convinced that this girl was that person.

The girl showed no sign of wanting to leave when the song ended and it lightened the burden of Luminita's sadness. It soothed her to let someone else lead. She closed her eyes as she played and let her thoughts drift ever so slightly toward her memories of *him*. He and his music had been as much a part of her as her own magic, and somehow, he'd made her even more powerful than she'd been before.

One song gave way to another, and she felt her young friend's desire to take the lead and play pieces Luminita had never heard. She happily bowed her head and took her bow from the strings. After listening for a moment, she began to pluck the strings to the tune the girl had started, letting her mind return to happy days long past, though she doubted they'd ever feel that far in the past to her.

Something changed, something she hadn't felt in so long that she failed to recognize it when it happened. Momentarily distracted, she forgot to play and opened her eyes which were still cast down at the ground before her. Someone stood directly in front of her, closer than any of her people would have dared. The desire to look up at him tore at her will. She needed it to be *him*. But she also feared it would be just another mirage, another bit of false hope to cast her down into the pits of despair.

She no longer knew if she was strong enough to survive any more confirmation that this world had no more miracles left to offer. But her gaze rose anyway, and she took in the strange shoes and short britches they wore in this time. The cello and piano built toward crescendo as the girl next to her played. But the music only whispered in Luminita's ears as she recognized the hands that had held her. In a rush her gaze swept upward, taking in the face she'd never thought to see again outside of dreams.

"How can this be?" she asked.

"I will always find my way back to you," Paul answered.

The surge of her elation brought her lost magic crashing in on them. No longer satisfied to feed on the sources of her lesser emotions, it gathered around Paul, wrapping him in layers of unfocused energy, threatening to crush him beneath the weight of her exile.

Perhaps it was the numb resignation of her long confinement that lulled her into inaction. Perhaps if she were truly honest with herself, she wanted it to draw him into this familiar twilight where nothing would ever separate them again.

But then she remembered him in the sun, and the way the light played across his face when they'd slept in an open field. She remembered the sound of his magic as it mixed with and magnified her own. She couldn't allow him to be confined here in the dark away from the sun he so loved.

She didn't remember bringing her bow to the strings, but her long clear note tore through the veil that protected her from the magic that she feared might consume him. Denied of its prey, the rogue magic poured into her, a whirlpool of molten sound. After two centuries of independent evolution, it had grown wild, lacerating her soul as it filled her to bursting and changing her as it came.

The wards surrounding Jubilee Field shattered and smothered the torches that marked the boundary of her confinement. Lights went dark and the stars and moon shone down from above.

Wild magic crackled through the air between and around them in equal parts agony and ecstasy. Her eyes held his while she played, and together they remembered not only the life they'd lived before the accident, but all the ones that came before, stretching back to the dawn of mankind.

Something was wrong. She saw her terror reflected in his eyes as she realized it was too much. The magic had grown during the years and she no longer had the strength or capacity to contain it all as she once had.

Then he pushed the violin aside and took her in his arms. As he kissed her, she realized why the magic had never obeyed her. It hadn't only been her magic that kept her bound within the clearing. His had been there as well, and it was only after he'd returned centuries later that their combined magic returned.

Their restoration ended long before the kiss, and they vowed without the need for any sound at all, that even if they had to storm the gates of heaven or hell, they would never be parted again.

Chapter XXIV: Picking a Fight

When the torches blew out and the sky fell, Bruce and Megan were standing in line at Gordon's new food truck. Whatever quality had permeated the air around them and brought their senses alive fell away, leaving a silence that had little to do with sound. And in that unnatural quiet Bruce heard a violin playing. But the notes of that instrument were like none he'd ever heard before. They passed not only through the air around him, but also spanned that place where thoughts traveled across space and time.

From where they stood in line, both he and Megan could see their big friend stiffen. All three of them turned toward the center of the Jubilee from where the surge of power still rippled outward. Then the electricity went out and plunged the entire carnival into darkness. Children screamed in mock terror followed by a buzz of irritated adult chatter.

"Ladies and gentlemen," a familiar voice boomed out from the darkness, "Good citizens of Nickelville. We beg your forgiveness, but it appears that the power lines leading into our festivities have failed and cannot be repaired in time for us to continue. Due to safety regulations, we cannot allow you to stay and must ask you to return to your vehicles."

Was that Paul? Megan asked. *His voice sounded so much deeper.*

And I don't think it was done with a megaphone, Sam sent as he passed out the rest of his wares for free and sent his customers on their way. *Go find him and make sure he's okay.*

"Did the Jones family stiff us for this part of the grid too?" someone yelled.

More complaints followed, many of them loudly demanding refunds of the parking fee which was the only thing anyone paid to get into the Jubilee. But in the end, everyone made their way back to the path that led to the parking lot.

"She's done it!" Bruce heard over and over as they made their way to where he could feel the familiar presence of his brother. "We're free! We're all free!"

Cell phones lit the ground around them, but he and Megan didn't need light to see.

Can you see his future? Megan asked.

No, but I haven't really been able to since the first night at the Sentinel tree. I know he's up ahead though. Jade and Andrew are off to our left, trying to get back to Sam.

I'll tell them to go home and that I'll take you two and Paul home after we get this packed up. Sam sent.

Moving as quickly as they could against the flow of exiting traffic, they made their way back to the area that the carnies usually sectioned off for their own use. As they approached, a large man moved to intercept them.

"The exit is the other way, my friends," he said in a very unfriendly manner.

"My little brother is back there," Bruce said, easily sidestepping him. "We'll collect him and be on our way."

"Maybe you didn't understand," another man said, appearing out of the darkness. He reached out and grabbed Megan by the wrist.

He landed several yards away. The first man brought his fingers to his lips and let loose a piercing whistle that brought a dozen more men running in their direction.

Bruce reached out and took Megan's hand before walking the shadows to Paul's side.

They found Paul kneeling next to a young woman who sat against one of the large trees that grew here in the clearing. An old gas lantern provided the only light, and at first Bruce blamed it for his brother's strange appearance. But as he looked closer, he realized that even the harshest shadows couldn't explain how much taller Paul looked than he had been in the car less than an hour before.

Noticing the strangers that had so suddenly appeared in their midst, the carnies quickly moved between these intruders and the man and woman at the base of the tree. The two men from before joined the group, one of them massaging his shoulder and walking with a pronounced limp.

"It's okay," Paul called out in that strangely deep voice from just after the blackout, and Bruce could feel power in his words as it softened the worry of the men and women around him. "They're with me."

Bruce and Megan rushed to his side, desperate to make sure he was okay. But when Paul looked up, they understood why his voice had changed. Very little of the boy they'd known remained in the man before them. And while they stared in horror, Paul's hair began to gray at the temples.

"I'm so sorry, my love," the woman said. "I didn't know this would happen to you when I broke the enchantment."

"As long as I'm by your side, I don't care," Paul said tenderly, holding her hand against his cheek. "We'll find each other again, just like we always do."

Megan reached for her mother before remembering her absence. Then her thoughts turned to Sam.

"There's no time," Bruce said, following her thoughts or maybe just answering one of the other versions of her that had spoken aloud. "Her name is Luminita, and she's the one from my vision…and from Jacob's memories. The only chance either of them has is for us to take them straight to Guarded Wood."

"August will know what to do," Paul agreed, seeing hope where there had been none before.

"I don't think we'll make it that far," warned the phantom violin player who'd been their unseen companion since Paul had seen her the previous year. "And what about the others? Are they aging as well?"

"We're okay for now," the fortune teller from the colorful tent said. "But we'll all die if you do. The boy is right, Eldest. The two of you must make haste. 'Tis the only way any of us will see the sun rise."

"Then take us where you will, Daughter of Crina," the not so goth looking violin girl said.

Megan reached out and took them with her to the hermit's darkened doorstep.

"Like a forest fire," the musician whispered in awe.

"Damn it!" they heard August yell from inside, and Fang began to bark loudly through the window. "How many times do I have to remind you that it's rude to open trans dimensional doorways on other people's doorsteps without so much as a warning!" Seconds later he burst from the door with the wolf at his side.

"We need your help," Bruce said, helping his brother to his feet.

"Of course you do," the hermit snapped. "Why else would you be here?" Then he saw Paul and the unexpected woman. "Get them inside."

Paul picked Luminita up and Megan was shocked to see that Bruce now had to look up at his little brother. He was lucky that he'd been wearing loose fitting clothing when whatever it was that changed him had occurred, because they were straining to contain him now.

Megan had only a second to notice how immaculate the interior of August's home was with bookshelves lining most of the interior before she got a better look at the previously youngest Grimble and panicked. In the light they could tell that the accelerated aging process had not stopped for him or Luminita.

August placed his hand over the woman's heart and closed his eyes, searching for something.

"How long ago was the enchantment broken?" he asked.

"Half an hour at most," Paul answered in that strange voice.

"She's the one from my vision," Bruce said. "The one who belongs here."

"You're sure?" August said skeptically.

"You don't remember me, do you hermit?" the woman asked. Fang came up and nuzzled her hand affectionately.

"If you're implying that we've met before, you must be mistaken," August replied, likely thinking she was delirious. "I've been confined to these woods for longer than you've been alive."

"Jacob introduced us," she said simply. "At the tavern inn where my sisters and I found lodging."

"Luminita?" he said in horror. "That's not possible."

"His attempt to free my sister from the underworld went awry."

"Misguided fool," the old man growled. "But that explains why Guarded Wood wants you. Do you have your instrument?"

She shook her head.

"Bruce," Paul said, "Mine is in its case on the foot of my bed."

Bruce reached out and plucked it from the air and handed it to him.

Luminita took it from him and tested its tuning, already becoming accustomed to people and things appearing out of nowhere.

"You still tune low," she observed, smiling up at Paul. "What am I playing for?"

"Come with me," August said, his white brows furrowed in thought and led them all outside.

"What are you thinking about?" Bruce asked.

"We need to show Guarded Wood exactly what these two can do for her," the hermit explained. "Megan, I'm going to show you and Bruce where to take them. All hell is going to break out when you show up in her lair."

"Maybe Paul shouldn't," Bruce began.

"I will never leave her side again," Paul growled, sounding menacing for the first time in this life. "Not in this life or any other. Besides, she needs me to amplify her bardic power the way you do with Megan."

"Bard?" Bruce asked. "Like Taliesin?"

Luminita fixed him with a cold stare.

"What did I say?" Bruce asked.

"Only women can be bards," Paul answered. "They really hate it when people talk about him. He was a bardic amplifier like me, and his bard was shy. No one really knows why she let him get by with taking all the credit for her work."

"Not the time," August pressed. "Bruce and Megan, one more thing. When you get there, you have to let these two take care of the siren. If Megan gets involved, Guarded Wood might take her instead, and I don't want to have to explain that to her mother when she gets back."

"They're taking on the siren?" Megan exclaimed. "But she almost ate Paul last summer!"

"She did what?" Luminita asked, her voice suddenly cold. Then, using Paul for support, she rose to her feet. "Hurry up and take us there. I'm going to have words with this creature. He's *mine*."

This older Paul still had the same boyish grin.

"I wish I could come with you," the hermit said gravely, "But we don't have enough time to ride there, and I fear another trip through Tyr Sgodl would kill me instantly. But remember, Paul and Luminita absolutely have to be the ones to defeat the siren. If either Bruce or Megan become involved it will ruin everything."

Pausing just long enough to pull them all close in an uncharacteristically August gesture of concern, he showed them where to go and Megan took them there.

A full moon shone over that part of the old growth forest, otherwise they wouldn't have been able to see anything at all, including the briar hedge that surrounded the clearing. Two ancient elms rose from the earth in the center of that forbidden place, their trunks fused near the ground. Roots radiated from them for dozens of feet in every direction, diving and breaking the surface of the soil like long petrified sea serpents.

Megan felt something stir within the clearing, though even her heightened senses detected nothing around them. Thinking that the siren might be like the giant ravens, Huginn and Muninn, she scanned the elms, looking for any sign of what might otherwise remain invisible.

Remember, August sent from a great distance, *this is their fight, not yours.*

Megan was just about to ask what exactly there was to fight here when the wisps began to gather across the enclosed space. They appeared, not one at a time, but in swarms that moved with a coordinated purpose not apparent out among the trees. Hovering just beyond this plane of existence dwelled amorphous beings of such hunger that Megan wondered how she'd ever failed to sense them that night under the Sentinel. Although human flesh held no lure for these beings, humans still remained their preferred prey for nothing proved sweeter for them than unbridled human fear in the last seconds of life.

Ethereal as the wisps might be, Megan still found them easier to sense than the predator in whose lair they now stood. Far up in the branches of the ancient elms a pair of eyes reflected the light of the wisps' dances, although the pinpricks of light were not enough to illuminate her form.

The mixed scents of rich earth and crops left to rot in the field filled the clearing with a cloying sweetness that Megan thought she'd be able to taste if she only dared to open her mouth. However, she clamped her lips shut against the pestilence she sensed hanging alongside it in the hot, humid air, whispering like the predecessor of every plague to torment humans since the days when their dominion over the world remained far less certain.

She almost failed to notice the faint song coming from within the darkened canopy of the elms, soft as the sound of an owl's flight. Yet it echoed through her, fanning her longing to such a consuming blaze that it ate away at her self-control. She and Bruce each took a single shuffling step toward the trees. Realizing what they'd done, he took her hand in his and she felt his shields harden around them.

Wisps writhed in an alluring kaleidoscope of invitation, soothing their fears while heightening some primal need that could only be fulfilled within the branches of the elms. Too late, Megan realized that

297

the shields she and Bruce layered over themselves had never been designed for a foe such as this. Nowhere in all of her mother's training had they ever needed to protect themselves from the hypnotic lure of auditory magic which slipped past their battle-hardened defenses without any opposition whatsoever, leaving them with only the strength of their combined will to resist the call.

Luminita stepped forward and brought the bow of her betrothed's violin to the strings and started to play. The first clear notes reverberated through the veil that separated the dancing lights from the puppeteers beyond. Wisps floated to the earth like the last leaves of summer on an autumn breeze, going dim and rotting away to nothing as they fell.

The irony of the siren was that even though her magic, like the bard's, manifested in the form of sound, she made no sound at all when she leapt from the darkened interior of the tree to land mere yards in front of Luminita as she played. Even in the faint light, they could see that she had the form of a young woman, clad in a short, flowing garment of white gossamer.

She was possibly the most beautiful thing Megan had ever seen. Her song continued to call them, promising such wonders as mortals could never hope to attain. But as she drew nearer, the illusion of her delicate stature began to fade. Her limbs were long and well proportioned, but even crouching in a vaguely simian manner as she drifted toward Luminita, her eyes remained level with Paul's.

Something in the siren's undulating movements reminded Megan of the way leaves moved in the wind, mesmerizing them all in the creature's subtle advance. Then the siren drew in on herself, eyes focused on the bard as she dug her sharp claws into the roots at her feet and prepared to strike.

When Paul stepped between them, Bruce broke through his

paralysis and started to move forward, gathering power as he went. He released Megan's hand, beginning to fade as he prepared to walk the shadows to his brother's side.

STOP, the hermit shouted through their minds, bringing Bruce to a halt just as Paul began to sing. Megan wrapped her arms around her best friend and held him close where she knew he wouldn't resist.

The siren froze as well, looking closely at the mortal who dared stand against her. The song softened, yet grew in intensity and her sinuous movements resumed toward him.

Luminita moved forward as she played, standing shoulder to shoulder with Paul as he sang. His words were foreign, and yet they spoke to something deep within Megan, as if some ancestral memory stirred within.

The siren ceased her progress toward them and held her ground. For what might have been hours or seconds, the three of them went on like this, their melodies weaving about them in an intimate conflict to which the onlookers remained largely unaware.

Then at last the siren began to move. First one step and then another, giving ground a fraction of an inch at a time until Paul and Luminita were stepping over the roots of the elms, chasing her back into the dark recesses where the moonlight didn't penetrate. When at last the siren was pressed into a hollow cavity at the base of the fused tree trunks, she folded back into it like a flower retreating back into the bud and her voice grew silent.

A shudder passed through the ground, reverberating in the branches overhead as Guarded Wood took the bard and her mate for its own. Tendrils of life force grew up like serpent vines, enwrapping their limbs and sealing the spiritual wounds from which their life force had flown since the breaking of Luminita's enchantment.

While Megan watched, the two lovers began to shed the years they'd gained since finding each other again, causing them to age in reverse until the bard returned to the early twenties of her previous life and Paul joined her there as well.

The howl of a nearby wolf split the air, followed by the sound of thundering hooves. With a rending groan the briar hedge split behind them, opening a path to the woods beyond and a very winded hermit.

"You're getting slow in your old age," Paul teased, holding Luminita close.

"I don't guess I can threaten to feed you to the siren anymore," August observed, swinging down from his lathered horse and pulling his staff from where it hung. "We can approach now that she's gone dormant." When the meager light he summoned failed to illuminate the clearing as much as they'd have liked, Bruce and Megan summoned their own.

As they moved closer, Megan noticed skeletal remains grown into the roots beneath their feet. Some of them looked as if they'd just been picked clean by carrion birds while others had blackened with age. At the base, next to the place where the siren now slept, several faun skeletons had been partially entombed by the elms that towered over them. Next to one outstretched skeletal arm the remains of a set of panpipes rotted on the ground.

"She's got green hair," Paul observed.

"That was amazing," Bruce said, clapping his brother awkwardly on the shoulder, unsure how to handle his younger brother being taller than he was.

"Thanks, bro," Paul said. Then he took the woman at his side in his arms, lifted her from the ground and spun with her there in the siren's lair.

"So you're the violin girl he's been driving us crazy over for the last year," Megan said when Paul finally put Luminita down again.

"And unless my eyes deceive me, you are a descendent of my sister, Crina," the young woman said. "Why did you not present yourself to me as tradition demanded?"

Everyone stared at her, but it was Paul that answered.

"Josephine died in childbirth and was unable to pass the secret on to her daughter, Emelia," he explained. "Thus, Megan did not know what was expected of her."

"I am truly sorry to hear this," Luminita said, placing her hand on Megan's shoulder. "I really liked Josephine. But as has happened often over the years, I entered the sleeping cycle and found her gone on the other side. I know she would be proud of you though."

"This really hurts my head," Bruce said, rubbing his temples. "I'm going to have to spend about a month working out the genealogy between you two. But I do know one thing."

"What's that?" Megan asked.

"I'm not looking forward to explaining all of this to Mom."

Chapter XXV: Confessions Under the Sentinel Tree

Along most of the futures Bruce looked down, his father remained calm and accepting, even proud of his children. His mother, however, took it badly in every single one of them.

Now that the aging crisis had been averted, they returned to the tree house so they could consult with Azarich and decide on the path of least conflict. Personally, Bruce wanted the one where someone else told his mother while he hid out in Guarded Wood until she cooled down. But since voicing that opinion would make Megan look at him in a way he'd rather not experience firsthand, he kept his mouth shut and agreed that the two of them should go to his house and get it over with.

He practiced what he wanted to say, but a strange spot occurred in the vision that he couldn't interpret, leaving him unsure how to continue past that point. Megan reached out and took his hand, trying to calm his nerves the way he always had when she'd been in danger of frying something. She continued to do so when they walked through the back door of his house and into the living room where they found both of his parents watching a movie and eating popcorn.

"Hey guys," his dad said when they walked in. "Sorry about the Jubilee. We can start the movie over if you want."

"No, Dad," Bruce said, recognizing the trenchcoated vampires at once. "Don't you ever get tired of that one?"

"It's a classic," his father answered defensively, but the way his mother rolled her eyes suggested she felt otherwise.

"We have something we need to tell you," Bruce said, taking a deep breath. Megan squeezed his hand in support.

He'd known that there was an awkward silence here, but this was one of the many muted visions he had, and he had no idea what came next. But now that he stood there with Megan holding his hand, he understood why his mother's eyes grew wide and then slid, heavy with unspoken accusation, to his friend.

"Oh, god no," he said quickly, letting go of Megan's hand. It felt like the heat in the room surged a good thirty degrees. "We're seriously just friends. I mean…we've never even…"

"Oh," Megan said, her own eyes wide with sudden understanding. She took a hurried step away from him, then another for good measure. "That's not what we're here to talk about at all…"

"Thank heavens," Dora said, her hand raising rather theatrically to her heart. "I'm sorry, it's just the way you two were standing there and looking so serious."

"Well," his father said, hitting pause and chuckling to himself. "Whatever it is can't possibly be too bad after that scare."

Bruce's mind went blank, not knowing how to start after the unintended irony of his father's remark. Luckily, Megan already had experience in such a discussion.

"Mr. and Mrs. Grimble," she started.

"It makes us feel so old when you call us that," his father said. "Bruce calls your mother and grandfather by name. You can do the same with us."

"I know your name is Doreen," Megan started.

"No one has called me that since I was in the third grade," the woman said. "Call me Dora."

"And my name is Ben," his father said. "Even though just about everyone calls me Mr. Grimble for reasons I've never understood."

"Okay then," Megan said, trying to start again. This was turning out to be every bit as difficult as the two of them had feared. "Dora and Ben, I don't know exactly how to tell you this, and I want you to know that we've wanted to tell you for a really long time now, but your son and I can work magic."

Both of his parents looked at her, uncomprehending, for several seconds before his father started to laugh.

"And you guys make fun of my vampire movie!" he chuckled.

Bruce held his hands about a foot apart and summoned arcing electricity between them, twisting and turning it about itself until it made a ball of crackling energy that threw long shadows behind them across the room.

"Show off," Megan said. "You could have used fire."

He allowed it to dissipate with a wisp of ozone.

"How did you do that?" Dora asked.

In reply, he lifted a piece of popcorn from the bowl and brought it to his hand before tossing it toward his mouth.

"No fair," Megan said, snatching it out of the air without moving and eating it herself, "we still haven't had a chance to eat. The blackout happened while we were still in line for pizza."

"You're serious?" Ben asked, putting the bowl down and coming over to them.

"Yes," Bruce said.

"For how long?" his mother asked.

"Ever since I came," Megan said. "He can see the future too."

"The first time was when I fell out of my window that day at the

Tribune," he said. "I saw her coming even though I didn't understand what was happening at the time."

"What else can you do?" Mr. Grimble asked, taking the whole thing fairly well.

Megan walked the shadows to the kitchen and then walked back in with two sodas from the refrigerator. She gave one to Bruce and then took a seat on the other side of the room from him. Apparently, she wasn't over their first impression of this conversation yet.

"Who else knows about this?" Dora asked, heading directly down a path he'd wanted to avoid.

"My mother and Sam are like us," Megan said while he tried to find the best way to proceed. "They've known about this since they were children. We had to tell my Grandfather a few months ago because Bruce saw that he was about to figure it out on his own."

"So you're the one who determines when and to whom this information is told," his mother said, eyes narrowing.

"No," he said in resignation. Why did he feel like he'd done something wrong? "The reactions of the people involved and the way it impacts the future determine who finds out."

"And you didn't think we could handle knowing what our own son was doing, but it was okay for the McGeehees and Sam Wise to know?"

"We already told you, everyone but Azarich already knew," Bruce said.

"And what proof do we have that these visions of yours are as accurate as you think?" she asked.

He knew it was irrational, but that hurt his pride.

"How about a man who's never bought a single stock in his life suddenly amassing nearly thirty million dollars in less than half a year? Or that he single- handedly pulled a town on the brink of financial collapse into the black for the first time in a century?" Megan asked.

"*Thirty million?*" his father gasped. "I had no idea he'd brought in that much."

"And almost every cent of it has been invested into local businesses," Bruce said. "He's even getting ready to update the library at the Academy and build a museum in memory of his people. I've wanted to tell you guys about this since the first time the power started to grow in me. But in every vision I've ever had, telling you leads to pain and misery. You're great parents. How could you not worry?"

"We would have managed!" Dora said, her voice flat with anger. This was the reaction he and his siblings avoided at all costs, but there was no way out but through to the other side.

"You would have been okay with knowing that Guarded Wood is home to monsters from legend and myth?" he asked, deciding it would be best to just rip off the bandage at this point. "Would you have been okay knowing that one of those things tried to eat Paul that first night that we stayed out in the tree house?"

"You said he got lost and August and Fang went in and saved him." Ben said angrily, but still trying to mediate. That was good, Bruce had hoped for his help.

"August did, but the only reason he could was because he's the six-hundred-year-old protector of Guarded Wood," Bruce said. He hated doing this to them, especially his mother. But these things had to come out before they could get to the part about Paul never coming home again. And as horrible as that part was going to be, Paul would need his parents before the night was out.

"That's not possible!" Dora said in a horrible merger of fear and anger.

"I assure you it is," Bruce said.

"Wait," his mother said, suddenly looking around the room and making him wonder if she had a hint of foresight herself. "Why are you telling us this now when you didn't see the need before? Where are Jade and Paul?"

"Jade is with her boyfriend," Megan said.

"Does she know?" Dora asked.

"She and Paul figured it out shortly after we finished the tree house," Megan answered.

"Where is Paul?" Ben asked.

"He's waiting for us at the tree house," Bruce said. "He has a part that he needs to tell you himself."

"Just tell me that he's okay!" Dora demanded, hastily slipping her shoes on.

"He's fine," Megan said. "Possibly better than he's ever been in his life."

They visibly relaxed a little after that, and even though Bruce couldn't tell exactly how the next part of the night would play out, his part was almost finished and he was grateful.

Just before they reached the back door, Bruce felt something subtle change in the night ahead and he chuckled to himself.

"What is it?" Megan asked, drawing the attention of his parents to him as well.

"It looks like it's a night for confessions," he said. "Jade just told Andrew about us. Will you guys excuse me for just a second?"

With an expression much the same as when he and Paul had woken his sister up by jumping on her waterbed, Bruce walked the shadows to Andrew's bedroom where the boy of no relationship and his sister were sitting on the foot of his bed, holding hands and thinking seriously about practicing more CPR. Bruce noticed with approval that his sister's

308

boyfriend had a lot of books himself and that they were neatly organized in bookcases.

"How could you!" shouted Bruce. *"Do you have any idea what you've done?"*

Andrew screamed, and Jade fell off the bed, taking him with her.

Bruce laughed so hard that he saw little lights travel across his vision and worried that they might be wisps until he remembered that they were gone. Then, without warning, he scooped up his sister and her future husband and brought them to the back porch of the Grimble house where his parents and Megan still waited.

"You jerk!" Jade screamed, coming to her feet so fast that he had no chance to avoid her. Truth be told, he knew he had the kick to the gut that doubled him over coming, but he also knew that given the opportunity a thousand times over, he'd pick the same path in *every single one of them*.

"Are you okay, Andrew?" Megan asked, helping him up while trying very hard to keep a straight face since she'd seen what her best friend had done radiating past his shields.

"Wow," was his only reply.

"Come here," Dora said, grabbing her daughter in a bear hug and refusing to let her go even after Jade started to complain.

"I take it Mom and Dad know too," she grunted.

"Come on," Bruce said. "The rest of the story isn't ours to tell. We don't know much more than you do at this point."

As they drew closer, Bruce realized he could hear music from the direction of the Sentinel tree. It wasn't loud, or even particularly pleasant to hear. But power radiated through that sound in the same way that the siren's song had called to him, subtly changing the ways in which his body reacted to the world around him.

A bonfire burned in the fire pit beneath the tree house they'd built just a few months ago, although it seemed like years had passed since those simpler times. Seated around the fire were Azarich, August and Sam. Fang stretched out next to the hermit's feet, looking as if he might fall asleep. Much to the surprise of Bruce and Megan, Paul stood off to one side, looking exactly as he had that morning.

"Hey guys," Megan said, eyeing Paul critically.

"Hey," Paul replied, in a voice at least a full octave higher than it had been when he sang in the siren's lair. "I take it everyone has pretty much been brought up to speed?"

"Yes," Dora said, irritated but relieved to see her youngest well and whole. "But you three are grounded for the rest of your lives," she said, pointing to each of her children in order and then adding, "I'm mad at the rest of you too. And Emelia is totally fired when she finally decides to come back from whatever it is she's doing!"

"I'd say that's pretty fair," Azarich said. "Are you feeling as left out in the dark as I was?"

"Very," Mr. Grimble answered but with more curiosity than anger. "So let's hear the rest of this."

"Did you have time to find Goth Violin Girl before the lights went out?" Jade asked.

"Oh yeah," Megan muttered under her breath. "He definitely found her."

Luminita laughed from somewhere nearby, but Bruce couldn't see her anywhere.

After prompting them to take their seats around the fire, Paul moved to stand near the Sentinel's massive trunk and began to sing.

"I had no idea your voice had gotten so deep," Dora gasped, smiling at the discovery.

Then the world around them changed and they no longer saw Paul or the fire, though they could feel its warmth. The complexity of his voice changed, seeming to split off from itself, creating countermelodies within its depths that strengthened the visions they now shared.

Three women rode together on horseback down a rutted dirt road. All three of the olive-skinned and dark-haired beauties flowed with the movements of their mounts, as if the horses were merely extensions of themselves as they rode. In the distance, a strange forest sprung impossibly from the otherwise vast expanse of flat grassland.

Although Bruce already recognized Luminita and her sisters from the memories he carried from Jacob Routh, the knowledge also flowed into his mind through the melody his brother and the bard created. The other two riders were her older sisters, Crina and Sorina. Their clothing was simple if colorful, but there was a wildness in the way they carried themselves that suggested there was nothing simple or ordinary about them at all.

Then visions born of fire and melody brought them further along, not only into the settlement that would eventually become the town of Nickelville, but also a short distance into the future. Sorina walked ahead of her sisters with her hand resting on the arm of a tall man. Her clothing looked startlingly bright compared to the drab women who looked at her with disdain. But even more so when compared to her companion, who would one day be known as The Dark Man. The yellow scarf tied about her head did more to contrast her long raven tresses than confine them, and matched the sash tied around her small waist.

Her sisters, Crina and Luminita, walked a discrete distance behind the courting couple. Although dressed similarly, neither of them radiated the seemingly contradictory impressions of contentment and potential flight that their sister gave.

As they walked, they passed buildings little more than board and beam shacks, and even though nothing of modern Main Street had yet been constructed, everyone beneath the tree house knew that was what the scene showed.

"Could you settle in a place such as this if the right man sought your hand?" Jacob Routh asked boldly, unaware that her sisters could hear.

"If that was a proposal, then I fear I must decline," Sorina answered sadly, even as her eyes danced with merry mischief. "I will only marry if I can do so in a church, and sadly, this humble place does not possess one."

"Then I shall have to remedy that problem," he said, unable to look away from her.

"Good sir, I'm not so easily tempted," she said loftily, smiling back at her sisters. "I'll settle for nothing less than a grand building with stained glass windows and stone steps. I'd wish to say my vows beneath a beautifully carved wooden cross. But alas, though both your face and your sweet words do tempt me, such an undertaking would leave us near the grave 'ere it's completion."

"Then I have a proposition for you," he said. "A wager if you will."

"How scandalous that you would make such an offer," she said, although her eyes sparkled and she listened just the same.

"Stay here within the shadowed embrace of these strange trees for a single year, and I will build you a church the likes of none you've ever seen," he promised. "And when it is complete, I will ask you to be my bride. I ask for no promise of how you might choose to answer at that time, only that you give me the chance to prove my love to you."

"You would have to be a wizard like the ones in the times of old to accomplish such a feat," she replied, looking at him with strange understanding.

"If any place could boast such a thing it would be this one," he said. "For it calls to those of us who claim legends in our lineage. Just as it has called to you and yours."

The scene shifted again and they now stood within a darkened clearing with the moon waning overhead. Trees surrounded them on all sides, hiding the wonders of the night to come from the eyes of common men. Jacob had only just returned that afternoon leading a caravan of wagons, each pulled by a massive team of oxen. It marked the first of the miracles to which his church would be attributed in that he'd managed to find and transport such massive materials safely through the untamed wild lands. By the time his wagon passed beneath the first branches of the ancient trees that circled the budding village, the wagons stretched off to the horizon. Laden with black stone and massive wooden beams, the weight of their passage cut the first real road into what would eventually become Nickelville.

Now the three sisters stood across the field from Jacob as he stood atop one of the still-laden wagons. Worried that his reckless actions might draw the ire of the superstitious residents of the settlement, Crina spread her hands out before them and warded the perimeter of the woods to hide them from prying eyes. Then she summoned hundreds of floating fires to ring the place where the church would stand.

Not to be outdone, Jacob began the construction of his church. As if an invisible giant reached out, the turf at the center of the field began to peel itself back, exposing the white bedrock that lay just below the surface. With a gesture of his hand, Jacob moved the dirt away from the freshly cleared ground. Then the massive stone blocks began to rise of their own accord and seat themselves around the perimeter of the bare stone, forming the foundation of the church.

"At this rate, you're going to have to give him his answer much sooner than expected," Luminita told her sister. "Are you sure a life here is what you want?"

"More than anything," Sorina whispered in reply. "After all, I can't follow the two of you around for the rest of my days."

Crina frowned as she watched him work.

The scene around the bonfire changed yet again and now they found themselves inside the newly completed church. Light shone down on the couple from the windows high overhead. Stained glass flanked the nave where newly crafted pews easily held the majority of the community's population. An ornately carved wooden cross hung over the pulpit.

Jacob Routh knelt in his usual dark clothing next to Sorina, who wore a pale green dress as they looked up into the face of the man who bound them in marriage. A short distance away, Crina and Luminita watched as their sister took a different path from the one they'd traveled together for so long.

When the vision shifted again, the scene burst into movement as the newlywed couple danced. The air overflowed with laughter and the sound of Luminita's music. Many had come to see the new church from the outlying farms and unfamiliar faces looked on from every side.

So focused upon her playing and watching her sister dance, Luminita didn't notice when the young man slid from between the other musicians, snatched up a drum and wove his beat into the song she played. A collective shudder passed through all present as their senses became stronger and their emotions deeper.

Luminita whirled toward this intruder, surprised anger filling her movements until her eyes met his and he began to sing. For the first time Bruce and the others could see that it was Paul. Then he dropped the drum and grabbed her by the hand so fast that she barely had time to hand off her violin before he pulled her with him into the midst of the dancers. The magic missed the beat and then found a new one in the sound of their combined laughter, for nothing made by the hand of man could produce such a beautiful sound, even in the hands of powerful bards.

Another wedding filled their vision, but this time it was stern faced Crina who married. Her groom also had a sour manner, except when he looked at his bride. They exchanged silver rings that looked like woven braids of hair and Bruce knew that she'd made them with her magic.

Jacob led them in their vows beneath the cross he'd carved with his own hands, and his wife stood nearby, full with his child. She held a sachet filled with cinnamon beneath her nose as it was the only thing that held her nausea at bay. Luminita looked often at her betrothed, and Paul smiled back at her.

The sound of the music turned grim and so did the vision before them. No longer in the church, but rather in the home that Jacob built for his family in its shadow. Sorina lay on the bed with her head in Luminita's lap as the bard sang. But although the bard could ease her sister's pain, she could not change the course of the sick woman's delivery. As they watched, the spark of Sorina's life grew dim.

Bruce recognized the seer from the Jubilee there in the room with them, but through the magic of the bards' music he also knew she'd been a midwife. He could tell from the way her eyes looked on the scene before her without appearing to take any of it in that she was searching for a possible future in which things turned out okay.

"Crina," Jacob begged from where he knelt at her feet, pulling at the hem of her blouse in desperation. "You have to help her."

"So many gifts have been given to our family," the eldest sister whispered, "and I would happily forsake them all to make her whole. But I have no more power over the ills of the body than you do. There may still be time to save the child."

"Yes," the midwife said reluctantly, giving a moment of hope before taking it away again. "But the boy is not destined to live past the dawn. Let me do what I can so Jacob and Sorina can have those moments together before they must part."

The scene shifted again, and those who watched beneath the Sentinel gladly left it behind because Luminita's grief passed through them while she played and they felt it as if it was their own. But their escape wasn't as clean as they'd hoped because just before they left, the dying woman let out one last wail of anguish in which she called her husband's name.

Jacob stood, facing the dwelling he'd built to live out his days with Sorina and Jonathan. Its darkened windows reflected the flashes of lighting called by his grief. Thunder rumbled through the clearing, shaking the black stone of his church. Remembering how clever he'd thought himself to build it for them, he clenched his fists at his side and his scream drowned in the thunder that overlapped it. Lashing out with his mind, the windows exploded outward, cutting deeply into his face and arms. Then the life he'd planned with them caught fire.

The trees surrounding the church bent and rolled in the wind, dancing with the turmoil that rolled out from within him. He could hear the frightened cries of the woodland creatures as trees uprooted and limbs burst. He'd either forgotten his boots or lost them somewhere along the way. He seemed to be drifting in and out of sleep while his body continued on without him. When he came to himself again, he stood in the corner of the church courtyard where he'd buried them. When the night flashed into brilliance he could see the wild roses he'd planted at the base of the stone cross she'd asked him to make for her. They were the same ones she'd worn behind her ear while they walked down the street that day.

When his grief grew too great for his body to contain, he called lightning over and over again. Each blast struck the earth between the graves and the wall of his church, drawn to something there that he could feel but couldn't see. Over and over it struck until the stone beneath the surface glowed in the darkness between each strike. And with each one he felt a bit more drained, a bit less alive, and a bit *closer to her*. For more than an hour he knelt there, and though he didn't find his way to Sorina and Jonathan, something in the earth broke, sending tremors through the entire town. At last he slept.

He woke from the dark place to which he had retreated, and in that first instant when he still straddled the chasm between the lands of dream and sorrow, he heard her voice.

His first thought was that sound must have perished along with his desire to live in a world where he'd never see her again. But that wasn't right, because he could still hear the cooing warble of the pigeons that had taken up residence in the bell tower. He could hear the sound of the water that dripped from the edge of the roof onto the muddy grounds of the courtyard.

As he listened, he realized that the silence wasn't silence at all. Rather it was a vast, roaring void in his senses that muffled the energies on which his extra senses relied. Within that void he could hear Sorina calling his name.

Leaving a trail of muddy footprints along the stone floors, he followed her voice to an interior wall where part of the flooring had collapsed. Moving the worst of the rubble aside with his mind, he climbed down into the dark, following the sound that wasn't sound at all.

In the center of a small cave he found a shimmering disturbance. Through that tiny rift in the fabric of the world, he sensed tremendous power, like a thousand voices whispering urgently to his soul.

The scene shifted again and now Jacob lead Crina, Luminita and Paul through two ornately carved wooden doors that looked familiar to all who had been to the school's library. Before they entered, Crina asked him if he had what she'd asked of him. He pulled out three pieces of metal that, when combined, formed a key.

"Are you sure this is necessary?" he asked.

"If you are correct in what lies down there," Crina answered, "it's too dangerous to leave open into the world."

She held the key up to the doors, concentrating as she did so. The parts of the key began to glow in her hands as did the doors. Then she separated the parts of the key, giving one to Jacob and another to her sister. The last she kept for herself.

The doors opened into a dark space beyond and descended into the cave below. Jacob had used his abilities to cut away the excess stone and create stairs leading down into the darkness to ease their entry.

Crina led the way, summoning flame above her hand as she went. Luminita and Paul followed, and Jacob brought up the rear.

The shimmering space still glowed faintly in the dark when they gathered below the church. Paul reached out to touch it, but Crina slapped his hand away without explanation.

"I had hoped you were wrong," she whispered.

"Can you hear her?" Jacob asked.

"I don't know what I hear," Crina snapped. "And neither do you. Even should you be able to open it without killing us all, there is no way of knowing what might lay on the other side! What if you are only half right? What if it leads to the dark side of the afterlife? What if it opens not on Heaven, but on Hell itself? I loved my sister more than anything, but what you propose is madness!"

"But I can hear her," he pleaded.

"I've known her far longer than you, and I do not sense her here," Crina snapped. "Abandon this foolishness, or you will kill us all! Come away with me," she commanded her sister and her betrothed.

"I'm not so convinced," Luminita said, studying the strange phenomenon before her. "There may be truth in what he believes."

"Suit yourself," Crina snapped, turning to go. "But don't expect me to return and clean up this mess when the three of you realize how ill prepared you are for such a task. I must return to my husband."

The three of them remained in the cave, bathed in the faint glow of whatever had been created during Jacob's night of overwhelming grief. For a long while they watched it, weighing Crina's warnings against the possibility of stealing a beloved wife and sister along with her newborn child from the underworld.

"How should we proceed?" Luminita asked. "I've never tried to use bardic magic in this manner."

"It is alive," Paul said, listening to it closely. "As such, we should have influence over it."

"You must think me insane to pursue this," Jacob whispered

"Insanity would be to give up without even trying," Luminita replied.

"I've never been to the underworld," Paul said eagerly, clapping his hands together in excitement. "It might be fun."

The look Luminita gave him proved that they had lived their lives together before, because the ability to express such irritated admiration could not possibly have been perfected in a single lifetime alone.

"Are we agreed?" Luminita asked. "If we fail this might very well kill us, and I would hate for the last thing I did in this world to prove my eldest sister right."

"If we fail, I will still succeed in being united with the ones I've lost." Jacob said.

"And if we fail, I will find you again," Paul promised, smiling and kissing her before she readied her bow. "Just like I always do."

Luminita began to play, layering her magic around the cave, strengthening it to make sure that the church didn't come down on their heads and clearing the way for the other two. Then Paul began to sing and the shimmering quality of the disturbance froze, making it look almost like a mirror suspended in time and filling the cave with urgent potential.

Eager to be reunited with his wife and son, Jacob focused his considerable power into a blade of raw energy and pierced the veil between this world and what lay beyond.

The following explosion threw Paul into the wall with a sickening crack. Luminita abandoned her enchantment, rushing to where he'd fallen. Still caught in the energy that poured out of the gate, she lost track of the preacher when the ceiling collapsed, burying Paul under several feet of rock. With her bow and violin forgotten in her hands she screamed her anguish, she screamed her longing and she screamed in one long note filled with the magic of all of the bards that had gone before her that if any gods listened, that Paul would indeed find her again.

The world melted around her and she found herself lying between two trees in one of the clearings next to the church. She sprang to her feet, leaving her bow and violin on the ground and ran toward the church where she might still save him.

But when she approached the tree line, her blood began to burn in her veins and she fell to the ground in agony, quickly crawling back toward the center of the clearing. Thinking to break free with the magic of her music, she ran back for her instrument before returning to the wall of pain, bringing the bow to the strings and summoning her power.

It refused to heed her call.

Over and over she tried until she collapsed. In her heart she knew that, if he lived, he would find a way to return to her side.

"Luminita?" a voice called from beyond the trees that kept her prisoner within this clearing. It was a voice she'd always counted on to protect her, especially since their parents had died.

Crina emerged from the trees along with the young seer that had accompanied them to this place.

"You have to go back to the cave and help Paul!" Luminita yelled before she drew close. "Don't come any closer. Something is blocking me from leaving this clearing. You have to go help him!"

As Luminita stood there, strange wisps of magic began to drift out from the trees, moving in languid lunges as if searching blindly for something they sensed nearby.

Crina ignored her pleas and ran toward her, passing blindly through one of the searching tendrils. She gathered her sister into her arms as if it had been a lifetime since they'd last seen each other instead of only minutes.

"Crina," her sister pleaded. "You don't understand. You were right, there was an explosion. But there might still be time to help Paul."

"Luminita," she said sternly when her sister continued to push her back toward the trees. "He's gone."

"No, he's not," the young bard whispered even though she knew her sister spoke the truth. But if she agreed then it would become real, and a world without him was one she would never abide. Then she noticed something odd. "When did you change your clothes?"

"The cave collapsed," her sister continued. "I thought you were gone too."

Unable to admit the truth of Crina's words, Luminita pushed her away and her eyes fell upon the young seer. When they did, there was a strange sense of connection that she'd never felt with the woman before, but it wasn't a healthy connection like friendship or love: more like a whisper of panic in the back of her mind. Tendrils of smoky magic began to converge on the seer, wrapping her in layers of opaque energy.

"Don't either of you see the magic in the air?" Luminita asked.

"Where have you been all this time?" Crina asked, glancing at the seer with concern.

"What do you mean?" the bard asked, watching the seer in horrified fascination. "It's only been half an hour at most since the accident. What is moving in the darkness around us?"

"Luminita," Crina said, blind to what was happening to the seer and worried about her sister's state of mind, "I came to the church to light a candle for you. It has been exactly one year since you and Paul..."

"That's not possible," Luminita whispered, shaking her head in denial.

"It's a miracle," the seer said quietly. The bard closed her eyes to block out what was happening to the woman even if she didn't seem to sense it herself.

"No, it's a miracle that I heard you playing out here," Crina said, making a sweeping motion of the clearing as she spoke. "The townsfolk have believed the church to be haunted since the night when Jacob called the lighting. I'm the only one who has set foot there since that night."

"She speaks the truth," the seer agreed. "I waited in front of the steps until she returned."

"Let me see if I can do anything to take down this ward that holds you here," Crina said, closing her eyes and reaching out with her mind. "I've never felt anything like this."

"Be careful," Luminita warned. "It bites."

"That only seems to be directed at you. For that matter, it doesn't respond to me at all. My magic has no power against it, in much the way it does not work against your bardic magic."

"Do you feel that?" the seer asked. "I feel so alive right now. It's almost exactly like I feel when Luminita plays her violin."

Over the next few hours, Crina tried repeatedly to break down the wards and free her sister, and several times Luminita attempted to summon her power. Neither of them met with success.

"It really is nice here," the seer repeated from inside her cocoon. Whatever it was that enclosed her didn't appear to be harming her in any discernible way.

"I'm glad you're enjoying it," Luminita muttered, lowering her instrument in defeat.

Then with a lurch, her sister disappeared and the angle of the moonlight changed.

"What just happened?" the seer asked, her cocoon of energy suddenly absent.

"I think we just disappeared and came back again," Luminita answered. "But this time you came with me."

"Crina," she called, hoping that if her sister had come with them, she wasn't far away.

"I'm here," Crina's voice came from the woods just as it had before. Moments later, her sister stood before her with a young man from the caravan that had brought their clan to this place. He wore a heavily laden pack on his back and carried a small writing table. Crina's clothing was much nicer than it had been before.

"It's been another year, hasn't it?" the bard asked.

"I'm afraid so," Crina answered. "I hoped it wasn't a onetime occurrence. I'm not sure how to stop this yet, but we'll figure it out. If it continues the same way as before, we'll only have a few hours to stop it before it happens again. I don't know if someone must go with you each time or what would happen if you were alone when you went," she said, motioning to the man at her side. "So it's best to keep everything as much the same as possible."

"You've put a lot of thought into this," Luminita marveled.

"I've had a whole year to ponder and plan," Crina replied as she directed the young man to set up writing materials on the table.

"Is that a pocket watch?" Luminita asked when her sister removed a round object from a fold in her dress.

"I need to know exactly when you arrive and disappear," Crina answered, writing something down after checking the watch. "And we should probably mark where you appear so we can make sure that nothing is in your way when you come back."

"This can't be possible," Luminita said, laying down on the grassy turf. "It only feels like a few hours ago that Paul…"

"I know," Crina said in an uncharacteristic show of compassion. "You don't feel the passage of time at all when you're gone?"

"Not a bit. I'm in this moment and then I'm in the next. There's nothing in between."

"I need to catch you up on some things," Crina said. "Much has happened since you've been gone. We are a real town now. We call it Nickelville."

"What a stupid name," Luminita said, making a sour face. "Who came up with that?"

"My husband," Crina replied coldly. "The mayor."

"Sorry," Luminita said, managing a faint smile.

"She speaks the truth," the seer said. "'Tis' a stupid name."

Tendrils of magic began to form, reaching out for the young man who had come with her sister.

"Can neither of you see that?" Luminita asked.

"See what?" the seer asked.

"It's like snakes made out of fog," she answered. "They came and surrounded you last time, and then you came with me when I…whatever it is that I did."

"What are they doing?" Crina asked.

"They're converging around him," she answered, pointing to the man in question.

"And you saw them do the same thing to her last year?" Crina asked, nodding toward the seer.

"Yes," Luminita answered.

"Then we have a way of telling who will be taken," Crina answered, writing that down as well. "Hopefully it won't be necessary, but if this goes on for many more years we're going to need a way to hide the fact that people are appearing and disappearing here. The town became official close enough to the night of the accident that my husband can decree a festival in celebration of this event. I've gathered enough of our people to perform as we did in the old country."

"You want to make the night my betrothed died a holiday?" Luminita snarled, but it sounded hollow without her magic.

"Stop being so dramatic," Crina said, brushing off the insinuation. "I'm just making sure that you are taken care of if I can't stop this."

"What do you mean?" Luminita asked, still irritated.

"Sister," she said, placing her hands on each side of Luminita's face to be sure she had her attention. "If this pattern holds true, by the time a full day has passed for you, roughly eight years will have passed here. Before the end of two weeks, I will have joined Sorina."

Still overwhelmed with the grief of losing Paul, Luminita could take no more.

"I need to rest," the bard whispered as her sister held her.

"You've had a long day," Crina said, comforting her as she had as a child. "But I do have one good piece of news."

"I could use that right now," Luminita mumbled, finally giving in to exhaustion.

"When you return next time, you will be an aunt."

Luminita woke to the cry of a child and opened her eyes to the sight of her sister holding an extremely loud bundle.

"She gets that from me," Luminita said, her head pounding with the effects of so little sleep.

"I hope not," Crina said. "You were already charming people into getting you out of your bed by this age."

"I thought it didn't come until I was much older," the young bard said, rising from the ground for a better look. There were several of their people present in the clearing this time and from the way they gathered around the surprised young man who'd come with her this time, she suspected them to be his family.

"You began to control it when you were older," Crina corrected. "You practically enslaved our sister to your will from the day you were born. Would you like to hold her?"

"What if that makes her be the one that comes with me?"

"I don't think it works that way." Crina said. "Otherwise you would have brought me with you that first time. But let me know if you see magic begin to pool around her and I'll get her clear of the clearing." She passed the child to her sister.

"She's not as small as I'd thought she would be," the bard said in wonder, taking in the dark hair and olive skin that matched her own.

"She's four months old," Crina explained.

"And she'll be walking in a few hours," Luminita said, at last understanding how much she was going to miss.

"I've never told you how proud I am of how well you're taking this," Crina said.

"If I withdraw into myself I'll miss it all," she cooed. "And I don't want to miss any of this. I'm proud to meet you, daughter of Crina."

"That sounds so formal for such a little one," Crina said, "like a royal title: Daughter of Crina. I think I like Megan better. It is, after all, her name."

"Well hello, Megan," she said and the child smiled at her. "I'm your Aunt Nita."

"I thought you hated it when we called you that," Crina said.

"I do when you call me that," the bard said, kissing her niece and holding her close. "But she's allowed. Megan and Paul can call me that." Her sister looked at her hard for a moment.

"You know he's gone," she said.

"Just for now," Luminita said, unable to be sad with the child in her arms. "He'll find me again. He promised he would, and he never breaks his promises."

"I think I may understand what caused this," Crina said, smiling at her child in the arms of her sister.

"And?" the bard asked.

"I think that in the heat of your grief, you cast an enchantment so strong that your magic left you to carry out your will," she explained.

"What does that mean?"

"I think your magic is doing two things," Crina said, sitting down on the ground next to her. "Because you believed Paul would come for you again, and that not even death could stop him…"

"He will find me," Luminita said defiantly.

"And because you did not give it a specific path by which to accomplish this feat," she continued, "it is keeping you alive until he returns to you again."

"But why is it taking others?" Luminita asked, holding Megan close to her as she noticed that her lost magic had begun to gather around another man who looked much like the previous.

"I think that it might need more energy to sustain itself," Crina said, looking at where her sister stared and nodding. "Or it might be that when it cannot find Paul it takes someone else, particularly someone who brings out strong feelings in you."

"But I don't have strong feelings for the seer," the bard argued.

"She'd just annoyed you when she was chosen," her sister explained.

"And the man last time?" she asked.

"He was the only person other than me."

"But why are you immune?" Luminita asked, smiling at the way her niece had nuzzled into her hair and appeared to be going to sleep.

"Your magic has never worked as well on me," Crina said.

"But it worked on Sorina," she reminded her.

"Our sister had no gifts to protect her."

"And the seer?" Luminita persisted.

"Maybe foresight doesn't count," Crina said.

Then the years began to flow by in a series of images, barely recognized before they were gone. Crina brought a son to greet her then grew old as her children grew into adulthood. The boy looked like a slightly overweight version of his sour father and never looked like he wanted to be there. Then they brought Crina before her, having held on for weeks in order to say goodbye. Without her power, Luminita couldn't even ease her sister's passing which was the most sacred of her duties as a bard. Crina's son brought a familiar face before her, one with impossibly blue eyes and blond hair. Megan was replaced by another and another and another. Even though Luminita was always pleased to see the next Daughter of Crina as they'd come to be called, the knowledge that she would see them grow old and die tainted what joy she could find in them. All the while she and the other cursedly smooth stones skipped across the surface of time unchanged. Each time the crowds came to hear her play, she scanned every single face for the one she'd been promised until at last she gave up hope and took solace in her sister's children. Eventually they forgot her too. But by far, the worst part of her curse came in the form of spending eternity with that damned seer telling her how good it felt to be in the clearing.

Then, only a year after the sleep cycle years, Paul found her as he'd promised. And in the instant she saw him, she knew he'd be the one chosen. Unable to allow that, and amplified by the bond that re-established itself when they saw each other, she finally summoned her power and broke free.

But as soon as soon as the spell was broken, time began to catch up to her, for she had lived long beyond the years she was allotted. Bound together, Paul also began to age and he was happy to do so.

Bruce could hear his mother crying even though he couldn't see her.

Then Bruce and Megan watched themselves take the two reunited lovers to Guarded Wood where they were restored. Given the highly edited version in which nothing of the siren was shown, Bruce realized that the bards didn't necessarily have to show what really happened.

The music came to an end and the illusion of Paul's youth evaporated while he stood before them, a man in his mid-twenties dressed in clothes borrowed from Azarich.

Dora rushed to him and held him close.

"Wow," Jade said, walking up and joining the embrace along with her father. "You've finally decided to go with the full old guy wardrobe and not just the pajamas anymore."

When their parents finally had enough time to accept that even though his brother was different, he was still Paul and he was okay, Bruce stepped forward and gave him a hug as well.

"So I'm named after Crina's first child?" Megan asked.

"And others who came after her," Luminita said, stepping into the light of the fire, still holding Paul's violin. "There were others before my time as well. It's a family name with a long history."

"But if Emelia didn't know about her mother's side of the family," Dora asked, "How did she know to use a family name?"

"I might not have known about the supernatural stuff," Azarich answered, "But I did know about my wife's favorite grandmother. I told Emelia all about her on many occasions."

"What I can't get over is the coincidence of Paul having the same name," August said, leaning heavily on his gnarled staff.

"It's not a coincidence," Dora said, holding Paul's arm in hers. "When I was pregnant with him we went to the Jubilee."

"We hadn't been able to settle on a single name we liked for a boy," Mr. Grimble added. "We were eating corn dogs between the two trees where they built that stage."

Paul groaned good naturedly.

"And this young woman came out and sang the most beautiful song I've ever heard," Dora said. "And I was in the middle of that horribly emotional part of the pregnancy where you just cry at the drop of a hat. So I was crying through the whole thing."

"And you had us put our hands on your stomach because he was kicking so hard!" Jade said. "I remember that!"

"And when you stopped singing," Dora said, looking straight at Luminita.

"I told the audience that I dedicated that one to Paul," the bard finished.

Chapter XXVI: Aunt Nita

Megan woke softly from dreams of music, and for once she didn't feel bad about her mother's absence. After all, she would only be gone for a few months. Compared to what Aunt Nita had been through, she didn't feel she had much to complain about.

When she cast her senses across the house, she found Azarich still asleep in his bed. It had been a long crazy night, and she knew that she'd had trouble falling asleep too. Not wanting to wake him if he needed rest, she walked the shadows to the side of his bed and listened to his breathing which was deep and reassuring.

"You'd be so proud of her, Josie," he whispered.

"Tell grandma that I love her," Megan whispered as she bent to kiss his forehead and then walked the shadows to the kitchen.

She thought about calling Bruce to see if he wanted to go watch the sunrise. But he'd need to be well rested for the race later that day, and she decided that she'd take his cue and go watch it by herself.

She made coffee, leaving enough for her grandfather to have a cup and pouring the rest into his thermos along with enough cream and sugar to make her happy. She kept expecting him to come down and join her, but when she reached out one last time, she found him still deep in dreams of days long past.

Megan reached the foot of the stairs before she realized that someone was already in the tree house. Two someone's in fact, although one of them still slept. She chided herself for not realizing that Paul and Luminita would stay there until they worked out lodging within Guarded Wood proper. She turned quickly to go back up the darkened path and watch the sunrise from the porch like she and Azarich usually did.

Don't go, Luminita sent.

I'm so sorry, Megan sent in reply. *I didn't mean to intrude.*

I feel your hand in the fabric of this strange dwelling as much as I do Paul's. I have no claim over this place. I've been watching the echoes of you and all of your friends when you built it. It is medicine for the wounds in my soul.

You can see the past too?

Yes, and I would be honored to teach you how to use the gifts you've received from our shared ancestors. I am in the tower if you would like to come up and watch the arrival of the dawn with me. I'm glad I never had to watch the sun rise over a world that didn't have Paul in it. That's a blessing when I think on it.

I have coffee, Megan sent, climbing the stairs.

Then you will forever be my favorite niece. They only had sodas from the concession stands when I woke up for the past several decades.

Remembering how difficult it had been to climb the ladder carrying the thermos and cups when they'd told her grandfather about their secret life, Megan decided to forgo the problem and walked the shadows to the tower where Luminita waited.

"That's quite a trick," the bard said quietly in the darkness, and even in conversation Megan could feel magic just below the surface of her voice. "And not one you inherited from my clan."

"It comes in handy," Megan agreed, handing her the cup she'd been carrying then filling it with coffee.

"I didn't mean to take your cup," Luminita said quietly enough to keep from waking Paul who they could hear snoring down below.

"It's not a problem," Megan said and reached through the shadows to get another from inside the cabinet at home. "I'm just glad I don't have to hide what I can do from you."

"It was the same for my sister and I," Luminita agreed, taking a sip from her cup. "I don't remember it being this sweet!"

Megan chuckled.

"My whole family drinks it that way," she said. "Although I can't really say that any more if you don't like it since you're my great great, with a whole bunch of more greats thrown in, aunt."

"You are the seventh generation of my sister's descendants," the bard replied.

"Wow," Megan said, noticing that the horizon was starting to lighten. "How do you keep up with that? I mean it's been close to two hundred years, right?"

"Not for me. I was only present for a little over three hours each time I returned to that field," she explained. "For me it's been a week since I last saw Josephine. It's been less than a month since the accident."

"So you really want me to call you Aunt Nita?"

"Heavens no," the bard laughed, and Megan realized she was going to have to reshape her shields to deal with sound. "When you get down to it, you are only a year or two younger than me. Just call me by my name."

Then the bard fell silent, drinking the sweet liquid and looking out over the treetops as the first light of dawn drew nearer. There were just enough clouds to give the morning some color.

"Now that I'm on the outside of that whole ordeal, I can think more clearly," the bard said, little more than an outline in the dark next to Megan. "On one hand I understand that I was born two centuries ago and everyone I ever knew except for a hermit that I only met once and the people who shared my fate are dead. That makes me feel the passage of time down in the marrow of my very bones. But on the other hand, I have no true sense of time's passage. I don't feel that much older than I did the day we descended into that cave. It's just so…"

"Confusing?" Megan offered.

"Yes, it is so confusing. I didn't sleep at all last night. I just held Paul while he did. It wasn't easy coming up here without him. But I have to be stronger than that, don't I"?

"I promise you that he didn't mind a bit," Megan chuckled. "We're just glad he wasn't crazy. He's been obsessing over you since last fall. We couldn't understand how he could be that fixated over someone he'd only seen for a few minutes. He's normally a very calm and reasonable person."

"We've found each other over and over since the beginning of time," Luminita explained, staring at the horizon. "Ah, the first dawn I've seen in a very long time. I don't remember it being this colorful."

"Pollution reflects colors more in the red and purple range," Megan explained.

"So it is a bad thing?"

"It's bad for the planet, but that doesn't mean we can't acknowledge that it makes for pretty sunrises."

All in all it wasn't the best sunrise Megan had seen since she started watching them with Azarich, but it wasn't bad either. The upper atmosphere moved faster than below, and the clouds in each part caught the light differently than the other. A gentle riot of color danced through the heavens and at some point, Luminita laid her hand over hers.

"So I was wondering," Megan began when the best part was over.

"If the Paul I love has pushed aside the one you've grown to think of as the brother you never had," the bard finished.

"How did you know what I was thinking?" Megan asked.

"My sisters and I always knew each other's thoughts. It was the only gift Sorina possessed, unless you count making Jacob fall so deeply in love with her the first time he laid eyes on her. You and I share the same bond."

Megan realized at once that it was true.

"To answer your unspoken question, he has always been the Paul I have known in this life and many others. The man I loved formed the foundation of the boy you've known. He still possesses all of the memories that made him Paul Grimble, but now he also remembers our short life together here in Nickelville. I still think that's a stupid name, by the way."

"Do you remember all of your lives together?" Megan asked, fascinated by the thought.

"Yes and no," Luminita answered. "All of it is in our memories, but unless something happens to trigger the older lives, they stay mostly dormant. The ones from our recent lives are more relevant and therefore more accessible. I think he's always had more of a connection to them than I have. He's always told me these fantastic stories about the animals that used to live when the world was younger. He even told me what the best ways to hunt them were before we learned to work metals. I thought he was just really imaginative."

"He's still fascinated by them," Megan said.

"I know," Luminita said, chuckling and realizing that her cup was empty. "He fell asleep late in the night telling me about all the things he's seen in Guarded Wood. I don't think any place would better suit us for the rest of our years together."

"Are you going to be okay with being confined there? I mean aren't you just exchanging one prison for another?" Megan asked, filling the bard's cup from the thermos.

"It was never Jubilee Field that made it a prison. It was being separated from Paul," Luminita explained. "I think we shall find much happiness here."

"He is pretty handy," Megan said, "He's a scout after all."

"Is that the boy soldier thing he keeps talking about? And this odd fixation with rope and tying things?"

"You might not want to call it that around him," Megan chuckled. The sun had risen enough for them to finally see each other, and she realized Luminita was wearing her clothes.

"I hope you don't mind," the bard said, reading her thoughts. "I told Paul that I wished I had something to change into, and he dragged out this huge bag filled with your clothing. He kept laughing and saying that you knew what you were doing after all. I promise I'll return them as soon as I find a way to procure replacements of my own."

"Don't worry about that," Megan said, putting her arm around her sister-like aunt. "You're welcome to keep anything you want, and I'll bring you some catalogs so you can choose your own wardrobe instead of being stuck in my old stuff."

"I don't have anything to trade," the bard said quickly.

Megan hugged her tighter. "You're family, and we take care of our own."

Luminita held her close, as if trying to make sure this was real. Megan knew she'd have felt the same were she in her place, so she opened her mind fully and showed her the years that she and her mother had spent on the run.

"And my brother is basically conjuring money out of thin air," Paul said, materializing out of the gloom next to them. "Is that coffee I

337

smell?"

"You didn't tell me he was an alchemist," Luminita said, impressed.

"Of a sort," Paul chuckled, eagerly taking the cup Megan summoned and filling it from the thermos himself. "Why didn't you wake me?"

"You helped me break an enchantment that killed you two centuries ago, grew several decades in less than an hour and then fought the siren that tried to kill you last year. I thought you could probably use a full night's rest."

"But you did all of those things too," he said, startled by the sweetness of the coffee, then shrugged and downed the rest of the cup.

"I slept a few years ago," she said with a dismissive shrug. "That's why you didn't see me before last year. I got depressed and slept in for a decade."

"How much sugar did you put in there?" Paul asked. "It's like syrup at the bottom of the cup."

"I like the last bit to be a little chewy," Megan said sagely.

Dad has gone into full overprotective parent mode, Bruce warned. *We will be there in a few minutes with a full-blown feast.*

Should you be eating that much before the race? Megan asked.

I'm not going to run, he answered.

Why? Paul asked, surprising both Megan and Bruce. *Did you see something bad again?*

Nothing like that. I woke up this morning and realized the race doesn't mean anything to me anymore. All I wanted last time was to beat Glenn and prove to everyone that I was more than just my asthma.

I haven't known you for very long, Luminita interjected, *but I doubt that was ever really a problem.*

I can tell I'm going to like you, Bruce observed. *I also saw two*

338

paths for Glenn. If I win today, he's going to end up working at the factory until he dies in a car accident a few years from now. If I don't run, he gets a scholarship and turns into a halfway decent human being. He needs this more than I do. I'm never going to be his friend, but I don't have to be his enemy. Glenn made my life miserable, but if this foresight has taught me anything, it's that no one should be judged by what they did in the past if it doesn't carry on into the future.

Mom and Dad are okay with this? Paul asked.

They're excited that they get to spend more time with all of us today. They're also excited that they get to get to know your fiancé better. I warn you, Mom has realized that the possibility of grandchildren to spoil is much closer than it was yesterday. I'm not sure if I should be insulted by how upset they were about the prospect when Megan and I talked to them.

What do you mean? Paul asked, confused by what they could be talking about.

Wait, does a proposal of marriage still count if one of the people has been dead for two centuries and is reincarnated? Megan asked before a discussion she seriously wanted to avoid became a possibility.

In response, Paul dropped to one knee, and Bruce appeared in the now crowded tower with his parents and Jade holding onto him.

"Luminita," Paul said in a voice that could probably out-cool Sam's now, "Will you do me the honor of accepting this offer of marriage, and bind yourself to me, body and soul in this life and every one of the ones that follow, just as you have done since there were words for me to ask you?"

"I'll think about it," the bard answered wistfully, "And maybe you'll get your answer if you feed me well enough. I haven't eaten in years!"

Chapter XXVII: Esther's Adventure

"It looks like we're going to Honeysuckle House today," Bruce said, glancing at the vine-entombed structure at the end of the road from the front driveway of Megan's house where he and Jade had just walked up.

"Seriously?' Jade asked. "I thought we weren't supposed to go there."

"It's okay now," Megan answered.

"I'll go get…" Jade said, frowning. "I keep forgetting that Paul can't."

"I know," Bruce agreed.

Nita and I can tag along if you let us, Paul sent. *Wait, August says to leave the front door open and we'll catch a ride.*

The front door opened, and Azarich strode toward them, still looking a bit tired even though he'd slept in through the sunrise that morning.

"Hey Grandpa," Megan said. "So you're finally ready to explore Honeysuckle House?"

"I don't think I'm ever going to get used to Bruce knowing everything I'm going to do before I even decide to do it," the old man chuckled after a moment of shocked surprise. "I just talked to Tom and he said Esther is having the best day she's had in a while."

"And you want to give her an adventure like the ones you guys used to have," Jade said. "Too bad Mom and Dad aren't home. I'll bet they'd like to go too."

"They're welcome any time they want," Azarich said. "So it's okay?"

"Let me check," Megan said, looking off into space and calling out, "Hey Charlotte."

The small-framed blond materialized out of a cloud of dust that rose from the ground at Megan's summons, all the more spectacular for having done it in the full light of the sun. She no longer wore the old bedgown from her long confinement to Honeysuckle House, but rather a faded pair of jeans and a leather jacket. Her long hair had been cut pixie style, and she wore sunglasses.

"Modern life seems to be agreeing with you," Bruce observed.

"It sure beats being locked in a trunk," Charlotte laughed with confidence, showing none of the timid shame that she'd radiated when they first met her.

Megan pulled her into a tight hug.

"I missed you too," the fear gorta chuckled. "So why did you summon me?"

"We wanted to know if you'd mind it if we entered Honeysuckle House," Megan answered.

"It belongs to your family," Charlotte answered, frowning. "You don't need my permission to go there. I've already said my goodbyes to the place. Although if it's okay with you, I'd rather I never set foot inside those walls again."

"I might have also been worried about how you were doing," Megan admitted.

"I don't think we've met," Azarich said, holding out his hand.

"Azarich, I watched you and your friends grow up," she said, ignoring his hand and hugging him instead. Then she paused. "I've always liked the way you MacGeehee's smell. Maybe it's just an echo, but you smell like your many-times removed grandmother after she'd been baking bread all day."

"What do I smell like?' Jade asked without thinking.

"You and Paul always smell like fresh earth," Charlotte answered. "And I'm sorry I scared you Paul," she added looking back toward the treehouse where she could see him and Luminita standing. "It's good to see you again too, Bard. I would have told them about you if I'd known you were still trapped there."

They waved in response.

"So how have you been doing?" Megan asked.

"I have found employment," Charlotte answered.

"Doing what?" Bruce asked.

"I'm a counselor at a women's shelter," she answered. "And so far, I have a perfect record. None of my girls have returned to the men who mistreated them. For that matter, none of them ever will. You'd be amazed at how many abusive men just…disappear these days."

"Is that so?" Megan asked. "I'm so glad to hear you're doing well. I worried that you'd have trouble finding a place you could call your own. Will you have to move every few years to keep people from noticing that you don't age?"

No sooner were the words out before the blue-eyed young woman began to age before their eyes. Then she changed into perfect replicas of Megan and then Bruce in turn.

"That is so disturbing," Bruce said, looking himself in the eye.

"You'd also be amazed at how many abusive people were terrified of someone while they grew up," Charlotte said, returning to her own form. "I still have to eat in order to retain the ability to look human, and since it's the fear of my prey that sustains me, it's useful to look like the people they feared most while I do so."

"Remind me to never get on your bad side," Bruce said with a shudder.

"I know what you did for Megan at that cliff," Charlotte replied. "I could never harm someone who would do something that selfless."

"I have no idea what you're talking about," Bruce said uneasily. "Besides, you saved her too."

"Thank you for that," Azarich said.

"It was seriously my pleasure," she said. "If you could have seen half of the things I saw in that man's soul you'd understand. It's also what gave me the idea to do what I'm doing now. He was a wife-beater among other things. But now, if you're serious about going into Bev... I mean Honeysuckle House, I should probably clear it away for you."

Then, looking down the road to the vine-covered structure, she focused her attention on it and drew in a sudden breath as if preparing to blow out the candles on a birthday cake. The honeysuckle withered in an instant and turned to dust, leaving the marvel of the mansion's construction open to the sunlight for the first time in over a century and a half.

"Wow," Jade said. "No matter how many times I see things like that happen it still doesn't get old."

"I should probably go open the front door before people start to arrive," Bruce said. "Or I guess we could just go back in the back like we did the first time."

"Just use the keys," Charlotte said.

"What keys?" Azarich asked.

"The ones that are hanging by your back door," she answered.

"Are you telling me that those keys are to Honeysuckle House?" he asked in excitement.

"They've hung on that hook since your family served mine," she answered with a smile. "I'm the one that put them there. But as much as I've enjoyed this unexpected reunion, I must go. I stepped into the restroom at the shelter when you called, and I'm afraid that someone will notice that I'm missing if I don't return soon."

"Thank you so much," Megan said, hurriedly hugging her again.

"No," Charlotte whispered with a happy smile as she returned the embrace, "Thank you." Then she was gone.

A short time later found the lawn before Honeysuckle House filled with vehicles. The Harrises had been the last to arrive, and Sam was currently helping Esther into her wheelchair. All eyes traveled the newly-revealed surfaces of the house, taking in the dark slate roofing tiles, the black stone that made up the entryway as well as the numerous chimneys that rose along intervals of the massive building. The gray paint had worn away in places where the honeysuckle had rubbed against it in the wind, but it would otherwise require little work to make it look new again. Several balconies opened to look out over the road and woods nearby. A large round window encircled a stained-glass letter B near the roof, reminding them that the road leading up to it had been named for the Beverly family under the guidance of Nickelville's first mayor.

"And you say that you woke up and noticed that all of the vines had just up and died this morning?" Alan asked, frowning in amazement.

"It surprised me too," Azarich said, without a single hint at the amusement Megan could feel coming from him. "Even stranger is how well-preserved everything underneath was preserved."

Esther looked at him with a smile and raised an eyebrow to say she already suspected something of what might have happened.

"And you own it?" the librarian asked.

"Yes," Azarich agreed. "It turned up when I was researching about the Academy ownership. The same ancestor of Josie's that inherited the school also lived here. It was a little more difficult to sort out though since the city surveys haven't recorded this place since the Civil War. But you want to know what the coolest part was?"

"What?" Alan asked.

Azarich pulled out the old ring of keys and held them up.

"Are those the keys from your back door?" Tom asked.

Azarich nodded.

"We must have tried those blasted things on every lock in town," Alan whistled. "Including every abandoned house on the block."

"All of them except for this one," Esther said with a smile. "Josie made us promise not to go here. I assume you've got a good reason to ignore that?"

"A little birdy told us it was okay now," Megan said, noticing three yellow ones perched in the overhang of the porch watching with an inordinate amount of interest.

"Paul made me promise the same thing," Jade said. "But he said it was okay now."

"How is he doing at that new school?" Kate asked. "To think that a boy I taught might be going to Julliard!"

"He's doing great," Bruce replied, covering for Jade's sudden unease. She didn't like to lie to her boss.

"Can we please go in now?" Sam asked. "I'm dying to see what's in there!"

"I've never seen you impatient before," Jade said.

"And yes," Megan said. "You can take some stuff to use in one of your displays at Gordon's."

It took a moment to get Esther's wheelchair up the steps, but between Sam, Bruce and Jade they managed without too much difficulty. Azarich handed her the keys when they reached the door.

"Why are you giving them to me?" the librarian's wife asked.

"It just seems right for you to be the one," Azarich answered. "I just wish Josie, Carl and Elizabeth were here with us."

The older members of their group all nodded in agreement as Esther fitted the largest key into the bronze plate before her and turned it smoothly.

"Not even a bit of resistance," Alan said in awe. "I don't know what guardian angel is watching over this place, but I sure wish she'd start moonlighting at the Academy."

"I'm pretty sure she's retired now," Megan said.

Alan looked at her in puzzlement.

As soon as the door stood open, the three birds flew over Esther's head and into the house beyond. Watching them flitter about, she giggled in contentment.

"I haven't seen warblers in years!" she cheered, clapping her frail hands together softly. "How remarkable!"

Megan couldn't help noticing how Alan frowned at the uninvited winged guests, likely thinking about what havoc they might cause if left inside and how difficult it would be to get them back out. After so many years of working at the Academy, that's just how his mind worked.

It looked much different inside with light streaming in through all of the windows. And it took Megan a second to realize that not only had all of the curtains been opened, but the one that had been missing in the dining room to their left had been replaced as well.

"Oh my," Esther whispered, "This is so beautiful. And it doesn't look like there's any dust or cobwebs anywhere."

"That's not possible," Alan said, frowning. "And it looks like all of the furnishings must have been left."

"Mysterious," Jade said in her best attempt at sounding suspenseful. When it failed, she looked to Sam for help.

"Mysterious," he repeated with a grin.

"Much better," Kate agreed.

When the rest had entered, Megan noticed that all of the shattered glass had been cleaned up from the broken mirrors. The mummified floral arrangements had been cleared away and with the light streaming in she could see much more detail than during their previous exploration.

Oil paintings of various sizes decorated the walls, covering much of the floral printed fabric that covered the walls above the dark paneling. They ranged in subject from portraits to landscapes and still lifes.

My sister painted these! One of the yellow birds sent, perching momentarily on Megan's shoulder as she looked at a picture of a wagon train stretching off toward the horizon. *I actually recognize the people driving that first one. The man was one of the first to be trapped with me.* Then the bird flitted away again.

"Hey Grandpa," Megan called into the dining room where the older group had gone. "These paintings are all signed by Crina. I guess Grandpa Josie wasn't the first painter in the family."

She shielded this place so tightly when she was alive that I could never see what was going on in here, August sent. *And Charlotte blocked me out after that. I tried to sneak in here as a mouse once and she killed it before I'd gnawed on the floorboards for more than a few seconds.*

I'll bet that wasn't pleasant, Bruce sent.

Let's just say it's the last time I tried.

"Oh my lord," Esther exclaimed. "This china is exquisite!"

347

Megan, Bruce and Sam reluctantly followed them into the dining room. The dishes had all been cleared away, cleaned and put back into their places in the china cabinets that lined the walls. The brass of the chandeliers gleamed in the light and the crystals that hung from them cast miniscule rainbows across the table. Like the mirror shards, the broken plates had been cleared away and discarded.

"I can't believe all of this has been left undisturbed for so long," Mr. Harris said. "And I don't understand why it wasn't packed up. These grand old houses had linen coverings to put over everything for when their owners traveled. This is all so strange. Beautiful, amazing and strange."

Esther surprised them by pulling away from him in her excitement to enter the kitchen that she could see through the door ahead. This brought a smile from the librarian who hadn't seen her so active in a long time.

I cleared all of the debris out of the wheel assemblies while we were moving her up the front steps, Bruce admitted. *It rolls a lot easier than it did before.*

You're a good man, Paul sent. Then one of the birds collided with Bruce's shoulder. *Sorry, that was intended to be a thump on the back. I guess it's the closest I can come in this form.*

Inside the kitchen, all of the pots and pans had been returned to the places where they hung from the ceiling, each catching the light from windows and dividing the room into pleasant patterns of light and shadow.

Esther moved around the room, picking up things that Megan couldn't identify and commenting about how long it had been since she'd seen anything similar. On a few occasions even she was stumped, although Paul could be heard in the backs of their minds, explaining a few of them which Megan then explained directly into the frail old woman's vibrant mind.

"Would you guys mind if Bruce and I went exploring back where we turned off?" Megan asked. "We saw this part of the house when we snuck in a while back, and we're curious about the rest."

"Not at all," Azarich replied, watching the way the place animated Esther, and in turn, the way she made her husband practically glow with happiness.

"Did you do anything that might have disrupted the honeysuckle?" Alan asked.

"Not that we know of," Bruce answered. "I didn't think it looked very healthy when we did though. It had a lot of wilt."

"Okay then," the janitor said, seeming to feel a bit better about the mystery. "It still doesn't explain how all of the vines just disappeared though."

"Some mysteries are meant to be enjoyed," Kate said, pulling him to the ceramic tiled stove and opening the door. "I've never seen one so fancy."

"These places always had a library," Mr. Harris called after the youngsters. "Yell if you find it."

"Gladly," Bruce called back.

"I'll catch up to you guys in a bit," Sam said, studying the way some strange iron contraption worked.

"Don't forget that you can take things for Gordon's," Megan reminded him.

"You should be careful giving me such freedoms with things like this," the big man said happily. "There is so much history here. I could spend months here looking and not become bored."

"Me too," Esther agreed. "Would someone please hand that case down that's on the top shelf. Let's see if it holds what I think it does."

"Gladly my love," they heard the librarian say as they made their way back to the front door which they'd left open under the guise of letting the birds fly back out.

The pictures along the hallway show our journey here from the old world, Luminita sent.

"That's a relief," Bruce said, pointing to the empty space above the mantle that they could see from down the hallway.

"What is?" Jade asked.

"There was a really spooky painting there," Megan answered, checking to make sure everyone else was still in the kitchen. "It looks like she burned it in the fireplace."

"Good," Bruce said. "That's one less nightmare I have to worry about." Then, looking into a side corridor he yelled, "Mr. Harris, I found the library."

"Thanks," they heard him call back. "We'll find our way there in a little while."

Jade quickly moved out of his way.

"What are you doing?" Bruce asked.

"I know better than to stand between you and books. There's only one thing you like better," she added, glancing meaningfully at Megan.

Stop, Megan mouthed at her after Bruce walked past.

Jade shrugged but continued to smile anyway.

If the rest of the house was considered luxurious, then decadent was the proper way to describe the library. A mosaic pattern took up most of the floor. Made up of three huge circles that touched but didn't overlap, the roughly triangular space in their center enclosed a huge three-sided fireplace. With openings on each side and facing the centers of the circles before them, it rose two stories before disappearing into the ceiling far

350

above. A second-floor balcony encircled the room with iron railing forged to resemble the entwined branches of a tree.

"We're never going to get Bruce out of here," Megan said, staring up at shelf upon shelf filled with books.

"I really hope they're already alphabetized," Jade added.

Too overwhelmed to be insulted, he stared in wonder.

"There are leaves carved into the stone circles," Megan noted as she passed. "These look like the oak trees in the woods near the school."

The other two are laurel and ash, Paul sent. *And the carvings between the openings in the hearth are of dryads. I think this is a representation of the woods that surround the Academy, Jubilee field and the one where the race starts.*

And there is a pair of trees at the center of each circle, Nita added. *My stage was situated between those two.*

"And those are the Gateway Oaks," Jade said, pointing to the ones on her side.

"What about the Academy field?" Bruce called over to where Megan stood.

"They're the ones in the courtyard!" she called over excitedly.

Yes, Nita added. *He built the church around them. This is Crina's work as well. I can still feel the signature of her power in all of it!*

I don't know what she did here, August added, *but she expended a tremendous amount of power over a long period of time in this place. Megan, you could probably see it all in time, but there are so many layers of past enchantment here that it might take years for you to unravel it all.*

Can one of you open the doors upstairs? Paul asked. *They're all closed and we can't fit underneath.*

"Gladly," Bruce replied out loud. "Paul wants us to go upstairs, but

351

you can keep looking around down here if you want."

"No, I'll come," Jade said. "I'm surprised you're leaving this so quickly though."

"I'll need a lot longer to sort all of this out than one afternoon," Bruce said, regretfully looking back over it all. "And let's be honest, I'm not going to be able to walk away once I start."

"The first step toward recovery is to admit you have a problem," Jade said wisely, leading the way up the stairs.

"Who are all of these people?" Megan asked as they climbed the stairs to the bedrooms.

Our ancestors, Luminita answered.

I thought you said Crina painted all of them, Megan said, *A lot of these look older than your time.*

She did, but I see what you're getting at. Crina could remember and reproduce just about anything she'd ever seen. Part of our training in the family included being shown who came before us. Knowing her, Crina probably wrote down everything she knew in one of those books you just saw. See the one at the end of the hall? Those are my parents!

Thank you so much for freeing Charlotte and making it possible for us to see all of this, Paul sent. *It's making Nita so happy.*

"Let's get these doors open," Jade said, turning a doorknob and looking inside. "Cool, this one has a piano." Then she walked in, lifted the cover to reveal the keys and hit one experimentally. The sound it made wasn't particularly pleasant to hear.

"After everything else being so perfect, I thought it would be in tune," Megan said with a grimace.

That's not a piano, Luminita sent.

It's a harpsichord, and that's just how they sound, Paul added, from down the hall where Bruce had opened another door.

Megan followed Jade into the room, taking in the four-poster bed, trunk and harpsichord. This room also had a fireplace, which most of the others did not. The carvings on the bed showed far more skill than the ones in all of the rooms except for the master, giving her the impression that this room had been intended for someone important.

Wait, Luminita sent. *Look back at that trunk. I'll be there in a second.*

Paul and Nita landed on her shoulders.

That's my trunk! the bard sent in excitement. *The one with all of my belongings!*

"Well that would have been hard to explain a few weeks ago," Jade said in surprise.

Looking up, Megan found Luminita and Paul looking down at her from a painting almost two centuries old.

Chapter XXVIII: New Beginnings for Old Friends

"I remember when doing that was still new," August said, looking overhead.

Bruce followed the direction of his gaze and felt the awareness of both Paul and his betrothed in the two falcons that streaked overhead. He'd never been to this part of Guarded Wood before, and he doubted he would have been there now except for the need to house two hundred Jubilee field refugees. He tried to fix the twists and turns of the paths in his mind as they moved from one pocket of stolen time to another, but where these enchanted woods were concerned, not all paths necessarily led to the same destination.

Megan followed close behind, riding alongside her Grandfather as they talked pleasantly about the sights. Azarich had been in high spirits ever since their adventure in Honeysuckle house the day before, and to be honest, Bruce had been pretty excited by it as well. How had he been able to make it this far into his life without discovering the amazing and mysterious side of Nickelville? When he remembered that first conversation with Megan on the bus, he realized she'd been right, and he was the one who'd been wrong.

He glanced at her, and she smiled back at him, making his heart race. Behind them rode his parents with Jade and Andrew bringing up the rear.

"What do you know about these ruins?" Bruce asked. "And are we sure that the rest of the carnies that are tied to Luminita can live in them without disturbing our present?"

"Most of her people came from lives similar to the people who once built this place," the old hermit answered. "As long as they stick to classical construction techniques for repairing the buildings and refrain from bringing modern materials here, it shouldn't matter. Before the modern era, people built their homes from local materials. Everything needed to rebuild should be on hand.

"And Sam is already up there?" Megan asked.

"We brought out horses yesterday," August answered. "Some of Luminita's folk repaired the paddocks for the domesticated ones, and the rest will be left wild to create a herd they can pull from in the future. Next year they hope to start planting crops and raising livestock."

"Have you two figured out anything new about the Baker mystery women?" Azarich asked, joining the conversation.

"My only contributions to that discussion are more questions," the hermit said. "And Sam says he can sense the Well of Dreams resisting him when he asks about the Fates. He's spent a lot of time working with the Well over the years, and he can tell that something is interfering with his attempts. It's almost as if someone in the past told it not to answer any questions about them."

"That would drive me crazy," Jade said. "But knowing Sam, he's all philosopher saint over the experience."

"No, he's very irritated by it," the hermit said. "The Well is the closest thing he has to living relatives that he can talk to. He's a gentle man, but none of us like to feel betrayed. I'd avoid the subject if I were you when we get down there."

"I've seen him irritated once, and I would happily go the rest of my life without repeating the experience," Bruce said, remembering the first time he'd been to his big friend's home.

"Are Luminita's people going to be okay living here long term?" Megan asked. "I'm not a huge fan of modern technology, but electricity and indoor plumbing are nice to have."

"You have to realize that what you consider to be normal has only been around for a few decades," Azarich answered. "Only the last three or four dozen of these people ever lived with modern conveniences. Just look at my own childhood. There were no phones, televisions or computers. The lives that the rest lived won't be that different from what they'll find here."

"Most seemed relieved to get away from all the noise," August added. "The majority were more scared of being forced to live in a modern world that they didn't understand than they were to return to the relationship they'd enjoyed with the land long ago. They don't feel like they're being locked away. To them this is being set free."

Without warning, the path left the trees and became rockier with the soil changing from the forest debris to a pale, sandy soil with many exposed rocks. Then it widened out and eventually became a poorly maintained road that cut deep into the earth.

They followed it around a hill and for the first time their destination came into view. Dominating the highest point in the region, ruins climbed the entire side of a huge hill. An undulating series of stone buildings seemed to be tucked into every conceivable surface up to the peak where a medieval castle looked out over the valley below.

"I wanna live there," Megan said longingly when she saw it, and Bruce had to quickly throttle the daydream of living out his life with her someplace like it before she could sense its presence or how much he wanted it.

"It's going to take a lot of work," Bruce said, his smith's senses already identifying structural issues that needed to be addressed soon.

"With two hundred sets of hands and centuries if not whole millennia to work on it, I don't think that will be an issue," Azarich said. "Are Paul and Luminita sure they don't want to live here with them?"

"They need to be closer to the boundary and in a section of Guarded Wood where time flows normally," the hermit explained. "Now that the protections have been restored, there shouldn't be many problems way out here. It's idiots coming in from Nickelville that will keep them busy."

"You mean keep you busy," Jade said.

"What?" the hermit asked.

"You said it will keep them busy like you weren't a part of it," she explained.

"Dora, Ben," the old man said irritably. "You really should have beaten your children more often. Then they wouldn't be so comfortable with interrupting their elders."

"I don't know about that," Azarich said pleasantly. "They seem like fine young adults to me."

"For that matter I'm your elder too," August said but with a smile.

Just then Paul and Luminita rode out at a gallop from the outbuildings in the distance and headed straight toward their guests. She was wearing the same clothing she'd worn in the vision when Paul had found her at the wedding celebration for Jacob and Sorina. Bruce smiled, realizing it must have been in the trunk they'd found at Honeysuckle House.

"This discussion is great and all," Jade began.

"Go ahead," her mother said.

With a whoop of excitement, she and Andrew took off toward her brother and future sister-in-law.

Do you want to follow them? Megan asked.

Not this time, he answered. *Jade's been pretty down with not being able to talk to Paul any time she wants to. I think they could probably stand a little time without us.*

"Are those olive trees?" Mr. Grimble asked, pointing to what might

358

have been an orchard near the outskirts of the abandoned city.

"Indeed they are," August answered. "I think that was the main crop when this place was last inhabited. If I had to guess where this was I'd say Italy. There were cities like this when I was last there. It's hard to say exactly when this is. I've found coins here before, but they're so worn they could be just about anything."

"I can probably narrow it down more if you let me take them to a coin shop," Bruce said.

"Won't that cause a stir if they're rare?" his mother asked.

"I'll just say I bought them in an online auction," Bruce said. "Stuff like that gets sold around the world all the time."

"So do we eat or explore first?" Megan asked, eyeing the ruins with interest.

"Whichever you want," August answered, smiling at her enthusiasm. "I think the work crews have already eaten and returned to clearing out some of the buildings that are in better condition. They hope to start repairing roofs in a few days to make enough dwellings habitable before winter gets here."

"They used clay tiles," Bruce observed, eyeing the distant structures thoughtfully. "Do we need to make more for the repair work?"

"Not yet," August answered. "There's a salvage crew combing through the buildings that are too far gone to repair. They've already collected two cartloads full of usable tiles. In time they will need to make new ones, but that's probably going to be a few years off."

"What's the castle like?" Bruce asked, studying the largest building at the summit.

"The shell seems sound," August answered. "The roof is intact, if in need of some maintenance. Paul was hoping you'd check it out and tell them if it's safe to work on before they go in too far. If they could focus their attention there and get it shored up before winter, it would make more sense than trying to get dozens of smaller structures prepared before the really cold weather comes."

"I can't wait," Bruce said eagerly. "But we should eat first. I have a feeling I'm going to be in there for a while when I start."

To Bruce's eye, the state of the ruins became paradoxically better and worse as they drew nearer. Walls that looked solid to the eye were actually in danger of collapsing to his smith's senses while some of the most age-worn surfaces needed only plaster to make them new again.

Sam fed them, even though the fare looked less like something from the Gordon's menu and more like the sort of thing that Paul might whip up to feed his troop. Most importantly, it tasted good without making anyone lethargic before the work that remained ahead.

"Do you guys mind if Bruce and I head up to the castle?" Megan asked when they'd finished.

"It's not an easy hike," Luminita warned, before remembering who she was talking to. "But I realize now that I've said it that you have no intention of walking, do you?"

"Not if we can help it," Bruce answered. "Does anyone want to come with us?"

"I think we're all content to take the beginner tour," Dora said, putting her arm through her husband's. "Old folks like us would just get in your way. But be careful."

"I promise I'll take good care of him," Megan said. "No harm will ever come to him under my watch."

"You always do," Mr. Grimble said fondly, smiling at her.

"Paul and Luminita promised to show us the exposed rock surfaces on the next hill," Jade said as she and Andrew pulled themselves back up into the saddles. "As great as all of this old ruin thing is, I'm still a rock hound. This geology is amazing! And if we're lucky, we can figure out where they quarried the stone for these buildings."

Moments later, Bruce stood with Megan at the castle's main gate. The view across the land from this high vantage point was breathtaking in its scale. The hill on which the ruins had been built was fairly large, but certainly not mountainous. Even so, it was the highest point in the landscape for what looked like hundreds of miles.

"I've never seen anything so beautiful," she said.

He stared at her a bit too long, and she caught him looking at her, admiring the way her hair absorbed the sunlight and shone off her perfect, pale skin. For just a second when she became irritated by his gaze, the brown of her eyes faded to violet, and he shrugged in apology.

"The tower on the right is sturdy enough to hold us without falling through," he said. "It's going to take me about an hour to get a true sense of what kind of state it's in. If you want to explore instead of sitting there with me I won't mind."

"Can I tag along?" she asked. "I'd like to see what things like this look like through your mind."

Smiling at this change, since she'd been irritated by his attention only seconds before, he took her hand and walked the shadows to the tower. There he took a moment to confirm what his foresight had suggested before sitting down on the warm stone across from her where they would be comfortable.

Even though they didn't need to have the contact any more to link up this way, she reached out and took both of his hands in her own, lowering her shields as she did so.

So what does something like this look like for you? she asked.

Reminded by the way it had felt to dance with her that night in the school cafeteria, he drew her essence close to him and plunged downward into the forgotten spaces below. He wished the hidden supports within the structure had been made of steel or iron like the ones at the Baker, so it would have felt like flying. But stone and wooden timbers didn't conduct his senses as well, so they would have to make do with the sense of running and crawling through the ancient fortress.

August had been correct in his assessment of the roof. It had held up surprisingly well considering the centuries of abandonment he'd personally witnessed. As far as Bruce could tell, most of the damage to this building at least, was fairly minor. He found no reason why Luminita's people shouldn't be able to clean out the bird nests and mouse burrows to make it habitable before winter came in earnest.

But this evaluation brought with it the question of why it had been abandoned in the first place. Had some plague wiped out its populace, or had they left during prolonged periods of drought or famine? Even though he couldn't see any problems with Luminita's people claiming this place for their own, it still made him uneasy. What if something lived out here that no one had seen yet? What if a dragon lived somewhere in this forgotten place that had only stopped hunting here because its prey dried up?

Paul and Nita will be living closer to the boundary, Megan thought. *And I can already feel her evolving to meet the needs of Guarded Wood. Before long they'll be hearing voices on the wind that tell them where something needs fixing.*

Do you think that's what August does? Bruce wondered.

I don't know for sure, but it does sound rather hermit-like. Are we done here?

"For now," Bruce said, bringing them up out of their trance. "I'll need to mend that beam in the ceiling of the great hall, but I'd rather be closer to do that and there's a lot of debris that needs to be moved out before it's easily accessible."

"It was neat seeing what this looked like for you," she said. "But it's weird. Even though it all felt perfectly natural while bound to you, I don't think I could do any of that alone. I might even damage things if I tried."

"Then you can always ask me for help with this sort of thing."

"And what will you come to me for?" Megan asked.

"Large scale destruction," he answered, grinning wickedly.

"I'm going to miss you," Jade said, standing on the tips of her toes to hug Paul properly.

"I do miss being able to talk to you anytime I want to," he admitted, hugging her back a little too tightly. He still hadn't become accustomed to his larger size and strength. "I wish cell phones worked out here."

"Wait a minute," Bruce said, handing the reins of his horse to Megan. "Dad, why do you have a silver dollar in your pocket?"

"I picked it up from the side of the paddock where we keep the horses. How did you know I had it?" he asked, then rolled his eyes. Paul wasn't the only one having trouble getting used to this new world they'd entered.

"Can I have it?" Bruce asked, holding his hand out. When his father placed it into his palm, he studied it closely. "This should do nicely."

"That's a Morgan dollar," Azarich said, glancing at it. "Those are pure silver if memory serves. I'll bet it's the one Carl lost when we were kids!"

"Another mystery solved," Bruce said. "Unfortunately it isn't going to be worth anything as a coin in a few minutes."

He broke it into two equal halves as if it were a cracker instead of a coin.

"Jade, Paul, come over here for a minute," he said. "I can't make it to where you can walk the shadows like Megan and I do, and I can't give Jade the ability to send and receive thoughts."

"Only the Beloved could do that," August said, and Bruce could hear the unspoken warning in his words.

"But I can make it to where you two can talk to each other even if Paul is deep in Guarded Wood," he said. "Jade, do you still want one of those bar earrings?"

"An industrial?" she asked, casting a quick glance at her mother. "Mom says I can't get one until I turn eighteen."

"And Paul, would you mind an earring?"

Mr. Grimble touched his left earlobe absently.

"No way," Paul said in horror. "Dad, did you have your ear pierced back in the day?"

His father's guilty smile answered better than words.

"We weren't as prudish as you three seem to think!" Dora added indignantly.

Bruce handed each half of the coin to his siblings. Then he placed one of his hands over each of theirs and began to concentrate.

"That feels horrible," Jade complained with a grimace.

"I haven't even started yet," Bruce said, opening his eyes and frowning at her.

"Well, your hands are really clammy," Jade complained.

"Do you want the cool earring or not?" Bruce asked.

"Can it have cool designs like Megan's ring?" she asked.

"Yes Jade, you can have cool designs since simple enchantment isn't enough for you," he mumbled under his breath. Then he began to shape the silver in their palms, forging it to suit their needs as well as his sister's questionable fashion sense.

"Cool," Paul added. "It's getting hot and moving. I can feel some of what you're doing too. Wait, the neck is too long. That's better. Oh that's perfect!"

When Bruce finished, he removed his hands from theirs and each of them held an earring of sorts. Jade's was an ornate silver bar capped on each end so it would stay once her ear was properly pierced. Paul's consisted of a simple curved hook from which dangled a perfect miniature violin.

"Any chance you can do this for them Sam?" Bruce asked. "Body piercing is not in my skill set."

"What makes you think it would be in mine?" the big man asked.

"You're the gentlest person here," Jade said. "You won't hurt us more than necessary." Then she looked to her mother for permission.

"I might as well say yes now so the rest of you won't gang up on me like you did with the treehouse," Mrs. Grimble agreed in exasperation. "And need I remind you how that ended?"

"Me first!" Jade said. "I want it on my left ear, so I can remember that my dad used to be cool!"

Mr. Grimble looked as if he were trying to take that as a compliment.

Hers was over in a second and then this new, older Paul also had an earring.

"I'll take you out into the edge of the woods," Bruce said, reaching for his sister's hand.

"I'll go," Paul answered, vaulting into the saddle of his nearby horse before coaxing it to gallop with the sound of his voice.

"Show off!" Bruce called after him. When Paul looked like a toy in the distance on the valley floor, he turned and waved at them.

"Okay Jade," Bruce said. "Think about Paul really hard and talk to him out loud as if he were right in front of you."

"Can you hear me?" she shouted.

Out in the valley, Paul's hand shot up to his ear.

"Not so loud!" they could hear him answer faintly from her ear. Being Jade, they could all see her thoughts as the implications of this gift sunk in. Then the girl ranked third in her division at state, sniffed and blinked quietly to keep from crying.

"Thank you so much, Bruce," she whispered, hugging him too hard just like she always did.

"And August," Bruce said, feeling a bit like Santa, "I've got something for you as well."

"What's this?" the old man asked, taking a folded piece of paper from his young friend's hand and reading it aloud. "August 2nd, 11,742 BCE. Likely an island roughly 600 miles southeast of Hawaii which no longer exists due to sea level rise and erosion."

"You have no idea how hard it was to figure that out," Bruce said.

"Is this my beach?" August asked, staring at it thoughtfully.

"That was the date when we took the pictures," Bruce answered. "I don't have any way of knowing when the exact date was when you and your wife found it."

"How did you track down the date without the location?" Paul asked from Jade's ear even though he was still riding back. "Without that, it should have taken thousands of hours just to narrow it down."

"Or a contest with a ten-thousand-dollar scholarship as the prize for the first person to verify it. We sent it out to universities across the country," Sam said. "It was money well spent as far as I'm concerned."

"I don't know what to say," the hermit whispered. "I never really thought you'd be able to find out. My wife and I had been in Guarded

Wood just long enough to suspect that time and place weren't as fixed here as it was in the rest of the world. One of the last things she asked me before she passed was where and when I thought we were. Now I guess I'll be able to give her an answer when I finally see her again."

Chapter XXIX: The Ghost of Detentions Past

At first Bruce thought Megan had noticed him adjusting the fuel mixture of her mother's truck as they idled at the town's only traffic light when he found her hand resting on his. He glanced over at her, but she continued to stare off into the distance without any indication that she'd intended to touch him. She'd already surprised him once by suggesting that the truck needed to be driven and that he should be the one to do it. He'd noticed an odd pattern to her affections. The more spur of the moment the situation, the more likely he'd find himself holding her hand. Furthermore, he often suspected she didn't do it intentionally because she seemed as surprised as he did when it happened. Then there were the moments when he'd catch her looking at him with a warmth that he swore reflected the feelings he had for her. But they never lasted for more than an instant and always preceded moments of agitation in which she seemed to forget what they were doing, like a computer recovering from an error in its programming. Whatever her reasons for this erratic behavior, it was nice to spend time alone with her as they drove to school. He just wished it wasn't going to be such a strange day.

Her hand still hadn't moved by the time they drove up to the school parking lot where he happily parked as close to the school as possible. Then he reluctantly pulled his own hand back to put the old gear shift back to park.

"Do you mind if I go talk to Mr. Harris for a bit?" Bruce asked.

"Not at all," she said. "Want company?"

"Always," he answered, getting out and walking with her to the front doors.

"But I'm going to talk with him about something that he needs to talk about, and he won't do it with you there for some reason. I have no idea what it's about."

"That must get really frustrating," she said, reaching out and squeezing his hand again before heading toward the left side of the cafeteria while he turned right toward the library. "I'll see you in first period."

A couple of balloons floating up near the roof gave testament that it had only been four days since they'd all spent a wonderful evening dancing there in the cafeteria. The cheesy decorations had been removed, and for the first time in a long time, he really looked at the cafeteria where he'd eaten lunch for the last ten years. It was hard to remember a time before his dark-haired friend had been a part of his life, even though only a year had passed. Maybe that was because so much had happened since that day when the bus driver had frightened them with threats of Old Man Biggerstaff.

The thought of the hermit made him smile. The grumpy old man would probably be pleased to know that parents still threatened bad children with his wrath. Of course, if those parents lived within a quarter mile of Guarded Wood, he'd probably heard them through the ears of his forest family.

Bruce paused at the carved library doors, his borrowed memories floating to the surface, making him wonder yet again how the cave could be behind them when there was no sign of it now. Maybe they'd covered it up after the collapse that had killed Paul.

Inside, Bruce found the librarian sitting at one of the tables with a catalog open in front of him, but he wasn't looking at it. Instead his eyes were focused on the space between two of the bookshelves.

Even though Bruce had always known that Mr. Harris was old, the man had never really looked that way until now. As he walked closer, expecting his friend to notice him at any moment, he took in the spots on his arm where the thin skin had torn and scabbed over. He hadn't shaved either, which was a surprise. The librarian normally kept himself immaculately groomed.

Bruce wondered what could have possibly brought about such a dramatic change in the few days since their adventure at Honeysuckle House. But in his heart, he already knew what it had to be.

He waited for a moment, sure that Tom would find his way back from whatever memory had trapped him and notice his young friend. When a full minute had passed, Bruce finally cleared his throat and made the librarian jump.

"Oh, hello there," he said, noticing Bruce at last. "I'm sorry if I'm not myself today. Esther made me promise that I'd come in."

"It's good to see you," Bruce said, pulling a chair over to sit next to him. "How is she?"

The old man didn't answer for a while, and his eyes returned to the same spot that had held his attention so thoroughly just a short time before.

"There's nothing more they can do for her," he whispered. "We took a nap when we got home that day. We were both tired, but we'd had such a good time with all of you. I woke up when she had the seizure…the worst one yet. I wanted to call your father and take her to the hospital when she came back to me, but she said she'd spent too much time there already. She doesn't want to die away from Nickelville. All of the people she loves are here."

"I'm sorry," Bruce said, knowing from the visions that it was okay to put his arm around his old friend. "You shouldn't be here."

"I promised," he said with a shrug, "And I've never broken a single promise that I made to that wonderful woman. Besides, there's a hospice nurse there with her, and she won't wake for quite a while yet. They've started giving her morphine for the pain."

The visions gave Bruce no guidance, and the unfairness of it all was almost too much to bear. How was it that he could see so much and steer the ones he loved to safety through these tragic waters, but not prevent this? If anyone deserved a happy ending, it was this man and his wife.

"All I can think about is that if she does wake, I'll miss it. She'd only be awake for a moment, mind you, and I don't think she'll know what is going on around her. But I can't bear the thought of missing a single one of her moments when there are so few left."

"You promised her that you'd come," Bruce said, "As far as I'm concerned, you've fulfilled that promise. Now go home to her."

"Did you know I was sitting in this chair the first time I saw her?" Mr. Harris said, his voice steadying. "One of the reasons I liked Megan so much when she came was that she reminded me of my Esther. They don't look anything alike, of course. In that your friend is pure Josie. But my wife wasn't born in Nickelville either."

"I didn't know that," Bruce said when the old man didn't speak for a while, lost again in memories of happier days.

"She was two grades ahead of us," Tom continued at last. "I didn't see the first time she walked up those stone steps outside. It was one of those rare cold winters here in Texas. I was sitting in this very chair when I heard the most beautiful sound in the world. I think I fell in love with her for the sound of her laughter even before I laid eyes on her for the first time."

371

"How do you know it was this particular chair after all these years?" Bruce asked when he became lost again.

Mr. Harris looked down at the armrest of the chair and pointed to where his initials were carved into the wood.

"I must have sat there a hundred times and never noticed that," Bruce said.

"Each of us had one," the librarian said, pointing at the arm of the chair where his young friend sat.

"AM plus JK," Bruce read. "Josephine Kennemur?"

Mr. Harris nodded, happy to be distracted if only for a moment.

"And how do you know it's the right table?"

"My predecessor gave us detention for carving these," he said, tapping the initials, "so of course we spent an afternoon carving all of our initials into the bottom of the table as well. I know it's just the foolishness of a doddering old man, but I put this table and these chairs back into place every morning."

"Josie's initials don't look like they're in the same writing as Azarich's," Bruce observed.

"That's because Azarich wasn't the one who carved them there. She did, although she didn't have to serve detention for it. She and Azarich were having lunch with me one day when she asked me if she could borrow the pin knife she knew I carried. We were about twenty-five at the time, just a few years after we came back home from the war. There's also a rather rude picture of Mr. Brown, the old principal, that Azarich drew during yet another detention. Azarich's a good man, but he was never much of an artist. That was Josie. She drew a picture of us all sitting on the check-out counter over there from a picture that's since been lost. I swear you could have mistaken it for a photograph. It was that good. She gave it to Esther since they were best friends. I always meant to have it framed, but like so many of the good intentions that got lost by the wayside, I never quite found the time."

"What are you doing?" Bruce asked, pointing to the catalog.

"Sam donated several thousand dollars to update the books, furniture and card catalog. I've wanted to do this for longer than you've been alive. But the only thing I can think about is that laugh. How am I supposed to walk into this room when I know I'll never hear her laugh here again? She's everywhere, helping me shelve, bringing her class here to check out books…"

Overcome, the librarian rested his stubbled face on his hands as if doing so could block out what was to come. Bruce stood up and held him, this man who was so much more of a grandfather to him than his father's father who lived far away and never came around anymore.

"This isn't going anywhere," Bruce said firmly. "You're going home. It doesn't matter if she's not awake. She'll know you're there, even if she doesn't open her eyes."

Mr. Harris nodded, taking a deep breath to steady his voice before he spoke.

"I'll take this with me and work on it while she sleeps," he said, putting the catalog into his worn leather satchel along with some paperwork.

"Would you mind if Megan borrowed the book on Irish folklore?" Bruce asked.

"Seeing as she more or less owns the school," Tom answered, trying to sound happy and doing a poor job of it, "I'd say she can do pretty much whatever she likes."

"We'll come in for an hour after school each day to let people check things out," Bruce added. "That way you won't need to come in at all. If anything comes up, I'll call you. And if you need anything, we'll bring it.

Just stay with her. That's your job right now."

"I'm so glad she got to meet you and Megan," the old man said, paused, and then wrapped his arm around Bruce affectionately. "She's enjoyed this last year so much. And Honeysuckle House was magical. She laughed more that day than she has in years. Thank you for that."

Bruce arrived late to his first class, and would have missed it altogether if Mr. Bob hadn't come to bat at his pen while he tried to write down everything his friend had said in his journal while it was still fresh in his mind.

Chapter XXX: Wild Rumors

Megan skimmed through the book Bruce had given her after returning from his visit to the library. However, unlike her friend, she'd never been particularly interested in any type of mythology, let alone Irish. But it was strange to see names she recognized from her mother's runestone memories. In particular, the Morrigan stood out. Although it seemed to Megan that there were wisps of truth that ran throughout each of the book's tales, she knew she wouldn't have a complete explanation for how they differed until her mother returned.

Bruce, having finally gotten over his dislike of going through the lunch line, currently waited to get those oddly shaped pieces of school pizza. In spite of the fact that they ate pizza from Gordon's at least once a week, they all still loved pizza day.

Jade sat down next to her and Andrew sat on the other side, frowning at Paul's empty chair.

"It's weird knowing that he's never going to be here again," Jade whispered. "I mean, why does that make me so sad? I just talked with him a few hours ago. He'll be sad he missed pizza day."

"Why is that stuff so good?" Megan asked. "It's nothing like actual pizza. Maybe Bruce or I can take him some the next time we have it."

"Genetic programming," Andrew answered around a mouthful. "My dad says everyone loved pizza day back when he was in school."

"My parents too," Jade said. "Dad says they had it at his school, even though he's from Oklahoma."

"Did everything go okay for Dora this morning?" Megan asked, watching for Bruce to come out of the line.

"It raised some eyebrows," the eldest Grimble answered, pausing between bites. "But she told them that he's going to be going to one of those exclusive prep schools to get into Juilliard."

"Anyone who's heard him play in the last few weeks would probably buy that," Andrew admitted. "Rumors are flying around the school like crazy. Everyone in my class is convinced that he ran off and eloped with the girl they saw him kissing just before the power went out at the Jubilee."

"Heads up," Megan said, noticing that Glenn had stopped Bruce on his way to the table.

"Should we do anything?" Andrew asked, turning to watch.

"He could handle both of the remaining members of the Trio even without using his abilities," Megan said. "I think he's got it covered."

"I did that," Jade said happily. "Before I took him under my wing, he was just a hopeless little bookworm. But look at him now."

"I just hope he doesn't dump the pizza on him," Megan said. "I'm hungry. If things go bad, I think I can snatch it out of his hands from here while everyone else is watching them."

After a short conversation, Bruce turned away from him and walked toward the table. He looked distracted as he approached, and Megan wondered if it was what Glenn had said to him, or if it was something he'd seen in the future.

"Everything okay?" Jade asked, finishing the last of her pizza and eyeing his plate.

"Don't even think about it," he said. "You'd have to fight both of us for them."

376

"Mine," Megan said, taking one out of his hand.

"Weird day," Bruce said, sitting down. "He wanted to know the same two things everyone else has asked today."

"Why didn't you run in the race, and where is our brother," Jade prompted, her hand moving slowly toward his plate.

"What did you tell him?" Andrew asked, since he'd already finished too.

"I thought about telling him that we had to drop him off at a deprogramming facility to get him away from a Satanic music cult, but knowing this school everyone would believe it."

"And the race?" Megan asked, already halfway through with her food.

"That the excitement of taking Paul to prep school made me forget about it," he said.

"I've only had one person ask me about him," Jade said, giving up on pilfering her brother's food.

"That's probably because you told the poor kid that you'd killed Paul for asking too many questions and given his body to Old Man Biggerstaff," Andrew said, chuckling.

"Seriously?" Megan asked, shoving the last bite into her mouth.

"It was one of the elementary kids," Andrew added. "The poor boy almost wet himself."

"You know," Megan said, pushing her plate aside and returning to the book. "It's like the stuff in this book. Everything we just said has a hint of the truth in it. Well, except the cult thing. But it's all twisted around, like these stories."

"Those myths have had about seven millennia to get mixed up," Bruce said. "It's amazing that anything from the original events survived at all." Then he spent the next few seconds eating. "Admit it, Jade," he continued when he'd finished. "What you're really upset about is that Paul will never have to take geometry."

"I hadn't even thought about that," Jade groaned, putting her head on Andrew's shoulder. "Life is so unfair. Hold me."

Andrew looked more than happy to comply.

"What's up with the book calling them Tuatha dé Danann?" Megan asked. "I never heard them refer to themselves with that last part."

"If I remember it right," he answered. "Medieval monks added that because they were calling the Jews something similar and wanted to make sure that readers didn't confuse the two."

"How do you know all of this stuff?" Jade asked.

"Some of us use the internet for more than online gaming," he answered. "Speaking of which, Megan, your house is currently being brought into the current century. Your new phone, laptop and printer should be set up by the time you get home. I'm rather jealous actually. They're quite a bit nicer than mine."

"Bruce," Megan scolded, "You can't just do things like that without asking!"

"Didn't I?" he asked innocently. "I could have sworn I did. It must have been in one of the other branches. Trust me, you were extremely grateful. After all, I had to replace mine as well recently for some reason."

"You're insufferable!" Megan said in exasperation.

"That's what Paul and I have been trying to tell you for the past year!" Jade said, losing her steam and looking at her brother's empty seat. "Why is this so hard? It's not like I can't talk to him anytime I want."

"Because you two have always been close. Besides," Bruce answered, looking at Megan again. "It was technically Sam who bought all of that stuff. I'm completely innocent, and I think you owe me an apology for being so mean."

Glaring, Megan looked down at the book which was suddenly buried under a purring mass of black fur.

"That cat just appeared out of nowhere!" Andrew whispered in surprise.

"Oh," Jade said absently, still resting her head on his shoulder. "Mr. Bob is some kind of ancient cat god or something. I may have forgotten a few things. The whole Paul thing was a bit distracting."

"Understandable," he mumbled, looking at the cat with concern.

When Mr. Bob stood up and stretched, Megan was no longer on the page she'd been looking at. In the middle of the page was the same woodcut image that Bruce had shown her from the internet. Below it was an entry on cat sidhe.

"Now you're just showing off," she said, passing the book over to Andrew. "Which means you not only understand what we're saying, but you can read as well."

He purred deeper.

"So if you can understand everything," she continued, looking him directly in the eye as he sat on the table in front of her. "That means that you understood that you were getting me into loads of trouble last year."

"He needed you to end up in the isolation room so Jacob could talk to you without me interfering," Bruce explained, sighing contentedly now that he'd eaten.

"Do you work for the Dark Man?" Megan asked.

The cat yawned.

"Do you still answer to the Morrigan?" Bruce asked.

This earned him a tilt of the head and a backward glance that suggested communicating with Bruce was beneath him.

"It's almost like he's the father of all cats," Bruce said, looking at the big feline. "You know, the one that taught them all to be so passive aggressive."

An irritated flick of his tail coincided with something falling hard on the ground next to the table. Bruce looked down to see what it was and then reached immediately to his back pocket.

"He just took my phone out of my pocket and dropped it on the floor," Bruce said, scooping it up and looking at the screen. "Ha! You'll have to do better than that! You can't spend this much time with Megan and not get the strongest case known to man for your electronics."

"Is it really wise to antagonize the cat god?" Andrew asked, still staring at Mr. Bob warily. "My mom read a story to me when I was little about the fair folk replacing children with changelings. It scared me worse than any horror story."

"Speaking of phones," Bruce said, deciding that he should probably head off any more talk of changelings since his friend still got offended by the term. "I wish the signal wasn't so spotty in the school. Will you guys remind me to call Sam and tell him what Mr. Harris wants for the library renovation?"

"That was fast," Megan said. "I thought you said he wouldn't make his choices for another three days."

"He won't," Bruce replied, still glaring at Mr. Bob. "But I already know what he's going to choose, and he's not going to return before it comes in anyway."

"They're sure there's nothing else they can do for Esther?" Jade asked. "Can you see anything about her dying?"

"No," Bruce said. "Things like this make me glad that strong emotions cause blank spots in my foresight. I don't want to have to see that more than once."

Chapter XXXI: Pucker up, Mr. Brown

A few days later, Bruce, Megan, Andrew and Jade went to the library after school to check out books to any of the Academy students who might show up, not that there'd been many so far. But as soon as they found the carved doors propped open, Bruce realized he hadn't been watching their future very closely. In his defense, they'd all been spending most of their free time in Guarded Wood with Paul and his future wife.

"I don't suppose you guys want to help me move all of these books over to the unused classroom?" Mr. Green asked.

"Sure," Jade said. "Do we just have the two carts?"

"That's right," the janitor said. "If you guys don't mind, I'll get started taking the measurements so we know how everything will fit."

After a quickly whispered discussion, Bruce and Megan started to run the carts back and forth down to the temporary new library while Jade and her boyfriend unshelved the books, careful to keep them in order.

What Mr. Green didn't know was that as soon as the carts were out of his line of sight, either Bruce or Megan walked the shadows with them to their destination and moved them the same way, a row at a time onto the floor. Distracted as he was, he didn't even notice the breakneck speed the eldest Grimble and her boyfriend had to work just to keep up.

When they'd finished, Bruce looked around and saw how empty his favorite part of the school looked. If he'd had his way, they wouldn't have changed this part of the school at all. He'd been tempted to avoid doing so. But Mr. Harris had always wanted to update his treasury of books and the resources available to the students. It would have been selfish to deny these renovations just because Bruce felt nostalgic.

"You can't possibly be done already," the janitor said, looking up from the clipboard he'd been using to store the figures. "It's not a mess over there is it?"

"Do you seriously think my brother would let us be anything less than organized?" Jade asked. "If we'd gotten even a single book out of order he would have made us spend the whole weekend putting them right."

"Good point," Mr. Green conceded. "The rats are still too impressed to go into my shed. I guess I might go home early to my blushing bride tonight!"

"Please," Jade said, looking skeptical. "I work for your wife, and I don't think that woman has blushed since the first space shuttle went up."

"You might be surprised," the janitor said.

"I never thought I'd say this to you or your friends," Jade said, looking ill. "But please don't finish that story."

"Hey Alan," Bruce said, eager to avoid any more knowledge about those two than already leaked past his shields when they were together in his presence. "Have you ever noticed that Mr. Harris keeps your chairs in their old places around the same table you guys used to sit at?"

"You mean when we were kids?" Alan asked, going over to look.

"What are you talking about?" Jade said, also relieved to have him distracted from his earlier line of thought.

"I'll be damned," he said, running the toughened skin of his fingertips along the initials carved into the armrest. "I haven't thought about that for at least twenty or thirty years. Mine should be the one on the other corner. And you say he makes sure they stay in the same place where they were back then?"

"He said that's how he starts off every morning."

"Hey Alan," Jade said, looking where he'd pointed. "You should look at this."

"What is it?" he asked, moving over where he could see. "Surely not!"

"Kate's initials are carved right under his," Jade said for everyone who couldn't see. "She had to have done it while she was still at the school."

"Let's just fix this," the janitor said, pulling out his pocket knife. When he was finished the four letters were enclosed in a heart. "I'm sure Tom won't mind."

"Are these my grandparent's initials?" Megan asked, finding Azarich's.

"This was our table," Alan said. "We used to come in here every morning when we got here. The whole school used to leave these seats alone when they saw us coming. Not because they were afraid of us. I don't think we ever really had any enemies here other than the principal's son, Christian Brown.

"Do I detect a forefather of the Terrible Trio?" Jade asked, sitting down in the librarian's old seat.

"Christian wasn't anything that bad," Alan said absently. "I wanted to restore this table a while back and Tom wouldn't let me. I guess I know why now. I think he put varnish over our carvings to make them last better."

"Do you know why he did it?" Bruce asked.

"No idea," the janitor said. "I wonder why he never mentioned it."

"The seat where Jade is sitting is where he heard Esther laugh for the first time," Bruce explained.

"She does have an amazing laugh," Megan admitted, enjoying this story.

"I used to be so jealous of my friends," the janitor confessed. "I hated feeling that way, but it didn't change anything. Azarich and Josie had been together since the first grade. Carl and Elizabeth were going steady for about three years before we left for the war. And it might have taken Tom the better part of two years to get Esther, but once he did, it was clear they never wanted to spend a single day apart. After we got back from the war, I don't think they've ever spent more than the hours when they worked apart. In the early days they didn't even spend that long apart because she taught second grade here."

"You eventually found your girl," Jade said. "She says she still remembers the first time you came into the movies when she worked there."

"Trust me, I remember it too. I'd never seen anyone so beautiful."

"That's not the first time you saw each other," Megan said, and Bruce could tell that she hadn't meant to say that out loud.

"What do you mean?" Alan asked.

"It was the day when the town threw the send-off for the men leaving for war," she said at last. "Esther and Josie saw it."

"She couldn't have been much more than a little girl," he said, frowning.

"You dropped your hat and she gave it back to you," she said.

"That was Kate?" he almost shouted. "I told her…"

"That she'd saved you getting into trouble and you gave her a stick of Wrigley's gum," Megan said, smiling at the look of wonder that came over the old man's face. "Esther said she could tell that girl fell head over heels for you. She stood on top of one of the seats so she could see you."

"Wow," he said, looking off into the room as if he could see it in his mind. "I guess that settles it. I am quite the cradle robber, aren't I?"

"Yes," Megan giggled. "You should be ashamed of yourself."

"But how do you know what kind of gum it was?" the janitor asked.

"Because it's taped over the pictures she has on the wall in her kitchen," she answered.

"Tell us about the drawing under the table," Bruce prompted.

"Tell me that's not still under there!" Alan exclaimed, distracted from the revelation of the gum wrapper and getting down on the floor with great difficulty to look at the underside of the table.

Soon all five of them were laying on their backs on the wooden floorboards, looking up at Azarich's drawing.

"Is that a Saint Bernard?" Andrew asked.

Mr. Green chuckled before explaining that it was a mule.

"That poor animal," Megan said. "What's wrong with it, and why is that man kissing its backside?"

"There's nothing wrong with it. Your grandfather was just a horrible artist."

"Azarich drew that?" Jade laughed, and then turned so she could use Andrew's stomach as a pillow. "Did he often go around drawing pictures of people kissing mule butts?"

"To my knowledge this is the only one," Alan replied. "There's a story about this one though."

"Does it involve a kiss?" Jade asked.

"No, just a mule, the four of us guys, Josie and Mr. Brown's office over a weekend."

"Damn I wish Paul was here for this," Jade said, then looked at the janitor apologetically.

"Don't be sorry," Alan said. "I think the whole school misses that boy. Have you talked to him since he left?"

Jade touched her left ear, screwing up her face in concentration.

"She talks to Paul all the time," Bruce said. "Get on with the story. I wish we had some popcorn."

"That's because you never worked the concession stand," Megan said.

"I love story time," Bruce said. "Don't keep us waiting."

"The principal's son," Mr. Green told them, "was named Christian. For some reason he decided one day that Josie was pretty sweet on the eyes. Even though she and Azarich had been going together for years, he asked her to the first dance we were allowed to go to when we got to the tenth grade."

"Just like us," Megan said.

"Yes, we were about your age. Anyway, Josie told him no. She was nice about it, but Christian wouldn't take that for an answer. His family wasn't particularly well off, but he seemed to think that just because his daddy was the principal, he should be able to do whatever he wanted."

"This still reeks of the Terrible Trio," Bruce said.

"When she finally got mad at him and told him she'd rather go to the dance with a mule, he became a bit angry and called her a name that no gentleman should ever use to describe a woman. She wound up to slap him, but Azarich got there first. He punched Christian so hard that the principal heard his son's nose break all the way in the office from the cafeteria."

"Man I would have loved to have seen that," Bruce said, now resting on his elbow so he could see the rest of them during the story. Azarich's drawing actually seemed to get worse the longer he looked at it.

"Azarich ended up suspended for three days, and then he had to clean gum off the bottoms of all the desks and chairs in the Academy. It took him over a week before and after school to get it done."

"It looks like he missed a few," Jade said, pointing out a few pieces that currently resided under the table.

"While he was under here, he drew this picture."

"But what about the office and the mule?" Megan asked.

"That was your grandmother's idea," the janitor laughed. "She suggested that we steal a real mule from the FFA barn that used to stand out past my shed. Azarich told his parents that we were camping out in my backyard even though we hadn't done that since we were on the elementary end of the school. It would have taken him all night to ride his bike down from Beverly Road otherwise. I grew up with farm animals and had no trouble at all getting the mule to come with me. What I couldn't figure out was how we were supposed to get into the school. Turns out Josie knew what she was talking about when she planned our little prank. She was scary good at getting locked doors to open."

Bruce flashed a quick grin at Megan, who listened blissfully at this chance to hear about her grandmother. Apparently, this Daughter of Crina wasn't as stern and serious as her ancestor had been.

"We locked the mule in Mr. Brown's office along with several buckets of water so he wouldn't dehydrate while he was in there," the janitor paused here, trying not to laugh as he spoke. "And that was the night that I decided I never wanted to get on Josie Kennemur's bad side. That girl brought a whole watermelon and a sack of green apples when she rode over here. I have no idea how she steered and rode with all of that. She wasn't very big full-grown, and she was still a few years off from that yet."

"Why did she do that?" Bruce asked.

"Mules can eat fruit, but if you give them too much without something with more substance, it tends to give them the runs."

"And you locked it into the principal's office for the whole weekend!" Megan cried in horrified glee.

"And that wasn't the best part," Alan said, finally giving into the laughter.

"Don't leave us hanging," Andrew begged, happily running his fingers through Jade's multicolored hair.

"Before we left, she pulled one of her father's Sunday ties out of her pocket and tied it around the mule's neck so there would be no mistake that she thought it would make a better date than Christian Brown!"

"Megan," Jade said when she could finally catch her breath. "Your grandmother sounds like she was quite the prankster."

"I wish I'd had a chance to meet her," Megan said, and Bruce knew she was thinking about the phantom who had guided them to the grove that day.

"This town wasn't the same without her," Alan said sadly.

"At least it still has the rest of you," Bruce said.

"I don't know about that," the old man answered, still looking at the drawing. "We had our time. The town has moved on since then. There are only a few places like this that still hold the marks we made."

"What became of Christian Brown?" Bruce asked.

"Everyone knew what we'd done," he answered, "But not even Megan's great grandfather would admit that the tie was his. As I recall, Josie got him a new one the next Father's Day, and he said he'd cherish it more than any other he'd ever worn. But Christian left us alone after that. I actually felt sorry for him after a while."

"What do you mean?" Megan asked.

"He became the unluckiest and clumsiest person I've ever had the misfortune of knowing," he answered. "Seems like he was always falling or having things fall on him after Azarich punched him. And every time some misfortune befell him, Josie and eventually her shadow, Esther, were there to laugh at him."

Megan laughed so hard she soon had them all cackling like children.

"Now this has been fun and all," the old man said when they settled down. "But I've got just one more favor to ask of you before we go."

"Anything," Jade said. "We owe you after that story."

"I'm going to have to get you young-uns to help me up. I've gone and gotten completely stiff on this cold floor. I guess the years are finally catching up to me."

Chapter XXXII: The Hermit's Secret

The two of you should probably come to Josie's Grove, the hermit's thoughts came while Megan and Bruce were catching up on some of their homework. *And bring the mirror.*

But Mr. Bob hasn't given me the next runestone yet, Megan sent, frowning from where she sat on the living room sofa.

The cat sidhe isn't the only one who knows where your mother hid them, and I've got the last one for you. I'll be waiting there by the time you two get there.

"I didn't see that coming," Bruce said, frowning.

"Me either," Megan said, reaching out and pulling the shirt-clad mirror from her backpack.

"No, Megan," he repeated, "I didn't see this in the future at all."

"I guess we'll have to find out the old-fashioned way then," she said, "I don't know how to feel about this. If it's the last one, then there must be something pretty serious in it. Otherwise I'm still going to have as many questions as when we started."

"I can't see anything for the next week or so," he said. "And everything after that makes no sense at all."

"That doesn't exactly fill me with confidence," she admitted. "Let's get this over with."

They walked through the shadows to where August already waited. Fang slept at his feet.

"I'm a little bit afraid of this one," Megan said, walking over and taking the warm stone from his gnarled fingers. "After wanting this for so long, I'm starting to realize that my mother was right in keeping some things from me until I was older. I'm not even sure that I'm ready now."

"All we can ever do is guess how we will react when confronted with situations that test us," August said. "Well, that might not be true for you Bruce, and I'm not sure if that's a gift or a curse."

"So far it's been a bit of both," Bruce admitted. "Are you still ready to get this over?"

"You promised that this one would tell me where she's gone," Megan said, turning the stone over in her hands.

"That's right," August said, sitting down. "Although you already know she's just outside of Haven. What you really want to know is why you spent the first part of your life running from the Wild Hunt. For that you will have your answer."

"Let's do this," she said, sitting down on the ground and placing the mirror in her lap for what she hoped was the last time. Then she placed the runestone in its center.

Emelia levered herself out of the bed she shared with her husband, careful not to wake him. It wasn't as easy or graceful as it had once been. Her time was growing close. Soon Megan would come into this strange world and eventually lead her people.

But this morning didn't feel particularly glorious. She'd spent most of the night getting up to go to the bathroom, and almost every part of her body ached as her body tried to reject Daragh's blood as it flowed through her veins. But that was a small price for the life she felt stirring within her.

She took in the lines and curves of his face in the shadows of the fire that burned in the hearth. She loved him as well as the life they'd carved in that strange world. Since the Battle of Mag Tuired, the Tuatha dé not only respected her, but they'd come to love her as one of their own even if her Gaelic remained rough at best.

Then the part of the Morrigan that had taken root within her stirred like the dark twin of the child in her womb. Emelia had just enough time to wonder if this unwelcome guest might not have infected just her, but her unborn child as well before the visions began.

In the first, she saw her daughter, twin to the mother she'd never known. After a lifetime of the venomous tales of the Children of Nyx, Megan rose up in the aftermath of her father's death, wielding the beautifully blended magics of her human and Tuatha dé heritage against her enemies with the might of her people behind her. Possessed of a cold and terrible beauty, the Dark Queen laid waste the Children of Nyx and sent them into the oblivion they'd once sought for the Tuatha dé. But this victory only whetted her appetite, and the following bloodlust led her to seek the subjugation of the mortals she disdained. She set world leaders against one another, flaming their animosity into war. Afterward, the Tuatha dé enslaved the ones left in its wake. In the end she ruled over a world in which whole cities burned and the future of mankind was no longer certain.

The first contraction of her labor clamped down, smothering her as she tried to make sense of the horrors she'd just witnessed. She slapped a thicker set of shields over the previous ones to keep Daragh from feeling her anguish and pain.

Then a second vision came to her, and in it she fled Tyr Sgodl before Megan took her first breath. Once again leaving everything and everyone she loved behind, Emelia gave birth alone in the world of her old life and raised her daughter on the run, never more than a few steps ahead of the Wild Hunt. This path held pain, anguish and at times it held despair almost too great to bear. But living outcast on the edges of society, the two of them would still survive. Megan would never find out who the Children of Nyx were and what they'd done to her people. She wouldn't know who she was or understand the depths of the power she would one day wield until she could do so without succumbing to its dark lure. And at the end of their long flight, her daughter, grown full of compassion, would become the savior of both the Tuatha dé and their enemies, the Children of Nyx, bringing about lasting peace.

With the absolute certainty that the only time for the choice to be made was at hand, Emelia quietly dressed, gathered a handful of things that she'd need in the lonely life ahead and paused only once more to watch her king while he slept.

She used his wedding gift one last time to walk the shadows to an isolated part of a forest where few ever traveled. Then she drew the Dagda's staff, still in the form of the blade she'd returned it to while still on the plains of Mag Tuired, and used it to sever her cherished wedding band. She couldn't allow him to follow her with it, no matter how desperately she wanted him to do exactly that. The backlash of power burned her finger badly, and she feared she'd lose it. But that was a problem for another time. Without the spells Daragh had forged into the ring's making, her labor intensified as her body sought to rid itself of the hybrid child.

Emelia, whose own mother had died in childbirth, gave birth far from the nearest trail with only the voice of the Morrigan for company. Then she made her way to a town where the whispers told her to sell the necklace that Daragh had given her in order to buy an old beat-up truck that reminded her of the one her father had driven. The woman who sold it to her even threw in a car seat for free.

393

The scene faded in Megan's mind, and she found herself standing in Josie's grove. She thought at first that the vision had ended, but unless August had changed clothes in the seconds since she'd sat down and Bruce had wandered off, this was still one of her mother's memories.

August held up the mirror that he would later give to Megan, so Emelia could see her reflection as she spoke.

"Now you know why we left our home with the Tuatha dé. I've never once thought you capable of becoming the woman I saw in that first premonition of the Morrigan, but even before you were born, our people had become a bitter echo of who they'd once been. The death of so many parents and friends left a mark on them that will not soon fade. I saw no way to protect you from that, and I knew from the vision that in the end you would become their greatest weapon. That was not the life I wanted for you. Even though the life we shared together was difficult, I cherished the chance to watch you grow into the woman that you are today. I'm so sorry you weren't given the chance to grow up with your father. I still love him as much today as I did when we first fell in love.

I have been shown that you will return from the shadows this afternoon, and that your own Scathlahm will watch over you from a distance while I am gone. I have given him the blade of his station, and he will use it in your defense should the necessity arise. Before morning, I will leave for Haven, the stronghold of our enemies. There I will meet with a man very much like you. Don't be afraid for me. I have been shown that he is not like his kin, and he will not turn me over to them. This journey is almost over, my miracle of a daughter.

But there is one last thing you need to know. Shortly after August began to help me make these runestones, he shared his greatest secret. You have heard my father and his friends talk about the night that they tried to camp in Guarded Wood. You and Bruce have both noticed that *none of them seem to be able to remember what happened on that night.*

In much the same way that young Paul drew the attention of the siren, my father and his friends did so as well. But unlike the night of the storm, August had traveled deep within the old places when he sensed their danger, and he did not reach them quickly enough. They'd already made their way to her lair, and she had drained their life force to the threshold of death. I have no idea how he fought back a creature like that who had just fed on four young men, but in the end, he won their freedom.

Using the skills that he'd learned in his long service to Guarded Wood, he bound their life forces to his own, saving them from the death that nearly claimed them that night. The irony is not lost on him that had he known how to do this in the beginning, he could have saved his wife.

The reason Azarich and the others do not recall what happened to them is because they were mesmerized by the siren at first and then unconscious for the rest. August carried them to the McGeehee house and left them there in the backyard, never knowing how close they had come to death.

The reason why they have lived for so long is because they will not die until the hermit does. That's why they've possessed the energy of youth in spite of their years. Until now. Shortly after the fauns came and restored the boundary, August began to feel his strength leaving him. His power began to wane, and he realized he was at last dying.

When he takes his last breath, the men he saved that night will pass with him. There is nothing that we can do to stop this. As difficult as these years on the run have been, the hardest part for me is that I will not be there when this happens. For reasons I do not yet understand, I must be just outside of Haven when it occurs. The Morrigan asks too much. But even as I say this, I know that I will do as she bids, for it is only on

395

this path that your future is secure.

My role in this is almost at its end, and I am so very tired. I am sorry to leave you with these burdens, but I have now fulfilled my promise. You know everything of importance now, and if by chance, I have forgotten anything you wish to know, I will never hide anything from you again. There will be hard days ahead for you, Megan, but I know that you and your friends will find a way through. I am so proud of you, not only for your abilities, but also for the amazing woman you have become. Tell my father everything, and let him know that I will be there at the end, even though he won't be able to see me. Tell him and the others that I owe so much of who I've become to the way they shared their lives with me. Tell Sam that I love him, and that a part of my heart will always belong to him, no matter how things turned out."

Megan withdrew into herself when the memory released its hold on her, and August was there to steady her. She clamped her shields down hard to hold in the maelstrom of grief and rage, lest she accidentally lash out at the ones she loved.

"What's wrong with her?" Bruce asked, kneeling next to his friend.

"She's just learned that most of her life here is about to come to an end," the hermit answered quietly.

"All of you?" she asked in a breaking voice, noticing that the ring on her thumb was growing uncomfortably warm. She hoped it held, or she might blow out every fuse in Nickelville.

"I'm sorry," August said. "It's cruel that after wishing I could follow my wife for so long, it's only here at the end that I have found a reason to stay."

"What's going on?" Bruce asked, his fear spilling past his shields. "Why can't I see anything in our future?"

"I love you August," Megan said, rising to her feet. "I'm so sorry we didn't figure it out sooner, but can you please tell Bruce so he can let his family and Sam know. I need to be alone for a little while."

Chapter XXXIII: Messengers of Bad Tidings

Bruce hadn't realized how much he'd come to depend on his ability to read the future until it suddenly became so unreliable. He'd never encountered such a large blank spot in the future, and he wondered if it was a coincidence that it coincided in events that involved the bard. He knew strong feelings could mimic the blurring effect of strong magic when they'd cornered Sam at his house. But maybe he had the whole thing reversed. Maybe it was the strong emotions of the situations when they used their power that made reading the future difficult and not the magic itself?

Whatever the cause, he really wished he could see how to proceed with Megan. She might have inherited her mother's stony facade, but this was too much for anyone to bear alone. She needed him, and she'd never admit that to herself. Furthermore, as much as he wished it might be otherwise, she only needed him as a friend.

"Why didn't we just tell all of them in the beginning?" she asked, pacing around his bedroom after appearing without warning a few moments before. "Then the worst part would have been over already."

It wasn't until much later that he realized that she'd done so in spite of his room's protections and without tripping his wards.

"Do you really think telling them about our abilities is going to be the worst part?" he asked.

"Good point," she agreed. "But why didn't we tell them when we told Grandpa?"

"We hid it from Mr. Green because no matter when we told him, he always managed to slip and then that person told someone else. In some of those paths he gets committed to an asylum."

"And we'd never want that," Megan agreed.

"Every time we tell Mr. Harris, his desperation pushes him toward the occult when he realizes that we can't heal her. It ruins the time they have left together."

"And you had no hint that it would turn out like this?" she asked.

"I don't think I can see much of anything when Luminita and Paul use their power. I didn't see anything about him at the Jubilee until it happened. To be honest, I can't see either of them even after we get past these next few days. Or our futures either. I don't know how I functioned like this before you came."

"I just wish we knew how to do this," she said, wrapping her arms around herself as if to keep herself from flying apart. As he watched, he knew what he had to do.

"You're not going to do this alone," he said. Then he walked over and pulled her close. He tried not to let it hurt him when she stiffened in his arms. "I'm here, and I always will be. But you've got to let this out, Megan. You can't hold this inside or it will break you when we tell them."

She shook her head violently and tried to push him away. He didn't let her.

"No," she said, and he could feel her power building.

"He's your grandfather, and they're all like family to us. You're not on the run anymore. You don't have to hold everything inside."

"I'm..."

"Your mother's daughter?" he finished. "I don't even think she would be armored enough to keep this inside. Even if she is sharing her head with the Morrigan."

Megan let out one blurt of laughter at that, then she stiffened once more. She balled her hand into a fist and worked it up inside his embrace to hammer against his chest once, twice and then finally a third time. But that was okay, because now she'd started to hold her breath to keep it inside. The armor she'd forged to protect herself from a world that would never understand her began to crack.

He held her tight enough to know that he was there, but loose enough that she wouldn't know how much he never wanted to let her go. Then with a tiny sob, her mind opened to him as she hadn't done since the early days of their friendship. The tides of her grief swept him away with her, and he wept as well.

Going on instinct alone, since they couldn't rely on Bruce's foresight to instruct them, they visited Tom Harris and his wife, Esther. Megan argued that they should tell Azarich first, but after telling his own parents about their abilities, he realized they needed to avoid having some people with all of the answers while some felt they'd been kept in the dark unfairly.

The librarian looked pleased though surprised to find the two of them on his doorstep before he led them into a house out of an old television show. Old photographs lined the walls, telling the story of their long lives.

"Please sit," Mr. Harris said, motioning to a long, low sofa in front of which sat a spindly coffee table, laden with books. "Can I get either of you anything?"

"No, but thank you," Megan said quickly, looking at one of the watercolors that hung on the wall.

"Josie painted those," he said, confirming what they already suspected as he took his seat in one of the two worn recliners that sat facing the television. "So what brings you here tonight?"

"We have some things that we need to tell you," Bruce said awkwardly. It was unpleasantly hot as an old gas floor heater radiated heat into the room. "Esther should probably hear this as well."

"I'm sorry," the librarian said after a quiet moment in which he looked as hard put to describe what he needed to say as they'd been on the way over. "It's unlikely that she'll wake again. The drugs they have her on are too strong for that."

"Why haven't you told anyone?" Megan asked.

"Azarich and Alan already know," he answered kindly. "But she didn't want either of you to see her like this. She wants you to remember her the way she was at Honeysuckle House. She had so much fun that day. So what have you come to tell me?"

"I'm so sorry," Megan said. "I was hoping that she could help us tell you."

"Tell me about what?" the old man prompted.

"Did you ever notice strange things happening when my grandmother was around?" Megan asked.

"Nothing was ever normal around Josie," Mr. Harris chuckled. "You're going to have to be more specific than that."

"The way she could open locks without a key," Megan began. "The way she knew things she couldn't possibly know about the past..."

"And the way she and my wife always seemed to be in the middle of some sort of mischief that only they understood?" the old man asked.

Megan nodded.

"I take it the two of you know something about it then?"

"Josie was descended from a family who had certain supernatural abilities," Bruce explained. "Almost all of the women had them."

"Are you trying to tell me that Josie Kennemur was a witch?" Mr. Harris said with a grin.

"Something like that," Megan answered. "Although what we do is nothing like the superstitions."

"But you are saying that you can work magic," he said skeptically.

Megan summoned the flame above her palm in what was quickly becoming a well-rehearsed show. Then Bruce brought a book from a nearby shelf to him without moving from the couch.

"But you're not part of her family," Tom said, frowning. "And not a woman either."

"I'm something slightly different," Bruce said. "I mimic her abilities and have a few of my own."

"But this is just a part of what we need to tell you," Megan said, then went on to explain the events of that night in Guarded Wood so long ago.

"Wait," Mr. Harris said when they'd finished. "If Old Man Biggerstaff was able to save us by binding our lives to his, then that means we can use this magic to help save my Esther!"

"August is dying," Bruce said quietly. "And I'm afraid that when he does, you and your friends will do so as well."

"When?" the librarian asked, oddly happy about the news.

"Just before the sun rises, two days from now," Megan answered, surprised that the Morrigan would choose that moment to become involved. Bruce cast her a startled glance.

"Esther and I can pass on together?" he asked.

"We can't promise that she will die the same time you do," Megan said. "She isn't bound to August's life force the way that you and the others are."

"She's only holding on because I won't let her go," Tom exclaimed with a relieved smile. "We owe August so much."

"What do you mean?" Bruce asked.

"If he'd let us die of our own stupidity all of those years ago, I'd have never met my wife. None of us would have gotten married," he said, then toward Megan, "And you wouldn't be here at all."

"I really hope I can be as strong as you when my time comes," Bruce said.

"This is a gift," the old man insisted, "I'm not nearly as afraid of dying with her as I was by the thought of living without her."

That part Bruce understood all too well.

"Have you told Azarich yet?" Tom asked.

"He knows about our abilities, but not about August," Megan answered. "We hoped you could help us."

"Of course I will," he said. "Azarich will handle it well, but poor Alan. He's the bravest man I've ever known, but he and Kate have had so little time together. This is cruel. But if we had died all of those years past, they wouldn't have met either. Only Azarich and Josie knew each other before that night, and even though I don't think they'd even held hands yet at that age, we all knew they'd marry one day. Let's have them come here and tell them at the same time. That way Alan won't feel like he's been kept in the dark while everyone else knew what was going on."

Kate had already known that her young friends were more than they seemed. She'd known every broken part of The Palace intimately and was not fooled when they said that nothing had been quite as bad as it had first seemed. They didn't even make replacement parts for the Grand

403

Theatre's projector.

"Why didn't you ever say anything?" Bruce asked.

"I know that this might come as a shock," Kate said, tossing her red hair for emphasis, "but I'm Irish. And I'm old enough that my family still talked about bogarts and how they would help if you kept their secrets and harm if you didn't."

What's a bogart? Megan asked.

It's kind of like a little troll or gnome, Bruce answered. *There's a lot of old stories about them fixing shoes.*

That's almost as bad as being called a changeling.

"How much do the two of you remember about that night when we went into Guarded Wood?" the librarian asked his friends.

"Not much," Azarich said. "August implied that we were better off not knowing."

"Unfortunately, that's not an option anymore," Megan said. Then she told them what she knew about that night and what August had done to save them."

"He's dying," Azarich said. "Isn't he?"

"I'm afraid so," Bruce said.

"That explains why I've been so under the weather these past few weeks," the old lawyer said. "As he fades, we follow suit."

"How long?" Kate asked, holding tight to her husband's hand.

Answering was the hardest thing Bruce had ever done.

Chapter XXXIV: Bruce's Gift

No one went to school the next day, and Megan laid in bed longer than usual, staring at the new alarm clock Bruce had ordered with the computer and phone. She'd spent the night watching the red lines that formed the numbers change configuration as the seconds bled away into minutes and hours. It somehow managed to feel as if the moments dragged by while simultaneously rushing by like the water in a narrow channel during a flood. Then she crossed the point she'd been dreading without knowing why. It was just numbers on a clock, but then again, she knew it wasn't really. By this time tomorrow, nothing would ever be the same again.

She reached out with her mind and turned on the coffee pot.

After they'd returned from breaking the news, her grandfather had set about making sure that she and her mother would be taken care of, and that his estate would pass smoothly to them. This was particularly important now that Honeysuckle House had been added to the family's ownings. The computer and printer she'd scolded Bruce for buying made it possible for Azarich to download and fill out all of the proper forms with Sam Wise serving as her guardian until her mother's return. They'd only had to leave the house once to go by and file the paperwork at the courthouse.

After that, she and her grandfather spent the evening in Josie's grove, watching the images she conjured in the flames and showing him everything he wanted to know about their lives on the run and why it had been necessary. And even though his strength drained away while she watched, he held onto the flames like a lifeline, and she understood at last how much he'd needed answers too.

But now it was half an hour before her new alarm clock would go off, and she remained unsure about whether she should wake him for their morning ritual. As the previous day had worn on, he'd begun to fade, and she feared how little of him might remain when the dawn came.

She became aware of a high pitch whine in the back of her mind just as she noticed that her room seemed brighter than it had just a few seconds earlier. She rose quickly from her bed, following the light that streamed in from her open door. The sound in her mind grew in volume, annoying, but not painful. Light had begun to pour in from the rooms facing Guarded Wood.

Worried that the new clock might be wrong and that the sunrise had arrived without them, she crossed to one of the guest room windows and looked out. But it wasn't the sun that lit the world outside. The treehouse tower shone like a beacon, illuminating the edge of Guarded Wood as well as the houses that stood at its edge.

She hardened her shields to meet whatever threat this might represent and walked the shadows to the tower, where she found Bruce, Paul and Luminita. Her first thought was that Bruce had gone insane. She'd never felt him so heavily shielded, even when he'd tried to spare her the anguish of his nightmares. Light pierced the night from a softball sized ball of light hovering between his outstretched palms, glowing as brightly as a welder's arc. His eyes were closed in concentration and she had the feeling that he couldn't sense her there.

Paul and Luminita both played their violins in a slow but powerful rhythm. But where Bruce faced Guarded Wood, the two of them faced the heart of Nickelville where she noticed a heavy fog had risen, denser than any she'd ever seen before.

Come down here, Sam sent from below. *It would be best not to disturb them right now.*

"What are they doing?" she asked, appearing next to where he sat at one of the tables with August. Fang was curled up on the deck at his feet, sound asleep.

"Making an amazing sunrise," August said quietly. His eyes were closed and a faint smile spread across lips. "That's some of the most beautiful magic I've ever seen."

Lightning crossed the sky and thunder rolled through the valley in which the town stood.

"He's making a sunrise?" she asked, confused.

"For you and Azarich," Sam said. "He told me to make sure you put a sweater on him. The low pressure front that Luminita is calling will drop the temperature. And Paul is raising the fog to make sure that no one from town can pinpoint what's going on here."

She stared at him, unable to fully comprehend.

Jade came out from the bunkhouse followed by her parents.

"What are you doing here?" she asked. "Aren't you supposed to be getting Azarich into position? The sun will come up any minute now."

Megan walked the shadows to the kitchen and poured a cup of coffee with a ton of sugar and cream, just the way her grandfather liked it. Then she went to his bedside and gently shook him awake.

"What's wrong?" he asked weakly.

"It's time for us to watch the sunrise," she said. "Do you want coffee?"

"That would be nice." he said, a little groggily, "I'm a bit chilled."

She put thick socks on him and laced up his shoes even though she had no intention of letting him walk down the stairs. Then she pulled his favorite sweater over his head and put his glasses on him, trying to find the hardened lawyer in the childlike expression he wore.

She helped him to stand and walked the shadows with him in her arms to the back porch.

"Weeee," he chuckled weakly. "Can we do that again?"

"I promise we will later," she assured him, helping him sit on the swing. Her eyes swept to the Sentinel where it held the tower above the other trees, resembling a lighthouse beneath a churning sea of dark clouds overhead.

"What's that?" he asked.

"That is Bruce showing off," she answered, calling the coffee to her hand and helping him to hold it.

"That boy really loves you," Azarich said.

"I…" she started to reply, breaking off in mid-sentence as she lost track of the thought. She leaned close to him while he watched, her hand cupping his while he drank.

"Mmmm," he said. "Perfect."

When the first bit of sunlight hit the undulating mass of clouds overhead, a shooting star streaked into the sky overhead from the tower, setting the tempest afire in a cauldron of rolling hues. Thunder shook the earth beneath Nickelville, accenting the music of the bards as they gathered the elemental power Bruce channeled through his body to shape the storm. Riots of color bloomed as they turned the maelstrom in upon itself.

"This is the best one yet, Josie," Azarich whispered.

"They've all been beautiful with you," Megan whispered back, both for her grandmother and for herself.

He fell back to sleep with her arm around him, and his head came to rest on her shoulder. She finished drinking his last cup of coffee for him.

"Grandma Josie?" she whispered. "I know you're going to take good care of him, just like you have with me. But I'm really going to miss him. And I know you don't have the power you did when you were alive, but if you know where Mom is, could you let her know what's going on here? It's kind of my fault that she's not here since, she's out there trying to keep me safe. But there's no one watching out for her, and I have a feeling she could really use someone right now."

A short time later she felt Bruce's power begin to wane, and the wall of force he'd created to keep them safe while he worked crumbled. When it did, the bards dissipated the remaining clouds to let the sun shine through just as Megan's awareness flowed over him like a second skin. Exhausted from the effort, he staggered and almost fell, but his brother scooped him up in his arms.

A whispered confession escaped Megan's lips as she looked toward the tower, and even though the memory of its passage faded from her mind like Paul's fog in the morning sun, Bruce smiled in his sleep.

Most of the time Azarich knew where he was and what was going on. He drifted off often, and when he did, Megan held his hand while he slept. When his dreams turned grim, she followed him down into the darkness and reminded him that his daughter had returned. She led him to dreams of friends and family. She reminded him that he was loved.

Near sunset he woke and asked her if she would bring the quilt that Josie had made. When she gave it to him, he told her his stories, and she hung on his every word even when she had to fill in the parts he could no longer recall.

"Megan," he said when at last he could think of no more to tell her,

"I want you to promise me something."

"Anything Grandpa," she whispered.

"Don't get so caught up in my stories that you forget to make your own."

"I won't," she promised.

"I think it's time for us to go," he said. "And I think you promised me another one of those whizzy rides."

"You're right, I did," she said, trying to hide how much she wished she could stretch this night out into eternity and hold onto him just a bit longer.

"Do you think I can bring this?" he asked, pulling the quilt up under his chin. "I used to cover Emelia with it when she slept, so my Josie could help watch over her. It has some stains from where she spit up on it that I couldn't get out," he added sadly.

"It gives it character," she told him.

Then she gathered him in her arms and walked the shadows with him to the place where he would leave her behind.

Chapter XXXV: Reunion

Luminita watched as Paul and his mother finished creating soft pallets on the tops of the stone benches in the enchanted grove behind the house where Megan lived with her grandfather. The surrounding trees held within their boundary a pocket of springtime promise, which she hadn't felt during the long duration of her imprisonment within Jubilee Field. A fire burned in the fire pit, casting shadows around the clearing and filling the air with the familiarity of her past.

She knew her reasons for wanting to keep Megan close ignored the girl's need to spend as much time as she could with Josephine's husband. But her time trapped in Jubilee Field had left scars on her soul, and she knew it would be a while before they began to heal. Until they did, her emotions coursed through her as wild and unpredictable as her recovered magic, burning or soothing in equal measure and blurring the edges of reality. She'd only managed to sleep a few times since her return, and when she did, she dreamed of being lost and forgotten.

A gentle breeze played nearby windchimes, and the yellow flowers that filled the clearing danced in the light of the fire and sang a song of homecoming that echoed throughout the night. Paul glanced up at her, hearing it as well. Then he pursed his lips and exhaled, releasing a wave of bardic energy that traveled up the length of her spine and warmed every nerve in her body. She'd forgotten this feeling, as every hair on her bare arms raised in the chill that followed.

Glad that no one could see her blush, she scolded him with a thought and the wicked grin he gave her made it impossible to think of anything else. She took her violin from its case and checked the tuning yet again. She hoped he wouldn't do it again all the while secretly wishing that he would.

She started to play without intending to, finding comfort in the familiarity of the movements and the sounds they invoked. While she did, her thoughts traveled back, trying to make sense of where she found herself now. She and her sisters had left the old world behind so many years ago because they wanted to ride on the crest of the world's innovations, to steer the wheel of their own destinies and discover all that they believed to be out there. None of them had intended to stay in the strange settlement that would eventually become Nickelville. Yet the town had snared all three of them just the same. Now here she was, two hundred years later, and instead of riding the crest of the wave, she felt like little more than the flotsam left over in some forgotten tidal pool.

She shook herself from the melancholy of those thoughts, once again reminded that it would take time for some of her scars to heal. Of course, part of her agitation might also stem from the fact that this grove, as beautiful as it might be, wasn't a true part of Guarded Wood. As such, it wasn't completely comfortable to be here, a dull ache manifesting itself in a vague sense of unease as if she'd forgotten something important.

A screech owl that perched in a tree close to the road noticed a woman walking toward the clearing from where she'd parked. She carried a large case that the bard recognized instantly.

"Our backup is here," Paul said, echoing her thoughts.

It took the woman a few minutes to find her way, but the light from the fire traveled a long way through the trees and she eventually came close enough for Luminita to greet her.

"We're back here," she called when the woman paused just out of sight, probably wondering what she was getting herself into. "I'd come to you, but I'm already as far away from the woods as I can go."

"So you're still trapped then?" the young woman asked, coming into view.

"Not trapped," the bard said happily. "Guarded Wood is not a prison. There are whole worlds hidden within its depths. I've been set free."

The woman looked at her skeptically and cast a thinly veiled glare in Paul's direction.

"We've still got a while before we'll play," Nita said, leading her over to sit on the edge of the bridge that linked the island in the spring with the land around it. Why don't we sit and talk?"

"As you wish, Eldest."

"Please don't call me that," the bard groaned. "Please call me Luminita."

The woman nodded.

"And I'm sorry that I didn't ask about it before," she said. "But what is your name?"

"Everyone calls me Anita," she answered awkwardly. She looked down at her feet, suddenly embarrassed before adding, "But I was named after you."

"You jest!" the bard laughed. "Why would your parents saddle you with such an old-fashioned name?"

"It's considered lucky," the woman answered, finally starting to smile. "I'm sorry if I seem upset, and I know it's a good thing that you're free. But for many of us there was an entire industry centered around protecting you and the people who were trapped with you. We're bound to all of you by history and blood. It was the proudest day of my life when I was chosen to play with you. And I know that I'm being selfish to think this way, but it was supposed to be a lifetime gig of practicing all year to play with you."

"And now you feel like you've been cast adrift to fend for yourself," Luminita finished.

The woman nodded, close to tears.

"You're all welcome to join the ones who were trapped with me in Guarded Wood," she offered.

"I can't give my music up," she whispered.

"Why would you have to do that?" Nita asked.

"They can't take anything modern," she answered. "My cello is a part of me. I can't leave it behind."

"I didn't realize how much of a problem this would cause," Luminita admitted. "I'm going to have a talk with my friends. They know far more about the ways of the modern world than I. Maybe Bruce in particular can find a solution."

As if summoned by the sound of his name, Bruce appeared next to them, his arms and shoulders bending backward as he yawned. Although his arrival made no sound, Nita felt him arrive without surprise. Antita glanced up at him and screamed, which of course made Bruce scream. He staggered back, outstretched arms wind milling as he fell off of the bridge, only to land on the ground next to where Paul and his mother stood.

"I'm so sorry," Anita whispered, horrified.

"That was almost as funny as Jade falling off the bed that time!" Paul laughed, lifting the spirits of everyone within the range of his voice.

"It's okay," Bruce said when Paul pulled him up. "I just wasn't completely awake yet."

"Do you often get out of bed at seven in the evening?" Anita asked.

"He had a busy morning," Luminita answered, remembering what he'd done and wondering if Megan had any idea how much danger he'd put himself into just to give her a better memory with her grandfather.

"But now that you're up," Paul said, ruffling his brother's hair affectionately, "Can you bring the piano out and put it over next to Anita's cello?"

"How did you know my name?" she asked. "We weren't talking that loud."

"We have extremely good hearing," Paul answered. "And how hard would it be to finally get orchestra classes at the Academy?"

"It could be done," Bruce said thoughtfully. "But you can't be thinking about putting that kind of a burden on Kate. She's great and all, but that's too much to ask of her."

"How would you feel about teaching?" Luminita asked Anita, following Paul's thoughts.

"But all I've got is a high school diploma," Anita stammered. "I'm not qualified."

"Maybe not in a big town," Bruce said. "But you'd be fine here in Nickelville. As you've probably noticed, we do things differently here."

"I did notice a thing or two," she replied with a grin.

"I'll see what we can do," Bruce said before turning to look where his brother had pointed. "We can't just put the piano there, Paul. It's uneven and the ground is soft. The torque of it settling would put too much pressure on the sound board. Best case it would completely throw it out of tune. Worst case it could make it crack again. We don't have time to make repairs. Let me see what I can do to shore up the ground."

They tried to return to their conversation, but it was difficult to concentrate with stones and pianos appearing and floating around. Luminita had never seen anyone with the range of abilities that Megan and Bruce possessed. Not even Jacob, who Crina had grudgingly admitted to be stronger than herself, possessed anywhere near this level of power.

"So we're going to be playing for a funeral?" Anita asked while Paul set about checking the piano.

"No," Luminita answered. "We're going to help them cross peacefully into death."

Anita stared at her, dumbfounded.

"Don't worry," the bard assured her. "I'll be handling most of the magical part and Paul will do the rest. But we need you to make parts of it more pleasant to hear. He'll guide you through what you need to do while you're playing."

"I don't know if I can do this," Anita whispered, frightened.

"I've played with you before," Luminita assured her. "You kept your head and played your best even when the sky was falling at Jubilee Field. You're a gifted musician, and like I said, Paul will guide you. If you make any mistakes, he can alter the sounds with his bardic magic."

Bruce walked over again, finally satisfied with the way the piano had been positioned.

"Okay guys," he said, looking a little bit nervous. "I'd better go. Sam and I should be back with August in no more than forty minutes or so."

"Be careful," she told him and gave him a sisterly hug that felt slightly less awkward than it had the first time. But Paul's family seemed to embrace a lot, especially Jade, and she wanted to fit in with them.

When he left, the three of them practiced the music if not the magic while Paul's mother listened. Anita began to relax as the bard had known she would.

Both Luminita and Paul saw the approach of his father's ambulance through the eyes of the creatures who lived there, and at last they broke off playing.

"Dad's coming down the road," Paul told his mother.

"I'd better go help him," she said, hurrying off down the path toward the house.

Paul rubbed his hands together as if to warm them, even though he'd already been playing for a while. His breathing was quicker than normal, and she could hear his elevated heart rate as well.

"You have helped scores pass with me," she assured him. "You have naught to worry on."

"You're a little bit nervous too," he said. "Your speech reverts when you are."

"These folks are dear to you," she whispered, wrapping her arms around him and putting her head on his chest.

"You two aren't doing anything for my nerves," Anita muttered, placing her instrument back into its case while they waited for everyone to arrive.

Dora appeared first, pushing the old librarian in a wheeled chair. He looked weak, but still managed to turn frequently and watch as Paul's father followed with the man's unconscious wife in his arms. She'd been wrapped in several blankets and she had a knit cap on her bald head.

Paul helped the old man rise from the chair and up onto the padded bench, where he gratefully settled back. And although his wife winced when they laid her down next to him with her head on his chest, she never woke.

"We're almost there," the librarian whispered in her ear, holding her close as if afraid that they might somehow be separated in the night to come.

Next came Alan and Kate, and although Luminita had never met them before, she could feel the love Paul had for them. He leaned on his wife heavily, and even though he was considerably taller than she, the bard could tell from the way that Jade and Andrew followed them closely that they'd both refused any offers of help.

When they reached the padded bench, Paul was there to help them.

"Paul?" the old woman with the red hair said, confused by what she saw.

"It's me, Kate," he answered, helping steady Alan as he moved into place.

"How?" she asked, shaking her head. "I thought you were going to Julliard."

"No," he said with just the right amount of grin to still be appropriate for their situation. "I'm somewhere much better than that."

As Paul's parents, sister and her friend moved to the edges of the small island, Luminita noticed that the flowers closest to the water's edge had wilted, many of them lying flat and lifeless.

Megan appeared next to the bard, and together they helped Josie's husband to his place. She'd draped him in an old quilt that, like the grove itself, held the texture of Crina's descendant. Luminita could see ancient designs of power in the way Josie had crafted it, perhaps knowing that they would watch over her family after she was gone.

Although Luminita had known little of the man, Paul's love for him filled her, and she found herself thinking of him as her own grandfather as well as Megan's. As she looked out across them, she realized that she felt that way about them all.

She felt Bruce and Sam approach before she saw them, and so did Megan. The big man strode into the clearing, carrying the frail hermit in his arms like a child. She could feel almost nothing of August and worried that they might be too late.

A restrained intake of breath escaped Megan as she fought to control herself just before Bruce stepped out from behind Sam. Most of the boy's upper body lay hidden behind the massive bulk of the wolf in his arms. But she could see the tears that ran unashamedly down his face to where the furry head rested between his cheek and his shoulder. She had no idea how he carried the beast curled around him like that, and given the stiff stagger of his steps, the stubborn boy refused to use his abilities to do so. The tail wagged weakly as he approached.

Sam laid August on the last remaining bench and both Jade and Paul ran up to help him arrange Fang along his side where the old man managed to place his hand on the grizzled head and bury his fingers into the fur of his neck.

"Bruce," Megan called softly.

"Yes?" he answered, smiling faintly at her in the light of the fire.

"There are some stains on the quilt that my grandmother made," she whispered, showing him as he drew closer. "Is there any way you could, you know?"

"Of course," he replied, holding the spot up where Azarich could watch. Then, brushing it lightly with his fingertips, he bent forward and blew across the stain which evaporated into mist and floated away on the night air.

Azarich caught his breath in amazed joy, smiling as he pulled it close under his chin like a child.

"Thank you so much," Megan said, reaching out to hug him.

He returned the embrace gladly, holding her tight against the sadness to come, but she stiffened and started to pull away.

But then, through the blood that linked the bard with all of her sister's descendants, Luminita felt a tension build within Megan as if the girl were attempting to push back against some vast weight that settled

419

over her. With the muscles along her jaw straining with the effort, she let out a snarl of determination and for just an instant, she held onto him with the same desperate need that Luminita had felt during her reunion with Paul. Then some door came crashing shut within Megan and she abruptly released him, shaking her head in confusion.

Worried for how this might affect Bruce, Luminita watched as he stoically accepted this change and kissed her chastely on the top of her head.

"Anything for you," he whispered before moving to stand with the librarian and his wife.

"I think they might be getting cold," Sam said, his deep voice filling the clearing.

Megan shaped a dome of energy around them, not for protection, but to trap the warmth. Bruce fed the flames until the chill left the air and they were ready.

Paul's fingers began to move, dancing across the keys of the old piano and bringing forth a slow, measured foundation for what she would build. For Luminita, it created the asymmetrical rhythm of water dripping from the trees after a storm. But she knew it would likely be something different for everyone who listened. No matter what form it took, it would be nothing less than exactly what each of them needed to find warmth, to find comfort and most of all to find each other. Pain fled before the melody he created and a shared sigh of relief escaped from the dying who'd been bravely hiding their suffering from the ones who loved them.

Then Anita joined him, nervous at first, sensing power she did not understand flowing beneath the surface of the sounds. Although her music held no magic of its own, Paul wove the long, rich notes into the imperceptible rhythm of each slow, steady breath. Within its ebb and flow Luminita felt the path open before her.

Recognizing the moment when it came, Luminita brought her bow to the strings. Building on the foundation Paul created, her notes gathered the minds of those who listened, weaving them into a tapestry of waking dreams in which she merged those who had been with the ones who would soon join them. Within the rhythmic shelter of the music, she created a new world in which loved ones would find closure before the cherished souls moved on.

The world beyond Megan's wall of power faded away entirely as the friends and family within found themselves bathed in warm sunlight. The stone benches remained, although they seemed less real than they had before, as if the padded surfaces had been replaced with one of Josie's watercolors.

Drawing on the power of those gathered, Luminita almost lost her concentration when wisps of errant magic began to dance through the clearing like fairy fire. She'd never felt anything like the power that Megan and Bruce radiated, not even in the lives she'd lived before.

Although the old men and women still remained solid, they no longer looked as they had before.

Azarich opened his eyes and sat up. His coal black hair covered his head in waves, short but mischievous like the eyes that twinkled below. The skin of his face was smooth and clean shaven, revealing a strong jaw as he threw back the quilt and sat up, looking around at the others. The contours of his body were that of a man in his prime.

Esther stirred next, raising her head from Tom's chest, her long auburn hair reaching halfway to the ground. The tips of her delicate fingers traveled the curve of her husband's lips as she raised herself up onto one elbow. She gasped when she noticed the way her hand looked in the shimmering light and reached up to cup her own cheek, exploring the extent of this unexpected miracle. Her laughter brought him awake, but before he could even draw breath she slid to the ground and pulled him after her. His fingers disappeared into the depths of her hair as he kissed her.

Kate had returned to her early twenties, sitting on the edge of the

bench in a floral sundress. Alan, once again wearing his uniform, stared up at her, scarcely able to breathe. She grabbed his hat and stepped quickly away from him, her long red hair whirling outward as she turned to look back at him.

"Hey mister," she purred, waving the hat back and forth. "I think you dropped this."

He sprung after her, his damaged knee no more than a memory as he took the hat from her hands and tossed it aside before picking her up. Her legs wrapped around his waist as he twirled with her, kissing her hard.

Fang's head shot up at the sound of Esther's laughter. Although he looked largely the same, brown patterns ran though his fur which had turned gray in his later life. He leapt down from the bench, spun around once like a puppy chasing its tail before standing on his hind legs and licking the hermit's clean-shaven face.

August climbed down with far more decorum than his furry friend, dressed in a deep red, toga-like robe. His sandal clad feet barely touched the ground before the wolf jumped up on him and nearly knocked him over before running off to greet everyone within reach, barking happily as he went.

Without warning, a new presence forced its way into the enchantment, making the bard hastily alter the weave of the musical tapestry lest the whole thing come unraveled and end before those gathered around her could find closure. Paul reinforced the magic with the sound of his voice, welcoming this stranger into their midst like a friend.

Laughter filled the grove as Alan lowered his bride to the ground. Then, never taking his eyes from hers, he pulled her close and at last gave her the dance she'd wanted at their wedding.

The sensation of the hand slipping into Azarich's felt so familiar that it took him a moment to realize he no longer stood alone. His eyes drifted over to the woman at his side and at first, he thought his granddaughter had joined him. But then a hundred subtle differences triggered an avalanche of recognition within him and his lips parted in a

soft intake of amazement. Before the man of a thousand stories could speak, Josie rushed into an embrace that left them both trembling with the strength of their need. They whispered things meant only for each other, pausing only long enough to kiss over and over again.

Fang grabbed the young hermit by the hand and spun him to face a woman Luminita had never seen before. August dropped to his knees, staring up at her in awe. As if fearful to find her an illusion, he reached out with trembling fingertips to touch her hand. Then he pulled her toward him and wrapped his arms around her waist. She smiled and held his head close against her as she kissed the top of his head. And were it not for the cavorting dance of the happy wolf as it rubbed against them, the picture they painted in their Romanesque dress could have easily have been a classical sculpture.

Megan walked over to where her grandparents stood, watching the dancing couple as they moved in graceful arcs between the trees. She embraced them both, and Luminita could see Josephine's face as they did. *Thank you for this,* the Daughter of Crina sent where only the bard could hear.

Not trusting herself to do more without breaking the enchantment, Luminita gave the slightest bow in acknowledgement as she continued to play.

Unwilling to be parted from Azarich for even a second, Josephine dragged him along behind her to embrace her best friend, Esther. Although lacking the passion of either woman in seeing their husbands again, the two radiated an energy to rival any teenager as they embraced, giggling all the while.

A blissful peace settled over the grove in the wake of their reunion, and they gathered at last around Kate and Alan who danced slowly near the fire pit. Jade stood with her back against Andrew's chest, holding his arms around her as she watched Kate. Paul's parents stood close as well, but the bard could feel that even though they found beauty is what they saw, they'd never completely understand the ways in which magic would shape their lives from this point forward. And of course Bruce, standing far enough away that he wouldn't interfere with these last moments between his friend and her family, had eyes for only one person.

426

But it was Sam who kept drawing Luminita's attention away from her work. In perfect timing with surges in the presence that now permeated the grove, he kept looking around as if hearing something, possibly his name on the wind.

At last Luminita felt her hold on the four men weaken, and she warned Megan with a wisp of thought that the moment drew near. Paul felt it as well, and he began to whisper words of healing beneath the surface of their thoughts, preparing them for the final ending and the moment when they returned to full wakefulness. As she lifted her bow from the strings, August released his last breath with a raptured smile and died, taking the others with him.

The men standing around the dancing couple faded from view first, leaving Esther with an expression of forlorn terror that lasted only as long as it took Josephine to catch her hand and pull her along into the afterlife behind them with their rich laughter echoing in the hallowed grove after them.

Alan lingered on, still holding Kate close. Whether he did so by the sheer force of his desire to stay by her side, or whether it was the stubborn love with which Kate clung to him, he still lingered no more than a single breath before he faded from her embrace.

Her arms held the memory of him for a few more seconds as she stood there, still dressed in the sundress next to the fire pit. Then her youth fell away from her like ash after a fire, and she stood dressed as she'd been when they'd arrived so long ago. Her hands slowly closed, and her arms dropped to her sides. She wilted when she released the breath she'd held, trying to hold onto him just a little longer. Then her lips moved as if she were trying to speak, but no words came.

For a horrible instant of shared understanding, Luminita felt like she was about to fade out as well, as if she too had stayed her stay and would now be cast adrift in time once again. Then Paul's arms closed around her and she could breathe again.

Jade rushed forward and held Kate hard against her, as if she thought that she could somehow hold off the knowledge that Alan was gone and keep it from reaching the old woman's heart. But Kate was made of stronger stuff than even Jade could understand.

"Don't be sad for me girl," she whispered, at last finding her voice. "I married a man that was nearly a hundred years old. A long life together was never in the cards for us. We may have only had a few short weeks, but we've each loved the other for most of our lives. So don't shed a single tear for me, Jade."

Then the old woman noticed something leaning against the edge of the stone circle that ringed the fire pit. She bent to retrieve it and came up holding the hat that Alan had playfully knocked from her hand.

"That's impossible," Paul said, staring at it in wonder. "It's not within our power to make something physically real with our music."

Both Luminita and Paul felt a strong pull coming from the direction of the woods as the flow of the spring slowed and the last of the hermit's magic faltered. Soon they would have to return to Guarded Wood.

"He couldn't stay," Sam said softly. "So he left you something to remember him by."

"Like I could ever forget him," Kate said, holding it lovingly to her chest.

"I didn't know him," Luminita said softly, hoping that these two had loved each other enough to find each other again as she and Paul had. "But he seemed like an amazing man."

"He was, wasn't he?" Kate said with a faint smile on her lips and eyes that were focused far away.

"Daddy," Emelia whispered, leaning over the still water. "I'm right here."

A single tear fell, casting ripples across the surface of the pool.

When they cleared, he was gone. Then, as the hermit's magic faded and his soul left Guarded Wood behind, the spring he had inadvertently created ran dry, and the link between the place where Emelia knelt and the one where she'd have given almost anything to be faded as well, leaving her hidden in darkness while the sun rose over a Nickelville that no longer held her father within it.

She was no longer alone.

"It's not safe for you to be here," said the man she'd come seeking. "There are many nearby who would see you killed for the things you have done."

"And what of the crimes that they have committed against me and mine?" Emelia asked, still searching the water's surface for echoes of what could no longer be.

"Their war is not mine," he said simply. "Even so, you are not safe here."

"How did you find me?" she asked, trying to unravel the tangled skein of the Morrigan's manipulations.

"I'm an empath," he answered. "Your pain called to me. No one should hurt as you do."

"I have no words for this grief," she admitted. "But I have come far, both in distance and in time to seek your aid."

"Why would you think that I'd help you when you have been the cause of so much pain for my people?" he asked.

"Because it was foretold," she whispered in reply, not liking the way the words felt even as she spoke them.

"I am mistrustful of such predictions," he sneered, "Such a foretelling led to the battle that almost killed both of our tribes."

"Then I will let you judge the purity of my intentions for yourself," she said, heeding the words of the Morrigan and lowering her defenses even though she was loath to do so. "I will hold nothing back from you."

"Aren't you afraid of what I will learn of the Tuatha dé Danann?"

"I am," she admitted.

"Then what could possibly motivate you to take such a chance with their well-being?"

"The love I bear for my daughter."

Chapter XXXVI: While She Slept

As had been planned beforehand, Bruce and Megan moved the bodies of her grandfather and his friends through the shadows to the librarian's house. They placed Esther and Tom in their recliners with their hands overlapping on the small end table as if they'd been holding hands when they died. Azarich and Alan took up places on either side of the couch where Bruce and Megan had explained what was to come just a few short days earlier. Bruce loaded a comedy that he'd heard Alan speak of at school into the old VCR and let the screen settle into static as if they'd been gone before the movie ended. The fact that they'd all died with smiles on their faces might raise some questions, but shouldn't point toward foul play.

Using the skills that he learned on the spot from his newly restored sense of the immediate future, Bruce caused their blood to absorb carbon monoxide from the air and then sabotaged the antique gas floor heater in such a way that it began to fill the room with the invisible poison. He leached the heat from their bodies, making it seem as if they'd died some time the night before.

"They look like they could be sleeping," Megan said, looking at them in the flickering light of the television static. "You're sure no one will suspect?"

"The last thing the new chief of police wants is a quadruple homicide," Bruce answered. "My dad will be the paramedic on the scene, and he'll give observations consistent with carbon monoxide poisoning. It will be seen as a freak accident, but the rumors will pass quickly."

"I wish we didn't have to do this," Megan whispered, taking one last look at her grandfather's smile and remembering the way he'd looked when he saw his wife.

"Me too," he agreed.

"I wish Mom had been here," she said.

"I felt her there at the end," Bruce said, searching for anything that might contradict the scene they'd created.

"She said she'd be watching in the last runestone," Megan said.

"What's that?" he asked, pointing to an envelope leaning against an old box of the type used to hold notecards. The front of the envelope read, "For Megan, after I've gone."

She picked up the envelope, opened it and read aloud.

"Megan, I'm so glad I had the chance to meet you," she read, her voice already growing husky. "It was such a pleasure to spend time with you and the others. I will miss the dinners and the adventures, but don't worry. Your grandmother and I will have many more while we wait for our boys to join us."

"She must have written it after Honeysuckle House but before her seizure," Bruce whispered.

"But while we wait," Megan continued. "I want you to promise me that you'll drag my Tommy out of this house. Don't let him abandon his precious library to mourn me, not when I'll still be there with him. And make sure that you make him come to your marvelous dinners. Remind him that they can tell all the stories I wouldn't let them when I was alive. Check in on him often, he's not going to be able to put the last piece into the puzzles he likes to work on. That was always my job. I'm leaving you my recipes so Paul can still get the deserts he loves. Just don't let your mother try to cook them. They deserve more respect than that. I'm always going to claim you as my granddaughter. I know Josie won't mind. Love, Esther Harris."

The two of them stared at the box in silence, unable to explore wounds that had not yet begun to heal. At last Megan folded the letter neatly and replaced it in the envelope before picking up the box of recipes and holding them possessively to her chest.

"We'd better get going," Bruce said at last. "Kate will call the police in a little while to report that Alan never came home and that no one answered the door when she knocked even though all of their cars had still been parked in the driveway."

Megan took one last look before walking them both through the shadows to the tree house, not yet ready to experience the spent magic of her grandmother's grove. As soon as they passed through the boundary, they could both feel the old man's presence fading like the scent of summer on a cold autumn breeze. In its place they felt the awareness of the bards settle over them.

Even though they knew the others were waiting on them, they both needed a while longer to come to terms with their time at the Harris home before saying goodbye to the hermit and his faithful companion. So they walked. She sent the letter and the recipes to the kitchen counter, where she planned to look through them at length later. Bruce filled her in on the things he'd learned from August the day of that unexpected meal. He told her about the old tower and why the hermit had moved from it when they passed. She pointed out fruit and nut trees she recognized from her mother's brief lesson. But when he showed her the pond she thought for just a moment that her grandfather could join him the next time he went fishing there since the lake was still too polluted. Then she remembered and the wound in her soul opened anew.

Several chickens ran out to greet them when they passed the hermit's home, likely wondering where August had gone and how they were supposed to sleep during the day without their wolf protector.

The climb up to the mausoleum remained treacherous, and the crowded peak provided a beautiful view but little space as they all gathered around the pyre that Sam and Paul had built. When they opened the stone monument, in preparation of adding August's ashes after the cremation, they discovered that he had preserved his wife's body with enchantments that only now after his death began to fade. So the living arranged the dead on the pyre, and like the loved ones left in the Harris living room, they looked as if they might at any moment wake from some pleasant dream.

Because they had no way of knowing exactly what the funeral customs of the Children of Nyx might have been, they each recounted their memories of them and marveled at the love that had led August and Aurora to this special place. Bruce ran his fingers through Fang's fur one last time and whispered something to him that only the wolf could hear.

Then the ones who could summon fire did so, and the ones who could ease their grief through the music they played did so as well. As the last notes died away, the quiet friends noticed that they were no longer alone.

As they had done on the night of the Sentinel tree's rebirth, the fauns gathered by the thousands. They clung to the sides of the hill where their cloven feet found purchase like mountain goats. They lined the distant peaks and filled the surrounding slopes with their strangely elongated faces bowed as they gave homage to the one who, like they, had served for so long.

A soft hum emanated from the childlike creatures, minor in its frequency yet almost overpowering by the sheer magnitude of its participants. It merged perfectly with the playing of the bards, and in an instant the bodies were no more, rendered to ash which the wind carried across the valley where the hermit had lived for so long. Then with a low rumble of thunder, it began to rain across Guarded Wood as the land mourned as well.

Even before Megan retreated into the solace of sleep in the house on Beverly Road, the world took on the haze of slumber. She often found the others staring at her, waiting for a reply to questions she hadn't heard. Police swarmed over the Harris home for little more than a day, puzzled by the uniform expressions of happiness but finding no signs of foul play.

She refused to sleep while they waited for the funerals although she apparently drifted off from time to time. The first time she woke in the darkness of Bruce's bedroom, holding onto him so hard while he slept that her arms ached the following day. She had no memory of walking the shadows to his side, but judging by the warm affection of his dreams he hadn't minded too much.

The next time she'd nodded off in her grandmother's hidden studio and woken in the treehouse with her head resting on his leg. He'd been awake this time when she'd arrived, and though her arrival surprised him, he'd continued to read while stroking her hair.

"Sam will be worried," she whispered, shaking herself awake.

"He knows where you are," Bruce said when she sat up, stretching his back. Apparently, it hadn't been a particularly comfortable position.

"I'm so sorry," she said groggily.

"Why?" he asked. "I always enjoy your company. But you seriously do need to get some real sleep."

"I will after the funerals," she promised, then fled through the shadows back to the questionable comfort of her own home. There Sam made her something to eat and she did so, although she had no memory of what it might have been later. Furthermore, the ghosts she found there on Beverly Road proved far crueler than any she'd encountered at the Academy. These whispered of what she should have done differently, of questions she'd never asked, and of untold stories lacking voices to be heard.

Several days later, they lowered Azarich McGeehee into the ground next to the woman who'd been his magnetic north since they'd first met at the age of six. And when Megan found everyone looking at her once again, expecting her to speak, the exhaustion became too much, and she just stood there, staring down into a carpet lined hole. All around her the world fell away, leaving her falling alone into the abyss where no one would even hear her silent screams.

Then she felt his fingertips brush the length of her arm as he reached out from the darkness to take her hand in his, anchoring her the way her mother and grandfather had before leaving and casting her adrift. He took her hand the way he had at the dance, taking her pain into himself and saying the words she needed to say. She thought he told one of her grandfather's stories, but she couldn't be sure. Something within her smoldered, threatening to catch fire with each of her indrawn breaths as she clung to him before dying away again.

No one expected her to speak for her grandfather's friends, but she still held onto Bruce's arm like a lifeline, her grip tightening in waves of conflict that rose and fell in a cycle of forgetfulness he noticed but would never mention. When at last the crowds began to disperse and she found herself alone with the Grimbles and Sam, Jade came up and wrapped her arms around her. Then the eldest Grimble rested the side of her head against Megan's so that the ornate silver earring pressed against her.

"It's finished," Megan heard Paul say in her ear, the words laced with potent mixture of bardic magic even though he stood miles away in the treehouse. "It's time for you to sleep."

The richness of his voice drained away the last of her strength, and Megan's eyes rolled back into her head. Bruce caught her and walked the shadows with her in his arms, rousing her as he carried her toward her bed.

"Not here," she mumbled. "Grandpa's room."

So he carried her to the bed where she'd roused Azarich just a few days before. She could still smell the old man's aftershave on the sheets as Bruce pulled them over her. Then, knowing what she wanted before she asked, he summoned Josie's quilt from where it lay on the sofa below and tucked it in around her.

She turned on her side to face him and found a black furry mass burrowing in next to her.

"Good boy," Bruce said, scratching the ancient cat sidhe under the chin.

"Bruce," she whispered, trying to hold on a little longer.

"Yes?" he replied, sitting on the edge of the bed and brushing her hair away from her face.

"I…" she managed to say before the cat's purrs swept away what she'd needed so badly to tell him and cast her adrift in the world of dreams.

While she slept, Megan watched the world around her. She watched as Bruce stayed by her side, guarding her slumber until Sam arrived.

Then he placed a chaste kiss on her forehead and walked home. There he changed out of the funeral clothes and put on his running shoes.

His mother hugged him on his way out the back door, and Jade offered to go with him. He shook his head, his lips pressed tightly together as he took off down the path into Guarded Wood. He needed to be alone.

But he wasn't alone for long. A scissor-tail crossed his path and darted in and out behind him, navigating the woods easily as he ran. Whether Bruce was too focused on his run to notice, or if Paul could somehow avoid detection when he wished, she didn't know. But any doubts she had about the bird's identity left when it traveled through the first of the interior boundaries without challenge.

She didn't know where he was going until she recognized the open green of the Irish highland. He passed through the familiar monoliths and barely slowed on the downward slope to the beach. Seconds later he stood at the water's edge. The sun burned down from directly overhead as he breathed, only slightly winded.

Then, as if not finding what he'd sought, he pivoted on his heel and sprinted back the way he'd come. In the twists and turns that followed, passing through different pockets of time seemingly at random, she began to worry that he might not be able to find his way back. He passed through jungle, rain forest and places that defied explanation for the brief times that he traveled there.

The desert crevasse hadn't changed much since they'd fled from the flood, except that the water had apparently returned to whatever land it had come from. She would have scolded him for his breakneck speed if she'd been able.

When he passed through the last boundary to the rusted plain, he put his head down and sprinted as hard as he could. But even that wasn't as fast as he'd moved the last time. None of the thunder cows could be seen, but that didn't mean that they weren't still about.

He stopped when he reached the cliff's edge, finally winded as he gulped down air and looked out over the broad expanse of the ocean before him. The scissor-tail landed on his shoulder, but Bruce didn't notice as he stood there, frowning down at the rocks below. Finally he shook his head as if to clear it and noticed the bird. Likely speaking mind to mind, he glanced up at the sky uncomfortably and nodded before turning to run back. When he did, she continued to follow, as insubstantial as the wolf that ran at his side.

Bruce returned to the school the next day while Megan slept on, riding in the front seat of Christine while his sister drove. Neither of them talked, each thinking about the empty seats as they passed through town and eventually through the ward that surrounded the school.

Students and teachers alike stared at the two Grimbles as they walked through the cafeteria, accompanied by whispers Megan could sense but not hear. Bruce reached up absently and grasped the stone necklace through his t-shirt, and when he did so, she could sense the flavor of his thoughts if not their actual content. He was thinking about how neither of the old men had known they'd worked their last day at the Academy when they'd walked out of the doors.

Bruce had forgotten about the library renovations until he walked through the carved wooden doors to find that the shelves had been replaced. Modern tables and chairs stood ready for a new generation of Nickelville students. Even the old carpet had been replaced, taking with it any sign of where the librarian had first seen his future wife. Megan felt him reach out with his mind and find the old ones in the shed out back, where Mr. Green must have moved them before he'd left.

Maybe it was strengthened by the purring presence at her side, but phantoms from the past rose up around Bruce as he walked to the unused classroom and began loading the books back onto the cart. All around him Megan could see her grandfather and his friends, living lives they'd only hinted at in their stories.

Mr. Danders found him just as he finished loading the cart. After watching him for a moment, the vice principal took off his coat and tie and tossed them in the corner before following Bruce's lead and loading up the other cart. Then he and the librarian's favorite student spent several hours moving books and meticulously placing them in their new home. Then Millie, the office secretary, stuck her head into the door of the library to tell him that Mr. Hambly hadn't come in again and that they needed him in the office. Before he left, Mr. Danders told Bruce that he could spend as long as he wanted setting things up, and that he could have any help he wanted.

Bruce thanked him, but said he'd prefer to work alone. By the end of that day, the new books had all been labeled and shelved. The computers had been installed, and all of the posters and decorations that Mr. Harris had requested had been placed throughout the library to Bruce's obsessive standards. The only thing that remained was setting up the new card catalog system which Bruce felt should be handled by the new librarian when the school found one. He knew he could look into the future and find out who it would be, but he couldn't bear the thought of anyone else taking his friend's place and chose to remain blissfully ignorant.

Then he sat in the corner, staring out over what had once been his favorite place in the school with a tired expression. When Jade came in at the end of the day, she looked at the room in silence and then told her brother that it was time to go home. But he shook his head and made her drive him to the Harris house.

Once there, Megan continued to watch over him while she slept. He spent several hours looking through old photographs and mementos until he had what he wanted. He even spent an hour finishing a puzzle that the couple had started sometime in the past, not realizing they'd never finish it. Then, walking the shadows to the deserted Academy shed, he cast wards against detection and intrusion so no one would discover him before he'd completed his task.

Megan's dream brought her to where Jade and Kate had just found a collage behind the couch in the janitor's living room. On it were displayed hundreds of tickets from the Palace, many of them going back to before the war. They also found a scrapbook full of Tribune articles that mentioned the town's only theater. But best of all, was an early color photograph from the sixties that had probably been taken by Tom Harris since he'd often carried a camera. The photograph was old and worn from frequent handling. In it, Azarich and Josie were standing in front of the concession stand at the Palace and next to them was Kate.

A short distance away from where the picture had been taken, Megan found herself drawn to the Baker Hotel. It was there that she realized that the protections that blocked out her ability to see apparently didn't apply to Mr. Bob, who still remained curled up at her side.

As they drifted from room to room, visions of the past began to impose themselves over the abandoned rooms and corridors, except now all of the visions piled up on each other without any respect for the order in which they'd originally occurred.

Long dead Joneses carried treasures out past the three mystery women as they went about their daily business, not that Megan could tell what any of that daily business might have been. Then she came to the tree once again, and she found it interesting that even though the Joneses had been present in every corner of the penthouse dwellings, they were nowhere to be found where the three dark-skinned women tended to the tree and the wild garden that surrounded it.

It was there that a single residual memory dominated the others that competed for Megan's attention. Once again, she watched the women in their final moments, coughing up blood that dried on their clothing and mouths.

What held her there most was that final act of colossal will that it had taken the old crone to place the hands of the others onto the rough bark of the tree before they died. Something about the dying woman's focus in that moment brought to mind the memory of Bruce creating her ring.

Then someone shook her, gently at first and then with more force.

"Megan, it's time for you to get out of that bed," Sam said.

Leave me alone, she replied. *I'm not ready yet.*

"And it's unlikely that you ever will be," he replied. "But you're going to get up just the same. And then, as a wise young woman once told me, you're going to take a shower because you really do smell."

"That's not fair," she mumbled. "Even when you say something insulting it comes out all nice. Damn but you've got a great voice."

"Thank you, but flattery is not going to make me let you go back to sleep."

When she finally opened her eyes, she realized she was lying on her side and Mr. Bob was curled into her with his back against her chest. He purred when she rubbed her chin against the top of his head.

"He's been there the whole time you were asleep," he said, reaching out and scratching the cat under his chin. The purr intensified.

"Is there any particular reason why your cat is shielded?" he asked.

"He's not my cat," she yawned. "He belongs to the grumpy lady inside my head that kicked you out that day."

"It's amazing that you can say things like that without making me question your sanity," he observed. "And if you don't take a shower for me, please do it for him. I'm sure his nose is much more sensitive than mine. Then we can go see what Bruce has been working on at the school."

"Whatever it is he's shielded the shed to block everything out," she said.

"And given that you've been here in this bed for the past two days, exactly how do you know that?"

"I was watching over everyone while I was asleep," she said, finally disengaging from her grandmother's quilt and climbing off the other side of the bed.

"Is this a new ability, or one I just didn't know about?" he asked.

"I don't know," she answered, frowning down at the cat, who had rolled on his back lazily. "It seemed so normal at first that I didn't really think about it. I almost think it had something to do with him," she said, nodding toward Mr. Bob, who promptly faded away.

"I see," he said, eying the spot where the cat had been only seconds before. "What else did you see?"

"Mr. Danders helping Bruce move the books back into the library. Jade helping Kate settle into Mr. Green's house. She found a bunch of old tickets and a picture of Kate."

"Which Jade told me a little while ago when she came over to check on you," he said. "I thought about letting her wake you up, but I've grown rather fond of her and didn't trust your mood."

"Like I'd ever hurt Jade," Megan said, crossing the hall to her room so she could get some fresh clothing. He was right, even though she didn't sweat, she still smelled pretty bad.

"Better safe than sorry when dealing with McGeehee women," he said sagely.

She stuck her tongue out at him and disappeared into the bathroom.

When she emerged, she felt much better as long as she kept her eyes from landing just about anywhere because then the memories of her grandfather began to surface. She wasn't ready for a world without him.

"If I'm going to do this I might as well make Bruce happy," she said, picking her phone up off of the dresser in her room and sending him a text. It worked flawlessly, and she thought once again about how simple the world had been just a few weeks ago when he'd given her the ring.

The phone vibrated in her hand and she almost dropped it in surprise. Sam seemed to find this inordinately amusing.

"Laugh it up," she said.

"I've seen old people catch on to technology faster than you," he chuckled. "Luminita and Paul have been asking about you as well. I'm glad you're okay. I was worried."

"Enough!" she said, then reached out and put her hand on his arm and walked with him through the shadows to the library where Bruce waited.

"I really don't like the way that feels," the big man said, sitting down quickly on one of the new chairs.

Although she'd seen the renovations in her dream, it was different being there in person. Even the smell was wrong. Gone were the scents of old binding and wood polish to be replaced with the chemical smell of new carpet. The faint ozone smell of the computers tainted the air as well.

"I absolutely hate it," she said.

"I know," Bruce agreed. "I went through with it because Mr. Harris chose all of this, but by the time I'd finished, I couldn't feel *him* here anymore. That's why I did this," he said, motioning for her to follow him.

Across the back wall of the library there was a new display case. Unlike the new elements that had been chosen to modernize the space, this one was dedicated to the preservation of the old. The ammonite that had once been in a display case in the middle of the room was now tucked away into a shelf that included pictures of the librarian and his friends standing around it as children. There were old pieces of library equipment displayed in cubby holes along with descriptions of what they did. But it was the picture in the middle of the wall that caught her attention. In a frame made from four heavily carved chair arms, each bearing the initials of the four boys and two of their wives, was the picture Josie had drawn of them sitting on the check-out counter.

"I wish I knew what Carl's fiancé was named," Bruce said. "I'd add Esther and her to the arms too."

Megan reached out and touched Carl's initials.

"Elizabeth Bennet," she said with a smile. "And unlike Andrew's parents, hers knew what they were doing when they named her that. It was her favorite book as well."

Under the touch of his finger, the final initials were added. And even though Carl had never gotten to marry his sweetheart, they knew he would have if he'd returned from the war.

"The display case itself is made out of their table," Bruce said, standing next to her. I left Azarich's contribution intact, but it's on the bottom where it doesn't show. "It wasn't exactly the look I was shooting for."

"It's perfect," she said. "She definitely was a better artist than he was, wasn't she?"

"I didn't see the picture you're talking about," Sam said, "But I didn't realize this was a drawing until you said so. She was indeed quite gifted."

"I'm ready to get out of here," Bruce said. "Everyone is planning to eat dinner at the tree house. Will you come with us, Megan?"

"I'm sorry I went AWOL for a bit there," she said. "And I'm famished."

"You needed some time," Bruce said with a shrug. "But we all really missed you. There aren't enough of us left to have anyone gone. And if you let Luminita and Paul play for you, it really helps. So what do you say?"

"Okay, okay," she said, "I'll come have dinner with everyone."

"Can I make one request?" Sam asked.

"Sure Big Guy," Bruce answered. "What do you want?"

"Please tell me that you drove here," Sam said, still looking a little bit queasy. "I really don't want to do that shadow thing again right before we eat."

"Sorry," Bruce said, "Jade dropped me off and I planned to just walk the shadows back when I was done here."

"If you guys don't mind," Sam said uneasily. "I'm going to walk over to Gordon's and pick up the catering truck."

"The Harris place is closer," Bruce said, pulling a set of keys out of his pocket and tossing them to his friend. "You can take their car if you want, they left everything to me in their will."

"Thanks," Sam said.

"Have you had any luck with finding out more about the women from the Baker?" Megan asked.

"Not yet," the big man answered, moving toward the doors. "I seem to have hit a brick wall."

"I was thinking about the way the oldest one made the others touch the tree just before they died," Megan said. "I don't think that was a random act."

"You think they were trying to do something with the tree?" Bruce said. "Or maybe they thought it could save them?"

"I don't know," she answered. "But whatever it was seemed to be pretty important to them."

"Interesting," Sam said, lost in thought. "Would it upset you guys too much if I stop off there and have another look around that tree?"

"Not at all," Bruce said. "Do you want us to come with you?"

"Not this time. I'm sure it won't lead to anything, but any lead is better than what I've been trying at the Well of Dreams."

Chapter XXXVII: Silly Man Who Talks to Trees

Bruce's father was cooking on the enchanted grill when they walked up. Jade squealed with delight in that not child but not adult way she did when she was really happy and hugged Megan so hard that she accidentally knocked them both over.

"Hey Megan!" Paul yelled down from the deck of the tree house above them. "It's good to see you. Sorry about knocking you out for so long. I haven't had much practice with that in this lifetime."

"That's okay," she yelled up at him. "I needed the sleep, and I could have woken up sooner. I just didn't want to. As a matter of fact, I almost woke up to go yell at Bruce for going back to that rusty field."

"Right?" Paul called back. "You should have. He wouldn't listen to me."

"I don't ever want to see you in that place again," Bruce said quietly, looking at her with a strange expression she couldn't identify.

She reached out and took him by the hand and led him up the stairs. At the top, they found Andrew and Kate setting out paper plates and cups on the table. Dora was sitting off to the side, talking on her phone about what sounded like *Tribune* business.

Megan walked up to Kate and gave her a hug, noticing that she'd cut her hair short and was letting her natural gray grow out.

"What's that for?" the old woman asked.

"I missed you," Megan said.

"It's only been a few days," she said, but she didn't look like she minded either.

Paul came out from the bunkhouse and Bruce was utterly lost for words. His brother was wearing a leather trench coat.

"Tell me you didn't order that," he said. "Have you been possessed by Dad?"

"No, from the sound of it, being possessed is more Megan's speed," he said. "It did come from Dad though. I mentioned that I needed to get a new coat with winter coming. I'm going to be spending a lot of time outside. He brought this out and said that I could have it if I wanted it."

"And you said yes?" Bruce asked.

"It's actually pretty nice," Paul said. "I'm obviously not going to be going out in public anymore and this will keep me warm on horseback. Besides," he said leaning in, "Luminita likes me in it."

"Which is why he's wearing a leather coat when it's still in the sixties," Jade commented, sitting down at the table.

"He does look rather dashing in it, doesn't he?" Dora said, walking up and putting her phone away. "I always thought Ben looked tasty in that coat when we were in college."

"And just like that I feel like taking it off," Paul said, stricken. "I'm not sure I want any part of something that makes you think of Dad and the word tasty together."

"Where's Luminita?" Megan asked, then looked up at the tower as if hearing something.

"Want company?" Bruce asked as she headed in to the ladder.

"I've got this," she said. "Unless you want to talk to her?"

"I think I'll stay down here and help with the food," he answered. "It is nice to have you back, though."

When Megan reached the top of the ladder, she found Luminita sitting on the rail, looking out across the trees. She was dressed in a dark t-shirt and a pair of jeans that didn't look familiar.

"Your clothes came in," Megan noted.

"Yes," Luminita answered, looking over at her. "Would you like your old ones back?"

"Not really," Megan said. "I sort of like knowing that you're wearing some of mine. I don't know how to explain it."

"I understand," Nita said. "I'm still so happy that my sister saved my old stuff. I know it's not really worth anything…"

"But when you don't have much, you really value what you do have," Megan said.

The bard looked through her, into her memories of the past and all of the paths that had eventually led her to Nickelville. It was nice to have someone who could truly understand what she'd been through, yet would never judge her for it.

"Dora brought me some of Paul's old shirts too," Nita said eventually. "Did you know he smells the same in this life as he did the last? I didn't expect that."

"I can't say I've ever spent much time smelling Paul," Megan said. "So I'll just take your word for it."

"That's probably the best answer you could have given," the bard replied with a smile.

"Are you guys moving into August's place?" Megan asked.

"We will in time, but right now Paul and I just don't feel like we belong there," the bard explained. "It's still so full of the old hermit."

"He did live there for several centuries," Megan pointed out. "I'd be surprised if it wasn't"

"Megan," Luminita said, suddenly serious, "I need to speak about something with you." Then she hopped down from the rail and stood before her sister's descendent.

"That doesn't sound good," Megan said. "I promise I've never had any interest whatsoever in Paul."

"No," Luminita said, smiling in spite of herself. "I had almost decided against telling you this at all for fear of something happening to you or Bruce."

"Something like what?" Megan asked, not liking the sound of this at all.

"Like what happened to Paul and me," she answered. "Shortly after we laid August and his wife to rest, I was visited once more. It has always been considered bad luck to speak of such visitations, but it was your aid that she sought."

"Crina?" Megan asked.

"No, Sorina."

"Jacob's wife?" Megan asked.

"And in her words, I found answers to questions we've asked about that night, "the bard answered, "particularly how Jacob still has power in this world."

"He's not dead either," Megan said, having already suspected this on several occasions herself.

"No," she agreed. "He's trapped in the partially opened gate."

"So it kept you both alive for all this time," Megan said.

"But unlike me, he did not leapfrog across time. He has been here in the present for two long centuries. And I'm not sure if anyone could possibly stay sane with what he's been through."

Bruce, you'd probably better come up here after all, Megan sent.

He appeared at her side.

"Jacob Routh is still alive and trapped in the gate under the Academy," Megan told him.

"We're sure about this?"

"Yes," Luminita said. "But I'm not sure if you should do anything about it. I don't want anything to happen to either of you. It might be too dangerous."

"I've looked everywhere around those doors for an entrance to the cave. Even if it's locked away I should have been able to feel its presence."

"That is odd," the bard said.

"Maybe the doors are enchanted to create a kind of portal," Megan said, "like when we walk the shadows. That would explain why the carvings never wear down. I remember thinking how strange they were the first time I passed through them into the library."

"What do they have to do with the library?" Luminita asked. "That's on the other side of the church from the graves and the cave."

"Wait," Megan said excitedly, "When you showed us the vision in the fire, Jacob walked right up to the wall behind the graves. Is the cave directly behind that wall?"

"Yes," the bard answered.

"The isolation room," Bruce and Megan said together.

"There shouldn't be anyone there right now," Bruce said. And there's no better time than the present. We don't have to do anything yet, but let's go check it out."

"Shouldn't we tell someone?" Megan asked.

"If you want to go down there and tell my mom where we're going you're welcome to do so," he answered.

"She won't care," Megan said with a grin. "I'm pretty sure Paul's her favorite now."

"Ouch," he said, and though he smiled when she said it, she thought she detected a bit of irritated concern as well.

Sam didn't like taking the elevator up to the penthouse. He didn't like the way it closed him off from the rest of the world and made him think about how it would feel to fall from that height if the antiquated machinery should fail. He also didn't like the thought of what it would be like if the massive roots that made up the sides of the shaft decided to squeeze in on him.

He thought about what it had been like to walk through the deserted corridors with the echoes of the past peeking through the present. But without Megan, it was just an old space which, like much of Nickelville, had never lived up to the intentions of its creators.

In spite of the foreign nature of what they'd seen in their previous explorations, there was still something familiar about this place that spoke to him. No matter how much he thought about that feeling, or how much he'd attempted to refine the sensation with the aid of the Well, it remained an amorphous wisp of memory that suggested he knew more about this than he realized.

His extra senses rendered his flashlight unnecessary, but he used it just the same. Unlike Bruce, he'd never been told that there was nothing to fear in the darkness. In fact, he'd been reassured growing up that there was truth somewhere at the root of every horror story, especially the ones that took place in the recesses where the sun never reached.

He passed through the rooms they'd searched before with little interest, focused instead on what the women might have needed so badly that they spent their final moments huddled beneath the strange tree that

455

grew so far from any of its brethren.

There was a huge eagle perched in the branches of the tree. He'd never seen one so big and reminded himself to tell Paul when he returned. It watched him as he approached, sublimely uninterested in the big man's presence.

Careful not to disturb the remains that had lain forgotten all this time, Sam slowly stretched out his arms and laid the calloused palms of his hands on the rough bark. At once he knew that Megan had been right. The Fates had not come here by chance to spend their last moments and furthermore, this was no normal tree.

It was an artifact, though he couldn't at first discern the purpose of its existence. The answers he sought were there, of that he was certain, but to access them he sensed that a key was necessary. But what could it be?

Closing his eyes and reaching down, both within himself and down into the roots below him, he realized something. Although the creation of the Well of Dreams had been lost in the passage of time, and the signature of the hands that created it had evolved since then, it was clear to him that both the Well and this tree had been created by the same three individuals. Furthermore, although he hadn't realized it until now, Guarded Wood also owed its existence to these mystery women.

"How long did the three of you live?' he asked aloud, and when he did so, something within the tree reacted to him. But though his words had drawn its attention, they were not the ones it waited for.

"I wish you were here, Squirrel," he whispered.

Silly Boy Who Talks to Trees, she whispered through his memories and he remembered the day that they'd met.

Taking a moment to rehearse the formal phrase his grandfather had made him practice over and over throughout his short childhood, he took a deep breath to steady his voice and thanked August for helping him to hone his rusty speech. Then he uttered the words he'd last spoken on that day when his childhood friend had given him his favorite name.

The world opened within him.

We dared not hope that one of our adopted children would survive and return, the voices spoke in his mind. *The seasons have passed many times since we last heard our names spoken aloud. Will you serve us as your ancestors once did?*

With respect, I must know who you are and what you would have of me before I can make that sort of promise.

Then with respect you shall know the answers to what you would know, but the seed of our tale was sown at the dawn of mankind. It is unlikely that you have days enough left for it all. Narrow the scope of your questions.

Why did you create the Well of Dreams?

To guide our children while we traveled elsewhere.

Why did it deny me answers to questions about you?

Because it called forth the knowledge of those who went before you, and none of them knew more than the barest glimpse of who we were. It could not tell you what they did not know.

Did you create what became Nickelville?

Yes.

Why?

To call those with the gifts of magic and be a haven for them. The one who created us made us barren, and only one of the Beloved can give us what we crave. We believed that by gathering families through which flowed the old blood, we could bring about the birth of another Beloved. For only such a one could bless us with children of our own.

What is the purpose of Guarded Wood?

457

It is a place of refuge for things that have passed beyond memory.

But that's not all it is, is it? Sam asked.

It is a prison, they answered. *But be careful of asking questions for which you do not wish answers.*

He considered this warning, and he recognized the truth in their message. Had he not already seen the mischief such knowledge had wreaked in Megan's life? But he'd lived with the torment of questions without answers for too long to pass up this opportunity.

What lies at the center of Guarded Wood?

Chapter XXXVIII: End of the Hunt

Bruce smelled mold somewhere nearby as soon as he and Megan walked the shadows to the isolation room.

"I'll bet it's that wall," Megan said, pointing at a section that didn't match the rest. "I thought it looked weird the first time I came here."

Bruce reached out with his senses and there was, indeed, a space behind this poorly constructed wall. He thought about simply walking the shadows to the other side, but wasn't sure what would happen if there was collapsed rubble in their way. He didn't particularly want to find out what would happen to him if he tried and failed.

"I think we're just going to have to take it down," Megan said, coming to the same conclusion.

"The doorway was here," he said, looking at the irregular surface from the side. Then, in much the same way he'd freed fossils from the limestone at the lake for Paul, he gave a slight twist of his hand and the outline of the door broke free of the wall around it. With a gentle push, the opening collapsed in upon itself, largely disintegrating.

"Pretty cool," Megan said.

"Not really," he said. "When Crina died, the wall must have pretty much broken down on its own. If someone hadn't plastered over it, it would have collapsed on its own decades ago."

Now that the wall was gone, they could see stairs descending into the dark.

"Paul would have loved to check this out," Megan said.

"I don't know," Bruce said, summoning a light before them in the darkness. "This cave may be why he hates being underground. I think he remembered this even before he found Luminita. I want you to promise me something before we go down there."

"What?" she asked.

"No heroics like the last time we went down into the dark," he said, holding out his pinky. "Promise me you will let me be the judge of my own fate, and that you won't leave me behind. No matter what happens."

"I promise," she said reluctantly, and hooked his little finger around hers.

He wasn't sure what special effects he'd expected to find at the bottom of the steps, but what waited for them did not measure up. There was a muted glow in the same place where they'd seen it in Luminita's vision, but otherwise the cave was empty except for a large pile of rocks that marked the grave of Paul's previous life here in Nickelville.

Megan stepped closer to the disturbance in the center of the cave and called out, "Jacob, can you hear us?"

The Dark Man appeared before them at once.

"Is this real or just another one of my dreams?" he asked.

"We're really here," Bruce assured him.

The apparition before them sagged in relief. "How long has it been?"

"Two centuries," Megan answered.

"I couldn't tell from here," he said, motioning to the cave around them. "It took me a long time to learn how to see anything beyond this place. Only the girls from Crina's line could see me when people finally returned to my church, but I was deep within my own dreams by then. I didn't fully wake until you came," he said to Megan.

"So you didn't know what you were doing when you saw my mother?" she asked.

"I was starting to wake by then, but I wasn't completely lucid until I felt your power cross the boundaries of this enchantment. I owe you both so much for clearing the graves of my wife and son. They deserve to be honored in spite of my shortcomings. Did I really hear Luminita play a short time ago?"

"Yes," Megan answered. "She's been freed from the clearing where she's been trapped since the accident."

"My brother Paul is the reincarnation of her fiancé," Bruce added.

"Truly?" Jacob said. "That is good to hear, and one less sin I shall have to atone for in the next life."

"Sorina told her that you were still alive, and she sent us to help you," Megan added.

He stared at her as if trying to make sense of her words. Then his shoulders sagged and his head bowed.

"I have caused much sorrow in my pride," he confessed. "I don't deserve her love. But in spite of my mistakes, we are all lucky that I failed in my attempt to open this gate. The world that lies beyond is broken and filled with such evil that I have not the words to describe it. I now block the passage with what is left of my earthly body, but I cannot allow what lies beyond to be released upon this world to feed. You must close this portal with me still in it or risk every living soul in this world."

"But you'll die," Megan warned.

"I wish I could say that after all this time, the fear of death holds no power over me," he replied, "but that would be a lie. I fear the judgment I will face for my sins."

"I don't think anyone would fault you for wanting a chance to have your wife and son back," Bruce assured him. "And if they did, what you have been through since then is payment enough for your sins."

"Crina did," Jacob said. "She is the one who blocked the opening after finding me here. She blamed me for the deaths of both her sisters."

"I know I shouldn't speak ill of the dead, " Megan said, "But even Luminita suggested that her sister was a bit of a witch."

"And a powerful one at that," Jacob agreed.

"August understood why you did it even if he didn't agree with it," Bruce confided.

"The hermit?" Jacob asked. "He lives yet?"

"No," Megan said. "He passed away just a few days ago. Not long after helping to save Luminita and Paul."

"I've missed much it would seem," Jacob said sadly. "But then not much at all either. All I ever wanted was to see my wife and son again."

"They are waiting for you," Bruce reminded him.

"Do you truly believe that?" the Dark Man asked quietly.

"Yes," Megan answered. "We have seen proof that the dead wait for the ones they love, or at least return for them when they die. Why else would Sorina still be waiting if not to welcome you to the other side?"

"I could do this with grace and dignity if I knew she'd be there," Jacob said.

"Then we promise you that she is," Bruce said.

"I am ready...no eager to leave this place," he said at last. "I only wish that our child had lived and that our line was as noble as the two of you have proved to be. I can never thank you for all that you've done."

"You're family," Megan said. "And you don't have to thank family."

Bruce took Megan's hand in his own.

"It's going to take both of us to do this," he said, "I can see just enough of our immediate future to pull this off. We're going to slam it shut so he doesn't suffer. Oh, and you and I are going to have one hell of a hangover when this is over."

She nodded and opened herself to him fully. Then, using a method that was oddly similar to the way he'd mended the cracks in Christine's windshield, he used his smith's skills to mend the damage that Jacob had caused. When it was done, he and Megan used all of their strength to close the gate.

In the instant that the ethereal door closed, they both felt the end of Jacob Routh and then the joy of reunion. But before either of them could leave, the white noise that camouflaged them ended. In the vacuum of that absent force, the outside world poured in, bringing with it a myriad of senses to bombard the two young people huddled beneath Nickelville Academy.

It was then that Bruce realized that it had never been the trees that protected them, but rather the energy from the partially open gate. Without it, their senses, so accustomed to the quiet, detected scores of minds in the distance turning to focus on the Heir of the Tuatha dé. After so many years of running, the Wild Hunt had found Megan at last.

Closer still, Sam Wise began to scream.

About the Author

Tom Barnett was a sick kid who escaped into fantasy books at a young age. As he grew, his asthma got better, but his love of reading never diminished. After three decades of leading teens toward a love of reading in which the stories of Nickelville have been percolating in the back of his mind, he's finally set them free.

Tom currently teaches middle school English in the Dallas area where he lives with his wife and children. He is also owned by several cats, one of which may or may not be the oldest creature in the universe.

www.ingramcontent.com/pod-product-compliance
Lightning Source LLC
Chambersburg PA
CBHW030535260626
47157CB00006B/2035